As DON DIEGO spoke, he stepped backward swiftly and whipped out his blade. Fray Felipe gave a cry of protest and started forward, but Don Carlos Pulido held him back. Don Alejandro stepped in front of Sergeant Gonzales, and glared at him.

"Fight!" Diego cried at the capitán. "Your blade, señor — draw and fight! Can it be that you are a coward?"

Rocha gave a roar of rage and whipped out the blade at his side. Steel clashed and rang. Light flashed from the flying weapons. The combatants breathed deeply as they advanced, retired, thrust, cut, parried.

The frightened servants crouched against the walls, watching from bulging eyes. There was a gleam in the eyes of Bernardo, who had watched his master fight before. And now Don Diego was laughing, like a man who knows that he is to be a victor. The beads of perspiration popped out on Capitán Rocha's forehead. Pressed back, he panted in a frenzy of sudden fear.

"Gonzales! Help me!" Rocha cried.

"Coward!" Don Diego taunted. His blade flashed forward, and Rocha felt it, gave a cry, reeled against the wall. "On guard! 'Tis but a scratch on your cheek," Don Diego called. "Three strokes for the Z this time, capitán!"

Under one cover — ***Zorro Rides Again***
and eleven Zorro short stories
by Johnston McCulley

Zorro: The Complete Pulp Adventures
Six-volumes collecting the original adventures of Zorro!

THE COMPLETE PULP ADVENTURES™ VOL. 3

Johnston McCulley

Featuring

Zorro Rides Again

Introduction by John E. Petty

"Zorro Rides Again" illustrations by Virgil Evans Pyles

Short story illustrations by Joseph A. Farren

Page 14 and 132 illustrations by Perego

Rich Harvey
Editor & Designer

Thanks to
Anthony Tollin, Doug Ellis, John E. Petty
David Saunders, Sheila Vanderbeek

Special Thanks to
John R. Rose,
a true caballero

ISBN-13: 978-1537128962
Retail cover price $19.95

Published by Bold Venture Press
www.boldventurepress.com

Contents

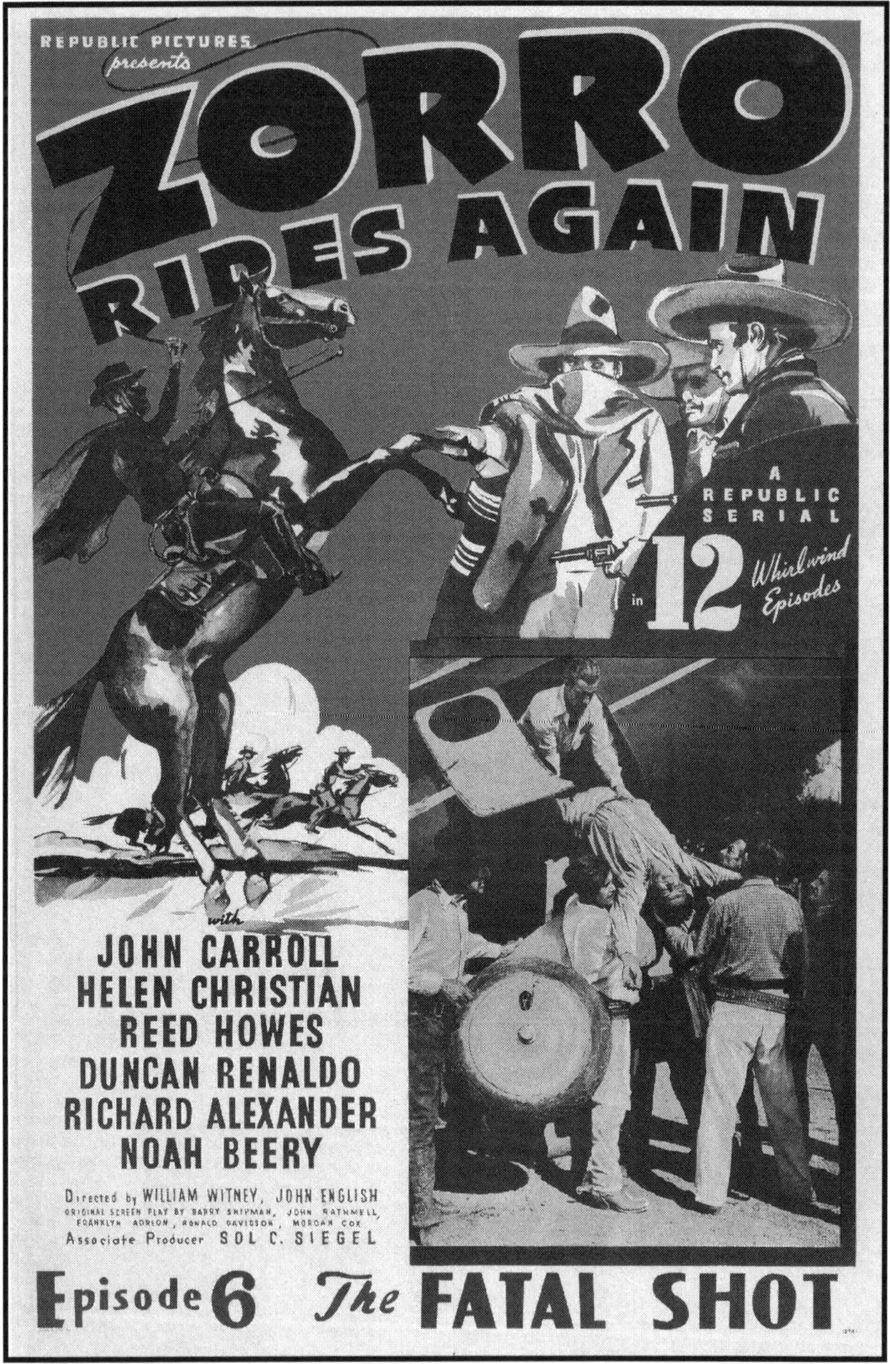

Zorro Rides Again (Republic Studios 1937) starred John Carroll in the first serial to feature Johnston McCulley's hero. The villain was portrayed by Noah Beery, who previously appeared as Sgt. Gonzalez opposite Douglas Fairbanks in *The Mark of Zorro* (1920).

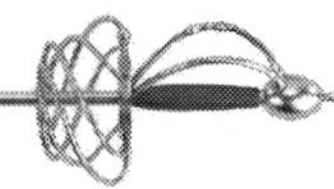

Zorro in the Serials

by John E. Petty

In 1919, *All-Story Weekly*, a leading pulp magazine, published the first chapter of a story called "The Curse of Capistrano," which would place author and former police reporter Johnston McCulley firmly among the gods of fiction. Within its pages, McCulley introduced the dashing Don Diego de la Vega, soon to be better known as Zorro, the Robin Hood of the West. A wealthy playboy, Don Diego wears a black mask and cape in order to strike fear into the hearts of criminals, thieves, and corrupt officials, as he stamps out cruelty, injustice, and oppression.

The first appearance of "The Fox" (the English translation of the Spanish "Zorro") on the silver screen was in 1920's *The Mark of Zorro* starring Douglas Fairbanks, who also starred in the sequel (of sorts), *Don Q, Son of Zorro* (1925). The character then lay fallow for more than a decade, until Robert Livingston starred in the first sound — and first color — Zorro film, titled *The Bold Caballero* (1936), released by the fledgling Republic Studios. In 1937, however, Zorro entered an entirely new medium: the serial.

Serials — so-called as they were released serially, a chapter at a time — had long been a standard in the literary world (all of Charles

Dickens's works were released in this fashion, for example). However, filmed serials first arose with 1914's *The Perils of Pauline*, and remained popular until the mid-1950s when television became the media format of choice for continuing adventures.

These stories were designed to be shown in chapters at a rate of one per week. Each chapter — there were generally either 12 or 15 chapters per serial — would run about 15 minutes (approximately the length of one reel of film), and would almost always conclude on a cliffhanger in order to entice audiences to return the following week. They were also filmed quickly, generally in 30 days or fewer, and were part of an entire theatrical package, typically including a feature film, a short or B-film, a cartoon, a newsreel, and a serial chapter.

Zorro Rides Again (1937), from Republic Studios, put actor John Carroll behind the black mask in the first serial to feature McCulley's hero. Carroll played James Vega, great-grandson of the original Zorro, set against J.A. Marsden (Noah Beery, who played Sgt. Gonzalez in *The Mark of Zorro*) and his plot to forcibly take the California-Yucatan railway from its rightful owners. Carroll's career was scattershot both before and after his stint as Zorro, but some clever land investments in the San Fernando Valley made him a millionaire almost overnight, at which point he retired to a peaceful life of golf and fishing in Florida.

Perhaps the greatest Zorro serial ever made was released in 1939, also from Republic, starring Reed Hadley as The Fox. *Zorro's Fighting Legion* (1939) depicted an epic battle between the original Zorro and the mysterious armor-clad figure known only as Don Del Oro, a would-be tyrant who intends to rule all of Mexico with an iron… er, golden fist. Directed by William Witney and John English, the team who also brought *The Lone Ranger* (1938), *The Fighting Devil Dogs* (1938), *Dick Tracy Returns* (1938), and many other great serials to the screen, this is a fantastic roller-coaster ride from start to finish, complete with landslides, exploding buildings, moving walls, collapsing suspension bridges, and more, as Don Del Oro seeks to eliminate Zorro in his mad grasp for power. Many fans consider this to be one of the high points of Zorro's screen career, and with good reason.

Zorro's Fighting Legion (Republic Studios, 1939) depicted an epic battle between the original Zorro and the armor-clad Don Del Oro, a would-be tyrant who intends to rule Mexico.

With Zorro more popular than ever, 20th Century-Fox (an appropriate name, to be sure) decided to remake *The Mark of Zorro* in 1940, this time starring matinee idol Tyrone Power. Like Fairbanks before him, Power also found that this role paved the way for more action/adventure parts, as opposed to the romantic leading man parts he had previously essayed.

The next serial to feature the black-clad hero (or at least a version of him) is an unusual one, considered by some to be a Zorro picture in name only. In *Zorro's Black Whip* (1940), Dan Hammond (Francis McDonald) and his gang commit acts of terrorism in order to prevent Idaho's bid for statehood. When the gang executes Randolph Meredith (Jay Kirby), the town newspaperman, his daughter Barbara (Linda Stirling, renowned as the Queen of the Serials) dons a fetching black costume (with lovely silver highlights) to hunt down the killers. A crack shot with both a whip and a gun, Barbara may not be the Zorro the movie-going public expected to see, but she does the name proud as a relentless and untiring force for justice. Interestingly, Stirling does not receive top billing in this chapter-play. That honor goes to George J. Lewis, who plays government agent Vic Gordon, Barbara's "sidekick" in her war against the Hammond gang. Whether this was an instance of blatant Hollywood sexism or simply the result of some savvy contract negotiation is anyone's guess.

McCulley's Zorro is back in 1947's *Son of Zorro*, this time portrayed by George Turner. When Jeff Stewart, descendant of the original Zorro, returns to his home after fighting in the American Civil War, he finds the town has been taken over by corrupt politicians who have been

Zorro movie posters Courtesy of HA.com.

Son of Zorro (Republic 1947) was re-edited for television broadcast in the early 1950s.

Don Daredevil Rides Again was a reworking of a Zorro script, necessitated by the ABC television series produced by Walt Disney. In *Zorro's Black Whip*, Linda Stirling took up the Zorro mantle to avenge a loved one.

oppressing the townspeople through high taxes, illegal tolls, and terrorist attacks. Appalled by what he sees, Jeff dons the legendary black garb of his ancestor and sets out to right the wrongs that have visited his homeland. This was one of a handful of Republic serials that would be re-edited for broadcast on television in the early 1950s, making it the first portrayal of Zorro on the small screen.

Ghost of Zorro (1949) is notable for several reasons. In this serial, Clayton Moore — who would go on to both big- and small-screen immortality for his iconic portrayal of the Lone Ranger — plays Ken Mason, grandson of the original Zorro, who dons his own black costume to prevent mob boss George Crane (Eugene Roth) from sabotaging the construction of the new telegraph lines in order to keep the law out of his territory. Aside from the presence of Moore, this serial is remembered as the most expensive of all the Zorro serials produced, costing Republic $164,895 (by comparison, *Ghost of Zorro*, filmed just two years earlier,

Courtesy of HA.com.

Before he portrayed The Lone Ranger, Clayton Moore starred as a descendent of Don Diego Vega in Ghost of Zorro (Republic Studios, 1949).

cost $156,745, while *Zorro Rides Again*, released in 1937, ran a mere $110,753). The amount of money spent shows Republic's confidence in the popularity and audience draw of Zorro, even though the serials were in their final days and budgets were increasingly tight (explaining the extensive use of stock footage in this one).

By 1949, the writing was on the wall for serials. Although they had a few more years to go, it was clear that the format was on the decline.

Republic, the studio responsible for releasing not only the Zorro series, but many of the best serials ever made, would close its doors completely by 1955, with other studios getting out of the serial business entirely at about the same time. The use of stock footage increased, and many — not all, but many — of the best serials were in the past. But the end hadn't quite come for McCulley's brave avenger.

In 1951, Republic went back to the well one more time for a final serial adventure with Zorro. By this time Disney had acquired the rights to the character — they would release the well-known TV show with Guy Williams behind the mask in 1957 — so using the name or anything else connected with McCulley's version was out. This was a frequent problem for serial producers, and one that they had become adept at handling. Rather than risk the wrath of Disney, Republic simply titled their new effort *Don Daredevil Rides Again*, and cast Ken Curtis (best known for his portrayal of Festus Haggen on *Gunsmoke*) in the title role. Trying to thwart the scheme of an evil political boss (played by the ever-dastardly Roy Barcroft) to criminally acquire the land of several honest ranchers, Curtis, as Lee Hadley (the secret identity of Don Daredevil), sports a black costume with lovely silver highlights — the same one worn by Linda Stirling in *Zorro's Black Whip* — allowing Republic to reuse footage from that previous film, regardless of the gender swap. Cost-saving, yes, but the serial suffered for it.

And with that, Zorro's serial career was over. But the Fox was hardly ready to retire. With a popular TV show in the wings, followed by a string of popular feature films, it can truly be said that Zorro, that black-clad champion of freedom, will always ride again!

John Petty is a Lecturer in Film at the University of Texas at Dallas. He is also the author of Capes, Crooks, and Cliffhangers: Heroic Serials Posters of the Golden Age, *available from Ivy Press at www.HA.com/serial.*

Illustration by Perego

Zorro

Rides Again

Zorro Rides Again

With a shock of disbelief, the old Spanish California village heard that its friend Zorro was now attacking the weak and helpless!

"Dead or alive" they wanted Zorro, and the gallant caballero himself, trapped in a Spanish mission, vowed it would not be alive.

Hated by those who once worshiped him, hounded by the Spanish California soldiery, the proud Zorro again becomes an outlaw to regain his stolen honor.

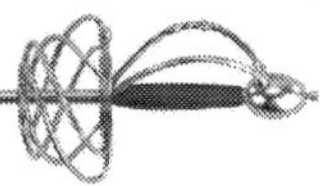

Chapter One
Marked by the Sword

ONCE more night descended upon the friendly little pueblo of Reina de Los Angeles, in the land of California, in the year 17 — , and tallow pans burned in the adobe huts of the natives, and gem studded candelabra sparkled and gleamed in the pretentious houses around the plaza, and over it all glowed the soft, cool, romantic moon.

Couples of natives, both neophytes and gentiles, slipped furtively through the shadows, ignorant of such things as chaperones, and giggles and coquettish squeals came from the dark patches beside the huts. A dainty señorita tripped by on the arm of her father, going for an evening visit at the house of a friend, her fat dueña bobbing along behind. A gay caballero hurried toward the inn, bent upon winecup and fling of dice.

Rough soldiers from the presidio swaggered about with sabers clanking, strutting before bronze native wenches whose physical beauty was something nobody could deny. Robed frailes of the missions moved with humble grace, now and then a hand uplifted in passing blessing. It was a fair evening in Reina de Los Angeles, an evening of peace and friendship and love, with nothing to indicate that it might be otherwise before the dawn of another day.

From the inn on one side of the plaza came a burst of raucous talk and ribald song. The door flew open, and a shaft of bright light shot out, and through the shaft of light flew a native with figure asprawl, to plop in the deep dust of the plaza. Another burst of laughter came, and the door of the inn was closed again.

"THAT is the way to handle them, señores!" It was the Señor Juan Sanchez speaking, as he pretended to be dusting off his hands. "Take not so much as a leering look from a bronze native, be he gentile or neophyte. A cuff on the ear, a kick where it will do the most good! Ha! By the saints, I know how to handle them! More wine, landlord, for these my friends!"

Saying which, this Señor Juan Sanchez went to stand in front of the big fireplace, his feet far apart and his arms akimbo, and look at the company before him. Soldiers were there, notably Sergeant Pedro Gonzales, the bully of the presidio. Travelers were there, men on their way up and down El Camino Real, the great highway which connected the mission chain from San Francisco de Asis to San Diego de Alcala. Loafers of the pueblo were there, wine guzzlers who intrigued for free drink, honest men spending an evening of leisure after a day of toil.

"What say you, big sergeant?" asked this Señor Juan Sanchez, little guessing that he was hovering on the brink of death.

Sergeant Pedro Gonzales hated a boaster, since he was one himself. And this Juan Sanchez had been holding the center of the stage since his arrival late in the afternoon. His boastings made those of Gonzales seem like the prattle of a child. He was a rover, a trader, a merchant of sorts, this Señor Juan Sanchez. From one end of El Camino Real to the other he plied his trade. At stated intervals he ceased his business bickerings and enjoyed life, at such times surrounding himself with numerous dainty señoritas about whom the less said the better, and drinking only the rarest wines, and scattering around gorgeous presents that would make any great landholder blink his eyes. At least so said this Señor Juan Sanchez.

Sergeant Pedro Gonzales had been listening to it, and drinking as he listened, and now the sergeant was in a dangerous mood. He was no man to cross even in his most peaceful moments, and when in his cups he was a human catamount. But word had been passed among the soldiery that these merchants were to be respected and even protected, since trade is a thing which builds empire, though a man of parts may sniff at it. So Pedro Gonzales had held his hand, though that hand itched to crack against the florid face of Juan Sanchez, or whip out a blade and run him through.

"What say you, big sergeant? Is it not the way to handle the scum?" Juan Sanchez asked. "A kick and a cuff, eh? Why were natives placed here if not for our service, eh? That fellow I but now tossed through the door — I did not like his looks. That was enough for me — merely that I did not like his looks. I remember once at San Juan Capistrano — "

"I shall go mad!" breathed Sergeant Pedro Gonzales. He groped for his wine mug as Juan Sanchez rambled on. His hand shook as he carried the mug to his lips and thrust it beneath his enormous mustache. Gonzales was at the point of explosion, and knew it.

"It is a great business!" said Juan Sanchez. "I buy hides from the native scum, and pay them what I please. The neophytes are too holy to complain, and the gentiles — ah, the gentiles! Many a hide and tub of tallow, cask of olives and jar of honey, do they steal from the *frailes* and bring to me. And then I rebuke them for theft and pay them but a part of the value. I am clever — not so?"

"Not so!" roared Sergeant Pedro Gonzales.

"How is this?" Juan Sanchez glared at him in surprise.

"A clever man," said Sergeant Gonzales, "would afterward steal back from the natives the few coins he had given them, and possibly whip them for having held the coins so long. A clever man would do the stealing from the frailes of the missions himself, say for the adventure of it."

"Do you mean to intimate, señor, that I am not clever?" Juan Sanchez demanded.

The face of Sergeant Gonzales purpled with rage. His suppressed emotions were choking him. He tore at his collar to loosen it, and his eyes rolled, and his breath came in great gasps.

The fat, greasy landlord of the inn rubbed his hands together and called upon the saints to witness that whatever happened hereafter was no fault of his. Pedro Gonzales now would get off his stool. He would advance and rend this merchant limb from limb, and toss his poor carcass out into the night!

But Pedro Gonzales did not, remembering the orders which had been given regarding merchants. He recovered a measure of his composure and spoke in a thin voice from which all life seemed to have fled.

"Si, señor! You are clever," Pedro Gonzales admitted. "You are also very fortunate. Had you been dabbling in commerce about three years ago, using such methods, your career would have been cut short, no doubt."

"How is this?"

Pedro Gonzales got to his feet. "When Señor Zorro rode the highway!" he cried. "Ha! What a man! Friend of the oppressed! How we chased him up and down El Camino Real — and prayed that we'd never catch him! He sought out those who robbed the frailes and abused the natives. He used his whip and his blade. On his big black horse he rode, darting about like a shadow. They called him the Curse of Capistrano — yet he was a blessing."

"I have heard the yarn," Juan Sanchez said. "Something like a legend, was it not?"

"A legend?" Gonzales cried. "I shall go mad! Know you, Señor Sanchez, that Zorro was none other than Don Diego Vega, a caballero if there ever was one, son of the rich Don Alejandro Vega — and my very good friend!"

"And did such a man stoop to defend natives and frailes?"

"Stoop?" Gonzales cried. "Stoop! Don Diego Vega stoop? His head rides the clouds, señor! A Vega stoops to nobody but his God!"

"No doubt he had his fun," Sanchez said. "No doubt he rode and played with his blade and made fools of the soldiers. But did he ever handle a proper man? I ask you that. Did he not enjoy himself punishing those it was not dangerous to punish? Did he not — "

"Ha!" Gonzales cried, striding forward. "I can endure no more! By the saints, Señor Sanchez, you are poised on the brink of death this instant! Merchant or no merchant, orders or no orders, if I hear one more word, one more insinuation against Don Diego Vega — "

Sanchez retreated a step as Gonzales choked with wrath. He lifted a hand as though to ward off a blow. But Gonzales stopped in time, stopped to stagger to one side and fall upon the nearest stool. He waved a hand weakly toward the landlord, who hurried forward with more wine. Sergeant Gonzales gulped the drink, so nervous that it ran down his chin and dripped from the ends of his mustache.

"If — if Zorro only would ride again — " Gonzales mouthed. "Only long enough to handle this — this merchant!"

"Zorro — the fox!" Sanchez was saying. "What was it he did? Ah, yes! He cut the letter Z on the face of his victims, did he not? The Mark of Zorro they called it, eh? A pretty caballero having his fun!"

"I shall go mad!" Gonzales breathed again.

However, this Señor Zorro scarcely will see fit to attack me," Sanchez continued. "He has had his fling. It is nothing to worry about. Landlord, my score! Do not rob me too much. I pay, and I go!"

"May the saints be praised!" said Sergeant Gonzales.

"There is a bronze native wench waiting beside a hut on the other side or the plaza," Señor Sanchez said. "I shall give her a string of beads, which cost me almost nothing in San Francisco de Asis."

"Open the door!" Gonzales cried. "Let him out before he changes his mind. And leave the door open a moment afterward. I ask you that much, landlord, if you are a friend of mine. Are you my friend?"

"Si, señor!" the landlord made haste to reply.

"Then leave the door open — and blow out the stench!"

Señor Juan Sanchez laughed, tugged at his belt, twirled his mustache, and went forth to his assignation.

Some minutes later Gonzales said, "I feel better now, I was weak for a time. What have I ever done that such a curse should be put upon me, that I must hold my hand when it itches for the feel of a blade hilt? Ha! He would belittle Señor Zorro, my good friend."

"Well do I remember when Señor Zorro rode," the landlord said.

"And now he is but an ordinary man," Gonzales said. "A woman ruined him. He fell in love with the Señorita Lolita Pulido, did he not? The fairest feminine flower in the garden of California! I grant you that! Yet, she is a woman."

"But naturally!" said the landlord.

"And hot blood turned to icy water in the veins of Don Diego Vega. He put aside his blade and his wild ways. He prepared to marry and become a family man."

"But it has been three years, and he is not wed," the landlord pointed out.

"There was some trouble, and the señorita was seized with a sickness. So her father, Don Carlos, must take her away to Spain. But now she has returned, her good health back again, and there will be a rich wedding. Zorro is but a memory." The sergeant sighed.

"In this very room he fought," the landlord said.

"Do I not remember it? He fought me. He played with me as a cat plays with a mouse. What a blade! He disarmed me, and laughed and hurried away. Such a man to weaken because of love for a maid! Love! Meal mush and goat's milk!"

The landlord refilled the sergeant's wine cup. It had grown quieter in the inn. Soldiers diced in a corner. Some, who had taken too much wine, slept. Sergeant Gonzales got upon his feet and adjusted his sabre belt.

"My friend," said he to the landlord, "there is no longer any spice to life. Why be a soldier when there is no fighting to be done? A man must listen to the boasts of a merchant and not rebuke him. Such a man! Boasting of robbing the natives and stealing from the frailes. Making presents to native wenches. These are mild days! Ah, for those days of yesterday, when Zorro rode the highway and played his game! At San Juan Capistrano tonight, whipping some thief! At Santa Barbara tomorrow, perhaps! Then back here in Reina de Los Angeles, with everybody looking for him elsewhere! Friend of the oppressed! Giving punishment where punishment most was needed! Dealing it out when the authorities would not, or delayed, or gave favors to those who did not deserve it. We need something like that now, my friend."

"That is true," said the landlord.

"The poor frailes are being robbed again, and the natives mistreated. And there is no Zorro to help them."

Sergeant Gonzales drained his wine mug and smashed it down upon the table. He tugged at his belt again.

"I go," he said. " At least, a man may sleep and cease his thinking. Señor, a Dios!"

"A Dios!" the landlord replied.

But there came an interruption as Sergeant Gonzales started toward the door. A man's wild scream rang out somewhere in the plaza. There came the sound of pounding boots. Into the inn rushed Señor Juan Sanchez, bellowing with pain and fear, holding his hands to his face.

"What is it?" the landlord cried.

"Some devil! Some devil attacked me!" Sanchez wailed. "He sprang upon me in the moonlight. He gave me no chance for fair fight. Call the soldiers, señores!"

"I am a soldier!" Gonzales reminded him. "Say more!"

"I know nothing more. He attacked me, cut me with his blade. I was compelled to flee — "

Señor Sanchez lurched forward into the light, and dropped his hands from his face. And those in the inn saw, on the man's right cheek, a new-cut, jagged letter Z.

"Ha!" Sergeant Gonzales cried. "My prayers are answered! Zorro rides again!"

Chapter Two
Enmity

Don Diego Vega, resplendent in a floundered dressing gown and with embroidered sandals upon his feet, sat at breakfast in the patio of his town house a short distance from the plaza of Reina de Los Angeles. Before him was a melon, and a dish of eggs, and fish fresh caught in the distant sea. At his elbow was a glass of thick wine which had come from Spain, and of which Don Diego Vega enjoyed the bouquet as much as the taste.

He was attended by Bernardo, his deaf and dumb servant, and he breakfasted alone. For Don Alejandro, his father, was out at the family's ranch, attending to the putting in of certain crops.

There came a summons at the front door, and Bernardo inclined his head in courtesy and left Don Diego to answer the summons. When he returned a moment later, there was a peculiar expression in Bernardo's face. He indicated by motions that Don Diego had early morning guests, and his face expressed the fact that Bernardo did not think much of them.

Don Diego stifled a yawn and got out of his chair. He gathered the dressing gown around him, and strode out of the patio and into the house, and so on into the great living room with its high ceiling and great fireplace, its grilles of metal work and its color-splotched beams.

Back and forth across the room strode a man in uniform, and Don Diego repressed a grimace at sight of him. He was Capitán Valentino

Rocha, commandante of the presidio, an officer who had been stationed there for less than a half a year. Don Diego Vega did not like him, and cared not that Capitán Rocha returned his dislike.

There was a second visitor also, a common-appearing fellow who seemed to be feeling out of place. Don Diego elevated his eyebrows at sight of him, and perhaps it was but a gesture that he brushed a perfumed handkerchief, edged with fine lace, across his nostrils.

Capitán Rocha bowed from the waist in what he fondly believed was the most approved manner, but which almost caused Don Diego to smile, though his inborn courtesy kept him from doing so.

"It is early for a call," Don Diego hinted.

"Don Diego, this is not a social visit," Capitán Rocha said.

"I presumed not, having issued no invitation."

Rocha's face purpled. "It is a visit of business, señor," he continued.

"But I have nothing to do with business. There is a manager of the estate, a superintendent in whom I put much trust — "

"My business is with you alone, Don Diego, and I should be pleased to expedite it."

"In such case," said Don Diego, "the pleasure shall be mine also. May I ask the name and station of this — er — person who seems to be in your company?"

The person lurched forward and announced himself.

"I am Juan Sanchez," he said. "I trade in tallow and hides."

"My nose should have informed me," Don Diego replied.

"I am an honest man! I work hard, and I take my fun. And — *look! Look!"*

Sanchez pointed to his cheek. It was purple, swollen, badly marred. But it was no great task to make out the jagged Z thereon.

His face immediately inscrutable, Don Diego bent forward slightly to look, and again he brushed the perfumed handkerchief across his nostrils.

"It evidently is a wound," he said. "But why come to me with it? The good Fray Felipe is a wonder with wounds, and he may be found at the chapel."

Capitán Valentino Rocha took another step forward, and his eyes flashed a bit as he confronted Don Diego.

"It is a letter Z." he announced. "Last night, this merchant was set upon in the plaza, by a man who carried a naked blade. That letter was carved in his cheek in three strokes. He is marked for life."

"It appears so," Don Diego said. "He should be glad that his assailant did not start with an A and work through the entire alphabet, instead of using only the last letter."

"It is the Mark of Zorro," Rocha accused. "And you are — or were — Zorro!"

" 'Were' is correct. It is quite true that, some time ago, I masked my face and rode to punish. Those were the days of enjoyment! Many a tight corner I avoided! Many a race I had over the hills!"

"Your pardon, señor, but I insist that we get down to our business," Rocha said. "This merchant had made a complaint, and, as *commandante*, I am compelled to give him ear. Can you convince me that you were not abroad last evening, that you spent the time here in your own home, in innocent pursuits?"

"Why should I take the trouble to do so?" Don Diego asked with a trace of indignation.

"Do you not understand? The Z was carved on this man's face — *and you were Zorro!*"

"Ha!" Don Diego exclaimed. "And does he intimate that I carved him? Is he ass enough to charge that I mutilated a face previously mutilated by nature? The Mark of Zorro, eh? Look at it, I ask you! Did you ever see the Mark of Zorro on anybody? You have not? I thought so! Observe the letter on this man's cheek. The upper bar of the letter, for instance, tilts a bit to the left. Did Zorro's Z do that? And the downward stroke, señor, is far too long. Made with three strokes of the blade? This man surely jests. The mark of Zorro was made with a single stroke of the blade, a quick twisting of the point that seemed like a flash of fire. I know, for I am the man who made it."

"Don Diego Vega, you are a caballero," Rocha said. "You are a man of honor, and your word is sacred. Do you give me your sacred word that you did not attack this man?"

"I do not give my sacred word in such trivial affairs," Don Diego replied, his eyes flashing a bit.

Juan Sanchez exhibited sudden anger. "He did it!" he cried. "I demand that you place him under arrest! What right has he to cut a man up? Don Diego Vega, eh? I care not what your name or station!"

Don Diego elevated his eyebrows again, and lifted one hand in languid gesture. From the shadows near the wall, Bernardo darted forward. He was a giant, this servant, both in body and in loyalty to his master, to whom he now looked for further instruction.

DON DIEGO made another gesture, and pointed suddenly at Juan Sanchez. Bernardo did not hesitate. He lurched forward and caught the merchant about his waist, lifted him off the floor, strode swiftly with him across to the door, opened it, and tossed Juan Sanchez out into the dirt.

"Don Diego!" Rocha cried. " This, señor, is a thing which — "

"You dare bring such scum into my house?" Don Diego cried.

"I have my duty. If you but say outright that you did not carve this man, it will serve. But you have not."

"Were I guilty, señor, what would you do about it?" Don Diego asked. "Place me in jail, perhaps? Or, possibly, suggest a duel with me?"

"Don Diego Vega, in this district I represent His Excellency, the Governor. And I warn you that I shall endure none of this Zorro business. A man must not take the law into his own hands. If he does, he must be punished. All soldiers are capable of preserving peace in Reina de Los Angeles. We need no help from — pretty gentlemen."

"Allow me to point out, capitán that you have interrupted my breakfast," Don Diego said. "Monstrous! Never before have I heard of such a thing! Is that a prerogative of the soldiery? Must we starve at the wish of men in uniform?"

"You may go too far in your pleasantries!"

"I am not inclined to be discourteous, but I must wish you a very good morning." Don Diego said. "And, since warnings are being passed about, allow me to warn you, capitán."

"Of what?"

"The commandante in office here prior to you was Capitán Ramon.

I believe he went to his grave wearing a Z on his forehead."

"You killed him?"

"In fair duel. Because he wronged me and insulted a lady in whom I was interested. I killed him in fair fight — as perhaps I would kill any man who impugned my honor. *Buenos dias, señor!"*

He motioned toward Bernardo again. But Capitán Rocha already was retreating toward the door.

WHEN Don Diego Vega returned to the breakfast table in the patio, there was a thoughtful expression on his face as he sipped his wine. He made certain signals to Bernardo, who hurried away. Don Diego entered the house and ascended to his chamber, where he dressed. And then he came down again and hurried to the front door.

Bernardo was waiting there with a horse, and Don Diego got into the saddle and galloped across the plaza, waving to such friends as he encountered. He took the south trail, toward San Juan Capistrano.

For several miles he galloped, passing natives who plodded along through the deep dust, and here and there a cart with big wheels carrying things to the town. Don Diego Vega scarcely knew what he passed, however; he was thinking deeply.

And, after a time, he turned off the highway and followed a road which ran to a ranch in the distance, the country estate of Don Carlos Pulido, father of the señorita Don Diego expected to lead to the altar one day. Now his manner changed and he brightened. But his face grew dark again when he saw a horse tethered in front of the great, sprawling house of the Pulidos.

"It is as I expected," Don Diego muttered.

A native servant came running to care for his horse. Don Diego got upon the wide veranda and started toward the front door. It opened, and Don Carlos Pulido strode forth to meet him.

"Welcome, Don Diego!" he cried. "Always welcome to this house! You ride early."

"There are others abroad," Don Diego observed.

"Señor Rocha but stopped as he was passing by — so he said. Allow me to whisper in your ear, Don Diego, that this new commandante is getting to be a pest."

"If he gets to be nothing worse, we may overlook it."

"Surely, Don Diego, you cannot look upon him as a rival? My fair daughter is betrothed to you, is she not? Moreover, it is a love match, is it not? Pulido women love but once — and they are true to their men!" There was a measure of asperity in the manner of Don Carlos Pulido.

"Are we to quarrel, señor?" Don Diego asked. "I am not questioning the integrity of the Pulido women. That is beyond question."

"I thank you, Don Diego. Let us go into the house."

They entered, to find Señorita Lolita and her mother talking to Capitán Rocha, who appeared rather put out at Don Diego's arrival. The señorita flushed as Don Diego clasped her hand, and her mother, being highly romantic, beamed.

Rocha bowed from the waist.

"I have met the capitán before this morning," Don Diego observed.

Rocha reddened.

"I feel, Don Diego, that I owe you an apology," he said. "I was compelled to call upon you and bring that person along. Orders have gone forth from San Francisco de Asis to treat merchants and traders with respect and give them every consideration. I am a soldier, and obey orders."

"It is forgotten," Don Diego said.

"He deserved to have his face carved. He cheats the natives, does things unmentionable. A fit subject for Señor Zorro to work upon!"

"Señor Zorro?" Señorita Lolita cried.

Rocha bowed before her. "There is a certain miscreant visiting in Reina do Los Angeles," he explained. "Last night he went forth from the inn, and was back almost immediately with a letter Z carved on his cheek."

"Ha!" Pulido cried. "So Zorro rides again! It is well! They have forgotten the work he did. A few passes with his blade, and fear will come to men, and they will cease from persecution."

"The capitán has warned me," Don Diego observed, "that a man must not take the law into his own hands. To do so puts him outside it."

"I was speaking for the benefit of that rascal," Rocha declared.

"Allow me to point out, señor, that you warned me after my servant had thrown the fellow out."

Rocha's eyes blazed.

"I — I perhaps was under the impression that he still was present," he said.

"Need we discuss it further?" Don Diego asked. "These fair ladies, I feel sure, are not interested in sordid happenings. It is not a pleasure for them to contemplate violence. Let us talk of music or the poets."

"My duties call me back to the presidio," Capitán Rocha said.

He took polite leave of them all. But the look he flashed at Don Diego Vega, as he passed through the door, was one of the deepest enmity.

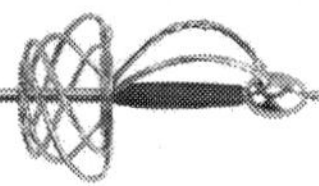

Chapter Three
The Tempest

AGAIN the night, the soft breeze, the moon. Again the tinkling guitars and the whisperings in the dark places near the huts. Once more, men in the inn held raucous revelry.

Sitting before his hut on the outskirts of the town, Bardoso smoked and listened. He had a jug of wine beside him, and now and then he took a swig from it. He curled his lips as he heard the din from the tavern.

Bardoso was a pirate, a retired and reformed pirate. For some years now he had been a man of peace. The rheumatism was in his bones during the rainy season, and a certain stiffness the year round, which informed him that his days of nefarious activity were at an end.

He had been converted, had Bardoso, and old, fat Fray Francisco was his friend. It was the custom of the fray to visit the pirate's hut.

Through the bright moonlight he came waddling, this fat Fray Francisco, his robe whipping about his legs. Bardoso arose and greeted him humbly, then seated himself again, with the fray at his side.

"It is a beautiful moon," said Fray Francisco.

"It reminds me of a moon I once saw at sea." Bardoso replied. "But you have told me not to remember anything about the sea."

"Bardoso, you have been a pirate, but now you are a good man," said Fray Francisco. "Your little charities are not unknown to me."

"Yet never will I live long enough to atone for what I have done."

"There is some work for you at the chapel tomorrow. Some of the masonry has become dislodged, and it must be mended."

"You can depend upon me to attend to it," Bardoso said.

"Is it good wine you drink?"

"It is excellent wine, Fray Francisco. It was a gift. You will taste it?"

Fray Francisco smiled. "I must make sure," he said, "that you do not drink poor stuff."

Bardoso grinned and handed over the jug. Fray Francisco drank.

"It is good wine," he said. "The grapes were grown on the estate of Don Alejandro Vega, were they not? I know the taste of it. Don Alejandro honored me with a jug also."

Out of the shadows on the hillside behind the hut of Bardoso rode a horseman. He approached slowly, but he made straight for the hut. Bardoso and Fray Francisco watched him. Some caballero on his way to the inn, they supposed. Fray Francisco shook his head. He hated to see gay young bloods wasting their time over the dice.

The horseman came on, trotted out into the bright moonlight, reined to a stop before them. Fray Francisco gave an exclamation of surprise and got to his feet. Bardoso did likewise, and crouched against the wall of his hut.

The horseman had a mask over his face. A large cape covered his costume. He held a long whip in his hand. "A fray drinks wine with a pirate, eh?" he growled at them.

"What sin is that?" asked Fray Francisco. "The wine is good, and the pirate a lost sheep returned to the fold."

"Silence, fray! Because you wear a robe, there are certain decencies to be observed."

"Who are you, señor?" Bardoso growled. "Who are you to rebuke my good friend, Fray Francisco?"

"If I carve a Z on your cheek, you'll know!"

"Zorro!" Bardoso gasped.

"Zorro?" Fray Francisco echoed. "Don Diego? Surely, then, this is but a jest. For a moment, I was frightened."

"Out here in the moonlight, the two of you!" the horseman ordered. "Side by side! The pirate and the pious, eh?"

Suddenly, he lashed out with his whip. It struck, stung. Fray Francisco gave a cry of pain, then bent his head and endured. Bardoso gave a bellow of rage as the lash cut into his body. He lurched forward, but the lash met him and drove him back. Fray Francisco felt it cut through his robe again, and could not prevent a moan escaping him.

"You are hurting my friend, the fray," Bardoso cried. "Touch him not. Punish me, for the fault is mine. I gave him the wine. He is a holy man — "

"A rat who drinks wine with pirates!"

"Rat? You dare call Fray Francisco a rat?" Bardoso cried. "You shall not, whoever you are!"

Fray Francisco prostrated himself on the ground as the lash bit into him again. And then Bardoso rushed, bowling like a maniac. The lash met him, cut him, drove him back. And now there was something else, too. As Bardoso brought up against the side of the hut, a blade flashed in the moonlight. The pirate screamed as the point bit into his face.

ON THE other side of the village a woman known as Carlotta also sat in front of her hut. She was the widow of an adventurer who had gone to his death in the hills, with two small children to support. She did what work came her way, took what pay was given, whether in money or in goods.

Now she sang, softly, a song of her youth. The children were half asleep on the ground beside her. She sang because of good fortune, of work which had come her way, of payment which would mean better food, and some new clothes.

She observed a horseman leave the highway and ride toward her hut, but thought nothing of it. Often riders cut across that way to get quickly to the town. None molested her. She was past the age of beauty, and her reputation was of the best.

But this rider pulled up his horse abruptly in front of her, and the woman Carlotta gave a little scream and sprang to her feet. The face of thc rider was masked, and through slits in that mask eyes gleamed at her malevolently.

"Dissolute woman!" the horseman cried. "Worthless lure of men!"

"Señor!" she cried. "I am Carlotta — and honest. You are making a mistake."

"Zorro does not make mistakes!"

The whip sang through the air. The children screamed, as their mother cried out with pain. Again the whip hissed and struck, and once more the scream of the mother rang through the night. It was heard in the plaza, and men started running.

But the horseman did not wait to receive them. He howled a curse at the woman, wheeled his mount, and charged away into the night.

MEN crowded the inn and thronged the open space in front of it. More men came hurrying to the spot from every part of the town. There was a bedlam of chattering voices.

"He has gone mad!" said Sergeant Gonzales.

"A mad dog should be exterminated!" That was the merchant shouting.

"I cannot understand it," Gonzales declared. "To whip Fray Francisco, the kindest man to be found the length of El Camino Real! And Bardoso, who has done no wrong for years."

"And the woman! Do not forget the woman!" Juan Sanchez cried.

Those in the crowd murmured angrily. They knew Carlotta, and the brave fight she had made to feed her children and herself. They knew that there was no evil in Carlotta. And now she was bleeding from cuts of the lash, moaning in shame because of what her assailant had said.

"Mad — he has gone mad!" Gonzales repeated. "I cannot believe it! It must be some other man!"

"Is this Don Diego home?" Sanchez asked. "There is a way of finding out, is there not? Where is your capitán?"

"He rode out to some estate to spend the evening, leaving me in charge," Gonzales admitted.

"Then take us to the house of this Don Diego Vega," Sanchez cried. "Let us see whether he is home. Such things as these cannot be allowed."

"On the morrow, I shall question him."

"You protect him!" Sanchez cried. "You protect the rich man who beats a woman and a fray!"

"Scum!" Gonzales cried.

"Do not dare to touch me! Do your duty! Lead us to the house!"

"Lead us, Gonzales!" the crowd howled at him.

Now, Pedro Gonzales believed that in all the world there was no man quite so splendid as Don Diego Vega. He was sorely troubled. If Don Diego had turned to Zorro again, and was doing these things, then of a surety he was mad and not responsible.

"Lead us!" the crowd howled.

Gonzales was forced to lead them. Across the plaza they trooped, kicking up huge clouds of the fine dust. They approached the Vega house, rushed upon it, surrounded it.

"Knock at the door!" Sanchez called. "Let us see whether the fine gentleman is at home. See whether his horse is in the stable. Let Don Diego prove his innocence, if he can!"

Men came running to say that there was no horse in the stable. Gonzales pounded at the front door. There was a short delay, and then a manservant opened it. He cried out in fright when he saw the throng, and would have closed the door again, but Juan Sanchez prevented it.

"Is Don Diego home?" Sergeant Gonzales asked, his heart heavy as he spoke.

"He is not, señor."

"If he is home, be not afraid to say so. You know me — Gonzales. Take word to Don Diego that I am here, and would like speak to him."

"I have told the truth, señor — he is not here."

"And where may he be found?" Gonzales asked.

"I know not, señor."

"Has he ridden out to his father's ranch, think you?"

"Not that, I am sure. Don Alejandro is expected to come home this night."

Juan Sanchez thrust his way forward again. "That is enough, is it not?" he asked. "This Don Diego rides afar, and nobody knows where. Can there be question of his guilt?"

"Are you the *commandante*, that you take charge of things so?" Gonzales snapped at him. "Back, everybody! We have no business here.

We can do naught but await his return. I shall make a report to my capitán."

HE TURNED and strode away from the house, and the crowd broke up, scattered, spread the gossip on the wings of the night. Natives carried it into the country, up and down El Camino Real. Old Don Alejandro, riding home with a servant, heard it, and put spurs to his horse.

He galloped wildly into the plaza and across it, scattering men out of his way. In the patio, he dismounted. He was furious that the privacy of his house had been desecrated, to find his servants frightened.

"Where is my son?" he demanded, once he was inside.

"I know not, Don Alejandro," a servant replied.

"Send a man to bring old Fray Felipe to me."

Don Alejandro marched back and forth from corner to corner of the big living room. He was erect, his eyes flamed, his mustache seemed to bristle. He could not believe it! Had the boy indeed gone stark mad? This thing would turn the entire country against him.

Don Alejandro howled for his servant again.

"Send a man on a fast horse to fetch Don Carlos Pulido," he ordered.

"Si, señor!"

Again, Don Alejandro paced the floor. He would feel better, he told himself, when old Fray Felipe arrived. He had a level head, that old fray. Perhaps he could suggest something. And he loved Don Diego, who had saved him from a whipping when Zorro had ridden before.

Fray Felipe came, with his bowed head and his gentle smile. He tried to soothe Don Alejandro, urging him to be seated, to drink a mug of wine, to control himself.

"I could understand the case of the merchant," Fray Felipe said. "But the others — no! Don Diego knows that Carlotta is a woman of worth. He never would touch Francisco, were he in his right mind. And, as for Bardoso, that pirate — Don Diego often visits him at his hut, listens to large tales of what Bardoso did when he sailed the seas."

"Can it be a sickness come upon him?" Don Alejandro asked.

"Such things have happened," Fray Felipe admitted.

"But the world will not believe it is a sickness. They will scorn him. They will say that he had a taste of power, and ran wild like a fire in the hills. And they will hunt him down like a beast — "

"Softly, my friend!" Fray Felipe begged. "This is terrible, but there must be some explanation for it. He is to be married in a month's time, to the señorita he loves. Would he do a thing, think you, to prevent that?"

Don Alejandro paced the floor again, while an hour passed. Fray Felipe continued trying to soothe him. Then Don Carlos Pulido arrived, to hear the tale.

"It was in my mind that Don Diego acted peculiarly when he was at my place this morning," Pulido said. "This will kill my daughter."

"For a thing like this to happen to a Vega!" Don Alejandro mourned. "A name that never has been touched by scandal! That filthy mob was here at my house! No doubt some of them are watching now, waiting for him to come home. They may even try to put hands on him, the scum!"

"It is not to be understood," Pulido declared. "Zorro rode to aid the oppressed. He did not attack frailes and women. It must be a terrible sickness."

"If he would only come home — " Don Alejandro cried.

And, at that moment, he did come.

Chapter Four
The Fugitive

THEY heard the pounding of a horse's hoofs, wild cries of men, shrieks and howls and hisses and curses. Don Alejandro ran to the patio door, Pulido and Fray Felipe hurrying after him. Don Diego came riding through the moonlight like a madman, shouting for all to clear his path.

He sprang out of the saddle as his mount skidded to a stop, sprang up the flight of steps, turned to face those who charged after him afoot. He laughed wildly, and then he was inside the house, panting, disheveled, his clothing streaked with dust.

"My son! My son!" Don Alejandro cried.

"So the wolves have gathered?" Don Diego asked. "It is to be expected."

"They have gone mad. They say that you have put on your Zorro mask again, and have done terrible things."

"I know. I heard natives talking."

"My son — " Don Alejandro stammered, stopped. "No, I will not insult you by asking," he added.

"I thank you, my father!"

"But, what does it mean?"

Don Diego sprawled in a chair. "It means," he said, "that I have an enemy. Why, I am not certain. But this enemy is trying to blacken me, make me a thing of scorn." He laughed mirthlessly. "How soon people forget!" he said.

"Forget good and remember evil," Fray Felipe murmured.

"They forget the things I did as Zorro. They are ready to believe anything of me. They would tear me to pieces. They believe that I — a Vega — would whip a woman and an aged fray. It is enough!"

"Do not harden your heart, my son," Fray Felipe begged. "In the end, all things are known, and justice is done."

Don Diego sprang to his feet. "Can't you see what has been done to me?" he asked. "This enemy of mine — he has struck in a clever way. He has aroused the town against me. And the countryside! Everybody thinks that I am a fiend!"

"Not everybody, my son."

"You do not. Neither does Fray Felipe, I am sure. Nor you, Don Carlos! And I know the heart of Lolita — she never would believe this of me. But that is not enough. The whole world must be convinced of my innocence."

"But who would do this bitter thing — and why?" Fray Felipe asked. "It is monstrous!"

"I think I know, but I am not certain," Don Diego replied. "I believe I know the motive, but I am not sure of that, either."

"What are we going to do?" his father asked.

Don Diego laughed again as he turned up the room. He strode to the wall, turned and came back nervously.

"Zorro rides again!" he said. "This time, he rides to save himself. He takes the trail against his enemy. He will be outlaw, with the soldiery hunting him, and almost all men against him. All men! The natives I befriended before — they will fear me now. They are simple enough to believe the tales. Outcast I'll ride — until I can prove the truth!"

"Ridiculous!" Don Alejandro cried. "A Vega ride like an outlaw? It is not necessary. I have influence, have I not? We laugh at the wild tales, have the soldiers protect us if others annoy."

"And have men saying that I am protected because of our family's wealth? That will not prove my innocence."

"How can you prove it by playing outlaw?"

"I'll run down the man who has done this thing. Let the soldiers chase me — as they probably will when Capitán Rocha gives the command. Let all men be against me! Zorro rode before against odds; he can ride again."

ONCE more, he paced to the wall and back. Outside, they could hear a chorus of voices as the mob gathered again in front of the house, somebody pounded at the door.

"Hold them for a time," Don Diego said. He whirled and rushed toward the stairs.

The pounding on the door continued. Frightened servants gathered in the big room to crouch against the walls. Don Alejandro growled his anger at the outrage. Pulido sank into a chair like a man suddenly bereft of all strength.

"I cannot endure this much longer," Don Alejandro said.

A strong voice reached them from outside: "Open! This is the commandante!"

"Get your soldiers and clear away that mob!" Don Alejandro cried.

"I am here on official business! I wish to see Don Diego. Open, in the name of His Excellency, the Governor!"

Don Diego came hurrying back into the room. The others looked at him in amazement. He had changed his clothes. At his side was the sword of Zorro. In his left hand, he held a whip.

He darted across to the door.

"Is that you, Capitán Rocha?" he demanded.

"It is! Open, I say!"

"And who comes in, if I do?"

"I come in with Sergeant Gonzales and some of my men."

"You come in with Gonzales, and no others," Don Diego told him.

"Very well! Open the door."

"If there is treachery, somebody dies! Your honor word!"

"You have it!"

Don Diego sprang back to the middle of the room, and waved a hand at the frightened servant nearest the door. He unbarred it, pulled it open slowly. Those in the room saw Rocha standing there with Gonzales beside him, saw beyond them other soldiers, and the white faces of the mob.

The door was slammed, barred again. From the outside came the crowd's throaty roar.

"What means this intrusion, señor?" Don Alejandro demanded.

"Need you ask? I warned Don Diego this morning that these Zorro tactics could not be tolerated. We have law and justice here!"

"Of what is he accused?"

"Wounding a merchant with a blade, beating a fray and a woman and attacking Bardoso, the old pirate."

"And do you believe in his guilt?" Don Alejandro asked, a dangerous gleam in his eyes. "Do you think a Vega could be capable of such things?"

"I have my duty, señor. I cannot look beyond that."

"You have not answered my question."

"It is not for me to answer. It is for me only to take Don Diego, your son, to the jail and hold him there until an investigation can be made."

"You would throw my son in such a foul hole?" Don Alejandro cried.

"I arrest him now, in the Governor's name!"

Don Diego threw back his head and laughed. "So you would take Señor Zorro to jail, eh?" he asked. "What a brave commandante! Is it promotion you seek? Capitán Rocha, I give you my word as a Vega, that I did none of those things of which you accuse me. What now?"

"Your word, under the circumstances, scarcely is sufficient."

"What?" Don Diego screeched. "You dare question my word? *On guard, scum!*"

As HE spoke, he stepped backward swiftly and whipped out his blade. Fray Felipe gave a cry of protest and started forward, but Don Carlos Pulido held him back. Don Alejandro stepped in front of Sergeant Gonzales, and glared at him.

"Fight!" Don Diego cried at the capitán. "Your blade, señor — draw and fight! Can it be that you are a coward?"

Rocha gave a roar of rage and whipped out the blade at his side. Steel clashed and rang. Light flashed from the flying weapons. The combatants breathed deeply as they advanced, retired, thrust, cut, parried.

The frightened servants crouched against the walls, watching from bulging eyes. There was a gleam in the eyes of Bernardo, who had watched his master fight before. And now Don Diego was laughing, like a man who knows that he is to be a victor. The beads of perspiration popped out on Capitán Rocha's forehead. Pressed back, he panted in a frenzy of sudden fear.

"Gonzales! Help me!" Rocha cried.

"Coward!" Don Diego taunted. His blade flashed forward, and Rocha felt it, gave a cry, reeled against the wall. "On guard! 'Tis but a scratch on your cheek," Don Diego called. "Three strokes for the Z this time, capitán!"

"You fiend! … Gonzales!"

Again, Don Diego's blade struck home, and again Rocha felt the hot blood trickling down his face. He knew that he had been marked. Fury engulfed him. He shrieked his rage and made a wild charge, tossing caution aside, and training. He felt a terrible wrench on his arm, and his blade flew through the air, to crash to the tile floor.

"Gonzales!" he screeched.

Gonzales winked at Don Alejandro, whipped out his blade, and charged forward, bellowing like a bull. He went at his adversary carelessly, purposely so, guard wide open. There was a flash in the light, and the blade of Gonzales joined that of Rocha on the floor.

"So!" Don Diego said, stepping back. "You will not believe me! You are driving me to the life of an outlaw! Hear you, Capitán Rocha! Zorro rides, until he can prove that he is not the beast men are thinking him tonight. Send your men after me — or come yourself — and be damned to you!"

He turned and darted to the patio door, thrust his gleaming blade back into its scabbard, laughed lightly at them.

"My son — " Don Alejandro began.

"It is an adventure, my father. Do not fear for me. I may drop in to see you at any time. Señores, a Dios!"

He opened the door, and sprang out into the patio. His horse was only a few feet away. But there were men in the patio, men who believed

Deftly Zorro flipped the blade from the capitán's fist

what had been said of Don Diego Vega and who knew Fray Francisco, and they were determined men now, prepared to forget Don Diego's station and punish him as they would have punished any other man.

Don Diego did not draw blade again. His whip sang through the air as he charged forward. Its stinging lash drove back the two men nearest. Then Don Diego was close to his horse, and got into the saddle. The whip sang again, as a man would have grasped the reins.

"Aside!" Don Diego called.

They fell back as he wheeled the horse at them. A pistol was drawn, and the whip curled out to flick it out of the man's hand. Don Diego jumped his mount over the low patio wall, thus avoiding the gate where some had gathered. Into the bright moonlight he galloped, leaving a chorus of howls behind him.

Across the plaza he flashed, a lifting cloud of dust trailing out behind to mark his progress. Somebody threw a clod, and it struck home. Don Diego reeled in his saddle for an instant, then recovered himself. Wild with indignation, he wheeled his horse and charged back at them.

They tried to scatter before him, but his whip caught some of them, stung them, sent them howling away. He dodged the soldiers and charged back through the crowd.

"Aside!" he cried. "Zorro! Zorro!"

Then he was out of the plaza again, on the south trail, and riding like the wind. Back to those in Reina de Los Angeles floated his mocking laughter.

Señorita Lolita Pulido could not sleep that night. She was wondering what wild summons had called her father to the town house of the Vegas. Her head tossed on its soft pillow, and sighs came from between her parted lips. Her mother slipped into the room and sat on the bed beside her.

"Do you suppose," Señorita Lolita asked, "that Diego is in trouble? Perhaps he has been injured."

"If that were true, my darling, the servant would have said so."

"But it is all so mysterious."

"When your father returns, he will explain."

"If anything happened to Diego — "

"You love him, then, so much?" her mother asked.

"So much that I'd die, if evil came to him!"

"I know, my pigeon. It was the same with me. That is the way the Pulido women love."

"I'm afraid — afraid that something evil has happened to him! If I could but hear his voice, could only know that he is all right — "

And just then she heard it. Drifting to her ears softly it came, a song she knew well, a serenade from Spain that Don Diego had sung for her often before.

She sat up quickly in her bed, her hands clasped at her breast. Then she slipped out and went shyly to the window. The song came to an end.

"Who sings?" she called, sweetly.

"And what voice did the señorita most wish to hear?"

"The voice of Don Diego Vega, my beloved!"

"It desolates me to disappoint, señorita. It is not the voice of Don Diego Vega, that pattern of a man. It is the voice of Señor Zorro, the outlaw!"

"And is Señor Zorro quite safe from capture?"

Señor Zorro laughed. "Quite safe."

But, even as he spoke, two men were slipping through the shadows toward him.

Chapter Five
Assassins

Señorita Lolita Pulido giggled a bit and timidly grasped the arm of her mother, who now was standing beside her at the window. And then the señorita, blushing furiously in the darkness, and somewhat aghast at her haughtiness, pulled aside the draperies for the space of half a dozen inches, that she might peer forth from her bedchamber and look at a man!

The room was in the blackness of night, and he could not possibly see her, but that made not the slightest difference, since she was fully conscious of her informal attire. The very thought of such brazen boldness made her face burn, and she wondered that her mother did not rebuke her. But her mother did not, and so she searched the moonlight until she found him.

First, she saw a riderless horse standing in the shadows against the patio wall. Then she beheld her Señor Zorro leaning against the gorgeous sundial her father had imported from Spain. He was singing again, in a voice soft and low, his attention centered on the house. And then — then Lolita saw two men creeping toward him through the shadows, one from either side, and the cold moonlight glinting on weapons they held.

In her sudden great fear for him, the man to whom she had given her maiden's heart, she forgot her unconventional attire, and the circumstances, and remembered only that he was in peril. She threw wide the draperies, grasped the metal bars over the open window, bent forward until her forehead touched them, and cried at him in alarm:

"Diego! On guard! Beware! At your back!"

Her mother was clutching at her now, demanding to know what was wrong, for she had recognized the unmistakable note of fright in her daughter's voice. Then Doña Catalina, too, looked through the window and saw the menace, and added her shrill cries to those of the señorita.

Don Diego sprang swiftly to one side and whirled, even as the two charged at him. He saw the flash of the moon light on a naked blade, saw it flash also on a dagger, and made haste to get his own sword out of its scabbard. He maneuvered, as swift as thought, to keep them out in the bright moonlight, when there would be no shadows to disconcert him.

"Saints preserve him!" the señorita breathed.

"Assassins!" Don Diego cried. "Cowardly dogs! Come to your fate, curs!"

Abruptly, they stopped their charge. That puzzled Don Diego for the instant, and then he learned the reason for it. There was a swish through the air, and a riata fell upon him, deftly cast by one of his foes. The noose was jerked taut around his body — but he managed to keep his sword arm free.

He braced himself quickly against the pull he knew was coming. It came, a tremendous jerk, but did not throw him off his feet, to roll on the ground and be a helpless victim for their steel. An instant later, he was rushing the man who had cast the rope, and who also held the dagger; rushed him before his companion in this murderous attack could get to his assistance. Don Diego was not inclined to exhibit mercy! Here were only cowardly assassins trying to strike from the dark, evidently bent upon his extermination, and a caballero could not afford to take chances with such. They did not regard the rules of fair conduct, hence could expect no mercy in return.

A FLASH through the air as the man hurled the knife, which passed over the shoulder of Don Diego as he bent quickly to one side. There was another flash as his own blade did its bloody work. A stifled cry, a gurgle, a fall — and Don Diego Vega sprang aside swiftly and prepared to engage the other.

He came at a charge, mouthing curses, making swift play with his blade. Steel rang, and they circled and fought. Don Diego caught sight of the other's face, and knew that he never had seen him before. It flashed through his mind that he had been set upon by rogues who had chanced to be near, perhaps cutthroats and highwaymen. There were many such prowling up and down El Camino Real, a threat to honest men and the despair of the soldiery.

But the fellow could use a blade! Don Diego Vega found himself facing an adversary he could not regard lightly. He could not dispose of this one by a simple feint and thrust. The man had a strong wrist and a sure foot. Some man of gentle blood turned from the path of rectitude, Don Diego thought, else a former soldier who now recognized no commander and made orders of his own.

And so Don Diego Vega fought seriously, carefully, as though his life depended upon it, which possibly was the truth. He advanced, retired, sought for a proper opening. He felt out his adversary, and presently knew that he was the assailant's master. The man was tiring rapidly.

Now the stranger was mouthing curses, and his breath was coming in painful gasps. In the bright moonlight, his face suddenly was drawn, haggard, his eyes wide — the face of a man who was looking at death. He gathered his remaining strength for a swift, reckless attack, hoping to crush Don Diego beneath this last effort. There was a lash of steel, a swift turning of bodies — and then Don Diego stood with lowered blade.

The other dropped his weapon, reeled, fumbled at his breast, and fell. He raised himself upon one elbow, sank back to the ground again.

"Oh, Diego … Diego!" the little señorita was calling from the window.

But Don Diego did not hear her. His mind was upon solving the reason for this cowardly attack. He stepped forward and looked down at the man his blade had pierced, and finally knelt beside him.

"Was it my purse you sought?" Don Diego asked. "You could have had money, had you asked for it."

"This — this is the end," the other said, his voice low and throaty. "The hour of death is a time to reveal all."

"We were hired to attack."

"Ha! Hired assassins!" There was loathing in the caballero's voice. "What man desired my death at the expense of gold? Should I feel flattered?"

"I know him not, señor."

"Is that a thing to be believed? You did not know the man for whom you worked?"

"It is the end approaching, hence I speak the truth — for once in my life."

"And the truth is — ?" Don Diego queried.

"Once I was a soldier, and knew the trade well. Then I became a wanderer, a scoundrel, a murderer and a thief. That other — he is but my companion of the trail, a man I know not, but another such as I. We met in Reina de Los Angeles."

"Come to the meat of it," Don Diego suggested, "for your time is short. I have seen such wounds before. There is little agony, yet they drain life swiftly."

"We were approached by a man who wore a mask, and who had a cape wrapped around his body. He gave us gold, and told us to await you here and slay you. Sooner or later, you would come this way, he said. We were to have more gold after the deed was done, for he promised to meet us and give us some."

"And you trusted him to do so?"

"Why not? By his speech and manner he was a man to be trusted — a caballero."

"And did he say why he desired my death?"

"He did not, señor. We thought that it might be a matter of a maid, and jealousy. We did not care as to the details … Oh, I am choking! … Dios!"

Don Diego stood to his feet He cleansed his blade by running it into the sandy ground, and returned it to its scabbard. And then he realized that the Señorita Lolita was calling to him from the window, and that Doña Catalina, her mother, was calling also.

He went to them, bowed, stepped close to the wall.

"I regret that you have witnessed such a miserable affair," he said.

"Diego, you were in danger! I — I was so afraid for you!" It was the Señorita Lolita who spoke. "What does it mean?"

"A pair of knaves bent upon robbery."

"And was that all? Is there not something else?" Doña Catalina asked him. "A servant came for my husband — "

"They were hired assassins, so one of them said," Don Diego admitted. "It is your right to know — and judge. Some unknown enemy of mine has done malicious things while posing as Zorro. The world attaches the guilt to me. I am riding outlaw until I can prove my innocence and find the guilty man."

"Riding outlaw — you?" Doña Catalina cried. "Who would dare cause you trouble — and why? What has been done?"

"Don Carlos will explain to you fully when he returns home. It seems that there is another Zorro abroad — a spurious Zorro who mistreats instead of defending. He has whipped a woman and attacked a fray, and used violence on two other men. I must find this man, ascertain his motive, and punish him as he deserves to be punished. So I ride as once before I rode with the hands of all raised against me."

"The hands of all? Cannot the soldiers of the presidio give you protection?"

"Ha! Capitán Rocha would have arrested me and put me in jail. We fought, and I put my Z upon his cheek. I can expect no help from the soldiers, except perhaps my old friend, Sergeant Gonzales."

"But — to ride outlaw — " the señorita began.

"A game with a thrill to it!" he said. "Again I am Zorro, the fox, and the hounds are chasing. I but came this way to sing my poor song for the daintiest ears in all California. And now I must mount and ride on. Doña Catalina, if some of your servants will dispose of those carcasses in the patio — "

He ceased speaking suddenly, and turned his head to listen. On the night wind came the sounds of thundering hoofs, the creaking of saddle leather, the jingling of accouterments. An order was bellowed in a raucous voice.

"Troopers!" Don Diego said. "Searching for me, no doubt. The odds probably are too great for fight, unless a man wish to be foolhardy, and I must live until I clear my name. I go — but I shall be near."

He rushed away from the window, lifted one of the men he had slain and put the body in the darkness near the patio wall. He did as much for the other, so it would not be found quickly if the soldiers stopped at the estate and searched. And then he got his horse, swung up into the saddle, and rode quietly around the corner of the large storehouse to disappear in the deep shadows.

Chapter Six
Bloodhounds of the Law

THE troopers came to a halt in front of the house, four of them, and Capitán Valentino Rocha one of the four. They dismounted, and the capitán led the way to the front door, against which he crashed the knocker.

"Ho! Within, there!" he cried. "Open, in the Governor's name!"

His three troopers shouted also, and native servants came awake inside the house, and also in the quarters in the rear. But these last, badly frightened, remained where they were, hoping that they would not be found, and that nobody would summon them.

Doña Catalina wrapped a robe about her, and bade Lolita do the same. Candles were lighted, and the women went forth into the great living room, where some of the male servants already had gathered. Doña Catalina approached the door.

"In the name of the Governor!" the capitán was shouting. He had abandoned the knocker, and was pounding upon the heavy door with the hilt of his sword.

Doña Catalina called to him. "Who demands entrance at this hour of the night."

"Capitán Rocha, of the presidio in Reina de Los Angeles, and certain of his men."

"My husband is in Reina de Los Angeles."

"I am aware of that, señora. Nevertheless, I demand immediate entrance. This is a matter of official business and will not admit of delay. Open the door at once, señora — or we break it down!"

Doña Catalina stepped back where the light from a swinging candelabrum played upon her and revealed her in all her haughtiness. She put a protecting arm around her daughter, and motioned for the servants to unbar the door. It flew open, and Rocha lurched into the room, his men close behind him.

Doña Catalina stood straight and proud, while Lolita clung to her, trying not to be afraid, telling herself that this intrusion surely would be punished at the proper time.

"What is it you wish, señor?" Doña Catalina demanded, giving the capitán no official title at all, and her black eyes dashing at him angrily as she spoke. "You have seen fit to upset my household. For your sake, I trust that you have sufficient reason for your act."

"We are searching for Don Diego Vega, sometimes also known as Señor Zorro. He was seen riding in this direction. I know that he is always a welcome guest at this house. Is it peculiar, then, that we should search for him here?"

"And why do you search for him at all?" Doña Catalina asked.

"Because he is playing at being Señor Zorro again. He has whipped a fray already, and cut several persons, and mistreated a woman. The prison yawns for him."

"Don Diego Vega is the soul of honor!" Doña Catalina declared. "He never would work an injustice."

"His blood is good, I grant you, but it seems to have soured in his veins," Capitán Rocha said. "Vega or no, he cannot run around the country mistreating men and women as he pleases. He has turned bad."

"That is a malicious lie!" Señorita Lolita cried.

The capitán bowed before her, mockingly. "I can readily understand the feelings of the señorita in the matter, and they may be excused," he said. "I know how it must irk you, when you find yourself sorely disappointed in the character of a man."

"Disappointed?" Lolita cried. "He is the finest man in the land, my Diego! And what sort traduce him? How dare you intimate that he has done things a caballero would not do? And what are those fresh cuts on your cheek, señor? Can it be that Diego put them there?"

Capitán Rocha paled with his wrath. "Ha! How did you know that, señorita, unless Don Diego Vega has been here to tell you?" he asked. "So he has been here, eh? And recently! No doubt he still is here."

"He is not here," Doña Catalina said quickly. "He was singing a serenade to my daughter, but did not enter the house. In the patio two men attacked him, and he slew them — "

"What is this?" Rocha cried.

"One of them, dying, admitted that they were hired assassins. Their bodies are by the patio wall. Can you not understand that some enemy is causing him trouble?"

"So he has been killing again!' Capitán Rocha cried. "We must take him — alive if possible. The man is a fugitive. This would be a friendly house for him, and no doubt he would be cunningly hidden here. It is my duty to search."

"Have I not said that he is not in the house?" Doña Catalina asked.

"Nevertheless, we search!"

"Señor!" she protested.

"Opposition to my wishes in this affair will avail you nothing, and may bring you trouble. I understand the relations between Don Diego Vega and this house. But, after these his late actions, Don Diego and his family will not be in favor with the Governor. It would serve you best if you were not too friendly with him."

Señorita Lolita left her mother's side and stepped forward quickly. "You mean, I presume, that we should desert him in his hour of trouble? Such a thought never would occur to a caballero," she said scornfully. "It might occur to you."

"You are doubly beautiful when aroused," Capitán Rocha declared. "May we not be friends? I stand high in the service of His Excellency, and a maid could do worse than look at me."

"Si, señor!" she agreed. "A maid could do worse than look at you. She might contemplate, for instance, *culebra de cascabel*, the snake which rattles before it strikes."

"Señorita!" Rocha cried, his face aflame.

"Señor!" she mocked.

"Search the place!" Rocha bellowed to the three troopers. "Leave no corner overlooked! Leave nothing unturned! Find me this Señor Zorro, that I may have him punished as he so richly deserves!"

He whipped out his sword, thrust the frightened servants aside, waved his troopers to different parts of the house. Doña Catalina and her daughter remained standing beneath the candelabrum, their dainty lips curled in derision, their eyes seeming to flash fire. They could hear the rough troopers tumbling furniture about, calling to one another.

After a time they descended the broad stairs to report that the fugitive was not on the upper floor. Rocha drove them to search further. He sent two outside, to investigate the other buildings. One man he kept with him.

"What room is that?" Rocha asked, pointing to a door.

"It is the bedchamber of my daughter," Doña Catalina replied.

"We search it!"

"You dare?" she cried. "I have said that it is the bedchamber of my daughter."

"Nevertheless, we search it. I have my duty to perform," Rocha said.

"For this insult you shall be slain!" Doña Catalina cried at him. "Every man of blood will resent it. Do you dare think that a man would be hidden in my daughter's bedroom?"

"Search!" Capitán Rocha ordered the trooper who remained with him.

The Señorita Lolita sobbed and hung her head with shame. Her mother clasped her tighter.

The trooper went to the door and opened it, not even looking into the room, but staring back at Rocha and the women.

"The room is empty, capitán," the man said.

"Outside!" Rocha cried at him. "Join the others there, and search. Since you are so timid about it, I shall investigate the bedchamber myself."

The trooper hurried to the front door and passed out into the night.

The servants who were huddled against the wall looked to their mistress, wondering whether they should make an aggressive move.

"That trooper of mine — he would ape the fine caballero," Rocha said, sneering. "He shall be punished for it later."

"And you surely shall be punished, if you enter that room!" Doña Catalina cried at him. "Have you no sense of decency? What manner of foul beast does His Excellency have for officer?"

"His Excellency will be to glad to learn of your words, señora. This foul beast happens to be His Excellency's nephew!"

"Do not search," she begged. "The intimation would be disgrace."

Capitán Rocha glanced at her swiftly, and saw pain in her face.

"I accept your word that Don Diego Vega is not in that room," he said.

"A caballero would not even ask that the word be passed," Señorita Lolita observed.

Capitán Rocha bowed before her again. "I trust that I do not merit your great scorn," he said. "I am truly one of your admirers. When this sorry business is at an end, I shall tell your father that I wish to pay you my addresses. It is possible that an alliance may be arranged between us."

"When this sorry business is at an end, you probably will have formed an alliance with the devil!" she snapped.

Rocha fought back his wrath and stalked to the door. He turned and bowed again, mockery in his manner. He opened the door, and let out a flood of light — and recoiled with a cry of mingled fear and rage.

Just outside the door, on the ground, were his three troopers. They were trussed up with ropes, and gagged with strips torn from their own serapes. And they were stretched out so that the three bodies formed the letter Z.

But they were not dead, and Capitán Rocha rushed to them and tore the gags away. Two of the troopers were conscious already, and the third was rapidly regaining consciousness. Capitán Rocha called for water, which a servant carried to him. He cut the ropes away, refreshed his men, meanwhile volleying questions.

Three of Captain Rocha's troopers lay stretched out like a letter Z

"What occurred? How came this about? Speak, Juan!"

"A blow in the dark — and I knew nothing more," the man moaned.

"Felipe?"

"It was the same with me, commandante."

"Are you soldiers? How many men attacked you? Do you go about serious business with your eyes closed? A month in jail, with little to eat and drink, might serve as punishment. Carlos, what happened to you?"

"At the corner of the patio wall, something struck me, commandante. I know nothing more."

"Dios!" Rocha swore. "Can none of you tell me the straight of it?"

But they could tell him little except that, one by one, in some dark corner where they had been searching for Señor Zorro, they had been felled by unexpected blows. And they had the bumps on their aching heads to show.

"The scoundrel is near at hand!" Capitán Rocha cried. "For this outrage, he shall die! We'll search till we find him! To horse!"

They rushed toward the spot where they had left their mounts tethered in front of the house. But the horses were gone.

Mocking laughter greeted them from the near distance, and a sarcastic voice called to them:

"Ho, señores! It is a long walk to Reina de Los Angeles, and the dust is deep!"

And then they saw their horses not far away in the moonlight, tied together and being led from them, first at a walk, and then at a trot, and then, as they watched and howled maledictions, at a furious gallop. Riding ahead of them, on his own mount, and leading them, was Señor Zorro.

Chapter Seven
An Indian's Wrath

SEÑOR ZORRO shouted wildly at the horses he led, rushed down the highway with them for a mile or so, and then released the animals, but continued to ride beside them, crying at them and lashing them with his quirt, until they were in a frenzy of a run which, he knew, would carry them into Reina de Los Angeles. There they would be found, and everybody in the pueblo would learn what had happened to the commandante and his troopers, and would laugh furtively. Señor Zorro knew the trick of turning laughter against his foes.

Presently, Zorro let the horses go. For a moment he watched them running furiously into the night, and then turned his own mount up into the hills. He knew this part of the country well, for often had he hidden here when he had ridden as Zorro before.

Now he cut through a tiny gulch, and then went up over the crest of a hill, and made for a certain little secluded canon where there was an excellent hiding place, and water and green grass. He wanted to be safe in hiding and his horse picketed before the dawn. He could do without food for a few hours, and could get water from a spring, but sleep was a thing he had to have during a part of the day that was coming.

He wanted to think and plan, too, while he rested. The bogus Zorro must be unmasked in such a manner that Don Diego Vega would stand revealed as innocent before all the world. He owed that to himself, his family, his friends, and the señorita promised to him as wife. Also, the bogus Zorro must be punished.

He guided his horse slowly and carefully through a fringe of brush, and came to a spot from which he could look down into the little cañon. In the distance, he saw red pin-points which he knew were camp fires.

That rather startled Señor Zorro, for this was not a usual place for men to camp. No vaquero looking for straying stock would spend the night there, when there was a big ranch house and free entertainment, wine and wenches, only a short distance away. And drifters through the land would have camped nearer El Camino Real, or gone on into Reina de Los Angeles for the night. It was better than an even wager, Zorro decided, that whoever was around those fires did not wish their whereabouts and present business known.

So his approach down the cañon was cautious, almost noiseless. He did not follow the cañon bed, but a narrow trail along the hillside, a trail he had used before. After a time, he reached a spot from which he could look down at the fires.

There were two fires, and natives grouped around them. Natives, awake and alert at this hour of the night! Natives busy with earnest talk. Another infernal uprising being planned, Señor Zorro thought. They were getting weary of persecution again, getting out of hand, and even the fraile of the missions could not influence them to remain peaceful.

Señor Zorro had held the friendship of the natives when he had ridden before. He had punished men who persecuted them, and they had hidden him, gathered information for him, aided him in a hundred ways.

So NOW he put on his mask, guided his horse through the trees, and sought a narrow trail which wound its way down to the floor of the little cañon. At the bottom, he rested for a time, then went forward. This was a box cañon, and Zorro was between the dead end of it and the fires. They would not have sentinels out in that direction.

So he managed to get close to them without being seen, and watched from behind a screen of brush. A tall native was making an impassioned speech.

"José of the Cocopahs," Señor Zorro muttered. "It must be serious, then."

José of the Cocopahs had led a former uprising, and had been strong enough to get immunity at its end. Señor Zorro had heard rumors of the Cocopahs being robbed and mistreated near the mission of San Luis Rey de Francia. Some of their tribe, he knew, even now were prisoners in the cárcel at Reina de Los Angeles.

Zorro touched with his spurs and rode on, straight toward the fires. A native glanced up and saw him, gave a scream and sprang to his feet. Others saw him, and sprang up also, reaching for all sorts of weapons.

But Zorro loped toward them, his hand held high in the peace sign. José of the Cocopahs called something, and the men were still. Zorro brought his horse to a stop near one of the fires. José growled something more, and the natives rushed forward and made a circle around the rider.

"José of the Cocopahs!" Zorro called. "I am a friend!"

José stalked toward him, his eyes burning. He stopped at the horse's head.

"It is, indeed, Señor Zorro," he said.

"And your friend," Zorro added. "Do not forget that. I saw your fires from a distance. Do not be afraid, for I rode alone, and no other man saw them. But it would be wise, would it not, to have no fires when there is no cooking to be done?"

Jose's eyes gleamed at this criticism of his generalship, and he growled for the fires to be extinguished. But he did not act in a friendly manner.

"I have no concern," Señor Zorro said, "in what business brought your men together here, except to say that you are fools if you plan an attack against the whites. I, too, ride with every hand against me. I would eat and sleep, and have protection while I do these things."

"Señor Zorro was friendly to us once," José said. "He attacked our enemies, and punished those who did us wrong. But I have heard strange tales today. He has turned on his brothers, the Cocopahs. Only this afternoon he entered a hut where one of our women was nursing a sick brother, and lashed them both with his whip."

Zorro could have groaned in dismay.

"It is being whispered that Señor Zorro rides again, but not in the name of justice," José continued. "He has gone mad, men say, and is hunted like coyote. Those who befriend him may find them¬selves in trouble."

"You believe Zorro did these things?" Don Diego cried. "Or if you do not believe them, you would turn your back upon a friend and brother because to aid him might bring you trouble. A noble thought!"

"It has been whispered, señor that you might try to lead us into trouble, by seeming to help our cause, learning our secrets, and then betraying us to the soldiers."

"Dios!" Zorro cried. " Do you think that I am so foul? Am I a snake to crawl among the rocks? Am I a skunk to stink? Who dares say such a thing? And what manner of men are you to believe it? This is my reward for fighting for your interests, as I did once at risk of my life."

JOSÉ made a sign, and retired a short distance to hold conference with some others. Señor Zorro watched them from gleaming eyes, his lips curled in a slight sneer. After a time, José returned to him.

"What is it you wish of us, señor?"

"By the saints! Do you have to be told? I want shelter, food and drink, want you to watch while I sleep. Attend me, José. Some enemy of mine is pretending to be Zorro. He has done the things of which you have heard, casting the blame on me. Can you understand that?"

"I hear you, señor."

"But do not believe? Do you dare say that you do not believe? Must I fight you, my friends? I had thought you might have a little gratitude, and be willing to help me. I wish certain information gathered, certain men watched. But the Cocopahs do not know the meaning of gratitude. They are only fair-weather friends! They hide their real thoughts behind lying faces!"

"Enough, señor!" José cried. "We do not know whether to trust you, after what we have heard. It is whispered that you have turned against your old friends. But we wish to be fair, and not do you a wrong. So you shall have food, and will be guarded while you sleep. Dismount, señor."

Zorro dismounted, and his horse was picketed, and he ate and drank. Then he retired to a little hut and stretched himself on some skins to sleep. The natives had gathered in close conference again.

He awoke, hours later it seemed to him. One of the little fires had been kindled again, for the night was chill, and the natives were gathered around it. The slight breeze carried their talk to Zorro.

"What are we to believe?" José was saying. "The tale has been told us that Zorro mistreated two villagers yesterday, and one a woman. Zorro says that another has done these things, to cast blame upon his name."

"Can any white be trusted now?" another asked. "Let us not forget our brothers rotting in the jail."

"We must serve our own ends," José said. "That is the way the whites do. I have in mind that we make this Zorro captive. Then some of us can go to the Capitán Rocha and offer to trade him for our brothers in the prison."

"That is a thought!" another cried.

"It is what the whites call cleverness. The commandante, it is said, wishes this Señor Zorro badly. When the whites fight among themselves, our cause is made stronger. Is it agreed?"

"Agreed!" they cried.

"Then when day comes I go to Reina de Los Angeles and bargain with the commandante. This Zorro once was our friend, but surely the stories are true, and he has changed. It is a queer tale that there are two Zorros."

There was silence for a moment, and then a stern voice spoke behind them:

"So José would betray his brother!"

They sprang to their feet to find Zorro standing there, his mask on, eyes blazing at them, his hand resting upon the hilt of his sword.

"Snakes!" Zorro cried. "You would trade me for those of your tribe in prison!"

"We do not believe your story," José told him. "You are a different Zorro."

"I have told the truth!"

"We think you speak with a crooked tongue. You have turned bad, it seems. You attack natives and whites alike."

"Do you desire that I draw blade and slay some dozen of you?" Zorro roared.

José made a signal, and suddenly they rushed. They surrounded him, grasped his arms and legs, held him helpless. But, to the wonder of them all, Zorro had made no move to defend himself. He did not offer to draw his blade.

"One moment!" he said. "You have forgotten, it seems, that I am a blood brother of your tribe. You made me so when once I had befriended you."

"Our brothers are in jail," José said. " We trade you for them. We cannot believe that there are two Zorros. And some Zorro whipped one of our brothers as he lay sick, and attacked the woman who was nursing him."

"You say it is so, and I say that it is a lie!" Zorro cried. "I demand the trial of truth!"

"Señor!" José of the Cocopahs cried.

"I am your blood brother, and I have the right! The trial of truth, José! And we abide by the decision!"

The natives murmured at that, glanced at one another, and seemed disturbed.

"Do you deny me the right?" Zorro cried. "Are you lost to all honor?"

"The trial with whom?" José asked.

"With you! With the strongest man here of all the Cocopahs! It is my right! Throw more wood on the fire, that we may see the better!"

José hesitated a moment, and then:

"It is well!" he said.

SEÑOR ZORRO was released immediately, and stepped back from them. Dry wood was tossed into the flames of the fire, so that it blazed and made the corner of the little clearing as light as day. Zorro removed his sword, his jacket, and rolled up the sleeves of his silk waist. José of the Cocopahs stripped the upper part of his body, so that his bronze skin gleamed in the light of the fire.

"You are entitled, señor, to the trial of truth," José said. "But it is not my wish to slay you, for, alive, you may be traded. I shall wound you merely."

"The boaster always likes the sound of his own voice," Zorro observed. "I have but one wish."

"And what is that, señor?"

"When the trial of truth reveals that I am in the right, I wish the help of all men here in this my trouble. I wish them to obey my orders, as coming from a brother, and help me in my difficulty. In return, I promise that your brothers in cárcel shall be set free."

"If the trial of truth reveals your tongue is straight, you may demand anything of us, and we'll serve you," José replied.

Now they stepped up to each other, and another man came forward with leather thongs and lashed their left forearms together. And then each was handed a knife.

This trial of truth was a simple thing. Arms lashed together like that, they fought with the knives. And the man who lived — he had spoken truth. And the other had been false, hence entitled to the death which had claimed him.

There was a moment of silence while the natives stood back and formed a big circle, and waited quietly save for their heavy breathing.

"You are ready, señor?" José asked.

"I am waiting," Zorro replied.

One of the natives near the fire snapped the word. The knives met above their heads, clashed. And the fight was on.

José of the Cocopahs was strong and had skill. Zorro had learned the tricks of fighting, and he had strong cause for victory. But he knew he was facing an ordeal, knew it before half a minute had passed. The trial of truth called to José like a clarion call of some religion. He fought as he never had fought before.

Zorro tried to pull his antagonist off his feet, and failed. In turn, he was whirled through the air, but regained balance in time to prevent the knife of José entering his breast. He felt a burning streak against his left shoulder, and knew that he had been struck a glancing blow, and that it had brought blood.

Back and forth, around the fire, they fought, tugging and straining, neither able to get home a blow. The perspiration stood out on their faces in great globules, their breathing was in great gasps.

Zorro felt himself growing weak. It came to him that this fanatical native would kill, because this was the trial of truth, and it called upon him to do his utmost. To die like this, when he had so much for which to live!

Through his mind flashed visions of his father, his friends, the little señorita. To die like this — with a stain upon his name!

New strength seemed to come to him, and he made a furious attack, forcing the giant José backward. They were in the edge of the fire, kicking up a shower of hot embers. They danced away, slashing with their knives, guarding, working each for an advantage.

Again Zorro felt a streak of fire across his shoulder, and knew that the knife had slashed. But he had wrenched aside in time to prevent the thrust. And his new attack seemed to be weakening José. The giant Cocopah was slowing. His breathing was labored, and Zorro could tell by the expression in his face that he was commencing to fear the outcome.

They surged back to the edge of the fire again, and again they kicked aside a shower of embers. The natives around them were muttering now, knowing that this fight soon must end. José made another heroic effort, exerted all his strength, cut and slashed as Zorro writhed away from the knife. And then their wrists were locked above their heads again, and they strained for the mastery.

Strained, until their faces were first purple and then white, as though the blood had been drained from them. Strained until it seemed that their arms would break. A wrist turned lightly, another forced it back. A knife slipped, another slipped to ward it off.

And then José of the Cocopahs gave a great sob, and Zorro a last twist of his wrist, and Jose's knife fell to the ground, to clatter against a rock. He seemed to sway and sink.

But he pulled himself erect, this José of the Cocopahs, and held up his head bravely. His eyes gleamed, and he waited.

"Strike!" he said. "It is your right!"

"Did I speak true?" Zorro demanded.

"The trial has decided. You spoke true."

Zorro drew back his arm, and José stood waiting, his breast heaving as though to welcome the thrust of the knife. And then:

"I do not slay my brother!" Zorro said, and tossed his knife away. "Unlash our arms!"

"You shame me!" José cried. "Strike!"

"It is the law that I may spare your life, if I so wish, and claim it in service."

"So be it, Zorro!"

Their arms were untied, and they staggered away from each other. A man came running with a gourd filled with water from the spring, and they drank and drenched their heads and arms and sweating breasts.

DOWN the cañon a pony came rushing. The natives sprang to meet the rider, weapons held ready. But he proved to be one of them, a man they had sent to spy in Reina de Los Angeles. He sprang from his pony and rushed to José. He did not catch sight of Zorro.

"More evil!" the man cried. "The Señor Zorro is indeed a madman and turns against his old friends."

"Speak!" José cried.

"He attacked Juan, who lives in a hut at the edge of the pueblo — old Juan, who raises melons to sell to the people in the great houses. He beat Juan, and cut him with a sword."

"And when was this?" José demanded.

"But a short time ago. I came at once with the word."

"Señor Zorro did this?"

"Juan says so. The man was seen by others."

"But Señor Zorro was here at the time," José said. "He has been with us since early in the night. So it is the truth, then — there are two Zorros!"

José got up, while the messenger gulped in astonishment, and walked across to Zorro, to clasp his left arm in the gesture of brotherhood.

"I have wronged you, señor," José said. "We Cocopahs are your friends and brothers. We will help you in your trouble. Do you tell us what to do."

And then, for the space of two hours, Zorro told them.

Chapter Eight
A Forgotten Disguise

IT was an hour before dawn, with the moon gone and the night its blackest, when a man led a horse to the public corral in Reina de Los Angeles, let down the bars, and turned the animal in with other horses put there to await the pleasure of their masters.

The horse had no bridle or saddle, only a halter with a rope attached. The man put up the bars again, and slipped away through the black night.

A short time later this man appeared at the hut of Bardoso, the pirate, at the edge of the town, and pounded upon the door.

"Who is it?" Bardoso roared.

"Amigo!"

"A friend, eh? And does a friend come in the dead of night to ruin man's honest sleep? Does a friend break into dreams? Ha! Such friend should have his throat slit from ear to ear, or his entrails cut out, or made to walk the plank! Such friend — "

"Cry aloud, and tell the world our business!" came the interruption.

"Wait, false friend, till I make light."

"No light, fool!"

"So that is the way of it, eh? Know you, I shall have a dagger ready, and you be a friend in name only — "

"Open the door, fool! Make a light when I am inside. Slayer of innocent babes and looter of churches — "

"Ha!" Bardoso exploded. "It is somebody who in truth knows me! One moment, fair señor."

The door was opened, and the caller stepped inside. He felt the prick of a dagger point against his ribs, and chuckled. The door was closed again immediately.

"Stand you still! I can see in the dark with my one good eye," Bardoso declared.

The caller stood still against the wall. He could hear the reformed pirate fumbling in the darkness. There was a tiny spark, a glow, and a tallow pan burned. Bardoso whirled quickly, weapon held ready.

"By the saints! It is a stinking Cocopah!" he exclaimed. "No friend of mine! A sneaking, thieving Cocopah! They overrun the town! They — "

The caller chuckled, and tossed his serape aside:

"Don Diego!" Bardoso gasped.

"No names, good pirate!"

"In other words, Señor Zorro, who lashed me and the good, fat Fray Francisco with a whip! You dare come here? By the saints — "

"The saints are better off your lips, Señor Pirate!" Zorro interrupted. "It was not I who lashed you, and you know it."

"I know it now, since Fray Felipe has told me so," Bardoso said. "What do you here, Don Diego? In what way may I serve you?"

"I am not Don Diego just now, but Zorro, and none other. And perhaps you do not care to aid me, since it might turn the soldiers and their brave commandante against you."

"Ha! Have I love for soldiers? Do I coddle them and buy them wine? I am reformed, good señor, but the heart of a pirate burns in my breast yet where soldiers are concerned. It is in the blood, my hatred for soldiers!"

Zorro sat down on a stool, and Bardoso put forth a jug of wine and sat beside him. They ate and drank for a while in silence.

"Do you not run a certain risk being here?" Bardoso asked. "Who is this man who pretends to be Zorro and gives you a bad name?"

"I am not certain yet."

"And why does he do it?"

"That remains to be seen, good Bardoso. "

"Ha! I would like to be present when you meet him," Bardoso said. "I would see you carve the wretch. Put your initial on both his cheeks, his forehead, then carve it on his heart! What help may I give, good señor?"

"At dawn make your way to my father's house unseen," Zorro requested. "Find Bernardo, my servant. Make him understand that my horse is in the public corral. Tell him my disguise. He is to loiter around the corral, and when he sees my need, have the horse out and ready."

"He shall be told. He can neither hear nor speak but I know how to make him understand."

"His affliction is convenient at times," Zorro said. "The commandante for instance, knows better than to waste time trying to get information from him."

"In what other way may I serve you, good señor?"

"Perhaps I shall let you know from time to time," Zorro said.

"There is on the wall of the chapel, and also on the wall of the inn, a certain placard concerning you."

"What does it say?"

"It says that there is a reward offered, in the name of His Excellency, the Governor, for the capture of Don Diego Vega, also known as Señor Zorro."

"That is interesting."

"The most interesting part, señor is that the reward reads — dead or alive."

"What!" Zorro cried. "They dare — "

"Even so, señor. They are that anxious to get hands on you."

"Does it not occur to you, good Bardoso, that Rocha is unusually zealous in this matter?"

"He is hot about it," Bardoso replied. "You did a little carving on his cheek, it is whispered."

"Dead or alive, eh? Have you some faint idea, Bardoso, of claiming the reward?"

"What did I ever do, señor that you think me so base?"

"I was but jesting."

"I do not like that, even in jest. Do you take good care of yourself, señor. In this emergency, Rocha has gone to the extremity of issuing guns to his troopers, and is himself carrying a pistol."

"A coward's weapon!" Zorro said. " I shall rely upon my blade."

"The blade is more gentlemanly, I admit," Bardoso said, "but cannot be used at such a great distance. You need have little fear, however. If they shoot at you, undoubtedly they will hit somebody else... Anyhow, you are not even wearing a blade."

"It is hidden beneath my ragged clothing."

"Ha! You would have made a great pirate," Bardoso declared. "Let me forget my reform, and do you with your money fit out a ship, and we will fare forth. There is profit in it!"

"At present I am busy," Zorro replied, laughing a bit. "I wish a charred stick from your fire."

"A charred stick? Are you mad? Do you also wish a pinch of dust from the floor, a spider's web from the roof?"

"I have use for the charred stick," Zorro declared.

"Take it, señor. Who am I to deny you a charred stick? Is there nothing else you wish?"

"Only that you do as I have asked," Zorro replied. "Now, I must go. It is almost daylight."

"I'll go to your father's house at once, señor and see your servant."

Bardoso extinguished the light and opened the door. For an instant their hands touched. And then Zorro was gone into the night.

ZORRO went across the plaza, moving carefully so as not to disturb some sleeping hound and cause a chorus of howls that might attract unwelcome attention. The first streaks of dawn were coming into the sky as he reached the inn. There, on the wall just outside the door, was the placard.

He strained his eyes to read it in the faint light. And then, with the end of the charred stick, he scrawled at the bottom of the notice:

> A LIKE REWARD FOR THE CAPTURE OF THE MAN POSING AS MYSELF — ZORRO

He left the inn and continued around the plaza, stalking with his body bent forward, shuffling like a lazy native. Doors were being opened, and men were commencing to appear. The scent of smoke was in the air as cooking fires were started.

It was growing light rapidly. Zorro continued toward the chapel, the door of which was standing open. Through the misty shadows of the early morning another man lurched toward him, a man in his cups, evidently returning to the inn after an all-night bout with wine and dice. They crashed together.

"Native scum!" the other cried. "One side, dog!" His fist crashed against Zorro's breast, causing him to reel back and almost fall.

Zorro's clothes were those of a poor native, but beneath them burned the heart of a caballero. Zorro forgot his disguise and even his purpose in wearing it. He did not stop to think, could not anyhow have endured to play his role in a situation such as this. The scornful language, the fist against his body maddened him. He growled his rage at the humiliation, struck twice, and sent his adversary crashing to earth.

It was Juan Sanchez, the merchant, he felled — Juan Sanchez who had asked for his arrest in his father's house. And, as Zorro stood over the prostrate man, glaring angrily, breathing heavily, Sanchez looked up and recognized him, penetrated his disguise. But he did not betray that he knew.

Then there came to Zorro a full realization of what he was doing.

Supposedly a timid, cowed native, he had dared show fight. He had struck down a man, had got out of character at an important moment. He strove now to rectify the error. He pretended to be horrified at what he had done. As Juan Sanchez struggled to get to his feet, Zorro turned and ran speedily toward the chapel, as though to seek sanctuary there.

He expected an outcry, an immediate pursuit, but these things did not come. Juan Sanchez dusted his clothes with his hands, and turned to go toward the presidio. Zorro hurried on, and entered the chapel. He did not notice that Juan Sanchez met a trooper at the corner of the plaza.

"Soldier!" Sanchez cried. "This Señor Zorro — dressed like a native — has just gone into the chapel. Inform your commandante at once. There is a reward offered. Bring help. I will wait here."

But Zorro knew nothing at all of that. Inside the chapel an old fray came from the shadows and through a streak of light caused by certain candles. Zorro shuffled toward him.

"You wished to see me, my son?" the fray asked.

Zorro chuckled. "Do you not know me, Fray Felipe."

"Don Diego! You, here? And in disguise? Is there not danger."

"And am I the one to run from it?"

"There is no question as to your courage, my son, though there may be some regarding your good judgment," Fray Felipe replied. "What has happened?"

Don Diego told him everything, speaking rapidly — of the affair at the Pulido estate, of the natives gathered in the hills, and of some plans he had made.

"I must find this impostor," he said. "And I cannot find him by riding through the hills."

"Truth will prevail, my son. Nevertheless, move with caution and carry a ready blade."

"If you see my father, tell him of this visit. Undoubtedly, they are keeping close watch at our mansion."

"Undoubtedly. I shall make it my duty to see your father and say to him that you are well."

"Send word to Don Carlos Pulido to guard well the little señorita.

This man who plays at being Zorro — he might attempt anything, if he seeks to hurt me."

"The señorita shall be protected," Fray Felipe said.

"Thanks, good fray. And now I must leave the chapel. I would not cause you trouble by having it known I visited here."

"This sacred chapel is open to all, my son!"

"Nevertheless, trouble is a thing to be avoided," Zorro declared.

"This statement from you, my son — from you, who always go to seek it?"

Fray Felipe laughed, put an arm around the younger man, and they walked to the chapel door. And suddenly they recoiled, darted back into the shadows. On every side troopers were creeping upon the chapel.

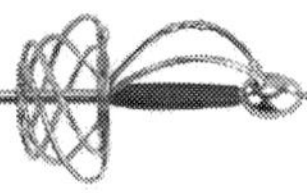

Chapter Nine
In A Close Corner

SEÑOR ZORRO had been in tight corners often enough. But trapped as he was now in the little chapel, he could see no hope of escape. His swift glance revealed the approach of the commandante and eight or nine men, including Sergeant Gonzales. They had spread out fan-fashion, to block an attempted escape in any direction. Capitán Rocha and two of his men stalked straight toward the chapel door, and the capitán held a pistol ready.

Zorro whirled to Fray Felipe.

"Your chapel shall not be desecrated by a brawl, good fray," he said. "I shall do my fighting out in the open. I carry my sword beneath my clothing."

"The odds are too great," Fray Felipe declared. "The commandante may bring you down with a pistol ball, my son. Stay here. The chapel is sanctuary."

Zorro shook his head. "I could not remain in the chapel forever."

Señor Zorro ripped open one side of his ragged garments and brought forth his naked blade, and started toward the door. But once again Fray Felipe gripped him by the arm.

"Come with me, my son, and ask no questions."

He moved swiftly through the shadows, back toward the altar, with Señor Zorro following at his heels. The soldiers outside were nearing the door. Fray Felipe led him to the wall behind the altar, where there was a little room used by the frailes.

"Be swift, my son," he said. "When this chapel was constructed, provision was made for retreat in time of trouble. There is a tunnel."

Fray Felipe had done something to the wall, and a small aperture appeared, and a gust of damp wind rushed out. Inside was nothing but darkness.

"Into it!" Fray Felipe ordered. "Feel your way, and do not worry about pitfalls. Caution, my son — and God go with you."

Señor Zorro felt himself thrust into the mouth of the tunnel, and the aperture was closed, cutting off the faint light of the candles. He was in a world of dampness, darkness and silence.

FRAY FELIPE walked slowly back to the altar and busied himself there. His aged face was serene and untroubled. Unpretentious, stoic Franciscan that he was, each day's events were only episodes in a long life of unselfish service.

There was a slight commotion at the door, and Fray Felipe turned his head in that direction. Capitán Rocha had entered the chapel, two soldiers behind him. The troopers took up position on either side of the door. Fray Felipe finished lighting a candle, then walked slowly toward the commandante.

"Where is he?" Rocha demanded. "Where have you hidden him? I know that you are friendly with Señor Zorro."

"Your voice is raucous for this, my chapel," the fray rebuked.

"I will endure no nonsense from a robed fray," said Rocha testily. "Delay not in answering. Señor Zorro was seen coming into this chapel a short time ago. He has not been seen to leave it. Where is he?"

"Do you see him here, señor?" Fray Felipe asked.

"Search the place!" Rocha bellowed. Take him, dead or alive!"

"Señor!" Felipe called, sternly. "Is this a place for such language?"

"I am a soldier, not a priest! If he fights, then it is Señor Zorro who desecrates the chapel. And where is he hiding?"

"I do not know, señor."

In truth, Fray Felipe could not tell where Señor Zorro was in the tunnel, if he was still in it at all. The search ended as swiftly as it had begun. There was no place, evidently, for a man to hide.

"There is some trick in this!" Rocha cried. "Listen you, fray! Tell me immediately where this Señor Zorro has gone, or I shall hold you accountable."

"Hold me?" Fray Felipe said, his voice lifting and his eyes glowing suddenly.

"Tell me at once where I can put hands on this rogue, or I shall put you under military arrest."

"You would dare?" Fray Felipe cried.

"I would. And put you in cárcel if you do not aid me."

Fray Felipe bowed his head. "If persecution comes, it is our lot to accept it," he said.

"Perhaps a dozen lashes might make you speak."

"You would dare?" Felipe cried. "The lash of disgrace, on my old back — if it gives you pleasure, señor, I cannot prevent you."

"There is a reward for this Señor Zorro," Rocha remarked. "Is it not possible that the money could be used to good advantage in your work with the poor?"

"Señor'" Felipe's voice was that of a man whose every sense of decency had been outraged. "Do you think a fray would take blood money, and use it for the poor?"

Capitán Rocha swept forward and seized the fray by an arm. Felipe flinched, but made no move to resist.

"Irons, here!" Rocha cried to his men.

His two troopers rushed toward him and offered the irons, but in a manner which said plainly that they did not relish this work.

"For the last time," Rocha said, "will you tell me what you did with this man known as Señor Zorro?"

"I have nothing to say, señor!" Fray Felipe replied.

"Very well!" The irons snapped. "Take him to cárcel!" he ordered the soldiers. "No — wait! Take him to the whipping post in the plaza, and detain him there until I come. I shall search outside with the others."

ZORRO fumbled his way through the tunnel, brushing his hands against walls that at times were dirt and at other times rough masonry. The dust was thick beneath his feet. Frequently, his hands came in contact with moisture. Now and then he bumped his head.

The air was damp, but not foul. It was excessively hot in the narrow tunnel. The perspiration streamed from Zorro's face and throat and arms, mingled with the dust and made mud. The tunnel curved to the right. Zorro lost all track of distance. It seemed that he had been in the stuffy tunnel for an age.

In the distance, he could see a faint streak of light. His blade was in his hand now. He came to a sudden turn, and crashed against the tunnel wall. There was more light just around the turn, and Zorro could see masonry. He could hear a voice which seemed familiar.

"Hunting him like hounds hunt a coyote!" the voice was saying. "There is something funny about this business. Though it be treason to say it, I declare Don Diego Vega has not done these things men say he has done."

"But everybody blames him, señor," another said.

"And do you blame him, ass? If I thought you believed it of him, I'd take off your hide in strips! I'd gouge out your eyes, limb of Satan! Get busy with the broom! Clean! No food until you have the place spick and span. This Zorro affair will be good for business!"

Señor Zorro grinned and went on along the tunnel. He saw more masonry, and was compelled to climb over some rocks. By lifting his head, he could see a huge kettle swinging on a crane.

The inn! The tunnel ended in the fireplace of the inn!

Zorro rested a moment, then got over the rocks silently and with extreme caution. He stood almost erect back at the side of the fireplace, trying to return his breathing to normal, endeavoring to wipe some of the perspiration and grime from his face and hands.

Then he stepped forward and peered into the big room. The landlord had gone into the kitchen. In a far corner, a native was brushing the floor with a broom, his back toward the fireplace.

Señor Zorro slipped into the room and to the nearest table. He sat down on the bench and put his blade beside him. He pulled his tattered clothing closer around him, and bent his head.

"Wine!" he called, in a voice sepulchral. "Serve me wine!"

The native turned, saw him, dropped the broom. The native was well aware of the fact that no man had been there a moment before, and knew that none had entered from the plaza. He gave a throaty yell that brought the landlord rushing from the kitchen.

"Wine!" Zorro growled again "Serve me! At once! And give me of the best!"

The landlord saw only a ragged native sitting at one of his best tables pounding upon it and demanding the best wine. Indignation almost caused him to choke.

"Wine?" he howled, grasping a club that leaned against the wall. "You dare to come into my place and ask for wine, you native scum? Out, before I beat you!"

The native got off the bench — and suddenly had a blade in his hand.

"What is this? You threaten?" the landlord cried. "You'll get cárcel for this — after a session at the whipping post. I'll call the soldiers — "

The man at the table threw back his head and laughed.

"Do you not know me?" he asked. "Do you recognize your friends only by their clothes?"

"Don Diego!"

"Señor Zorro, if you please!"

"Saints preserve us! It is you — and in those rags? Are you, then, indeed mad?"

" 'Tis but a disguise, fat one. Even now the soldiers are searching for me in the plaza. Give me wine!"

"How came you here?" the fat landlord asked, as he filled a mug.

"That is a secret." Zorro gulped the refreshing wine. "Give me something to eat, also — cold meat, bread, anything. My time is short."

As THE landlord rushed into his kitchen, Señor Zorro hurried to the nearest window. Soldiers were fussing around the plaza, acting as though they did not know what to do. Juan Sanchez, the merchant, was howling at them, mentioning the reward of which he claimed a share, urging the troopers in their search.

The landlord returned with cold meat, bread, honey. Zorro rushed to the table and wolfed down the food.

"No trouble shall come to you because of this," he said to the landlord, his mouth filled as he talked. "I compel you to feed me. You may tell the soldiers as much. Will you do me a favor?"

"Si, señor. Gladly."

"Get word to my friend, Don Audre Ruiz. Tell him to await me at the witch's hut on the Capistrano road. He must go there alone, and unobserved."

"It shall be done, Don Diego." The landlord hurried to the window. "They are still searching around the chapel."

"A futile search. Do you see the brave commandante?"

"Ha! He is just emerging from the chapel, señor. They have Fray Felipe! His wrists are ironed!"

"What?" Zorro left the table and rushed to the window.

"They are taking him to the whipping post, señor. The poor old fray — "

Señor Zorro said nothing more. He left the window, wrapped his ragged serape around his body so that it hid the sword he carried, and went into the kitchen of the inn. From the back door, he stepped behind the building, skirted the corner of it, and started slowly across the plaza.

Two soldiers were leading Fray Felipe toward the whipping post, as the commandante had ordered. Rocha himself was ordering more troopers about, urging them to search the buildings. Juan Sanchez, the merchant, was making a nuisance of himself howling for a capture. Natives were scattered around the plaza, and some men of quality had appeared to learn the cause of the din.

Señor Zorro shuffled along like a reluctant native going to work, but he was alert, watching the scene carefully. His steps took him in the direction of the public corral. Looking ahead, he could see Bernardo, his deaf and dumb servant, standing beside the corral gate. Bardoso had got word to him, then.

Fray Felipe had been conducted to the whipping post, but had not been tied to it. The soldiers were awaiting further orders, watching those in the plaza, having no fear that Fray Felipe would attempt an escape. The aged fray sat upon a stone, his head bent.

Señor Zorro went on toward the public corral, and when he was certain that he was not being observed, made a little signal that the watchful Bernardo saw and understood. Bernardo entered the corral instantly, got Zorro's horse, and led him to the gate. He let down the bars, brought the animal out, and put the bars back into place again.

Señor Zorro shuffled on, with a little more speed now, looking back every few steps to find that the scene had not changed. He came to the gate, thanked Bernardo with a glance, and motioned for him to be gone home, that he might not be blamed.

Zorro buckled his sword to the leather belt he wore, and picked up a mule whip somebody had left near the gate of the corral. A moment longer he waited, then mounted his horse.

At the far side of the plaza, Capitán Rocha was shouting to his men. Natives were trying to get out of the way, knowing from sad experience that the wrath of the commandante might turn on them. Juan Sanchez, the merchant, continued his raucous howling.

And suddenly there was a thunder of galloping hoofs, and a cloud of dust, through which charged a horse ridden bareback by a man who seemed to be a native. A chorus of cries rang around the plaza. It appeared that this horse was bolting, was out of control, might charge wildly into those before him.

Men rushed for places of safety. The horse dashed straight at the whipping post. The two soldiers darted aside, howling for Fray Felipe to save himself. The aged fray got slowly to his feet, glanced about bewilderedly, and turned to walk away.

But the horse swerved toward him, and there was another chorus of cries — cries of warning and pity. It seemed that the fray would be ground to death beneath the pounding hoofs. The horse swerved yet again, and seemed to skid to a moment's stop. The rider bent from the saddle, and his arm encircled the aged fray, lifted him from the ground.

A wild yell came from the throat of the horseman. The mount he bestrode, without guidance, darted straight at the soldiers. They rushed to clear a path for the charging beast. A whip sang, to snap at backs. Juan

Sanchez gave a screech of pain as he felt the lash bite into him.

Realization came to the commandante.

"It is Zorro!" he screeched. "To horse, and after him! An extra reward to the man who gets him! Fire at him — fire!"

But the bewildered soldiers did not fire. They had no wish to send a bullet into the body of the fray. Capitán Rocha discharged his pistol, without effect save to scar the wall of a house. And then, before the soldiers could make another move, the horse was gone in a great cloud of dust, gone toward the Capistrano road, Señor Zorro carrying the aged Fray Felipe with him.

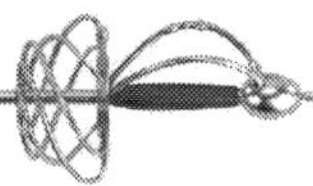

Chapter Ten
In Hiding

OVER a hill went the dust cloud in the center of which Zorro rode. It would take some time, he knew, for the pursuit to get mounted and after him. He shifted Fray Felipe to a position behind him, laughed, rode on. When he came to the next hill, he let his mount walk and have a breathing spell.

"Let me go, my son," Fray Felipe begged.

"And have you whipped and blame myself for it? You go to a place of safety, fray, until this affair is at an end."

"But I am a burden that delays your escape. Drop me beside the highway, Don Diego."

"Hold on, and ride!" Zorro ordered.

They came to the top of the hill, and once more the horse was sent to a run. Fray Felipe wrapped his arms around Zorro's waist and did considerate bouncing. Around a curve in the road they dashed, scattering a flock of sheep and frightening their native shepherd.

Then they approached a rocky gorge which opened upon the road and at the mouth of it was an adobe hut. Zorro began pulling up his horse.

"We stop at the witch's hut," he said.

"The abode of evil!" Fray Felipe declared. He would have crossed himself, no doubt, but dare not take an arm from around the waist of Zorro.

"The abode of a native woman who has more brains than men give her credit for having," Señor Zorro corrected. "Fear not, fray."

"They will overtake you, my son, if you stop here."

"There are mysteries about this hut, regarding which few know nothing. When I rode as Zorro before, I made use of it. Certain natives did the work for me," Zorro replied.

"I hide in the hut of no witch," Felipe declared.

"She is not a witch. She is a neophyte and goes to chapel regularly."

He skidded the horse to a stop in front of the hut in a cloud of dust and flying gravel. The door of the poor abode was opened. A native woman stood in it, a bent, gnarled woman of great age. Her eyes were bright as she looked up at Zorro, and she worked her lips as though muttering.

Zorro sprang off the horse, and pulled Fray Felipe down after him. The native woman hobbled to one side of the door.

"You know me?" Zorro asked.

"Si, señor!"

"You have heard certain tales regarding me, no doubt."

"But they are not true, señor. José of the Cocopahs has told me so."

"He is here now?"

"He is waiting, Señor Zorro."

"Good! This fray is to be hidden from the soldiers."

Fray Felipe looked surprised. "How may a man hide here, Don Diego?" he asked. "There is nothing but this poor adobe hut braced against the side of the hill."

Zorro laughed. "Come, fray!" he said. He motioned for the woman to stand aside again, and led the horse straight to the door. Into the hut he went with the animal, which scarcely was able to squeeze through. Fray Felipe followed, wondering.

And now the aged woman entered the hut also, and went to the rear of it, where there were some old boxes covered with a litter of skins. She pulled the boxes aside, lifted the skins out of the way, and exposed a jumble of rocks.

Señor Zorro laughed yet again and strode forward. He pressed against the rocks in a certain manner, and they fell aside. A dark hole yawned.

"The frailes of the missions were not the only ones to plan cunning retreats," Zorro said. "Within, there! It is safe to make a light now."

An instant later a tallow pan glowed. Zorro led the horse through the hole, and Fray Felipe followed. They were in a cave, and a hole in the top of it furnished ventilation.

Zorro turned to the old woman. "You have not seen me," he said. "It is a lie in a good cause. You heard a horse gallop past, going toward San Juan Capistrano."

"I understand, señor."

"Don Audre Ruiz may come. If he does, I wish to see him at once."

"Si, señor!"

"Brush away the tracks the horse made. That is all."

The hole was closed again. A man got up from a corner of the cave and came forward. He was José of the Cocopahs.

"You have news?" Zorro asked him.

"The men have scattered, Señor Zorro. What they discover will be reported to me."

"And they will gather in the plaza as I said?"

"Si, señor."

"If things happen as I expect, the men will keep from violence unless I give the word to fight."

"That is understood, Señor Zorro. Your blood brothers of the Cocapahs will serve you well."

"As I shall serve them well, José, whenever I have the opportunity."

"You can forgive us, señor, for thinking evil of you?"

"Freely," Zorro said.

SUDDENLY Zorro extinguished the light and hissed a warning for them to be silent. Side by side, they crouched in the darkness in the cave, close to the rocks which opened into the hut. The pounding of horses' hoofs had come to their ears.

"The commandante mounted his men in good time," Zorro whispered. "He is eager for the chase."

"It passes understanding," Fray Felipe whispered in return. "Generally, a commandante is not so zealous, especially where a caballero is concerned."

"This particular commandante has an itch for duty, it appears," Zorro said, chuckling. "Listen!"

Horses were brought to a stop in front of the hut. They heard a raucous voice.

"That is good Gonzales," Zorro whispered. "The commandante does not relish an early morning gallop, perhaps."

Sergeant Gonzales was bellowing at the crone in front of the hut.

"There has been a horse gallop this way?" he demanded in a voice that could have been heard above the roaring of a storm. "This horse had two men upon its back, one of them a robed fray."

"My eyes are not good, señor."

"Nor your memory," Sergeant Gonzales accused. "You wish a taste of the whipping post, eh?"

"If you harm me, señor, I shall cast a spell upon you!"

"Cast your spells elsewhere. I am plagued enough already," Gonzales declared. "Did the horse gallop on along the highway?"

"I know nothing, señor. Horses come and go," the woman said.

Sergeant Gonzales bellowed an order, and the cavalcade rode on.

Zorro called to the woman.

"How many soldiers." he asked.

"Ten, besides the big sergeant."

"Which leaves only two in Reina de Los Angeles with the commandante," Zorro observed. "And the sergeant will take his squad an hour's ride along the highway, no doubt, and stop at some rancho for food and wine. I know the good Gonzales. It is time for me to strike a blow!"

"A HORSEMAN comes, señor," the woman said. "A caballero."

"Those bad eyes regarding which you spoke to the sergeant — are they good enough to identify the caballero at the distance?"

"I think, señor, that it is your good friend, Don Audre Ruiz."

"I would see him," Zorro replied.

Then there was silence again for a time in the cave. Then somebody spoke on the other side of the rocks.

"Diego! This is Audre!"

"Ha, my good friend!"

"Do not come out. Speak from the cave. Command me, Diego."

"Good, my friend! Pass the word to the proper ones. Have them gather naturally in Reina de Los Angeles, hang around the inn and my father's house. The ringing of the chapel bell shall be a signal for them to gather."

"Who is to ring the bell — and when?"

"I do not know when. I'll send a man to ring it at the proper time."

"Stop playing the fox. Stop letting the hounds chase you," Don Audre Ruiz begged. "Come out and be Don Diego Vega. The commandante will dare not touch you."

"That would only be defiance."

"'Tis the chase you love," Ruiz declared. "You have the chance to play Zorro again."

"As you will. A Dios!"

"'Dios!" Ruiz replied.

SOME fifteen minutes later Señor Zorro led forth his horse from the cave. He had put bridle and saddle on, and Zorro had put off his native-attire, and was garbed in clothes more fitting.

Now Señor Zorro cut up over the hills and presently came to a crest from which he could see El Camino Real winding across the land like a great yellow serpent. Far in the distance he saw a cloud of dust where men rode, and knew they were Gonzales and his squad. He grinned when he noticed that the soldiers were nearing a great rancho noted for its hospitality.

Señor Zorro did not return to the highway, but made in the direction of Reina de Los Angeles by means of half-obscured trails. And finally he emerged a short distance from the pueblo, but on the opposite side.

It was the presidio at which he gazed long and thoughtfully. Two horses were tethered in front of it, two soldiers were sprawled on benches there. At the side of the building, another horse was tied, a big white animal which the commandante rode.

Señor Zorro approached the presidio from the rear, so that the two soldiers did not see him. Behind the building, he dismounted, and fastened his horse to a post in such a manner that a single quick jerk of the reins would untie him.

He stopped to listen, but heard nothing to cause him alarm. The cook was singing in the kitchen as he rattled his pots. The door of the armory stood open. Zorro hurried inside, and selected a pistol from a case, but did not load it, though he took some ammunition. He picked up the riata also, and tied it to his belt. Then he went out in the corridor of the building again, and tiptoed along it toward a door which was ajar.

He peered through. Capitán Rocha was sitting before his big desk, making out some reports. His brow was furrowed as though with deep thought.

Like a shadow, Señor Zorro slipped inside the room. He closed the door behind him noiselessly. He held the pistol in a menacing position, and then he spoke.

"ATTENTION, señor!" he said, in a low, tense voice.

Capitán Rocha gave an exclamation of surprise, sprang from his chair, whirled.

"Not a sound, or you die!" Zorro growled at him. "Be seated again! You are quite at my mercy, señor."

"I have but to cry out — "

"And die!"

Beads of perspiration popped out upon the forehead of the comandante. His face had gone white. He dropped back upon the stool and braced his elbows upon the desk, and his breath came in quick gasps.

"Talk in low tones," Zorro instructed. "We are to have an understanding, you and I. Why have you posed as Zorro and stained my name by evil deeds?"

"I have no wish to discuss it with you, señor."

"Perhaps you do not have the courage to admit your guilt."

Capitán Rocha snarled at him. "And why not?" he asked. "No one is here to listen. You have guessed it, Señor Zorro. What are you going to do about it?"

Señor Zorro straddled a stool, facing him, continuing to hold the pistol.

"You puzzle me, capitán," he admitted. "Why have you done this?"

"I came to Reina de Los Angeles for the purpose," Rocha declared. "The former commandante here, Capitán Ramon, was my friend. You killed him."

"Yes — in fair fight. That is not the reason you came here, my capitán. You are not a man to risk your life without thought of gain."

The capitán's face reddened. "You carried things off with a high hand when you rode as Zorro!" he flared. "You even humbled his Excellency, the Governor!"

"Forced him, rather, to dispense justice here in the southland."

"Humbled him," Rocha repeated. "And the Governor is my uncle!"

"Ha! I can see it now," Zorro said. "His excellency sent you here to undo me. With Zorro out of the way, you would be free to turn all of the southland to your own selfish ends."

"I intend to ruin you before I am done. You shall come to trial — or be slain," growled Rocha.

"Indeed?" Señor Zorro got off the stool and took a few turns around the room. But always he watched closely and always he held the pistol ready. "Now that we have had an understanding, I have only to make a fool of you and take my leave," Zorro added, as he took the riata from his belt. "Be careful how you move, capitán, unless you wish to die. Stand, turn your back,

"Not a sound, or you die!" Zorro growled at him.

and put your hands behind you."

His face livid, Capitán Rocha got up and turned his back, while Zorro watched him carefully. Zorro stepped forward swiftly, and slipped a noose over the wrists of the commandante, jerked the rope taut. Then, working swiftly, he bound his man hand and foot, threw him to the floor, tied him to the leg of the heavy desk.

He grasped a cloak from a stool, and gagged his victim with it, while the capitán gurgled and glared, then stood up and looked down at the man he had handled. But he was not yet done. He went to the desk and scrawled a sign, and pinned it to the capitán's blouse:

With the polite compliments of Señor Zorro.

Then he laughed lightly, and backed to the door.

"I should slay you," Zorro said, "but I must keep you alive until I can prove my innocence. When the proper hour comes, you shall die by my blade. Then news shall be sent north to his excellency, the Governor, with the request that he send a better man the next time he wishes to dispose of me. *Señor, a Dios!"*

Chapter Eleven
Decoys

SLIPPING out of the room, Señor Zorro passed swiftly through the corridor and left the building through the rear door. Sergeant Gonzalez and his men were just entering the town on the opposite side of the plaza.

Zorro swung up into his saddle and rode leisurely away from the presidio. He got behind a row of adobe huts and rode slowly until he was behind some of the great houses of the town. Zorro had a daring thought now, and immediately put it into execution. He rode into the patio of his father's house, and found Bernardo waiting. To the deaf mute, Zorro made certain signs. Bernardo took the horse and led him to the stables, where he was rubbed down and put into a stall. It would be the last place the soldiers would look for him.

And that house undoubtedly would be the last place, also, where they would be liable to look for Señor Zorro. So he entered the house from the patio, and emerged into the great living room, where he startled his august father so that he sprang out of his chair.

"Diego!" he cried. "You come here? Rash boy!"

"I know...Capitán Rocha has just informed me that it was he who impersonated me."

"What? We shall face him, denounce him — "

"And have the world still believe that I am guilty?"

"What else can be done?"

"Catch him at his work, my father. Let the world see two Zorros … Now I go to my little secret room and get some sleep."

Don Diego yawned and went up the broad stairs, while his father looked after him in mingled admiration and wonder. In a corner of that upper floor was a tiny room, reached through a hidden door in a wall. Don Diego passed through the door, undressed, and tossed himself upon a couch.

REFRESHED at the inn, Sergeant Gonzales and his men rode to the presidio. They were hot and dusty from their futile chase. Gonzales drew off his gloves, slapped some of the thick trail dust from his shoulders, and stalked into the presidio to report. The door of the capitán's room was closed, and the big sergeant knocked upon it. He got no summons to enter.

It was not unknown for the present commandante to entertain in his office some señorita with careless feet, and so the sergeant cleared his throat and knocked again, louder this time, giving Rocha ample time to hide the señorita in a closet.

There came no reply to his second knocking. He opened the door a crack, and peered inside.

What he saw caused good Sergeant Gonzales to draw in his breath sharply and choke back a cry of surprise. His capitán was stretched on the floor, bound and gagged. But Gonzales was a good soldier. He did not cry for help, knowing better than to expose his commander's plight to the world. Instead, he hurried into the room and closed the door. He worked furiously to get off the gag and the riata with which the capitán was bound. He helped his superior to his feet and to the nearest stool, and brought some water.

"Thanks, Gonzales!" his commandante muttered, working his sore jaws.

"I beg to report, capitán, that this Señor Zorro escaped us," said Gonzales.

"He has been here," Rocha said.

"Here, capitán?" Gonzales pretended surprise. He had glanced at the placard Zorro had left.

"Gonzales, this man must be caught. It would please me were he shot while trying to escape. I am not a fool. I know it is difficult to catch this Zorro. So — he must be decoyed. We shall do something to attract him into town. Men shall be posted around the plaza."

"Understood, capitán!" Gonzales agreed.

Capitán Rocha turned to his desk and reached for certain papers, wrote furiously. When he had finish he got up and paced the floor, as though trying to arrive at a decision, while Gonzales stood against the wall at attention, and waited.

"A brave idea!" Rocha muttered at last. "It drove Zorro to madness when my friend Ramon did even less, years ago." He stopped his pacing, faced the sergeant.

"Here are orders for arrest," he said. "Aiding enemies of his excellency. You will send the corporal and six men to make the arrests."

"And the prisoners, capitán — what is to be done with them?"

"Have we not a cárcel?"

"If the capitán will pardon me for saying so, the jail is a foul place, and at present there are some persons in it — " Gonzales ceased speaking and waved a hand eloquently.

"I am aware of it," Rocha said. "In the cárcel at present are two insane natives, three arrested for drunkenness, and two women charged with gross immorality. What of it?"

"I was only thinking, if the capitán pleases, that there might be a public feeling against the capitán — "

"That is my sole concern, sergeant. Here is another order for arrest, also same charge. Don Alejandro Vega."

Sergeant Gonzales gasped. Don Alejandro Vega! Leader of the haughty hidalgos! This would, indeed, create a sensation, and perhaps a deal of trouble.

Gonzales was a great admirer of Don Diego. He esteemed Don Alejandro, the father. He realized that his friend, Don Diego, was the victim of a plot. Sergeant Pedro Gonzales was in a tight corner, from which he could not fight his way free with a blade.

"He is to be put in cárcel?" Gonzales asked.

"At once. Send the squad after the Pulidos first. Make the arrest of Don Alejandro yourself, taking a couple of men with you. Endure no resistance!"

"It is an order, capitán!"

Chapter Twelve
Storm Clouds

Don Diego Vega came from the midst of a pleasant dream to find somebody shaking him gently and whispering in his ear. He sprang off the couch to find Bernardo and another native servant in the little secret room.

"Bernardo brought me, master, because he cannot talk swiftly," the servant said. "The soldiers have come and arrested your father. They took him to the cárcel."

"To that filthy hole — my father?" Don Diego cried.

Bernardo, standing at the window, made a peculiar gurgling sound. Don Diego whirled to find him excited, beckoning, and ran to the window also. And then he saw a sight which made the blood surge boiling through his veins.

A squad of soldiers were conducting two more prisoners toward the cárcel — Señorita Lolita Pulido and her gentle mother.

Don Diego's first impulse was to rush from the house, naked sword in hand, vigorously attack the soldiers, and rescue the prisoners and bring them into the house. Common sense told him that such a course would be useless and would only be playing into the hands of the enemy.

He stood back a short distance from the window, so he could not be seen if anybody happened to glance that way. He watched the soldier escort conduct the prisoners across the plaza and to the cárcel. Then Don Diego motioned for Bernardo to come to him, seized the tablet the man always carried, and wrote swiftly:

Don Audre Ruiz — somewhere around plaza — get him.

Bernardo nodded that he understood, and hurried away.

Don Diego paced back and forth from corner to corner of the little room. It was not long before Don Audre Ruiz came to him.

"This is not to be endured!" Don Diego raged. "We must take action."

"It will be the end of this commandante. Don Audre Ruiz assured him. "A score of blades will be at his throat!"

"He belongs to me!" Don Diego cried. "Pass the word for all others to keep their hands off him."

"And what is to be done?"

"Arouse the caballeros and have them gather around the plaza. I'll have the chapel bell rung, and that will bring the Cocopahs. They, too, will loiter around the cárcel."

Don Audre was standing at the window, looking down into the busy plaza.

"Look!" he cried. "Capitán Rocha goes to the cárcel."

"He goes to accuse them, or taunt them," Don Diego groaned. "I cannot endure it, Audre! Whatever befalls, I must take my sword — "

"Softly — softly!" Don Audre Ruiz begged. "I'll hasten out and talk to some of the others. We may find a way to get the prisoners released."

"Send me word, whatever happens," Don Diego begged.

Capitán Rocha strutted across the plaza to the jail like a conquering hero newly returned from the wars, with two soldiers at his heels. The prisoners had been detained in the office of the jailer.

"What is the meaning of this outrage, señor?" Don Alejandro Vega demanded.

"Where is Don Diego, your son?" Rocha countered.

"If you wish him, seek him."

"He is a fugitive, and you are helping hide him," Rocha charged. "You place yourself in opposition to the wishes of the Governor."

"The Governor? Bah! Were he here, I should demand your instant dismissal."

Rocha smiled. "Take it up with his secretary, Don Esteban Garcia," he suggested. "He is coming south on a tour of inspection within a day or so."

"Tell me, then," asked Don Alejandro quietly, "why are you holding gentle ladies in this foul place?"

"Señor Zorro was at the Pulido estate and slew two men there."

"They were hired assassins who tried to kill him," Señorita Lolita cried. "Perhaps, capitán, you know something of that?"

Rocha's face burned with anger. "Zorro mistreated some of my troopers at your estate, also," he said.

"He also carved your cheek with the letter Z, did he not?" the señorita asked.

"Enough of this!" Rocha cried. "Jailer, conduct Don Alejandro to the common detention room."

Don Alejandro arose in all his dignity. "Take me," he said quietly. "I prefer the company of those poor wretches to the commandante's."

The commandante closed the door and faced Doña Catalina's stony glare, and the little señorita's flaming eyes. Capitán Rocha smiled.

"Doña Catalina, in the absence of your husband, I have the honor to ask you for the hand of your daughter in marriage." He bowed.

"Are you jesting?" Doña Catalina asked him, motioning for the angry señorita to remain silent. "Surely you would not offer your grand name to a maiden in prison."

"I make the offer in all sincerity."

"My daughter is betrothed to Don Diego Vega."

"But he is a fugitive from justice," Rocha protested. "Think well, señora, before you refuse."

"I consider your proposal an insult," Doña Catalina replied.

Capitán Rocha's face turned purple. "Then you may expect scant mercy from me," he declared.

The doña turned her head contemptuously.

Rocha suggested: "Look with favor upon my suit, and I will withdraw the offer of reward for Don Diego Vega, forgive him his trespasses against the laws and ask only a parole from his father. Refuse me, and my men shall have orders to slay him at sight."

"You would dare?" Doña Catalina cried.

"Why not? He is a menace to men. I have the law at my back. I shall give you a chance to consider what I have said."

ROCHA left the room, went out of the cárcel, was joined by his two troopers, and gave a swift glance around the plaza.

He saw groups of men standing around in whispered conversation — caballeros, natives, citizens — and he did not doubt that they were speaking of him, and speaking ill.

The bell of the chapel started sounding, but Capitán Rocha paid little attention to it. The confounded frailes were always ringing their bells, a nuisance at times! It was enough to get on a man's nerves, that steady hammering of wooden clapper against bell made of leather stretched tight around a frame.

Flap, flap! … flap, flap! … flap, flap!

That was the way it sounded — a sort of flat, dismal sound. Capitán Rocha did not guess that it was sending out a message for his enemies to gather, that certain of the caballeros heard it and moved toward the plaza, that natives heard it and drifted in the same direction.

Rocha knew he must put on a bold front and justify his position. It was his nature to confront those who despised him, sneer at them to show that he had no fear. He went toward the inn, with his two troopers at his heels.

He strode along as though oblivious of the sour glances cast his way. He entered the inn with his two men. The place was deserted save for Juan Sanchez, the merchant, who was bathing his sorrows in wine.

Rocha settled himself on a bench beside one of the long tables, and waved his soldiers toward another bench.

"Wine!" Capitán Rocha ordered.

The fat landlord made haste to serve him, nervously spilling the wine over the edge of the mug. Capitán Rocha directed that his troopers be served also. He sprawled on the bench, sipping his wine, and looking at those in the room through narrowed eyes.

Juan Sanchez, the merchant, arose and reeled toward him.

"Greetings, commandante!" he called. "You have not yet caught this pest of a Señor Zorro?"

"We are searching for him."

A couple of caballeros entered the room. They glanced toward Rocha as though he had been something inanimate. Capitán Rocha flushed at the night. Two more entered the inn, to sit quietly at a table near the door. They ignored Rocha's presence.

Juan Sanchez raved on concerning his rights and wrongs, while Rocha sipped at his wine and wished the man would have done. More caballeros slipped quietly into the inn, to sit at tables or stand against the walls with their arms folded. They were silent and stern of face, like men bent on some grim purpose.

Capitán Rocha commenced feeling uncomfortable. In whatever direction he glanced, he found accusing eyes, eloquently curving lips, saw hands toying with the hilts of blades as though itching to draw there. He noticed that Don Audre Ruiz was among those present. Ruiz moved around the big room, speaking to each of the men in turn.

"RUIZ!" the commandante snapped.

The manner of his speech scarcely was courteous, and there was an instant of ominous silence in the inn. Don Audre Ruiz turned his head and observed Rocha as though seeing him for the first time, and his eyebrows lifted questioningly.

"You address me, señor?" Don Audre asked.

"I do. Come here."

"Pardon me, but I am not in the habit of taking such orders."

Rocha sprang to his feet, his face livid. "Do you dare dispute my authority?"

"I do," Don Audre replied.

"Ha!" Capitán Rocha cried, as he lurched forward. "This is not to be endured! You rally to the defense of this Señor Zorro, a beater of natives and women, author of attacks only a coward would make!"

Some of the men stepped forward angrily, but Don Audre motioned for them to be patient.

"Señor Zorro needs no defense from us," Don Audre said. "He is a gallant gentleman."

"He has, indeed, done some gallant things recently," Rocha replied.

"We do not believe he did them," Don Audre said. "And we resent the arrest of Don Alejandro and the ladies of the Pulido family."

"Indeed? They were guilty of abetting this Zorro. If he commits another atrocity — "

"If he really does, commandante, then we might agree that you should take measures to preserve the peace."

"Ha! I shall remember that."

Capitán Rocha fought himself to keep back a smile. Events were shaping themselves to suit him. Señor Zorro surely would commit another atrocity; Rocha himself would see to that.

If that failed, Rocha had an ace up his sleeve. He would soon welcome Don Esteban Garcia, secretary to the Governor. There was a man to hurl terror into the heart of one like Zorro! Don Esteban was the real power behind the throne; a brilliant swordsman himself, with a band of well-trained fighters always at his call. Even the Governor himself feared the man.

Don Esteban and Capitán Rocha made a great pair. This brace of consummate villains had worked together in the north with such fervor that the Governor had separated them by sending Rocha to Reina de Los Angeles.

Chapter Thirteen
By Force of Arms

NATIVES gathered and shuffled around the plaza, especially certain Cocopahs, and drifted in the direction of the presidio, where Sergeant Gonzales was in command.

"There seem to be more natives than usual abroad today," Sergeant Gonzales observed to his corporal. "Whisper to the men to be on the alert. There may be trouble."

A certain horseman came riding from the corner of the plaza, on a magnificent black. He bent forward in his saddle and got speed out of his mount. Straight across the plaza toward the jail he raced, scattering men out of his path. A mask obscured his face. He skidded his mount to a stop in front of the cárcel and sprang from the saddle. He rushed to the door. Holding a pistol ready, he thrust the door open, and came face to face with the jailer.

The jailer gasped in fright.

"I have come for Don Alejandro Vega," said Zorro. "Open up!"

"It is against the law to release a prisoner by force of arms."

"It is also against the law, I doubt not, to shoot down a jailer. Move, señor!"

"I am compelled." the jailer announced, as he reached for his keys.

Down the corridor he was forced to go with his hands held high, and Zorro immediately behind him with the pistol ready. The door of the common detention room was unlocked and opened.

"Don Alejandro, come forth!" the jailer called.

The proud Don Alejandro emerged from the darkness, blinking because of the bright light. He blinked yet again when he beheld Señor Zorro.

"Don Alejandro, hurry out of this foul place," Zorro ordered. "Take with you certain gentle ladies. Where are they to be found?"

"They are in a room in front," the jailer said.

Down the corridor they hurried, and another door was thrown open, and Doña Catalina and the señorita sprang to their feet.

"Zorro!" the señorita cried. "I knew you would come to the rescue."

"Come with me!" Zorro exclaimed. "Lead the way to the door, jailer."

On they went, Don Alejandro aiding Doña Catalina, and the señorita clinging happily to the arm of Zorro.

"Go to my father's house," Zorro instructed them. "The caballeros will protect the place."

"And you — " she asked.

"I have work to do."

"Be cautious, my Zorro!"

Then they were outside the cárcel in the bright sunshine. A cart was passing, and Zorro seized it. Don Alejandro helped the ladies, and Señor Zorro mounted his horse.

"Are you not afraid of capture! Señor Bandit?" the little señorita asked.

"Bright eyes already have captured me," he said.

"How much is the ransom?"

"A million kisses."

"It is not possible for a frail girl to resist an armed robber," she replied.

The cart came to a stop, and Don Alejandro helped the ladies out.

"Hasten into the house," Zorro said.

Then Señor Zorro gave his black horse a dig with the spurs and was gone. In a cloud of dust he rode around the house. But instead of making a wild dash for the Capistrano road, he raced into the patio, turned the horse over to Bernardo, and darted to the plaza again.

Turmoil was in the plaza now. The soldiers at the presidio had witnessed the rescue of the prisoners. They had rushed to get at their horses, but a group of natives seemed to get in their way, and had to be kicked and cuffed.

The big Sergeant Gonzales had some difficulty getting into his saddle. When he finally had done so he looked around as though bewildered.

"The capitán is not here," he observed, "and I scarcely know how to proceed without his guidance."

"Would it not be best to chase the fellow?" the corporal asked.

"Are you presuming to instruct me, your superior, in my duties?" Gonzales roared at him.

"But the man is escaping!"

"So he is. But what am I to do without specific orders?" Gonzales asked, his eyes twinkling. "However, I shall take it upon myself to ride out the Capistrano road a distance and see whether we can find our man."

Sergeant Gonzales grinned and led the way at a gallop.

In the inn, Don Audre Ruiz was standing in front of Capitán Rocha, and the others in the room were facing the commandante also. The native servants had hurried, frightened, into the kitchen, and the fat landlord hovered about, trembling with fear.

"You came to this post from San Francisco de Asis, did you not?" Don Audre was asking. "You did a foolish thing."

"Are you threatening me, señor?"

"I am not. But nothing would give me greater pleasure, capitán, than to cross blades with you."

"You have an injured wrist, perhaps?" Rocha sneered.

"It is not that, señor. You belong to another, when he is ready to claim you," Don Audre explained.

"This Señor Zorro, possibly? But that pretty gentleman fails to honor me with his presence," Rocha said. "He is too busy running from my troopers. He is — "

Capitán Rocha ceased speaking suddenly. He almost choked, his face turned white, his eyes bulged. At the other end of the room, near the fireplace, stood Señor Zorro, his mask over his face again, his arms folded across his breast.

"Zorro!" Don Audre cried. "How came you there?"

The others cried their surprise also. Señor Zorro walked forward slowly, his arms now swinging at his sides, his eyes gleaming through the holes in his mask.

Rocha started to draw blade.

"Detain him!" Zorro commanded.

Rocha suddenly found half a dozen caballeros before him, swords out and ready.

"So!" Rocha cried. "The brave Señor Zorro calls a small army of friends to his aid."

"I do not desire to fight you now," Zorro said. "I am here to give you certain orders. You will send your resignation to the Governor and quit Reina de Los Angeles at once."

Rocha laughed. "Are you mad? You are a fugitive from justice. These men helping you are liable for punishment also. And you stand there and demand that I surrender my rank. Yes, you are mad!"

"I also have released certain prisoners you had in cárcel," Zorro told him.

Juan Sanchez, the merchant, thrust his inebriated way forward into the room.

"Commandante!" he cried. "Seize this man! He is the one who attacked me. Call your soldiers!"

Zorro laughed. "The soldiers are chasing shadows out along the highway," he said.

"Dios!" Rocha swore. "Draw your blade, señor, or be termed coward!"

As HE SPOKE, Rocha whipped out his own sword. At a sign from Zorro, the caballeros fell aside. Zorro sprang lightly toward the wall, drawing blade as he did so. A light laugh came from behind the mask.

"So you will have it, eh?" Zorro said. "Then show us that you are a credit to the service you ornament."

Rocha howled his rage and rushed. Zorro retreated and let the man get over his wild burst of wrath.

"I could have had you then," Zorro said. "Never let anger rob you of caution. Now, commandante, fight in a proper style, guarding yourself well, attending to wrist and eye."

"Do you tell me how to handle a blade?" Rocha cried.

"Somebody should," Zorro replied. "For instance, look how you are holding it now. When it is held so, this happens."

Zorro's blade darted in like the tongue of a snake, there came a sharp cry from the capitán, and his weapon was jerked from his hand, to describe an arc in the air and fall clattering to the floor.

Zorro laughed and sprang backward, dropping his point. Rocha paled and his breathing suddenly became deep and rapid.

"I spare you, señor," Zorro said. "I fully expect to slay you, but this is not the proper time."

"If you are wise, you will kill me now!" Rocha cried.

"At the proper time," Zorro repeated. "I insist upon having my own way in this affair, señor. Do not be in so great a hurry to die."

Zorro laughed again, and the caballeros laughed with him, while Capitán Rocha swore great oaths that he would some day wipe out this stain. It was a wild cry from one of the native servants that caused them to whirl quickly, Zorro swiftest of all.

Juan Sanchez, the merchant, had thought that here was an opportunity to square accounts and also reap rich reward. Unobserved, he had picked up the sword of the capitán from where it had fallen to the floor. And now he rushed forward like a madman, charging with the blade.

Zorro danced nimbly aside, yet the blade scratched his left arm. His own sword flashed forward, and came back red. Juan Sanchez coughed and fell.

"It should have been a mortal wound, though it is not," Zorro said. "Such a foul attack merited one. Reina de Los Angeles will be the better for your absence, señor, when you are able to travel. See to it!"

Then Zorro sprang backward again, toward the end of the big room.

"A favor, señores," be begged. "Do all of you face the other way, and keep so for a moment. Don Audre, kindly see that the capitán does as I request. Landlord, view the front door, and do not turn if you value your skin. Quick, señores!"

They complied with his request, wondering at it. They heard him laugh lightly again, and then there was silence. And, after a moment, Don Audre Ruiz turned.

Señor Zorro was gone.

"After him!" Rocha screeched at his two soldiers. "Get outside. He went through that open window."

They rushed out, but Señor Zorro was not to be seen. And two men were standing just outside the window, and swore that nobody had come through it.

Señor Zorro, meanwhile, was making his way back through the tunnel to the chapel. He came to the chapel wall and listened. He could hear voices on the other side. So he dared not leave the tunnel now and so disclose its existence. He owed it to old Fray Felipe not to reveal the secret. It was likely that the tunnel would be of great use in the near future.

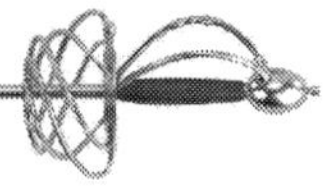

Chapter Fourteen
Mutiny

SOME time later, Señor Zorro opened the hole in the wall and slipped quietly into the semi-dark chapel. He crouched there in a corner for a moment, scrutinizing the place and listening to the sounds outside. Then he sped silently across to the door and peered out into the plaza.

He could see the troopers down by the presidio, and could make out the white horse of the commandante. Then he saw Capitán Rocha himself, waving his arms and evidently shouting orders. Men were scattered through the plaza but women were absent, which was a sure sign that trouble was expected.

Señor Zorro stepped forth and cut across the corner of the plaza at an ordinary rate of speed, so as not to attract attention. He gained the rear of his father's house, slipped through the patio and entered the building.

Don Alejandro was in the big living room, and Doña Catalina and the little señorita also. Don Audre Ruiz was there, talking to them.

"Rocha will scarcely make a hostile move," Don Audre was saying. "If he does attempt it, we are prepared to resist him. He will think twice before causing a battle."

"Diego!" the little señorita cried as she caught sight of him. With an utter disregard of the strict conventions, she rushed up to him and clasped him by the arm, and held up her face to be kissed. Also disregarding the strict conventions, Zorro kissed her.

"Where have you been, my son?" Don Alejandro asked.

"In hiding," Zorro explained. "I cannot explain the exact way of it, for it is a secret."

"And how did you escape from the inn?" Don Audre asked.

"It is the same secret," Zorro replied, smiling. "What is the news?"

"José of the Cocopahs has sent word that the commandante will be watched closely. And our friends are prepared to act, if the commandante decides to regain possession of these his prisoners."

A cry from a servant watching at a window engaged their attention. Zorro rushed to the window with Don Audre at his side. The soldiers had mounted, and were coming across the plaza toward the house.

"Diego, go into hiding," Ruiz said.

"At such a time?"

"Do not be foolish and risk yourself. There is no danger for the rest. The caballeros are waiting for this to happen. Do not forget, my friend, that the false Zorro must be unmasked if you are to clear your name. You must live to do the work. Even a wound might prevent."

"Go to your secret room, my son," Don Alejandro said.

"Go, Diego — please!" the señorita begged.

That settled it. Señor Zorro hurried up the broad stairs and went to the little secret room, where he stood at the side of the window to watch and listen.

THE SUN was sinking, and the shadows were long in the plaza, and through the shadows rode the troopers with Rocha at their head. They rode slowly, and in formation.

Then Señor Zorro noticed a thing which pleased and amused him. From almost every direction, caballeros started wandering toward the Vega casa. They sauntered along as though merely taking the air, or on parade for the benefit of ladies' eyes.

One by one, two by two, they drew together at the Vega house. They stood in front of it to gossip. Some wandered around to the rear, and into the patio. As Don Diego watched, he saw Don Audre Ruiz leave the house and join his friends in front of it.

Capitán Rocha led his troopers on across the plaza and straight toward his destination. His head was up, his eyes were flashing. Inwardly, he was seething. He sensed that the town was laughing at him, and he was sensitive to ridicule.

He shouted an order, and the troopers spread out in line and kept on. He brought them to a stop a few feet from the front of the house, and looked down at Don Audre and the caballeros who were with him.

"Disperse!" Capitán Rocha shouted.

"Do you dare address us as though we were plotting natives?" Don Audre Ruiz snapped at him. "We are gentlemen and citizens, and have a right to gather and talk."

"Under ordinary circumstances that would be true," Capitán Rocha said. "But I give this order as a military necessity."

"How is this?" Ruiz asked.

"We have come to retake escaped prisoners, and your presence here hampers our plans."

"We are aware of that fact," Don Audre replied. "It is our desire to hamper them."

"A caballero should have respect for authority."

"When it is not abused," Ruiz told him. "Capitán Rocha, those you seek are in the Vega house. And there they shall remain until they choose to go elsewhere!"

"They face charges — "

"It is your official right to file charges and hold an examination on them," Don Audre interrupted. "But it is not necessary to place gentle folk in a foul cárcel with drunken natives and dissolute women. When you wish to hold a trial, your prisoners will appear. Until then, you must accept their parole through me."

"Enough!" Capitán Rocha cried. "I have come for the prisoners, and shall take them. If there is resistance — "

"Undoubtedly, you'll find a quantity of it, señor!" Don Audre interrupted again.

He gave a signal, and the caballeros immediately drew their blades. They stepped back and formed a line in front of the door. All of them were smiling, and some of them were humming songs. They swished their blades through the air, whipped them, cut and thrust as in preparation for fight.

The troopers viewed this play with keen interest. They knew better than to turn up their noses at these pretty lads with their fancy swords. Each was a man of blood and breeding, and the majority had been taught the finer points of fence by sterling masters. Combat with such was not a thing to be regarded lightly.

Capitán Rocha suddenly faced his troopers. "Draw!" he commanded. "Prepare to dismount and enter the house. If any stand in the way, clear the paths!" He looked down at the caballeros again. "And to the cárcel with any who are able to be taken there after it is over," he added.

"One moment, capitán!" It was Sergeant Gonzales who thus addressed his superior officer.

"Well, sergeant?"

"If I may make the suggestion, commandante — I have been stationed here in Reina de Los Angeles for a long time, and know its people and its customs well. Let me suggest that it would be best to allow the prisoners to remain in this house, and take their honorable parole."

"You dare make such a suggestion!" Rocha cried.

"I dare do so. I know these fine caballeros. They fight as though the devil guarded them. I am prepared to die at any moment, being a soldier and dying my trade, but I prefer not to die in such an unworthy cause."

"Is this mutiny?" Rocha cried.

"Certainly not! I am only trying to give you some good advice," the sergeant said. "It is in our articles of training that a noncommissioned officer may give advice if he has knowledge, and it is treason not to do so."

"Perhaps you fear for your thick skin," Rocha suggested, sneering a trifle. "Dismount!"

The troopers obeyed the order mechanically, because of the discipline of training. They drew blades also, and Rocha placed himself at their head.

"I again order you to disperse!" he said to the caballeros. "It is the last warning!"

There came no reply to his order. Don Audre Ruiz whispered something to the others, and they braced themselves and stood ready. Rocha marched straight toward the door, his men following.

A blade came up. Capitán Rocha howled an oath and brought up his own. There was a quick exchange, and the commandante reeled back with a scratch on his right forearm, and his sword on the ground.

"Charge them!" he bellowed at his men. "Capture or slay! In the Governor's name!"

But the troopers made no move forward. And suddenly Sergeant Gonzales was in front of them, holding up his left hand.

"Fall back!" he commanded. "Two of you instantly take charge of the commandante. Mount, and return to the presidio."

"What is this?" Capitán Rocha screeched. "Treason! Mutiny! For this, Gonzales, you shall die at the end of a rope!"

"It is the rule," the sergeant informed him, "that when an officer suddenly becomes insane, the next in rank may take charge, depose the mad one, and have him placed in custody."

"You dare say that I am insane,"

"That is my present judgment, Capitán Rocha. None but an insane man would act as you are acting now. Perhaps it is a touch of the sun."

"I'll prefer charges against you!"

"It is possible, capitán, that you'll die before they can be preferred, if you continue along your present path," Gonzales said. "I am acting for your own good, and I do not doubt that the Governor himself will agree as to it. Do you go to your horse quietly, capitán, or do I have the men bind and carry you?"

"This is something that cannot be overlooked," Rocha said. "We return at once to the presidio, and hold a court-martial! Don Audre Ruiz!"

"Yes?"

"I accept the parole of the prisoners for the time being."

"It is given in honor, commandante."

Capitán Rocha turned swiftly, got up into his saddle, and galloped back across the plaza, almost running down several in his path. He was like a madman in truth, now. Unable to command his own troopers! And scores had seen and heard, and would spread the tale!

At the presidio, he retired to his private quarters, there to pace the floor and think on the situation. Everything had gone against him! The town and countryside were laughing at him! They were making a hero of Don Diego Vega, this detestable Señor Zorro. There remained but one thing to be done. Señor Zorro must commit some new atrocity, something that would shock greatly, that would cause a demand for him to be hunted down like a maddened cur.

But first — there was the matter of the rebellious Sergeant Pedro Gonzales. The sergeant must be punished, and immediately. However, Capitán Rocha did not have the chance to punish him just then. For there came a knock on the door, and upon the capitán's call to enter, the sergeant presented himself.

"The secretary of His Excellence, the Governor, nears the town," Sergeant Gonzales announced. "One of his escort has come ahead with the information."

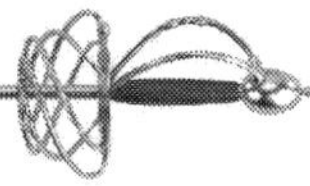

Chapter Fifteen
A Fiend Abroad

DON ESTEBAN GARCIA, secretary to His Excellency, was more than a man who merely obeyed orders and attended to details for his employer. Don Esteban was the power behind the throne, and held the State together. His decisions carried very great weight with the Governor.

For Don Esteban was renowned throughout California for his brilliant swordplay, and the band of daring swordsmen who rode with him struck terror into the hearts of natives and whites alike. So strict was Don Esteban in enforcing the laws to the last letter, that none knew when he might be taken to task. It had gone hard with those who had dared to oppose the Governor's secretary.

So, receiving news of Don Esteban's approach, the capitán made haste to arrange his toilet, don his most gorgeous uniform and his finest sword with its jeweled hilt. He had the troopers clean quarters and get out rare wines, and sent certain important orders to the presidio cook.

An hour later, just before dusk, Don Esteban Garcia arrived. A dozen men rode with him as escort. The party made grand entrance to the town, swept across the plaza, and dashed to the presidio. Capitán Rocha received the secretary of His Excellency in proper fashion, as the soldiers fired a salute.

Being conducted to the private quarters of the commandante, Don Esteban tossed his sword aside, sprawled on a bench, loosened his tunic, and grinned.

"Wine, my friend!" he demanded. "It has been a long and dusty journey. Food! Entertainment!"

"All shall be forthcoming," Rocha declared.

"And how are things going with you here, my friend? Was my arrival timed correctly? By the saints? Your face has been badly scratched!" Don Esteban bent forward to see better. "It's a letter Z! Did that fellow — "

"He did!" Capitán Rocha interrupted, getting up and storming around the room. "Everything's gone wrong. I have failed to avenge Ramón."

"Tell me of it," Don Esteban ordered.

Capitán Rocha told the story, omitting nothing, giving all the minor details. Don Esteban sipped his wine and regarded him thoughtfully.

"A maze of errors, my friend," he passed judgment. "You went at the thing with too much strength, rushed the affair. However, the evil is done and the situation must be remedied."

"There is but the one sure way to remedy it," Capitán Rocha declared.

"There must be more evil acts, committed in such a fashion that everybody will believe this Zorro did them."

"An excellent idea! And where is this Señor Zorro now?"

"I do not know," Rocha replied, as he prepared to light the candles.

AT THAT instant Señor Zorro was leaving his father's house, creeping across the patio through the dusk. Those inside were unaware of his departure. He had slipped away, deciding that he would look over the situation and have speech with José of the Cocopahs, could he locate him.

He knew of the arrival of Don Esteban Garcia, and guessed that the secretary of His Excellency wished him no good. Even now, Zorro supposed, Don Esteban and Capitán Rocha were discussing him, possibly planning to undo him.

The spirit of dare-deviltry entered the breast of Señor Zorro again. Why not, he asked himself, overhear the conversation in which he undoubtedly was a principal topic? So he went on through the gathering night, avoiding all men, and neared the presidio.

Crouching in the darkness, he watched and listened for a time. Some of the troopers were in the building, and some out in front of it, while others had gone to the inn. The garrison cook was singing as he rattled pots and pans.

There was a dark window not far away, an open one, and through this Señor Zorro entered the building. He found that he was in a small wine vault adjoining the capitán's office. Rocha and Don Esteban were talking.

"The principal thing," Rocha was saying, "is to act at a time when the whereabouts of Zorro are unknown to others, so he will have no defense."

"And what atrocities will you commit?" Don Esteban asked, laughing.

"Leave that to me, my friend. What I shall do will make the name of Zorro hated. There will be no further opposition when I run him down."

"Let us get at it," Don Esteban said. "His Excellency will be displeased if the thing is not done. He has small love for this Señor Zorro or any of his friends. He must be disgraced, then imprisoned or slain."

"He shall be slain!" Rocha decided.

"As you wish it! Let's have an end of it, and then some entertainment. Now, more wine!"

"I'll attend to that immediately, and by myself," Rocha said.

In the dark vault where Señor Zorro was crouched near a grilled opening, there was rich wine of the sort the capitán was giving his guest. Suddenly, the door was flung open, and light streamed into the room. It revealed the crouching Zorro to Don Esteban and the commandante.

"Zorro — here!" Rocha cried.

Don Esteban was at his heels, and the pair lurched forward in the streak of light. Zorro, half kneeling, was caught off balance. They were upon him, hurled him to the floor before he could make a move in defense. A blow found his head, and he passed into oblivion.

Zorro returned to consciousness to find himself bound and gagged and propped against the wall in the capitán's room. Pains were shooting through his head. He opened his eyes and moaned.

"I am for slaying him," Rocha was saying, "and then giving out the story that he crept in here to attack us. You can verify the statement."

"That would be a quick end of it, but not the best one," Don Esteban declared. "The man must be discredited utterly. The thing must be done in such a way that none will say there is a possibility Zorro was not guilty."

"Well, then?" Rocha questioned.

"Here is your chance, my friend. We have him here. Do you go out and impersonate him now, commit your atrocities, knowing that he cannot pop up and confront you. If any man says Zorro did not commit the acts, ask where, then, was Zorro when they were committed."

"It shall be done!" Rocha cried.

"Ha! The fellow has returned to life and is glaring at us," Don Esteban said. "What a chance do we have now! I shall remain here and guard him. Your men believe we are in conference, and will not dare bother. Nobody can say this fellow was not abroad doing wrong."

"Capital!" Rocha cried. "But I would — "

"I know! You itch to run him through," Don Esteban said. "But the other is the better way. Shame him and his family and friends. Then turn him loose, run him down, slay him prettily. And then, my friend, possibly a quiet promotion at the hands of His Excellency, and a return to San Francisco de Asis, where the two of us may have great times!"

"Ha!" Rocha's eyes sparkled at the prospect. "It shall be as you say, Esteban, my friend! Let us have off his gag and let him talk."

Don Esteban removed the gag, but did not touch the bonds, nor did he allow Señor Zorro to change position.

"So we have you, my pretty one!" Rocha hissed at him. "And now the world shall learn what a cur you are! A caballero gone mad! Your relatives will hang their heads in shame. And the little señorita — perhaps she will listen to my suit in her agony to forget she ever knew you."

"You are making a deal of noise," Zorro told him.

"I shall now go forth and create for you a name burdened with such shame that, for years to come, men will hate the sound of it. Think on that, my proud caballero!"

"You are your troop's own trumpeter," Zorro informed him.

"Bah! Gag him again, Esteban! Guard him well! If any man comes to the door, send him away again!"

Though Zorro tried to prevent, Don Esteban gagged him again, and left him propped against the wall. Capitán Rocha left the room, to remove his fine uniform and dress in the semblance of Zorro. He returned presently, laughed a bit, drank wine, and then was gone.

ROCHA slipped quietly through a window and went from shadow to shadow like a skulking thief, until he came to a jumble of rocks behind which a black horse was picketed. Working swiftly, he got bridle and saddle upon the mount. Then he mounted, listened for a moment, and rode slowly and carefully away from the trail and up over the nearest hill, cautious not to show himself against the starlit sky.

Apart from the highway was a certain adobe hut inhabited by a family of natives. Now they were out in front of it, gathered around a fire over which a pot of meat was cooking. Two men, two women, three small children were there.

They were happy, singing natives, neophytes taught by the frailes. The three children were playing with a goat. The men were indulging in gossip, and the women were tending the fire and pot.

Out of the night dashed a big black horse with a masked man upon his back. Men and women sprang to their feet when the firelight revealed horse and rider.

"It is Señor Zorro!" one of the women cried.

But this horseman did not come as a friend of the oppressed, as Zorro often had ridden. He charged down upon them, screeching like a madman, a whip singing as he brandished it. They turned to rush into the hut, but the horseman was before them, driving them back.

He cut with the whip, lashed unmercifully. He rode over one of the women, crushing her beneath the hoofs of his mount. The frenzied horse reared and struck, and one of the men went down. The whip sang again, and brought blood from the back of a child.

"Dogs!" the pseudo Zorro cried.

So he drove them into the darkness, and then dashed on. They heard the thundering hoofs of his mount. Behind him he left curses and cries of pain.

Down the highway, two merchants approached in a cart. Out of the night came the masked horseman, to drive them from the cart, whip them, scatter their goods. One had a pistol, and fired and the masked horseman turned and ran him through. The other fled into the night, to creep toward the town with the tale.

And then, into Reina de Los Angeles, came stories of more atrocities. It appeared that Señor Zorro was riding on all sides of the town like a madman, seeking to destroy. He had met another cart, struck down a man, insulted a señorita of gentle birth. He had whipped more natives.

There was a hush in the town. Could it be possible that Señor Zorro did these things? Had he gone mad? Certain caballeros carried the stories to the Vega house.

"Where is Don Diego?" one demanded. "Let him come out and show himself in the plaza. Let him reveal that some other man is doing these things."

"I do not know where he is," Don Alejandro was compelled to say.

"Can it be possible that — "

"Do not dare to contemplate such a thing!" Don Audre Ruiz cried.

"If a sickness has come upon him — "

"Even with a sickness of the brain, a caballero would not act in such a manner," Ruiz defended.

Don Audre sent a servant to pass word for José of the Cocopahs, and after a time José came to the house.

"My brothers will search," he said. "They will find Señor Zorro."

"They must make haste. Do you understand what it means?" Ruiz asked.

"Perfectly, señor."

"Is Capitán Rocha at the presidio?"

"Our people have been watching for some time, and have not seen him leave. It is said by the soldiers that he entertains a great man from the north."

"Go and find Zorro," Ruiz begged.

José hurried away on his mission, to spread the word that close search should be made. And into Reina de Los Angeles came stories of yet more atrocities. Even some of the caballeros began whispering that perhaps Don Diego Vega's brain had been turned a little, and that he was like a wild man of no responsibility. But José of the Cocopahs believed it not.

"Señor Zorro is not doing these things," he declared. "We shall search and find him, and so prove it. And we shall find this other, too!"

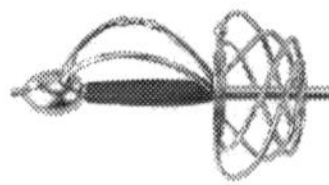

Chapter Sixteen
A Broken Goblet

BOUND and gagged, and propped against the wall, Señor Zorro felt uncomfortable in both mind and body. But he ceased abusing himself for carelessness, decided that his capture was only an accident of ill luck, and focused his mind on the thought of getting free. He could visualize Capitán Rocha riding abroad, casting shame upon the name of Zorro, and his helplessness and inaction became agony.

Don Esteban Garcia was partaking copiously of rich wine. A spell of oratory had come upon him.

"When we have finished with you, my pretty bird, I shall return and take Rocha with me," he said. "We shall have some great times, some famous hours. Ha! But you will not be in a position to hear of it!"

He filled a big glass goblet with the sparkling ruddy wine, drank a bit of it, waved the glass as he talked. The goblet slipped from his hand and crashed to the floor.

Don Esteban volleyed strong curses because of the mishap, and filled another goblet. He continued his pacing and his bombastic oratory, while Zorro remained propped up against the wall. A gleam of hope had come into Zorro's eyes, but he quenched it, lest the other should see and understand.

Zorro had been working at the rope which bound his wrists. It was a small rope, tightly tied. The knots had given a little, and the rope was loose, but Zorro knew he could not work free of it. However, he could twist his wrists to a certain extent, and touch the rope with his fingers.

And now he saw on the floor, only a short distance from him, a piece of the broken goblet — a jagged chunk of the heavy glass. He watched Don Esteban Garcia closely, and inched his body toward the objective. He toppled over, twisted, managed to clutch the piece of glass. Then he struggled to prop himself against the wall again, while Don Esteban roared with laughter at his helplessness, thinking that he had toppled over accidentally and because of fatigue.

Behind his back, Zorro held the piece of broken goblet in the fingers of his right hand, and sawed at a strand of the rope which bound him. He cut through the strand and attacked another, watching Don Esteban as he worked. But the secretary to His Excellency did not seem at all suspicious. Zorro was bound and gagged, and the sword which had been taken from him was on the long table in the middle of the room, while Don Esteban's blade was at his side. Don Esteban felt no fear.

Zorro sawed through another strand of the rope while the secretary drank wine and paced and boasted. His wrists finally came free, and he rubbed them vigorously behind his back. But his ankles were still tied, and he was gagged.

IN THE corridor of the presidio there was a sudden tumult as some of the troopers indulged in rough play with the soldiers of the escort. Don Esteban reeled to the door, unbarred it and jerked it open. He stepped out into the corridor.

"Silence, scum!" he roared. "Outside, if you must howl and screech!"

Zorro could hear the frightened men scampering through the corridor and out into the night, fearful of punishment. Don Esteban returned to the room almost immediately. But, during his absence and while his back was turned as he closed and barred the door again, Zorro managed to free his ankles.

He remained propped against the wall, the gag in place, his hands behind his back. He was feverish to spring up, get his sword, escape from the presidio, but held himself in check, waiting for the proper moment.

Don Esteban lurched to the table to fill the wine goblet once more, turning from Zorro to do so. Zorro tore off the gag and sprang to his feet. He darted lightly across to the table and seized his sword.

"Ha, señor!" he cried, almost in Don Esteban's ear.

Don Esteban gave a screech of surprise and turned swiftly, so swiftly that he tottered and was off balance. He fumbled for his sword. But the heavy hilt of Zorro's weapon crashed against the side of his head, and he swayed and collapsed to the floor.

Through the adjoining room Zorro dashed, to leave the building the same way he had entered it. Through the darkness he darted, and crashed against one of the Cocopahs.

"Where is José?" be demanded.

"By the hut of Bardoso, señor. We have been searching for you."

Zorro rushed on, and found José. In a moment he had learned all that had happened. "We must pick up his trail," Zorro said.

"My men are watching, my brother. Bernardo has your horse ready in the patio."

"You have done well. I'll get it and return."

Capitán Rocha was still running wild, committing atrocities piling up shame on the name of Zorro. But he was growing tired of it. He would do one thing more, he decided, and then would return to the presidio. Then he would arrange to have a semblance of capture of the real Zorro, and have the man slain.

On he went, this Capitán Rocha, until he came to a little dry gulch, and into that he descended cautiously, to follow the sandy bottom. Presently, he brought his horse to a stop. Ahead of him was an adobe hut, where Old Marcos lived. There was a light gleaming in the hut.

It was away from the traveled paths, this hut. Old Marcos was the sort to live away from the haunts of men. There were many tales concerning him. Some said that he was a retired pirate with a price upon his head. Some said that he was a man of rank, forced to flee his proper associations because of a crime the law would not overlook. But all agreed that Old Marcos had wealth, and that he kept it hidden. When, once or twice a year, he came out into civilization, it was to spend lavishly for a few days.

Capitán Valentino Rocha, his eyes agleam, rode forward slowly, and cautiously. He made certain that there has nobody near him. He stopped his horse in front of the hut, and got the whip ready.

"Ho! Marcos!" he roared.

There was a moment of delay, and then the door was opened, and Old Marcos was revealed standing there in the candlelight. His body was bent, his hands gnarled, he squinted as he peered out into the night.

"Who calls Marcos?" he asked, in a thin voice.

"Out here, Marcos! I need help!"

Old Marcos stumbled forth from the adobe hut, straining his eyes and ears to ascertain what this was all about. A whip sang through the air, a lash stung.

Old Marcos gave a cry of pain, another as the lash hit home again. The whip hissed and sang, bit and cut. Old Marcos tried to turn and get back into his hut, but could not. The whip always blocked his path.

"Mercy! … Mercy!" he cried.

"Where is your money? I demand your money!"

"I have none," Marcos wailed.

"Do not lie to me! Tell me where you have your wealth hidden!"

The whip sang and stung again. Old Marcus dropped to his knees, tried to protect his head with his arms. His shrieks and cries riddled the night.

"Tell me!" the demand was repeated. "I am Zorro! Your money, or I whip the life out of you!"

"I have no money, señor! For the love of the saints, do not whip me again!"

Capitán Rocha could always use gold. He drove Marcos back into the hut, then dismounted and followed.

"A liar's tale!" the masked man raged at him.

As Old Marcos crouched in the corner, he began a furious search of the poor hut, scattering the few articles of furniture, wrecking the fireplace.

"You have it hidden outside," he accused. "For the last time — where is your money!"

"I have told you, señor — "

The lash hissed and sang and cut. Marcos gave a screech of pain and huddled against the wall. But the masked man had no intention of slaying him with the lash or otherwise. He wanted Marcos, bleeding from his cuts, to stumble and stagger into the plaza at Reina de Los Angeles and tell the tale of his mistreatment.

THROUGH the night, figures were stealing toward the hut. The bogus Zorro had been located by the Cocopahs, and word had been passed back in a way they knew. And now, on their tough, speedy little ponies, they were surrounding their enemy, while he raged and fumed and beat with his whip.

Marcos made a dash for the door, trying to get out into the night. He eluded the masked man for a moment, and won free.

Capitán Rocha went after him, howling curses. He caught Marcos and beat him back. He got up into his saddle again. Capitán Rocha felt disappointed, for he sensed that the old man was telling the truth. And he wanted to be gone, to get back to the presidio, and attend to Señor Zorro. He would give Marcos time to get to town with the story of what had happened to him. It would be the last needed straw to infuriate the populace.

He lifted the whip for a last cruel cut, but this time the whip did not strike.

Something else whizzed through the air with an ominous, sibilant sound. A riata fell true, was jerked taut. Capitán Rocha was yanked out of his saddle, to crash to the ground half stunned.

Forms emerged from the night and rushed toward him. Suddenly Cocopahs were surrounding him, their angry eyes gleaming at him in the faint light.

And then the real Señor Zorro, who had cast the riata, rode forward and coiled his rope.

Chapter Seventeen
A Fateful Command

BACK in the pueblo of Reina de Los Angeles, the bell of the chapel was sounding. It was Fray Felipe who worked it, and there was a peculiar gleam in the eyes of the old fray, as though the labor was one of joy. A crowd answered the summons of the bell — townsmen, visitors, travelers, natives. Through the gathering crowd hurried certain of the caballeros, and with a few words they prepared the people for what was to come.

Soldiers came hurrying down the slope from the presidio, led by blustering Sergeant Pedro Gonzales. The caballeros gradually grouped together at one side of the square. Natives appeared from several directions, slipping silently through the gloom, to group by themselves on the other side. From the houses of the wealthy came men and women of station, to ascertain the cause of the commotion.

Fuel was heaped and a bonfire was started. The flames sprang up, spread, grew in volume, and illuminated the night. Down into the plaza raced José of the Cocopahs on his spotted pony.

"Zorro has been caught!" he cried. "He was beating Old Marcos, and trying to rob him. He was whipping him, so that the old man cried for mercy."

A ripple of indignation ran through the crowd. More ponies came racing into the plaza. And then came a big black horse led by a Cocopah, and across the saddle a man was lashed, a man with a black mask over his face.

There was a chorus of exclamations, and the crowd surged forward as the cavalcade came into the big circle of firelight. For there was another black horse, and another masked man, only this latter sat erect, command in his bearing.

"Unbind him!" this one ordered. "Put him on his feet upon the ground!"

While his orders were being obeyed through the crowd lurched Don Esteban, with a band of soldiers at his heels. An expression of consternation was in Don Esteban's face.

"What is this?" the Governor's secretary cried. "You are gathering here in riot! Disperse, everybody! To your homes! My soldiers shall — "

But suddenly the caballeros surged forward, and Don Esteban found himself thrust back with his soldiers, found a milling throng always between him and the scene of action.

The bound man was taken from the horse and stood upon the ground, and the ropes removed from him, but the mask allowed to remain over his face.

"Hand him his sword!"

It was the second Zorro who commanded this. And now he sprang out of his own saddle and whipped out his blade.

"Señor, you have seen fit to impersonate me and do many cruelties in my name," he said. "You have caused me much trouble and distress, humiliated my friends, caused men to curse my name. On guard, beast!"

The other snarled, leaped forward.

NOW ROCHA fought with what skill he could master, for he knew well that he was fighting for his life. He fought with a determination to win, regardless of the proper rules of combat. But the other met his foul with foul and held his own, taunted him, played with him.

Perspiration streamed down from beneath their masks. Around them as they fought, surged the crowd. Steel clashed and rang, and it seemed that a dozen blades were playing.

"Fight, beast!" the real Zorro cried. "Fight well — for this fight is to be your last!"

A volley of curses answered him. Then came a furious charge, a last attempt at victory. Again sparks flew from clashing steel.

Suddenly Don Esteban slipped through the crowd and was in the center, his own blade out and ready. He rushed to the attack, rushed to the aid of the man who was fast tiring. Don Esteban was still reeling from the wine, Zorro noted.

The crowd roared its wrath at the unfairness of it. Certain of the caballeros started forward.

"Back!" Zorro shouted, as he fought. "Back, my friends! I need no help in this!"

He sprang backward as he spoke, and the two others came side to side and rushed forward to engage him. But they faced a master of fence who was enraged. The sword of Zorro was like a live thing as it played with their blades. His foes tried to separate, that they might not hinder each other, but Zorro kept them side by side.

Then there came a great sigh from the throng which watched. Never had they seen such swordplay. One of the combatants reeled backward, dropped his blade, clutched at a breast from which the blood was streaming. He swayed, tottered, crashed to earth.

Don Esteban cursed and pressed forward. Zorro played with him a moment, then made a swift attack, and to the astonishment of those who knew Esteban's reputation as a swordsman, disarmed him.

"Seize him, and hold him!" he cried.

Some of the caballeros rushed forward and made Don Esteban prisoner.

"As for the other, it is an ending," Zorro said. "Take off his mask!"

It was José of the Cocopahs who sprang forward and removed the mask. And in the firelight all saw the features of him who had been Capitán Valentino Rocha, commandante of the presidio.

Don Esteban Garcia urged his way forward again.

"A trick!" he cried. "This is murder which has been done! Arrest this man! To cárcel with him!"

Zorro strode up to the man.

"It was a trick — si!" he cried. "This man came to Reina de Los Angeles to undo me. And you, also, were in on the plot!"

"What is this?" Don Esteban cried.

"You arrived to see the finish of me, eh, señor?"

"The Governor shall know — "

"Ha! The Governor!" Zorro cried. "You and this dead man failed him. I know the Governor's disposition well. He will say he had nothing to do with it. He will cast the blame on you. Your plot has failed."

"We shall see, señor!" Don Esteban cried. "I shall ride at once to report this affair."

"One moment! There is something yet to be done," Zorro said. "You made a foul attack on me while I was fighting your friend. Now, señor, we fight properly! Pick up your sword!"

"You would dare — "

"Your sword, señor, unless you wish the world to know you for a coward!"

Don Esteban screeched his rage, and rushed to where his sword had fallen to the ground. But there he stopped, to remove his jacket. He was working for time in which to control his rage, and let the last of the wine fog clear from his brain. This would be a serious affair, and he wished to be at his best. And he knew that an enraged man is never that.

His eyes narrowed and gleamed. Don Esteban was sure of his prowess in the use of a blade. His mind was clear and determined now. Here was an opportunity to end Señor Zorro forever, and in a fair fight which could not be questioned later.

Silent, motionless, Zorro waited. Don Esteban picked up his sword, made a swift examination of it, and advanced. The blades clashed.

THEN began swordplay which was the talk of El Camino Real for months. Here were two worthy antagonists. Swift victory would come to neither. They felt each other out, used caution. Then the speed of their combat increased.

Señor Zorro fought coolly and with cunning. He felt the point of the other's blade rip a sleeve and scratch his arm. In turn, he gave the other a scratch. Back and forth, around and around as they shifted positions in the firelight, the two fought. Each sought the advantage of position and light. Each used what skill he had.

The blade play slackened a bit. Now came the time of danger, when they were commencing to tire. Now it was not only a test of skill, but also one of stamina and strength. This was a matter of life and death which might be settled by a wrist suddenly grown weak.

Zorro pressed the fighting again, and Don Esteban gave ground. His face became ghastly. He sensed that he was outdone, that the end would not be long in coming now. He backed away, sought a new position, and cried into the night:

"Troopers! Help! Arrest this man!"

Discipline is a thing that controls men who are slaves to it. Tense with excitement as they watched the fight, the soldiers heard an officer's command. They had no time to think of the situation. Mechanically, they started to obey.

But a grim-faced horde of caballeros surged forward, too, and some of the natives. Sergeant Gonzales was far in the rear, and a corporal in charge of Don Esteban's men was in front.

"Rescue the Señor Garcia!" the corporal commanded.

Don Esteban's agile troopers drew their blades and surged forward to obey. Behind them came the men of the presidio. They crashed against a determined wall of the caballeros, quietly but tensely gripping their fine blades, with Don Audre Ruiz in command.

"Back!" Don Audre cried. "It is a fair fight!"

But the troopers went on. Blades crashed. Don Audre shouted an order. A mighty roar went up. Suddenly there was a battle in the plaza at Reina de Los Angeles.

Yet it was a queer battle. Here and there a scratch, a ripped sleeve, a slashed coat. Fine blades playing against the heavier though fast-flying swords of Don Esteban's soldiers. Experts in brilliant fence dealing with men taught to use force.

The heavy blades were at a disadvantage in this. The caballeros were light and swift on their feet, also. The troopers found that now they were not fighting rebellious natives. And soon they sensed that the caballeros were making mock of them, that they could have caused casualties had they wished.

A sword flew up from the hand of a soldier, made an arc in the air. Another followed. Up and down the line, the soldiers were being disarmed.

"Stand to them!" the corporal cried.

But it was a thing that simply could not be done. It is true that two of the caballeros received wounds which put them out of the fighting, and one of the troopers fell back clutching at his shoulder. But there were no deaths. One by one the soldiers of Don Esteban's band and the troopers from the presidio were disarmed. One by one, they were tossed backward into the midst of the Cocopahs, who surrounded them, smothered them, took charge of them in the manner Don Audre Ruiz called to them to do.

The other fight went on. Don Esteban felt his strength going, now. He saw that the soldiers could not help him. In the flickering firelight, his face took on the queer expression of a man who looks upon Death.

"That all men may know you faced Zorro!"

As he spoke, Zorro darted forward, and his blade went in, and he stepped back again. There was a cut on the forehead of Don Esteban. Zorro laughed, pressed his man, and used his blade again — another cut!

"And now to complete the Z!" Zorro cried. "Be glad, señor, that I do not carve the letter on your black heart!"

Don Esteban made a last effort to avoid the indignity. He rushed forward like a wild man, disregarding all teachings of fence, hoping only in a last effort to bear down his enemy and get home an unexpected thrust.

But Zorro only laughed lightly again, side-stepped prettily, awaited the proper moment — and cut again. On the forehead of Don Esteban Garcia was a bloody letter Z.

"Curse you!" Don Esteban cried.

Again he rushed. And now Zorro deftly disarmed him, sent his blade flying through the air again, and stepped aside as Don Esteban rushed past to drop upon one knee, all strength gone from him, the last of it expelled in that futile mad rush.

Zorro's voice was cold as he gave the command to which victory entitled him.

"Get your horse, señor, and leave Reina de Los Angeles! Sergeant Gonzales is capable of commanding the garrison until a new officer can be sent from San Francisco de Asis. And tell His Excellency the Governor to send a better man next time!"

DON ALEJANDRO VEGA slowly sipped wine at the head of the table in the big living room of his mansion. He smiled in contentment as he looked at Don Audre Ruiz, at Doña Catalina, at Don Carlos Pulido, who had just got to town. He smiled also as he regarded Sergeant Pedro Gonzales, who was there to consult with Don Alejandro about what was to be done until a new commandante should arrive.

"A pretty pair!" Don Alejandro observed, nodding his head toward a corner. Don Diego and the señorita were sitting there, holding hands and looking into each other's eyes.

"We must get them married at once," Don Alejandro declared. "Until he becomes a family man, Don Diego Vega probably will continue playing with natives and pirates, riding the highway, wearing a black mask and wielding a blade. Ha! We must get them married!"

Then they saw Don Diego bend forward slightly, so that his lips met those of the little señorita in a lingering kiss.

"Ah, youth!" Don Alejandro breathed, his eyes misty.

"Meal mush and goat's milk!" said old Sergeant Gonzales.

But the old warrior's eyes were misty, too, when he said it.

Illustration by Perego

The West

Short Stories

Part 1

Zorro in West Magazine

Zorro made his world debut in *The All-Story Weekly* in 1919 in *The Curse of Capistrano* (later retitled *The Mark of Zorro*). The Frank A. Munsey Company merged *All-Story* with *Argosy*, and the masked hidalgo made sporadic appearances throughout the 1930s.

Beginning in 1944, Zorro became a continuing feature in *West* magazine. Johnston McCulley penned 51 stories of varying length, ranging from 3,000 to 40,000 words. During this time, Zorro also appeared in numerous matinee serials (see John E. Petty's introduction).

In addition to *West*, Better Publications, Inc. published the adventures of The Black Bat in *Black Book Detective.*

Zorro Draws His Blade

Swiftly out of the night rode the masked and cloaked Zorro, with flashing sword, ready to right a great wrong!

GAUNT and gray, with his head held high and indignation flaming in his eyes, Fray Felipe stood before the door of the chapel at Mission San Gabriel that afternoon, alone between a frenzied mob and the terrified cringing man they sought to slay.

The strong wind whipped the fray's tattered robe around his emaciated form as his thin arms were uplifted in a gesture that demanded silence. In front of him was the seething mob–peons, natives, travelers off the highway, traders, vagabonds of the hills–all acting like maniacs as the blood lust turned them from men to beasts.

"Back!" Fray Felipe shouted in his shrill voice. "Are you mad, my sons? Would you desecrate the chapel? The man has claimed sanctuary until dawn tomorrow, and shall have it. Such is his right."

A chorus of wild cries answered him:

"Give us the murderer! … Give us the rogue who slew Don Esteban Sanchez! … Let us hang him!"

Fray Felipe silenced them again with a gesture. "The man has sanctuary until dawn tomorrow. That is the law. I shall talk to him meantime and learn the truth."

"We know the truth already, fray," a man called.

Fray Felipe recognized the speaker as Miguel Cortez, superintendente of the rancho owned by Don Carlos Martinez. He was middle aged, short and stout, and notorious for his cruelty to those who worked under him. He was the right sort of man for his employer.

For Don Carlos Martinez, despite his hidalgo blood, was a wastrel and licentious, forgetting the responsibilities of his rank and station, and received only cold and distant nods from others of gentle birth.

Two years before, Don Carlos had inherited properties on the death of his father. Because he gambled heavily, and spent huge sums in lavish entertainment whenever he visited Monterey, he was becoming impoverished. Men whispered that he had mortgaged his estates heavily. He left management of the rancho to Miguel Cortez, and cared little what methods Cortez used.

Now, Cortez stood out before the others and spoke to Fray Felipe.

"The half-breed known as Juan killed Don Esteban Sanchez with a skinning-knife he took from the sheep pens, where he had been working. I saw him, and caught him robbing the body, and brought him to San Gabriel. The rogue managed to escape me, and rushed here to claim sanctuary."

THE priest did not flinch. "Which he shall have," Fray Felipe said, sternly.

"As you will, fray! Confess the rogue, shrive him, pray with him through the night. But at dawn he leaves sanctuary, and we hang him. And we will camp here to make sure he does not get away."

"Enough!" Fray Felipe shouted. "Remain on guard if it pleases you. But act in an orderly manner, and do not desecrate the mission."

Men in the mob began muttering, and the crowd started breaking up into small groups. Fray Felipe watched them a moment, his mind troubled at this blood thirst and violence. Then turned to reenter the chapel.

But he came to an abrupt stop and gave a sigh of relief at what he saw. A carriage drawn by prancing black horses was entering the mission compound. A native coachman handled the reins, and a native footman sat beside him.

In the carriage, reclining on fat silk cushions, was a young caballero dressed in resplendent attire, who brushed his nostrils with a scented handkerchief and stifled a yawn with a hand the fingers of which were adorned with jeweled rings.

THIS was Don Diego Vega, son and heir of Don Alejandro Vega, one of the wealthiest and most prominent men in Alta California. But the hidalgo blood which coursed his veins never seemed to set Don Diego afire. He did not join other young caballeros in their feverish adventures, but read poetry and cultivated roses, which made men decide that he was nothing but a fop and a spineless jellyfish.

The coachman shouted a warning, and the crowd parted to let the carriage through. It stopped in front of the chapel. Don Diego looked around at the crowd, turned up his nose slightly as if at an unpleasant odor, and stepped from the vehicle and upon a strip of crimson carpet the footman had been quick to spread.

"Welcome, Don Diego, my son!" Fray Felipe greeted, cordially. "What wind of good fortune blows you here?"

"I was visiting in the neighborhood, padre, paying my respects to a beautiful señorita and her estimable parents, and thought I would stop to break bread with you and spend the night in your guest house," Don Diego replied. "Usually, it is so quiet and peaceful here. But now I find a tumult that makes my head ring. What is the meaning of this riot?"

"Come into the chapel, Don Diego, and I'll explain," Fray Felipe said.

Don Diego followed him inside, and the fray closed the heavy door in the faces of the mob. Don Diego saw a barefooted, ragged man kneeling before the altar. Fray Felipe gestured toward him, and spoke to Don Diego in hushed tones.

"He is Juan, a neophyte. He would not tell me a falsehood. He says Miguel Cortez caught him and tied him to a tree beside a trail, stuffing a cloth into his mouth so he could make no outcry. Cortez took his skinning-knife from him, and waited in the brush. Don Esteban Sanchez came riding along the trail alone."

"Sanchez is a dear friend of my father's," Don Diego said.

"Your father will grieve. According to Juan, Cortez sprang out of the brush and stopped Don Esteban, pulled him from his saddle and stabbed him to death."

"Monstrous!" Don Diego cried.

"Juan heard Cortez say, 'Now, Don Esteban, you cannot press Carlos Martinez for payment he cannot make.' Then, Cortez untied Juan, and made an outcry, which called workers from a field. He accused Juan of the murder and brought him to San Gabriel. That is the story. And who would believe the word of a nameless ragged half-breed against that of Martinez' superintendente?"

"I would, for one," Don Diego said.

"Sí. And I, for another, my son. But possibly nobody else. Juan told me his story and I believe him. It has been thought that Don Esteban held a mortgage on Martinez' estate. No doubt he hoped to seize the property and drive the notorious Martinez from the country."

"How came this Juan here?" Don Diego asked.

"He twisted away from Cortez and ran here to claim sanctuary. Cortez aroused the mob. If Juan leaves sanctuary, the mob will kill him. That is bad enough, but there is more."

"And that?" Don Diego questioned.

"I know I may speak freely to the man I christened and who confesses to me," the fray said. "Evil times have come to Alta California. Unscrupulous politicians rule the land. Favors are sold or given to friends. The missions have become wealthy through the toil and sweat of the padres and neophytes, and the politicians covet that wealth."

DON DIEGO nodded his head. "That is true," he admitted.

"There is strife between the missions and the political rogues. They would seize our herds and flocks, the goods in our warehouses, and turn us out. And look where I stand in this affair. If I free Juan, knowing he is innocent, it would be said we Franciscans are protecting our neophytes though they are murderers. That would arouse men against us."

"I can see that, padre."

"If I surrender Juan at dawn, it will be worse. For the natives we have converted believe they have a refuge in their faith, that it protects them from injustice. If I do not protect Juan, they will think there is no truth in our teachings, will desert the missions and return to the spiritual darkness from which they came."

"You are in a tight corner, padre." Don Diego judged.

"Juan can be saved, and I be freed of this dilemma, if the real murderer could be unmasked before dawn."

"The mob would have to be convinced of his guilt," Don Diego interrupted.

"I know one man who could accomplish it."

"And he is — ?" Don Diego questioned.

"Señor Zorro. The man who rode the highway and helped the oppressed, and punished evildoers without mercy. It has been some time since he was active. He should become active again."

"Señor Zorro, the fox," Don Diego muttered, looking straight into the old fray's burning eyes. "I wonder how many men know his real identity?"

"Possibly only two, his father and his father confessor," Fray Felipe replied, smiling slightly. "What say you, my son?"

Don Diego glanced again at the altar, where the terrified Juan was imploring help. He faced Fray Felipe once more, and his reply was a whisper: "Zorro will ride tonight."

"I thank you, my son. Providence must have sent you this way today."

"I need some help. I must have a man to take a message to Bernardo, my body servant."

"Let us step outside, and I'll call a man."

They left the chapel, and Fray Felipe summoned to the one he wanted, a man he could trust. Don Diego instructed him:

"Ride at top speed to my father's house in Reina de Los Angeles," Don Diego instructed him. "Find Bernardo, my body servant, and tell him I will spend the night here, and want him to come immediately on his fast riding mule, fetching my heavy sleeping robe."

"I understand, señor."

"Bernardo cannot speak, having been born dumb, but he can hear and will understand. Tell him I said, 'Bring everything I need for the night.' Those exact words. Here is a bit of gold for your trouble."

The man accepted the gold, grinned, knuckled his forehead in respectful salute, and hurried away.

Bernardo reached the mission an hour after nightfall. He had been a loyal servant to Don Diego for years, and knew his secret. Being unable to speak, he could not reveal Zorro's identity even under torture, and the written word was beyond him.

Bernardo tied his mule, tucked a bundle he had brought beneath one arm, and hurried to the guest house, where Don Diego was waiting in the room assigned him. Bernardo bobbed his head and unrolled the bundle, which contained only the sleeping robe.

"You understood, Bernardo?" Don Diego asked.

Bernardo grinned, and nodded that he had.

"You brought the clothes of Zorro and his horse and hid them in some safe place near by?"

Bernardo nodded in the affirmative.

"Get my couch ready, and remain here until I return."

Don Diego strolled across the main room of the guest house to the open outside door, and looked out into the compound. Fires had been built, and men were sprawled around them. There was a sliver of moon, which would give just enough light to make moving shadows deceptive.

A sudden tumult at the gate attracted Don Diego's attention, and he saw two troopers riding through. One was Sergeant Manuel Garcia, from the barracks at Reina de Los Angeles.

Don Diego drew back swiftly out of sight. As Zorro, he had clashed with Garcia often enough. He did not fear the man, nor did he make the mistake of underestimating him.

GARCIA had brains and instinct, he was a good horseman and an expert swordsman. And he had sworn long before to unmask Señor Zorro some day and stretch him lifeless on the earth with a deft thrust of his blade.

Don Diego watched the troopers dismount and tie their horses, and saw Fray Felipe welcome them and send them to the eating hut. The fray then approached the guest house and joined Don Diego in the doorway.

"They heard in Reina de Los Angeles about the crime, and soldiers have come," the fray reported. "But even the Governor's troopers dare not violate sanctuary, so Juan is safe until dawn. The troopers will save him from the mob, but that will not help."

"What mean you, padre?"

"Our alcalde is on a journey. So the magistrado will come from Reina de Los Angeles in the morning to judge the case. It will be Juan's word against that of Cortez, and the magistrado is an unscrupulous rogue and will not affront the mob by a moment's hesitation. He will order Juan hanged forthwith, and the soldiers will carry out the sentence."

"Then Zorro has work to do tonight. If any ask for me, padre, say you believe I have retired."

"I have learned that Miguel Cortez has gone to the tavern down the highway, and that Carlos Martinez is there for the night. Martinez has engaged a room on the patio."

"That information saves me considerable time," Don Diego replied. "I have plans in mind."

"Everything must be accomplished before dawn, if Juan is to be saved and the situation cleared," Fray Felipe reminded him. "*Buenas noches*, my son!"

Fray Felipe shuffled away with his hands thrust into the sleeves of his tattered robe. Don Diego returned to his room and closed and bolted the door. In whispers, he explained to Bernardo what had happened and what he intended doing.

On a sheet of parchment, he scrawled a message, and tucked it into his sash. He paced the floor for a time, thinking, then extinguished the tapers in the candelabra, so the room would be dark and it would appear he had retired. He opened a window in the rear of the room, and he and Bernardo dropped through it and crouched in the darkness outside the wall of the compound.

Keeping to the dark spots, they got away from the mission and into a coulée, followed this for a short distance, and in a mass of brush-shrouded rocks came to where Bernardo had tethered the black horse Zorro rode. From beneath a clump of brush, the mute pulled a roll of clothing, Zorro's attire. Another bundle contained Zorro's blade, his pistol, powder horn and a pouch of bullets.

In the darkness, Don Diego Vega changed his attire and became

Zorro, dressed in black and with a black mask over his face. Into his belt he thrust the charged pistol and the parchment he had prepared in the guest house.

"Remain here," he instructed Bernardo. "If I am chased and reach this spot, you will know what to do."

Then Señor Zorro mounted quickly and rode away through the darkness.

He circled the mission at a distance and approached it cautiously from the opposite direction, eyes strained as he watched shadows, ears attuned to catch every sound.

The rabble around the fires were laughing and shouting, and evidently were passing wineskins around. The gate of the compound stood wide open. Zorro felt in his sash for the message he had prepared. On the parchment, he had scrawled:

> *The man Juan is innocent. The slayer of Don Esteban Sanchez is known to me, and soon I shall expose him.*
>
> *— Zorro*

He rode toward the gate of the compound, approaching it slowly through the shadows. When he reached a spot where he could look through the gate, he surveyed the scene well.

Suddenly, he touched his horse with spurs. The big black sprang into action. With thundering hoofs, he dashed through the gateway and straight toward the fires and the men scattered around them.

Zorro gave a wild screech that rang out above the din and attracted the attention of all around the fires. Some men sprang to their feet, and others struggled to stand.

In a shower of gravel and dust, Zorro stopped his horse within the circle of light cast by the largest fire, so they would have a good look at him.

"Señores, atencion!" he shouted. "Read this — if any of you can read." He tossed the parchment toward the nearest man. "And tell that pig of a Sergeant Garcia that Zorro is here. Perhaps the sergeant would like to capture me, and earn a fine reward."

"Zorro!" the men began shouting. "It is Zorro!"

Zorro menaced them with his pistol and backed his horse away from the fire. He held them off until he saw Sergeant Garcia lurch from one of the buildings with the trooper behind him.

"Ho, Garcia!" Zorro cried. "Glutton and wine soak! Are you able to climb into a saddle? Can you use a blade?"

"By the fiend, you need a lesson," cried Garcia, and hurried toward his horse with the trooper running after him.

Zorro rode through the gateway, but did not urge his horse to speed until he saw Garcia and the other follow through and take after him. Then, Zorro began maneuvering to keep just beyond pistol range, playing with the pursuit, knowing that the horse he bestrode could give distance easily to the mounts of the troopers.

Reaching the highway, Zorro turned toward the tavern a mile distant. This roadside inn had a reputation not of the best. It was known as a haunt of smugglers and other rogues, where dice and cards attracted some and wine others. The presence there of troopers or any other representatives of law and order was not desired.

The tavern was a long, low building built around a patio in which there was a well. It was set in a grove of huge trees and thick brush, with a winding lane leading to it from the highway. Two torches burned outside the front door.

Now that he had revealed to the pursuit that he was riding to the tavern, Zorro used his spurs and distanced the troopers. They would follow there, he knew, and being only two in number they would be cautious about entering the place because many rogues were gathered in the big main room. Nothing would delight such gentry more than to slit the throats of a couple of the Governor's troopers and leave the bodies beside the highway.

Nearing the tavern, Zorro left the lane, pulled his horse down to a walk and rode him into the depths of the grove, where he dismounted and tied the black, then hurried back to the building.

He heard the pursuit coming. But there was a sudden cessation of hoofbeats, and he knew the troopers had pulled up and were riding beneath the trees. Undoubtedly, they feared ambush, possibly thought that Señor

Zorro had lured them here to their undoing.

Zorro desired their presence, for he wanted official witnesses. His one fear was that Garcia and the trooper might interrupt proceedings too soon. That was a chance he had to take, but he had taken desperate chances before. He shifted his scabbard, made sure of the pistol in his belt, and slipped noiselessly along the side of the tavern to the front door.

Glancing through a window he passed, he saw that the big main room was half packed with men. Thieves and vagabonds they were, smugglers and possibly a few wanted murderers among them. They were drinking, playing at dice and cards. The fat landlord was shuffling around, watching his native servants as they poured from the wineskins and collected coins.

Smoke swirled across the room from the fireplace and from cigaritos and pipes. It blackened the strings of peppers which dangled from the rafters, and gave new flavor to the haunches of meat being cured. Reeking torches illuminated the place, save where a couple of the larger gaming tables were decorated with old, battered candelabra in which tapers burned.

At one of the large tables Don Carlos Martinez was sitting on a stool, with Miguel Cortez beside him. Martinez had a heap of coins before him, and was playing cards, while Cortez guarded his master and his gold.

Zorro ran to the door, jerked it open and entered swiftly, slammed the door behind him and dropped the heavy bar into place. He ran across the room to the other door, which opened into the patio, and stopped there and turned to face those in the room.

"Ho, señores!" he cried. "I am Zorro! Troopers pursue me, and may be here soon."

INSTANT silence fell in the big room as all turned their heads to stare at him.

"Zorro," some man muttered. *"Zorro!"*

"There is a reward offered for my capture, as possibly you know," Zorro said. "Is any here mean enough or brave enough, to try to earn it?"

A man lurched to his feet.

"So you are Zorro, and the troopers are pursuing you, eh?" he asked.

Zorro began to press the fighting.

"Only two of them pursue."

"And do we here fear only two such scum?" He turned to the others. "This is Zorro, who whipped a *magistrado* once because he defrauded a poor peon. Are we friends with a *magistrado* or with the man who whipped one?"

A chorus of howls answered that, and Zorro knew he had nothing to fear.

He whirled and dropped the bar across the patio door, then confronted them again. And suddenly he seemed to see Martinez and Cortez for the first time. His eyes gleamed through the slits in his mask as he strode toward them, his right hand resting on the pistol in his sash.

"Señores!" he cried to the men in the room. "Have you lost your wits? Are you trying to put nooses around your own necks?"

They shouted questions as to his meaning.

"Is it not true," Zorro asked, "that there has been an informer busy recently? Have not some friends of yours been taken, testimony given against them? Have not men been hanged, and others farmed out at hard labor?"

Growls and expressions of rage answered that. For these men had friends who had been seized by the Law recently. Such were always being arrested and punished, but now that it was called to their attention, the rogues in the tavern remembered vividly that there had been an epidemic of such seizures for some little time.

"That means a spy at work, does it not?" Zorro asked, standing back against the wall and looking directly at the table where Martinez and Cortez were sitting. "Fools! You gather here to have your fun. Wine loosens your tongues, and you talk of things which would hang you. Ears are open to catch that talk."

"Whose ears, Zorro?" somebody shouted.

"What man in this room is not one of you? There sits Don Carlos Martinez, a hidalgo, a man of broad estates, and the superintendente of his rancho beside him. They are hearing everything you say. Because they play at cards and dice with you, you are foolish enough to accept them as friends."

Exclamations of rage came from a score of throats. Some men got up from their stools and benches. They stood with feet far apart, shoulders hunched, hands working like claws, rage suffusing their faces.

And, at that moment, Zorro saw what he had been waiting to see–the faces of Sergeant Garcia and his trooper at one of the small open windows. Whatever happened now would be seen, whatever was said would be heard officially.

Don Carlos Martinez sprang to his feet with Miguel Cortez beside him. Fear showed in their faces. The ruffians before them would tear informers to pieces, torture them brutally before killing.

"Wait, señores–amigos!" Martinez shouted. "Who is this man who makes such an accusation? Have you ever seen his face? Does he not always wear a mask?"

"If my face ever is known, my work is done," Zorro said. "Perhaps

I am a man well known. Perhaps, as my own self, I am in a position to learn the moves of the soldiery, and so escape them."

The ruffians howled with delight at that, then turned toward Martinez again.

"We trust the masked man who once whipped a magistrado," their spokesman said. "We trust a man the soldiers pursue. But how do we know we can trust you, Don Carlos Martinez? What have you and your superintendente ever done to make you one of us? You are a rich hidalgo. You often go to Monterey and visit the Governor."

"Seize him!" another shouted. "Get his superintendente, too! Knives for them!"

"Wait!" Martinez shouted. "I tell you that Miguel Cortez and I are your friends. We like men of your stamp. We like to gamble and drink with you. Landlord! Bring out a fresh skin of wine. Give my friends what they want."

"He would buy you off," Zorro said.

MARTINEZ scowled. "As for you, Señor Zorro, it will please me to cross blades and carve you," he shouted, angrily. "What does it profit you to arouse these men against me?"

"We'll attend to these rats, Zorro," the leader of the rogues shouted.

They surged forward, and Martinez and Cortez retreated to stand with their backs to the wall. Cortez got a pistol from his belt, and Martinez reached to draw blade. But they knew they could not hope for a victory against their foes. They might kill or wound two or three, and then the knives would be carving at them.

But Zorro sprang forward, and got between the two against the wall and those who would use their knives.

"Wait!" he shouted. "My friends, I have only been showing you that you are careless. Don Carlos Martinez and his man could easily have been informers. You accepted them without using any care. Let this be a lesson to you. If you value your necks, be careful in your talk hereafter when strangers are around."

"But, Zorro, you said — " the leader began.

" 'Twas but a lesson I hope you will take to heart. You have nothing to fear from Martinez and Cortez. They are one with you, as I happen to know."

"Explain!" they shouted.

"You all have heard how the rich Don Esteban Sanchez was slain today. A nameless half-breed even now crouches in the chapel at the mission, accused of the crime. In the morning, the troopers hope to hang him. But he did not kill Don Esteban. I happen to know who did."

"Tell us!"

"Don Carlos Martinez says he is your friend. Is that true, Don Carlos?"

"It is," Martinez replied. "I would be the last to betray them."

"You will not care, then, if your friends know something of your affairs." He faced the rogues. "Señores, because Don Carlos has been a good fellow, because he likes wine and games, he has been losing his estates. Don Esteban Sanchez had a mortgage, and demanded payment."

"Enough!" Martinez cried.

"Let your friends know the truth, señor. Let them learn they have nothing to fear from you, or they may yet use their knives."

"Tell us more, Zorro," somebody shouted.

"I tell it all. Miguel Cortez today plotted well. He seized the half-breed, tied and gagged him. He slew Don Esteban, then untied the nameless one and shouted for help. He accused the half-breed of the crime and brought him to San Gabriel. But the nameless one escaped and ran to the mission and claimed sanctuary until dawn.

"By doing this, Cortez helped Don Carlos, for it will take time to settle the Sanchez estate, and by the end of that time Martinez can prepare to pay. The pair planned the murder, and Cortez executed it. Does that not make them one of you?"

Cortez' eyes were bulging at this recital of the truth, and Martinez' face had paled. Zorro glanced toward the window again, to see Sergeant Garcia and the trooper still there, interested listeners.

"How dare you say such a thing?" Martinez cried at Zorro. "With my blade, I'll split you like a goose!"

"You are with your friends, señor," Zorro pointed out. "Possibly every man here has slain another. They will not believe that you and your superintendente are informers now — if there is truth in what I have just said."

"But how do we know it is truth?" the spokesman of the rogues demanded. "Perhaps you, Zorro, have been misinformed."

"Use the knives!" another man howled.

They surged forward again, eyes agleam and knives ready. Terror came into the face of Martinez. He threw up a hand to stop them.

"Wait!" he shouted. "It is true. It is as Zorro told you. Now you know that I am one of you, and that Cortez is, also. And any of you are welcome on my rancho whenever you care to visit. I will even show you fine hiding places, if you are pursued."

The ruffian stopped.

Some turned back to the tables in order to gulp wine.

"And, since I am one of you, I settle personal differences your way," Martinez went on. "This rogue who calls himself Zorro — were I sure he was of proper blood, I'd cross blades with him and carve out his heart."

ZORRO laughed. "My blood is better than your own, Carlos Martinez," Zorro said. "I swear it!"

"A fight!" somebody cried. "Let blades ring!"

Miguel Cortez had returned his pistol to his sash, but now he drew from it a knife. Martinez whipped out his blade and Zorro retreated a few steps swiftly and got his own from scabbard.

The rogues tossed tables and benches aside and made a cleared space in the middle of the room.

"I'll run you through," Martinez was shouting. "Then I'll tear the mask from your face and see what manner of man you were."

Zorro knew Martinez was trying to rivet his attention. From the corner of his eye, he saw the swift move Miguel Cortez made, saw the knife gleam. Zorro's left hand dropped to his own sash to jerk out his pistol. It spoke, but the ball sang past Cortez' head and struck the hard adobe wall to ricochet with a whine.

Cortez hurled the knife, which grazed Zorro's shoulder and clattered to the floor.

"Treachery," Zorro cried at the rogues. "Seize Cortez and hold him while I fight this man."

They shouted approval, rushed forward as Cortez tried to get out his pistol again, seized him, disarmed him, and held him back against the wall. Zorro tossed his useless pistol to the floor.

Blades held ready, he and Martinez met in the middle of the room.

"I'll see your blood," Martinez cried.

Martinez attacked furiously, and Zorro retreated, keeping on the defensive while he felt out his opponent. Martinez was good with a blade, but Zorro knew after those first few moments that he had nothing to fear.

He stopped retreating and stood firm, then began pressing the fighting. He heard a tumult in the patio, heard the native servants screeching in fear. Zorro glanced at the window again, to find that Sergeant Garcia and the trooper were there no longer. The front door, and the one opening into the patio, were barred inside, but the small door opening from the kitchen of the tavern was not. And through this door now stormed Sergeant Garcia and his trooper.

"Soldiers!" Zorro shouted at the rogues. "A troop of them. Save yourselves! Out the front way!"

They rushed to the door and took down the heavy bar, and many ran out into the night. But others remained, those having no particular fear of the soldiery at the moment. The door remained open.

"Grab that man Cortez," Garcia shouted to his trooper. "He is under arrest for murder. Handle him quickly! Bind him! Try to have a poor half-breed hanged for murder, will he? And this fine gentleman, who instigated the crime, will get his desserts, also." He started toward where Martinez was fighting with Zorro.

"Back, Garcia," Zorro shouted. "This is my business. Help your trooper with your prisoner."

Martinez was making a fresh onslaught and Zorro pretended to retreat before him, edging his way toward the open door. Too late, Sergeant Garcia understood the ruse. He could not squeeze past those flying blades and get at Zorro now. "You — Zorro!" Garcia cried. "Highwayman! There is a price on you."

"Try to collect it, señor," Zorro said.

He had stepped back to the door now, with Martinez after him and pressing the fighting. And through the ring of steel he heard the wastrel's plea.

"Do not let them hang me," begged Martinez. "If you are a hidalgo, slay me now with your blade. End my life. Do not let me die on the gallows."

Martinez attacked with fury, then, Zorro found it necessary to defend himself. The blade he sent home through Martinez' heart was in self defense. Martinez gave a sigh and collapsed in the doorway.

Before Sergeant Garcia could struggle over the body, Zorro was outside and speeding through the darkness.

He reached his horse, untied him and sprang into the saddle. The black spurned the ground with his hoofs.

SWIFTLY Zorro left the highway and circled, out-riding the trooper Garcia sent in pursuit, while the sergeant prepared to take his prisoner back to the mission in custody. The rogues had scattered, and would not bother Garcia by going to the defense of such a man as Cortez, who blamed his crime upon another.

In time, Zorro reached the spot where Bernardo was waiting.

"All is well," he said. "Rub down the black while I change clothes. Then come with me to the mission for your mule, return here and get the horse, and be on your way before daybreak. If you are missed, I'll say I sent you back to Reina de Los Angeles with a message."

He changed clothing swiftly, and they hurried to the mission carefully through the darkness. They got into the room through the window. Working swiftly, Don Diego half undressed, lit the tapers in the candelabra while Bernardo cleaned telltale dirt from his boots, then opened the door and strolled into the main room of the guest house.

There was a tumult in the compound. Somebody had brought word of what had happened in the tavern. Don Diego walked to the door and strolled toward the chapel, meeting Fray Felipe almost in front of it.

"I honor myself by being your guest for a night, padre, and you reward me with an air-splitting din," Don Diego said, yawning. "Is there nothing but turbulence in the world?"

"Thank you, my son," Fray Felipe whispered. "I am going now to give the good news to Juan. After this, his faith and that of other neophytes will be stronger."

"Let me go with you," Don Diego begged. "I want to see the expression in the man's face when he learns he has been saved. And then I will need your ministrations, padre. I was compelled to take a human life tonight."

Zorro Upsets a Plot

Again the bright blade of Zorro flashes — to snip a web of intrigue tarnishing his honor and to rescue a girl held prisoner!

WHEN darkness closed down that day there was a drizzle of rain, and a heavy fog had rolled in from the sea to engulf the hills of Alta California with its sticky dampness. It would be a miserable night for honest folk, though no doubt it was a night favorable to such as did their nefarious deeds under cover of darkness and inclement weather.

In his tiny adobe hut on the outskirts of the pueblo of Reina de Los Angeles, Pedro Perez was he content as he sat on a stool in a corner and watched the dancing flames in the fireplace. His young, motherless daughter, Juanita, moved gracefully around the hut, attending to the stew in the pot which swung on a crane over the blaze.

Juanita's bare feet pattered on the beaten earth floor as she went to a tiny table where she had been fashioning tortillas. She was almost seventeen, and Pedro Perez feared she would be marrying soon and leaving him alone in his hut. But that was a thing to be expected. He would miss her smiles and laughter, and the throaty songs she sang. She was so like her mother at the same age.

The wind died down for a moment. And during that moment hoofbeats could be heard approaching the hut. Pedro Perez got up from the stool with alarm in his face. None of his friends rode horses. Only one or two of them were rich enough to have broken-down, cast-off mules to drag a cart. Either same wayfarer was approaching, or one of His Excellency's soldiery. This might mean trouble.

Juanita ran quickly to a corner of the hut and got behind some hanging skins, peering around the edge of them with her eyes wide and her mouth agape. As he waited, her father was thinking of the state of affairs in the country.

Why should an honest, hard-working man feel fear when a horseman approached his habitation? Why did not the laws, and those named to enforce them, protect the poor and helpless? Why should aggression stalk a land the good God had made beautiful and drenched with alternate rain and sunshine to make the earth bring forth its bounty?

The hoofbeats stopped at the hut, and there came knock on the door.

"Open, Perez!" a harsh voice called. "At once!"

Pedro Perez took a deep breath, unbolted the door and pulled it open.

LIGHT from the fire and the burning tapers on the table streamed out into the night and revealed a huge black horse, and a rider dressed in black, with black cloak and hat and a black mask over his face. A pistol was in his sash, and a blade was hanging at his side.

"Do you not know me, Perez?" he asked. "I am the man they call Señor Zorro."

"Ah!" Perez cried, happily. His face lighted up with a smile as he took a quick step forward. "The good Señor Zorro, who rights wrongs with his blade! Friend of the poor and helpless!"

"Enough of that!" the masked man said. "Is your daughter, Juanita, at home? I would speak with her."

Perez beckoned, and Juanita left the corner timidly and went to the doorway to stand in the light. Her eyes were wider still as she looked up at the masked rider.

"Closer, child," he ordered. "You do not fear Zorro, do you?"

"No, señor," she replied. "Each night I pray for your safety."

He reached down and took her hand, gripping it so that she winced.

"Rest one foot on the stirrup and swing up behind me," he ordered. "Be quick, señorita!"

"What would you do, Señor Zorro?" Perez asked, hurrying forward. "What has happened? Where would you take my daughter?"

"To my hideout in the hills, fool," the rider replied. "I grow lonesome there without the company of a woman."

"But she cannot go alone with you, Señor Zorro. She is a good girl. Of course, it would be a great honor for her to be the wife of Señor Zorro. But how could you dare stand before a padre? You would have to remove your mask and disclose your true identity."

"Bah, marriage is out of the question!" the rider answered. "I want your daughter, Perez, and I take her!" That is all. Perhaps I may send her back to you some day."

"No — no!" Perez cried, lurching forward.

Juanita had been pulled up behind the masked rider, but now she tried to get down to the ground again. He laughed and wheeled his horse and used his rowels. The black horse disappeared into the night, the girl's wild cry came back to Perez on the wind.

For a short distance, the hoofs of the big black pounded the sodden earth. Then, the horse was pulled up. Other riders approached.

"Here come some troopers, señorita," the masked rider said. "They will pursue me, and my horse cannot outrun them while carrying double. So I'll drop you here. Perhaps I'll come for you again. Scream, and they will find you and take you back home."

Juanita screamed for help as the masked rider thundered away into the night. There were no pursuit, for two troops came to a stop beside the screeching girl. The masked rider rode on to Reina de Los Angeles, approached the barracks there, stabled his horse in an adobe hut, removed his mask and changed clothes swiftly. Then he strode through the drizzle to the front of the barracks and went inside. Halfway down a passage, he stopped before a door and knocked.

"Enter!" a voice called.

He entered, closed and barred the door behind him, stiffened and came to a salute. Before him, sprawled in a chair, with a goblet of wine in one hand, was Capitán Carlos Ortega, commandante of the post.

"Report!" Ortega ordered.

"It was perfect, Señor el capitán. Everything went off smoothly. I left

Perez howling for help and shouting maledictions. The men have the girl."

"You are a clever man, Sergeant Garcia," Ortega praised him, getting up and stretching his arms. "It is a pretty plot, you conceived. This unknown Señor Zorro is adored by all the riffraff in the country because he rights wrongs, aids the oppressed!" The capitán ceased speaking to laugh raucously. "Sí, you have a crafty mind."

"The riffraff will not adore him so much now," Sergeant Garcia said. "Perez will shout around that Zorro stole his innocent daughter and carried her away to the hills. No more will the peons and natives think this Zorro is a saint. Even the robed Franciscans, who pray continually for his welfare, will turn against him now. He will not find help and sanctuary on every side."

"You thought up a splendid plot," Capitán Ortega declared. "It will start the downfall of this Zorro. Since you are such a noted swordsman, it shall be your pleasure, I hope, to cross blades with the rogue and stretch him on earth. And Garcia–do not forget, when we have the rascal and the reward is paid, we shall share equally in the gold pieces. They will dazzle the eyes of the señoritas, and possibly bring promotion to us both."

THERE was a sudden tumult at the door of the barracks.

"That probably is Perez coming here to lodge his complaint," Ortega said. "We must appear indignant. The girl is safe in a prison room by this time, and we'll keep her there without anybody knowing except us two and the couple of troopers who aided you. When the time comes to release her, we will give out that she was held after being rescued because we thought Zorro might learn she was here, come to rescue her, and ride into a trap."

"Any further suggestions, Señor el Capitán?" Sergeant Garcia asked.

Ortega tossed him a couple of pieces of gold. "Better go to the tavern on the plaza with a couple of the men after Perez has departed, as you originally planned. Stir them up against Zorro. Use this gold freely and buy wine for all. You know how to do it, Garcia. Play upon the riffraff until they are ready to go for Zorro's throat."

"It is likely that the affair may bring Zorro out of hiding to protect his good name," Garcia reminded Ortega.

Capitán Ortega smiled. "I hope so," he replied. "That is the most ingenious part your plot."

That same evening, Don Diego Vega was in his father's house on the hillside near the pueblo. Dressed in silks and satins and wearing a heavy embroidered robe, Don Diego reclined before a fireplace as he munched fruit and read poetry.

He heard a tumult in another part of the house, and an expression of annoyance crossed his face. As he tried to concentrate on his reading, the door was opened, and his father, Don Alejandro Vega, stood before him. Behind Don Alejandro was Diego's body-servant, Bernardo, who had been born dumb.

"Do not arise, my son," Don Alejandro said, as Bernardo closed the door. "One of the servants just brought word from the pueblo that Señor Zorro has been at his tricks again."

"Indeed?" Don Diego lifted his eyebrows slightly.

"A short time ago, this Zorro stole Pedro Perez' daughter, Juanita, and carried her away to the hills. There is a great hue and cry about it. Perez is like a madman. The soldiers are making loud talk about Zorro not being such a friend of the common man as he pretends."

"Interesting," Don Diego said.

"What do you think of it, my son?"

"It is understood," Don Diego said, "that Zorro is often aided by the peons and natives, and that the good padres of the missions wish him good fortune in his work. If they should turn against Zorro because of this affair, it may cause Zorro trouble. Not to mention that it will ruin his reputation as a just and merciful man."

"You are right, Diego."

"I do not believe — nay, I am sure — that Zorro would do such a thing. So, there are a couple of possibilities. Perhaps, for his own benefit, some scoundrel is posing as Zorro. Or, perhaps this is a trick of the soldiery to arouse the people against Zorro."

"I have thought of that, my son."

"If Zorro is wise, he will investigate immediately, clear his good name, and punish those who have wronged him. It is a thing that cannot wait. Bernardo!"

The dumb body-servant stepped forward, grinning, and bobbed his head.

"Zorro rides tonight, at once!" Don Diego said.

Bernardo opened the door and hurried out. Don Alejandro touched his son's arm. "Use great care, Diego," he whispered.

A few minutes later, Don Diego Vega slipped from the house through a rear door, and went through the foggy night to an adobe hut some distance away. Bernardo was there, and Zorro's horse was ready.

"You will follow me on your riding mule, as usual," Don Diego said, as he changed clothes rapidly and got into the costume of Zorro. "I shall investigate matters at the barracks, and then possibly at the tavern."

They rode carefully through the fog and mist until they were behind the barracks, and then Señor Zorro dismounted and went forward alone. He crouched against the rear of the building and listened. None of the troopers' horses was saddled and tethered to the hitching rail in front. Nor was there a tumult coming from the men's lounging room.

ZORRO went through the darkness along the wall, and came presently to a window in the guards' room. He heard voices, and listened.

"The girl weeps her head off in the prison room," one of the guards was saying. "A pretty wench, for a peon. And a pretty plot it is."

"You think so," another replied. "Not for us. We fetch the girl here, and Sergeant Garcia and the other take the capitán's gold and go to the tavern to spend it freely and arouse men against Zorro. What do we profit?"

"One of us is enough to be on guard."

"Sí. But here we both are."

"Do you also go to the tavern and have some of the free wine," the other said. "Garcia will not care. Possibly he will not even question you. If he does, say we are taking turns. And do not forget to come back in time for me to go there and do some drinking. If you do, forget me not."

"I'll see that you have your turn," the other said.

Listening at the window, Zorro heard him scurry away. Zorro continued along the wall. At another window, he heard a girl weeping and listened for a moment.

"Señorita!" he murmured softly. "You are Juanita Perez?"

"Sí, señor. Who calls?" She appeared at the window, her hands clutching the bars.

"Attend me closely, señorita. It was not Señor Zorro who carried you away, but another man posing as him. It was a trick to cause Zorro difficulties. Do not be alarmed when I come soon to rescue you."

"Ah, I did not feel that Zorro would do such a thing," she said.

"Careful! Do not speak and let the guard hear. Be quiet until I come."

"Who are you, kind señor?"

"I am the real Zorro, señorita. Be quiet, and wait."

He left the window and hurried on through the darkness. A torch burned in front of the main entrance of the barracks, but nobody was in sight. Zorro slipped along the wall to the door, peered in and found the main corridor empty.

He felt of the pistol in his sash, took it out, and entered the building. Noiselessly, he went along the corridor and turned off into another, and approached the open door of the guards' room. He looked in, and saw the lone guard sprawled on a bench in front of the fire.

"Do not make a sound!" Zorro called out in low tones.

The guard's head jerked around. Then he gave a squawk of surprise and sprang to his feet. But there was no belligerency in his manner. He flattened himself against the wall, gulping, his eyes bulging as he regarded Zorro's pistol, which menaced him.

"What a fine guard you are!" Zorro commented. "I could ransack the place, no doubt!"

"Wh – what do you want here, señor?" the guard asked.

"Keep your voice down."

"All the others are gone, señor. The capitán is visiting a friend. The sergeant and my comrades are making merry, drinking at the tavern."

"Where are the keys to the prison rooms?" demanded Zorro.

"On that ring on the bench, señor."

"Stand still!" Zorro ordered.

He strode forward and picked up the ring of keys, and attached the ring to his sash. Then he went on to the wall and took down a coiled reata.

"Stretch on the floor on your face, and put your arms behind your back," Zorro ordered.

"Thanks, Señor Zorro, for not slaying me," the guard blubbered. "I am only a poor trooper of the lowest grade. I have no ill feeling toward you, Señor Zorro. Tie me up well, so I may say a dozen men overwhelmed me. Kick over the benches and stools."

Behind his mask, Zorro grinned at the other's fear. He made a noose and fastened the guard's hands behind his back, then rolled him over and tied him well from head to feet, and fastened the end of the reata in a ring-bolt in the wall.

"Has the señorita been harmed?" he asked sternly.

"No, Señor Zorro. Just frightened. We only took her from where she was dropped by the sergeant."

"Then Sergeant Garcia acted the part of Zorro tonight?"

"Sí, señor. But do not let anybody know I told you, or they will whip me."

"I'll gag you now," Zorro said, and did so with the man's own neck-cloth.

He hurried along the semi-dark corridor and unlocked the door of one of the prison rooms, to face the frightened girl.

"Come!" he said, grasping her hand. "Ask me no questions now, for there is not time to answer them."

He got her out of the building, led her through the swirling fog to the darkness behind it.

"Wait here," he ordered. "If you run away, you will be ungrateful, and may also cause your father trouble."

"I trust you, señor."

"You know I am not the same man who stole you away from your home?"

"I know, señor. He was shorter and heavier in body, and his voice was harsh."

"Stand!" he shouted, brandishing the pistol.

"Remember that," Zorro said. "Now, wait!"

He left her and hurried through the darkness to where Bernardo was waiting.

"I have the girl," he said. "I will take her to the tavern and leave my horse behind it. Be near with your mule, but be careful the girl does not see you and identify you later as my servant. If I call the signal, ride your mule and decoy the pursuit."

Zorro mounted and rode carefully back to find the girl waiting. He helped her up behind him.

"It is not thc same horse either, señor," she whispered, "and the saddle is different. Ah, I felt that Zorro would not do such a wicked thing as steal me from my father's hut."

"Be silent," he cautioned.

In time, he stopped the black some distance behind the tavern, where it was dark. He dismounted and helped the girl down, tied the horse to a stunted tree, took the girl's hand and led her forward slowly.

"You are to do just as I say," he instructed her. "If you do, soon you will be clasped in your father's arms, and be safe. Come!"

They reached the side of the tavern building and stopped beside a large open window, which let the fog drift into the big main room of the tavern and smoke roll out. As the girl crouched against the wall, Zorro lifted his head cautiously and peered inside.

Sergeant Garcia was strutting around the room with a goblet of wine in his hand. Some of his troopers were sprawled on the benches. Men of the town and travelers off the highway were drinking with the soldier, and the native servants were scurrying about, filling goblets and mugs from wineskins. The fat landlord had a grin on his face. Business was good tonight.

"This Zorro has proved himself to be a rogue instead of a man who aids the oppressed," Garcia was declaiming. "He has fooled you all. But we of the soldiery expected the scoundrel would do something like this in time. It is another crime marked up against him. Abductor of innocent girls! We will never cease effort till we run him to earth!"

Zorro looked over the place carefully as Sergeant Garcia continued his tirade. Half the men in the room were intoxicated to a point where they had slow wits and slower muscles. Of the other half, most were of the sort who would recoil from combat with anyone, especially a man with the reputation of Zorro. He made his plan swiftly.

"Your father is there, señorita," he whispered, bending down beside her. "I will take you to him."

"Oh, señor! They may fight with you and take you."

"It is a risk Zorro always runs, señorita. Hasten to your father's arms, and be sure to declare aloud that I am not the man who abducted you. I will attend to the rest."

He took her hand and led her cautiously toward the front of the building. Because of the fog and mist, the plaza was deserted. Only a couple of torches burned, and those were in front of the little chapel not far away.

Nobody observed them as they went slowly along the front of the tavern and toward the open door. Sergeant Garcia was still declaiming.

"It is a monstrous thing this fellow Zorro did! Think of it, you who have daughters and sisters! Should he not be swinging with a rope around his neck?"

They howled their agreement, and called for more wine.

"Look at poor Señor Perez, sitting there and weeping into his goblet," Garcia continued. "His pretty daughter was all he had in the world. Now he is bereft. There he sits, weeping, and his fair daughter — where is she?"

At this moment Zorro, holding his pistol in his right hand, thrust the girl through the doorway.

"She is here, señores!" he shouted. "Make no move, or I shoot!"

There was deep silence for a moment as the face of every man in the room was turned toward the doorway. Then the señorita gave a glad cry and rushed to her father.

"The real Zorro did not steal me," she cried, as she was clasped in her father's arms. "He just rescued me, from the jail."

"How came you in jail?" Perez demanded.

"The man who stole me dropped me, and two troopers picked me up and took me to the barracks, putting me in a prison room. That is the real Zorro — there in the doorway. And the man who stole me, who pretended to be Zorro, is there." She pointed at Sergeant Garcia. "I recognized his voice when he was talking."

"What means this, Sergeant Garcia?" Perez thundered, putting his daughter aside and reaching for the knife in his belt.

Others in the room came to their feet, their attitude menacing. The troopers there were waiting for orders from the sergeant.

"It was a trick, Señor Perez, to lure Zorro out of hiding and into a trap," Garcia said. "Your girl has not been harmed. And now we have Zorro here, and will deal with him. At him, men!"

The troopers sprang to their feet as the others in the room rushed to get back against the walls.

Zorro had made plans for this moment. He could not fight them all, and it was Garcia he wanted to meet on even terms. He had moved from the doorway, and saw he could not get through it now, for two of the troopers had rushed there. He darted across the corner of the room to the window.

"Stand!" he shouted, brandishing the pistol. "It was a trick — *sí* — to make everyone think ill of Zorro. Now you know I did not do the thing of which I was accused."

"Seize him!" Garcia shouted. "There is a reward!"

He started forward himself, whipping out his blade, despite the fact that Zorro held a pistol and the sergeant had none. His troopers jumped forward also. Zorro sprang to the window, and his pistol roared and spewed smoke and flame and a slug which struck the adobe wall and ricocheted.

An instant later, he had gone through the open window head first, to strike the muddy ground outside.

"After him!" Garcia shouted to his troopers. "To your saddles, and run him down! Fetch him back here!"

The troopers ran for the doorway. Outside, Zorro gave a peculiar cry which was a signal to Bernardo, waiting somewhere near. As the troopers got into their saddles, they could hear the pounding of hoofs.

"There he goes!" Garcia shouted. "After him! Catch me the rogue!"

The troopers dashed away through the billowing fog in pursuit. But they pursued, not Señor Zorro on his black horse, but Bernardo an his fleet riding mule. Zorro laughed silently as he crouched against the back of the tavern. He had no fear that the troopers would capture Bernardo.

The tavern had been emptied of men during the tumult, and not many cared to return. There would be no more free wine, they rightfully guessed. Now that the plot had been exposed, Sergeant Garcia would not toss away any more money.

Those who did re-enter the tavern finished emptying their mugs and then grouped before the fireplace to dry themselves. Sergeant Garcia was unable to claim their attention. There were men in that room who had entertained a friendly feeling for the unknown Zorro and his works, who had known a moment of distrust concerning him, who had faith restored in him now and scorn for the man who had tried to besmirch him.

Garcia finished a goblet of wine, went to the doorway and turned.

"When this Zorro is taken, we will commence looking for those who have been his friends," he threatened. "He always runs away, the rogue. 'Tis fortunate for him that he has a swift horse."

"'Ho, Sergeant Garcia!" somebody outside in the night shouted.

Garcia went to the doorway. "Who calls?" he yelled.

"Señor Zorro calls, poltroon! Abductor of girls! Man who makes clever plots that go astray! Ass and dolt! Can you fight, fellow?"

SERGEANT Garcia howled a curse and sprang outside. Some of those in the room followed him swiftly. A short distance away, Zorro was standing in front of the chapel, in the circle of light cast by the torches.

Garcia whipped out his blade and started forward, and some of the men in the tavern followed.

"Do not be afraid, señor," Zorro taunted. "My pistol has not been reloaded. Dare you fight me fairly with a blade, Señor Sergeant?"

"Nothing could give me more pleasure," Garcia shouted, as he charged forward.

Zorro whipped blade from scabbard and stood ready. The mist was still falling, and fog swirled, and the torches cast a flickering uncertain light, but what was fair for one was equally fair for the other.

Their blades met and rang. The men from the tavern came up closer and spread out to watch, and others came running, and shouts that there was a fight rang around the plaza.

A robed padre came from the chapel, lifted his hands imploringly, then retired quickly to pray, for he knew he could do nothing to stop such a combat.

Garcia attacked with a rush, and Zorro retreated with skill, maneuvering to keep the light out of his eyes. So they felt each other out a moment, eyes agleam, nostrils distended with their deep breathing. Garcia expected a duel to the death. Zorro knew that failure would mean death or capture, exposure, pain for his father, possibly execution as a highwayman if the sergeant did not slay him.

Garcia pressed the fighting. Here was an exceptionally skillful swordsman, Zorro found. Here was no ordinary, clumsy sergeant of the governor's military. Zorro felt that the other would call forth all his skill with a blade.

"This is your end, highwayman!" Garcia said, as they fought. "We'll soon have that mask off and see what manner of face is behind it."

"Fight, poltroon!" Zorro answered. "With your blade instead of your tongue!"

More men had come running, and Zorro feared that some might not be his friends, or that a trooper might appear to use a pistol against him. He pressed the fighting in turn. The blades darted in and out and sang and flashed in the light of the torches.

Once, Zorro slipped on the wet stones in front of the chapel, and Garcia's blade flashed over his shoulder. That was how narrowly the sergeant had missed. But Zorro sprang to his feet again, and now was with his back to the torches, which bothered the sergeant until he tried to turn slightly aside.

In a frenzy, Zorro attacked. He brought into play all the tricks of swordsmanship he knew. Sergeant Garcia, he found, was a worthy foe. But Garcia was tiring. His reactions were growing slower. He tried to press the fighting again, and this time Zorro did not give ground before the onslaught.

"I could kill you now, Garcia," Zorro said. "But you have not done anything against me to merit death. So far, you have only done your duty."

" 'Tis my duty to slay you — and also my personal pleasure," Garcia howled.

"I always mark my foes — so that all men may know them," Zorro said.

He had Garcia where he wanted him. He avoided a wild thrust, his blade darted forward, and Sergeant Garcia recoiled with a scream, dropping his blade and clawing at his face.

The tip of Zorro's sword had done some fast writing on Garcia's left cheek. Carved there was the letter Z.

"Seize him!" Garcia howled. "The reward!"

Zorro sped away. Some few men started after him, but only to make a showing. Zorro reached the black horse waiting in the darkness, mounted and sped away, his shout carrying back on the rushing wind.

Some time later, Señor Zorro turned over the black to Bernardo, who had out-ridden the troopers and was waiting at the adobe hut. With a change of raiment, Zorro disappeared, and Don Diego Vega got cautiously into the house, removed his sodden boots, put on comfortable slippers and his embroidered gown, and sprawled on the divan in front of the fireplace.

PRESENTLY, his father entered the room. Don Diego looked up at him.

"Here is a beautiful passage in this poem," he observed.

"Read it to me at another time, Diego," his father said, his eyes twinkling. "Just now tell me, if you care to do so, about another passage — the passage at arms which I understand occurred a short time ago on the plaza."

Don Diego answered in lowered tones. "This Sergeant Garcia is a man to be reckoned with," he said. "I was compelled to extend myself. The man knows how to handle the blade. Caution must be my watchword in the future."

Then he picked up the book of poems again. His father smiled and went slowly from the room.

Zorro Strikes Again

When a despoiled peon pleads for justice, the cloaked Zorro thunders through the night, his flashing blade bringing retribution to tyrants!

DON DIEGO VEGA yawned as he slowly crossed the patio of his father's house in the outskirts of the little town of Reina de los Angeles. He brushed a scented, lace-edged handkerchief of the finest linen across his delicate nostrils. He bent over a rose bush, and inhaled deeply of the fragrance. Then he strolled on, like a man to whom daily existence is wearisome and without interest.

Don Diego's attire was resplendent — trousers and jacket of thick brocaded satin, a ruffled white shirt of heavy silk, boots of the finest leather made by skilled workmen, a wide silk sash of brilliant hue.

He had been languid in his extreme youth, and he had returned to his father's California estates after schooling in Spain, with the appearance and manners of a fop. He was the scion of the Vegas, an only son. Not only must he inherit the broad estates in days to come, and operate them for the credit of the family, but also he must carry the honor and dignity of that family on his shoulders and guard them with his life.

At first Don Alejandro, his proud white-haired father, had felt a measure of shame because his only son had seemed so utterly devoid of spirit. He had nothing in common with the other young caballeros. He drank wine sparingly, did not care for gambling, seldom gave the eye to a pretty wench, and was not sensitive enough to brawl now and then at an affront. He even said that riding a spirited horse at breakneck speed was not sport but a sort of fatigue-inducing labor.

It was about this time that a mysterious Señor Zorro began riding around, helping the oppressed and punishing the oppressors, dodging the soldiers of the unscrupulous Governor and mocking those who tried to catch him. With the tip of his sword, he carved the letter Z on the cheeks or foreheads of men he fought, until it became known as the Mark of Zorro.

It was a happy day indeed when old Don Alejandro learned that Zorro was none other than his languid son, whose dispirited attitude was nothing but a pose. Don Alejandro felt himself compelled to choke back his pride, for the identity of Zorro must not be disclosed. But he smiled after that whenever a friend pitied him because his only son and heir had cold blood in his veins and read poetry.

Now, Don Diego paused beneath the arches at the side of the patio. He had heard voices in the house, and did not wish to enter until he ascertained the identity of the visitor talking to his father.

THIS was Don Alejandro's birthday, and before sunset the guests would be arriving for the birthday fiesta. There would be feasting, dancing, music until the dawn. Young caballeros and beautiful señoritas of noble families would be there, filling the air with their merry laughter. Older persons would sit around and smile and talk of the days of their own youth.

Don Diego made out his father's voice, and the first words told him the visitor was a certain Estebán Morales, a good man though of peon blood.

Morales had worked for Don Alejandro, and in middle life had acquired a wife, the start of a family, and some land which he worked day and night. He was an honest, industrious fellow, and Don Alejandro helped him when he could, saying that the country needed many such to give it substantial growth and progress.

"I am like an animal caught in a trap, Don Alejandro," Morales was saying. "Capitán Carlos Ortega had me arrested by his troopers, and I was taken before Pedro Ruiz, this magistrado, without knowing with what fault I was charged."

"And with what did they finally charge you, Morales?" Don Alejandro asked.

"It was a monstrous lie, Don Alejandro. I started out as a poor peon; and have had some success because of hard work and thrift. So they would take from me, bit by bit, that which I have earned by my sweat, thinking I am helpless to prevent it — which I am."

"Explain in detail, Morales," Don Alejandro said.

"The other day, Don Alejandro, I sold some hides to a traveling trader. He said he was making up a cargo of goods to take to Monterey to ship. This morning, the soldiers came and hauled me before the magistrado. The trader was there. I was accused of changing the bundles of hides, Don Alejandro, and substituting inferior ones. They listened to the trader, but not to me. When I tried to tell the truth, they said I lied."

"No doubt," Don Alejandro said. "We live in mean times, Morales. The present Governor is a rogue, and most of the men he names to office are rogues also. Capitán Carlos Ortega, stationed in Reina de los Angeles, is one such. Pedro Ruiz, the magistrado, is another. They do as they please, and no doubt send a share of their ill gains to His Excellency. What was the result of your trial, Morales?"

"I must deliver to the trader twice as many prime hides, and without payment. I must pay as a fine twenty pieces of gold. It will impoverish me. My hard work will go for nothing. My wife and children will be hungry. They would strip me, Don Alejandro. When I told them this, the capitán laughed and said a peon should not have property."

"The rogue of a capitán is nothing but a peon himself," Don Alejandro said. "Pedro Ruiz is another."

"You will help me, Don Alejandro?" Morales begged.

"I wish I could, Morales. But I am not friendly with the present Governor of Alta California — who is another peon. He hates all men of blood. If I appeared in this as your friend, they would only double the punishment."

"Then I am ruined," Morales said. "How I wish Señor Zorro rode these days and punished the wicked! But it has been a long time now since he helped men like me. No doubt he has left this country, or has lost his life somewhere. How he would deal with a case like this!"

Don Diego Vega strolled through the open door and into the big main room of the house. He was yawning again, and brushing his nostrils with the scented handkerchief. Estebán Morales got to his feet quickly and knuckled his forehead in respectful greeting.

"My son, Estebán Morales has just been telling me of a certain injustice," Don Alejandro began.

"I had the misfortune to overhear it," Don Diego said. "Is there anything in the world except trouble and discomfort? I was trying to meditate on the poets. Why must men always be having controversies and annoying other men with them?"

"I beg your pardon humbly, Don Diego," Morales said. "I did not mean to annoy you."

"Even mentioning that fellow Zorro fatigues me," Don Diego said. "I remember when he rode the highways, dashing here and there with the troopers always chasing him, upsetting everything and wrecking our tranquility. A pest!"

MORALES made a distracted gesture. "There is no chance for a poor man to better himself," Morales declared. "When those in high places oppress him, what can he do?"

"Do not ask me questions," Don Diego begged. "It makes my head ache to think up the answers."

Don Diego picked a pomegranate off a dish on the table and strolled on across the room. His father gave Estebán Morales his hand.

"Do not despair, Morales," he said. "Something may happen to aid you."

After Morales had backed to the door and left the house, Don Alejandro sat at the head of the table again and looked at his son. Don Diego came back slowly across the room and sprawled in another chair.

"Estebán Morales is a good man, and I hate to see him swindled of the goods he has worked so hard to attain," Don Alejandro said.

"It does seem a pity," Don Diego admitted.

A barefooted servant dressed in white entered the room silently and went across toward the patio. He was carrying a huge platter heaped with little cakes, the sort guests ate when they drank wine. The servants were commencing to get ready for the birthday feast.

Bernardo was always looked upon as Don Diego's personal body servant, though he helped the others when his master did not need him. He was a huge man, strong in his shoulders and arms and quick of wit for a man half peon and half native. He could hear and understand, but could not speak. Bernardo had been born dumb.

He glanced toward Don Diego as he crossed the room, and Don Diego lifted a hand languidly and beckoned. Bernardo grinned and turned toward him, to stop a few feet from the chair and stand waiting.

Don Diego ignored the servant and looked at his father again.

"It occurs to me, my father," he said, "that the man Morales was right in one particular. If Zorro were riding now, he probably would attend to the affair in a proper manner."

"No doubt, my son," Don Alejandro said, his eyes glistening suddenly.

"My father, this day is the anniversary of your birth, and there will be many guests this evening. No doubt all the turmoil will give me a headache. Do I have your permission to retire for a time during the festivities, to rest? I shall reappear before it is time for our guests to depart, of course."

"Certainly, my son," Don Alejandro replied, smiling broadly.

Don Diego looked up at the waiting Bernardo, then. He made a peculiar gesture. Bernardo straightened his huge shoulders and tossed up his head, and his nostrils dilated as if at the thought of excitement. Don Diego motioned for him to go away.

It was enough. Words did not have to be spoken. Don Alejandro understood and Bernardo understood. For Bernardo was Señor Zorro's helper, a man always eager to aid his master in his good work — and a man who could not talk to the soldiers if questioned. He would have everything ready. Señor Zorro's black attire would be where he could don it swiftly. And his powerful big black horse would be waiting. That night, Zorro would strike again!

Three hours after sunset found the merrymaking at Don Alejandro

Vega's casa well under way. Long tables creaked beneath a weight of food. Wineskins were scattered around, gurgling continually as the servants filled goblets. Musicians were playing in the big main room of the house and in the patio.

Guests from prominent families made merry in the house and patio, and those of lesser degree had their feast beneath the huge pepper trees around the huts in the rear. This birthday feast was an annual event, something to which everybody looked forward.

At a certain time, Don Diego approached his father, who was talking to a group of guests, and said he had a headache. After receiving permission to retire, he said he would return later, and left the room. Don Diego had already danced a couple of times with the prettiest of the señoritas, who was much disappointed to see him leave.

As Don Diego strolled languidly through the corridor near his own quarters, he noticed the fat figure of a friar lounging upon a bench near the door of his room. This mendicant monk had visited the casa frequently of late, and Don Diego remembered noticing the man several times near the soldiers' barracks at Reina de los Angeles. For a moment the young man's eyes narrowed and he slackened pace. Then he nodded pleasantly to the monk and passed on. In his room he found Bernardo waiting.

"Everything is in readiness?" Don Diego asked.

Bernardo grinned widely and nodded his head.

"Your own mule is ready, also?"

Bernardo nodded his head again. Don Diego gave him a keen glance.

"By the way, Bernardo, I see that Fray Sabio is again visiting the casa tonight," he said. "I observed him, just now, seated upon the bench, as if he were watching my door. Before you leave be sure and tell the servants to give him plenty of meat and wine."

He smiled significantly and winked at Bernardo, who ginned broadly and bobbed his head emphatically up and down to show that he understood.

Don Diego slipped through a window with Bernardo close behind him. They went through the darkness and away from the scene of festivities. In a secluded place, there was a hut not used by any of the workers on the estate. Behind the hut was an adobe stable, usually empty. But it was not empty now. The big black horse was in it, saddled and waiting.

Don Diego worked swiftly changing his attire. He got into the saddle, and Bernardo opened the stable door and let him out. Bernardo rode a huge mule bareback. They went slowly and cautiously through the shadows, down a long slope, toward the road which ran to Reina de los Angeles.

It was only a short distance to the town. But, before they reached it, Señor Zorro stopped and gestured to Bernardo. He slipped off his mule and disappeared in the darkness, going toward where a fire burned at a camp traders had made not far from the highway.

He was back within a short time.

"The trader is there?" Zorro asked.

Bernardo nodded assent.

"How many are with him?"

Bernardo held up two fingers.

"Are they heavy with food and drink?"

"Yes," Bernardo nodded.

"Are many of the horses saddled?"

Bernardo shook his head in the negative.

"Remember all I have told you," Zorro ordered.

He listened a moment, to make sure no travelers were near, then rode out into the highway and urged the big black horse along it. Slackening speed as he neared the fire, he suddenly swerved off the highway and toward the spot. He could see three men around the fire, emptying a wineskin.

They sprang to their feet when they heard the horse coming. They recoiled with fright when they saw the masked man dressed in black.

"Stand still!" the rider commanded. He held a pistol in his left hand and a whip in his right, and the reins were looped around his saddle horn.

Zorro looked then over. The one in the middle was the trader who had conspired with Capitán Ortega and Ruiz, the magistrado, to despoil

Zorro's long whip lashed out and the man screamed

Estebán Morales.

"You see Señor Zorro before you!" His voice had a ring to it. "Step forward!" he ordered the trader.

"In what way may I serve you, señor?" the trader asked, his voice shaky.

"I do not allow myself to be served by such scum as you," Zorro said. "Robber of men! What you have done has come to my knowledge. I mean this affair of the man Morales. So you would help swindle an honest, hard-working man, eh? You cannot do such a thing in this neighborhood, you dog, and escape punishment."

The whip cracked through the air and the lash bit into the trader's body. The man screamed and dropped to his knees, wrapping his arms protectingly around his head. The whip sang again and again, and the lash bit.

The trader's two friends were stunned to inactivity for a moment. Then there came to them a realization of what was happening. Here was the notorious Señor Zorro, and there was a big reward for his capture.

They leaped forward, howling, one holding a bludgeon and the other a knife which flashed in the firelight. Señor Zorro swerved his horse, and the whip lashed out and cut across the face of the man who held the knife. He screamed, dropped the weapon, and put his hands to his bloody face. The one who held the bludgeon dropped it and sprinted away through the darkness.

Again, the whip cut into the back of the dishonest trader.

"Get up!" Zorro ordered. "Hitch your horses to your cart and start down the highway. If I see you again after dawn, I'll use pistol or blade instead of a whip."

"I'll go, Señor Zorro," the trader whined. "But I — I was only a tool for the use of others."

"I know that. I'll attend to the others, you may be sure."

ZORRO put his pistol back into his sash, grasped the reins and wheeled his horse. Hoofs spurned the flinty ground as he rode away from the trader's camp.

He left the highway as he neared the town, slowed his horse to a walk, and listened. Everything appeared to be serene in Reina de los Angeles as usual. Song and loud talk came from the tavern at the corner of the plaza.

Lights burned in houses and huts.

Pedro Ruiz, the magistrado, lived in a rather large house off to one side. He had acquired the property within a year, though he had been poor and in debt when he had received the appointment as magistrado. It was no secret that his money had come from misuse of his office, that he and Capitán Ortega had conspired together, and that in their deviltry they had the backing of the Governor.

Ruiz' house had a garden in front of it, surrounded by a low wall. Señor Zorro put his horse at the wall, and the animal cleared it easily. He rode to the front door, reached out and hammered on it with the butt of his pistol.

The summons, in itself, was an insolence, and Zorro hoped that the magistrado would answer it in person. A servant pulled the door open, but Ruiz was only a step behind him, his face a picture of wrath. The streak of light shot out and revealed the masked man on the black horse. A pistol menaced Ruiz.

"Step out here, Señor Ruiz!" Zorro commanded. "At once, or I fire!"

"What is this outrage?" the magistrado demanded.

"Tell your servant to come out also, and not give an alarm. At once!"

Ruiz came out of the house, the quaking servant behind him.

"What do you want?" Ruiz asked. "Who are you? How dare you come to my house masked, which is against the law since that thrice-accursed Señor Zorro brought his lawlessness to this province?"

"I am Zorro!"

"You — you are Zorro? And you have the insolence to approach the residence of a magistrado? For this, you will be hanged. There is a reward offered for your capture."

"Do you aspire to gain it?" Zorro asked. "Do you hope to capture me here and now, perhaps?" He gestured to the servant. "Close the door! I can do my work by moonlight."

"What would you do?" Ruiz cried, as the door was closed.

"Your evils are well known, Señor Ruiz," Zorro said. "You are perfidious to the core. But the affair which interests me now is that of the man Morales, which has come to my attention. He is honest and hard-working, and you would despoil him. That calls for punishment."

"Do you presume to dictate to the courts?" Ruiz asked with a show of bravado.

"Not to decent courts, but to such as that over which you preside. I know the demands you have made on Morales. The trader has been sent away by me. You will erase your judgment from your books in the morning, and let the original hide deal stand."

"Very well," Ruiz said.

"You comply too easily," Zorro told him. "No doubt you think I will ride away now, so you can inform Capitán Ortega what has happened, be guarded on the morrow, let the judgment stand, and possibly persecute Morales some more for this act of mine. Rest assured, Morales knows me not, nor does he know I am acting in his behalf. In reality, señor, I act in behalf of all the oppressed who cannot help themselves."

"I — I'll do as you say, Señor Zorro. If the trader is gone, I can state that no doubt he gave false testimony and feared to remain, and so reverse my decision in the case."

"You will also resign your office at once," Zorro said.

"You ask too much, señor. I shall not!"

The whip cracked. Pedro Ruiz gave a cry of pain and fell back. Zorro urged his horse forward, and the whip sang again and again. Ruiz' screeches rang through the night as he howled for mercy. The servant ran away, and Zorro guessed he had gone to spread an alarm. He knew, also, that the man who had run from the trader's camp had gone to the inn to shout that Señor Zorro was about.

Zorro ceased whipping. "That is enough for now," he said. "There will be greater punishment if you do not do as I say. Resign your office and make public announcement of the fact. You are not fit to be a magistrado. If you do not do as I say in all things, I'll visit you again. And all the troopers of His Excellency cannot keep me from getting at you."

ABRUPTLY Zorro put his horse at the wall and cleared it and galloped away. He turned from the town and cut up over a slope. Men were shouting down by the plaza, and he knew an alarm had been given.

He stopped and listened, then circled and approached the town again. This time he went toward the soldiers' quarters.

Troopers were leading out their horses and saddling them. Zorro heard Sergeant Garcia bellowing orders. Some of the men rode toward the plaza immediately.

Zorro left his horse in a dark spot and went forward afoot, to come to the wall of the building and follow it around to the window of the capitán's quarters. Ortega was inside. Sergeant Garcia was with him.

"It is this Zorro again, without a doubt, Capitán," Garcia was reporting. "The description fits. He whipped the trader and ordered him down the highway. He whipped Pedro Ruiz and told him to resign. The Morales affair was mentioned."

"I was not stationed here when Señor Zorro rode before," Capitán

Ortega said. "But I have read all the records. It was suspected at one time that Zorro is Don Diego Vega."

"Ridiculous, if the capitán will pardon me," Garcia said. "Five minutes in Don Diego's company would convince anyone differently."

"I know. He dresses like a fop and is always yawning. People think he has water in his veins. But I have looked at Don Diego closely on occasion. I have noticed his back and arms, which are not those of a weakling. I have noticed his stride when he thought nobody was looking. It is the step of a fencer, Sergeant."

"But Zorro is here in Reina de los Angeles, or was a short time ago," Garcia protested, "and Don Diego no doubt is out at his father's place. This is Don Alejandro's birthday and there is a big fiesta. I had intended riding out myself when I got off duty. There is food and wine for all. Don Diego would be there helping entertain the guests."

"That is easy to settle, Sergeant," said Ortega. "We'll ride out to Don Alejandro's place, taking a detail of troopers with us. I'll pay my respects, and we'll see if Don Diego is at home, or whether perhaps he is riding around with a mask on his face. Also for the last few weeks, I have placed a friend in Don Alejandro's casa, to watch Don Diego's movements. He is a wandering monk named Fray Sabio. He will tell us the truth. Saddle my horse."

Outside the window, Zorro heard the sergeant reply and leave the room. There was a rear door, and Zorro got through it quickly. Nobody was in the corridor. Zorro went swiftly to the door of the capitán's quarters, pulled the door open and entered.

Ortega was winding his sash, and turned quickly, enraged when he heard the door opened without somebody first asking for admittance. The capitán reeled back against the wall at the sight of a masked man threatening him with a pistol.

"Do not call for help unless you wish to die!" the intruder ordered.

"Who are you?"

"I am Zorro, as perhaps you have guessed."

"Indeed? And you dare come here to my quarters? You spare us the necessity of running you down, you scoundrel!"

"For some quaint reason, I refuse to be frightened," Zorro replied. "I know you have sent your sergeant for your horse, and he will be returning soon to say the mount is ready. So we have but a moment."

"A moment for what, señor? For you to confess your errors to me before I have you into jail?"

"A moment for me to punish you," Zorro said. "You are but a cheap swindler, capitán. You disgrace the uniform you wear. You should wear a mark of shame, and I intend to mark you. You have a blade at your side!"

"And you have a pistol in your hand," Ortega reminded him.

"I return it to my sash, señor — so! Now, if you will draw your blade, we are on even footing."

Capitán Ortega gave a glad cry as he whipped blade from scabbard. In the same instant, Zorro backed to the door and shot the bolt. Then he darted aside as Ortega made for him, and whipped out his own blade.

Ortega kicked a stool aside, and Zorro tossed a bench back to the wall, so they had ample room. Flickering tapers in a huge silver candelabra illuminated the scene.

THE blades touched, rang. Light flashed from them as they sang a song of combat. Feet shuffled on the floor of packed earth.

Capitán Ortega was noted for skill with a blade. But after he had felt out his adversary for a moment, he knew he had met his equal, if not his master. He redoubled caution and set to work seriously.

Ortega pressed the fighting, and Zorro gave ground. The masked man worked along the wall to get the flickering of the tapers out of his eyes. Then he, in turn, pressed the fighting.

Zorro's blade seemed like a live thing as it darted. Ortega felt himself being driven backward. The perspiration stood out on his face. Zorro was playing with him, he knew.

There came a knock on the door.

"Garcia!" Ortega shouted. "Zorro is here! Get help!"

"Poltroon!" Zorro cried at him. "So you need help, do you? It will not arrive in time, señor."

As he fought, he could hear boots pounding the floor of the corridor. He drove Ortega back against the wall again. Zorro's blade darted in, he gave a quick twist of his wrist, and Ortega reeled aside, and almost collapsed against the wall, dropping his blade.

"Now, you bear my mark on your cheek, señor," Zorro told him. "Surrender your post here to some honest man, or we may meet again and my blade find your heart."

Men were trying to smash in the door now. Zorro slapped his blade into its scabbard and ran to the window. He was through it and gone before Ortega could lurch to the door and open it.

"Get your mounts!" Zorro heard the capitán shouting. "I ride with you."

A trooper running around the building appeared in front of Zorro as the latter hurried toward his horse. Zorro whipped pistol from his sash and fired a ball past the man's head to make him dart aside. Zorro ran on.

As he got into his saddle, he heard hoofbeats back by the soldiers' quarters. He urged his big black along the hillside, and as he rode he gave a peculiar strident cry which pierced loudly through the night. That was a signal for Bernardo to mount his mule and ride to a certain rendezvous.

Bernardo was waiting when Zorro rode up, and side by side they went along the highway.

"The troopers are close behind," Zorro reported. "Their capitán leads them. He suspects me, I think. We must work swiftly, Bernardo."

They got top speed from their mounts, and knew they were gaining slightly on the pursuit. Over a stone fence they jumped, to cut across a field where the going was slower. At the hut Zorro sprang out of his saddle and handed the reins of the big black to Bernardo.

Bernardo rode his mule away, leading the horse. He would go to a pasture a half mile distant, unsaddle the wet horse and turn him loose with the mule. Capitán Ortega and his troopers would find no wet horse to increase their suspicions.

In the hut, Don Diego divested himself of the Zorro costume and put it in a safe hiding place. He washed the dust from his face and hands, wiped it off his boots, brushed his hair. Darting from the hut, he kept to the shadows as he got to the house.

Through a dark side patio he made his way to a door which let him into a hallway which ran to his own rooms. As he got in unseen, he could hear a commotion at the front of the house. The music stopped, some of the women squealed in fright, and he heard his father's stern voice demanding an explanation:

"What does this mean, Capitán Ortega? Have you taken too much wine? How dare you bring your men here in this boisterous manner and frighten my guests. And your face — it is slashed and covered with blood!"

"It bears the mark of Zorro, señor, if you must know," Ortega replied. "The rogue is riding again, and caught me off guard and wounded me when I was unable to fight him fairly."

"And must you ride here to tell me this?"

"We pursued him in this direction. We could hear the pounding of his horse's hoofs up to a few minutes ago."

"No doubt he passed and rode into the hills," Don Alejandro suggested.

"Or he may have stopped here," Ortega insinuated. "I have no desire to interrupt your merriment, Don Alejandro. I hope my troopers will be welcome to join in it."

FOR a long minute Don Alejandro stared at the capitán coldly. "They are," he said at last.

"When they have finished with their duties," Ortega added. "I do not see your son, Don Diego. Does he not attend his father's birthday fiesta?"

"My son has retired for a little time because of a headache. He will appear again presently."

"Indeed? May I visit his room and suggest a remedy for his headache?" Ortega asked. "I am eager to see Don Diego — here and now."

Don Alejandro drew himself up haughtily.

"I do not like your manner, Señor el Capitán, and fail to find a proper meaning in your words," Don Alejandro answered haughtily.

Perhaps he would have said more, but he saw Don Diego entering the room from the hallway. Don Diego was in his usual splendid attire. He was brushing a scented handkerchief across his nostrils, and he yawned.

"What is all this turmoil, my father?" Don Diego asked. "My head is splitting already."

"Some troopers are here, my son. They have been chasing Señor Zorro, their capitán says."

"Is that rogue abroad again? Now we shall have constant excitement, I suppose. These are turbulent times. A man cannot muse on the works of philosophers and poets. And what is wrong with the capitán's face? Is that a sight for gentle ladies?"

Capitán Ortega was watching him closely, listening carefully. Don Diego's voice certainly was not like that of Señor Zorro. He began wondering whether he had made a fool of himself with his suspicions.

Then he remembered something — his best card — his ace, known as Fray Sabio. Turning to a servant, Ortega motioned him to approach.

"Fetch Fray Sabio to me at once," he ordered in loud tones. Turning to Don Alejandro, who had suddenly grown pale with dismay, Ortega smiled maliciously.

"Fray Sabio is an honest monk," the Capitán said. "We can all believe what he says. We will question the good friar regarding your son's whereabouts tonight."

Don Diego patted his hand against his lips and stifled another yawn.

The portly monk entered hurriedly. His eyes were red and swollen. He looked inquiringly at Capitán Ortega.

"Fray Sabio, you have been here all evening?" Ortega asked.

"Sí, señor." The monk nodded vigorously. "I have been out in the corridor, seated on a bench near Don Diego's rooms. I have not moved from that spot for hours."

"Ah!" Ortega grinned with satisfaction. "Doubtless you saw Don Diego leave. At what time did he return?"

Fray Sabio showed surprise. "I do not understand, Señor Capitán. Don Diego retired to rest several hours ago and did not come out again until just a few minutes ago. I should have seen him otherwise."

Ortega scowled. "You are lying!" he cried.

The monk drew himself up with offended dignity. "I do not lie, señor," he said stiffly. And without another word, he turned and left the room.

Capitán Ortega, his face crimson with baffled rage, glared at Don Diego, who smiled serenely.

"My father, have some servant bathe the capitán's face, so he will be more presentable," Don Diego suggested. "And there is Sergeant Garcia, looking like a thundercloud. Let him take his troopers out to the tables under the trees, and fill them with food and wine. This is the anniversary of the day of your birth, my father, and nothing must mar it."

Don Alejandro, his face a mask, clapped his hands for the same servant who had executed the previous errand. Don Diego stepped closer to the capitán, brushing the handkerchief across his nostrils again, almost significantly.

"This Señor Zorro marked you well," he said.

"It shall be my delight some day to see him twisting and squirming at the end of a rope," Ortega replied.

"Before you can experience that delight, capitán, this Zorro will have to be caught," Don Diego remarked. "Ah, well! Something is always ruining our pleasure."

Don Diego bowed slightly, and turned toward where a bevy of hopeful señoritas were waiting as they eyed him over the tops of their fans.

In the meantime Fray Sabio had left the casa and was pacing back and forth beneath the trees, in the orchard. Spears of light from the nearby windows showed that his fat face was creased with worry and indecision.

"I wish the good servant Bernardo had not ordered that servant to give me that meat and wine," he muttered aloud to himself. "He knows it always makes me sleep. I wonder if I did tell the truth to Capitán Ortega?"

Zorro Saves a Herd

Behind the thundering stampede rides Zorro — his toledo blade a match for the pistol hidden in the sash of Carlos Lopez!

ROLLING up the tree-bordered driveway which led to the great adobe casa on the rancho of Don Manuel Sandoval, the ornate carriage was an imposing sight.

Imported from Spain by way of Mexico, the vehicle was truly a conveyance for a proud "hidalgo." Not in all Alta California was there another. It was drawn by a splendid pair of blacks with flowing manes and tails. Everyone in that part of the country knew the carriage was the property of old Don Alejandro Vega, and used by him for ceremonial visits and on feast days.

But the splendid conveyance was not being used by Don Alejandro now. He was taking his ease in his house near Reina de los Angeles. The carriage was being used by Don Diego, his only son.

Don Diego was rather resplendent himself. Attired in garments of brocaded satin, ruffled white silk shirt, boots of the finest leather, and a sash which contained all the hues of the rainbow, Don Diego reclined on the silken cushions in the rear seat of the carriage. He covered his mouth and nostrils with a scented handkerchief to keep out the fine dust.

The native coachman driving the blacks was glad the carriage was nearing its destination. For his ears rang with Don Diego's complaints. When the coachman brought the horses to a stop in front of the Sandoval home, a footman sprang down to spread a length of crimson carpet on the ground and help Don Diego out.

A Sandoval servant witnessed the arrival and hurried to inform his master.

Don Diego strolled languidly to the front door. When it was not opened immediately at his approach, he turned toward the patio.

Gray-haired Don Manuel Sandoval was standing beside the fountain in the patio, stiff and stern, his eyes flashing, his hands clenched at his sides. Before Don Manuel stood a man whom Don Diego knew to be Carlos Lopez. Lopez held some sort of office under the Governor, and was reputed to be an unscrupulous rogue, as were most of the Governor's appointees at that time.

Don Diego overheard their conversation.

"But this is nothing less than robbery, señor," Don Manuel Sandoval was saying to Lopez. "In whatever guise it is presented, it still remains plain robbery."

"You defy the orders of your superiors, Don Manuel?" Carlos Lopez asked.

"My superiors?" A quality of amusement was in Don Manuel's voice as he spoke. "We have not been talking of my superiors, señor. We have been speaking of the Governor and those who serve him, men such as yourself."

"Your rash words shall be reported to the proper authorities," Lopez declared. "There are certain penalties for treason, Don Manuel."

"No doubt," Don Manuel said, "you are ignorant of history, not being an educated man. From the earliest times, señor, there have been periods when oppressors gathered power, and for a time made life miserable for honest men. They despoiled, robbed, slew. But never once, señor — and mark this well — never once did the oppressors last for long. With the loot they gathered, they also gathered the wrath of those they wronged, until it became a seething sea and engulfed them."

"I am not here, Don Manuel, to listen to any high-sounding words," Lopez broke in. "I came merely to state the case. You did not pay the special taxes which were assessed against your name. You even protested. So I was sent with my men to take over the herd. The animals will be driven to San Fernando and slaughtered. The value of the hides will be credited to your account. There will be little credit, however, since expenses of the operation must be deducted."

"In plain words," Don Manuel remarked, "you would steal my herd, kill the animals for their hides. Whatever the hides bring in the market will only offset the expenses. Despite the loss of my herd, I will still owe the original, exorbitant tax. Is that correct?"

"I do not make the laws, Don Manuel," Lopez said. "I merely obey orders."

"My vaqueros have just finished gathering the herd," Don Manuel said. "Now you come with your ruffians to seize it after the work is done."

"That is wisdom," Lopez said, smiling.

"It might honestly be called by some other name," Don Manuel hinted.

"I have stated the case," Lopez said. "We will camp for the night at the mouth of the canyon, and drive the herd away at dawn. I desire to inform you that the men I have with me are lusty fellows and well-armed. If your vaqueros make an attack, they will be dealt with harshly."

At this moment, Don Diego Vega disclosed his presence. He strolled into the patio, brushing his scented handkerchief across his nostrils.

"Good afternoon, Don Manuel," he said. "I have done myself the honor to drive through the heat and dust to extend my father's compliments and my own to you and your charming daughter, Inez."

"Ah, Don Diego! A Vega is always thrice welcome at my house," Don Manuel replied.

"There seems to be a stench in your patio, Don Manuel," Don Diego observed. "It overpowers the fragrance of the roses and other blooms. It puzzled me at first, but now I have the answer to it. I am standing to windward of the creature beside you, and the stench comes from that direction."

"Don Diego Vega, I shall remember that remark," Carlos Lopez said angrily.

"As long as you do, señor, you will also remember that you cast a stench," Don Diego countered.

Lopez' face colored with wrath. He walked swiftly to the garden exit, where he stopped.

"Don Manuel Sandoval, I have told you what I came to say," Lopez called back. "I shall report your words, and those of your visitor, Don Diego."

"If you make the report as strong as your stench, señor, it may travel even as far as the ears of the Governor in Monterey," Don Diego said. "Kindly do not annoy my friend, Don Manuel, any further."

"You speak in a loud voice for a cockerel without any spurs," Lopez replied. "Your lack of spirit and indolence are the jest of the country. If hidalgo blood flows in your veins, I am thankful it does not run in mine."

"No doubt your veins are charged with swill for swine," Don Diego observed. "Perhaps we shall learn some day regarding the truth of that. It is being said in Reina de los Angeles that Señor Zorro is riding the highway again. It appears to be his particular task to attend to rogues like you. When his blade lets blood out of your body, we shall see the color of it."

Carlos Lopez' eyes widened and his lower jaw sagged at the words. He turned and hurried to where his horse was waiting.

Don Diego turned to Don Manuel, who sought a bench beside a gurgling fountain. But, before Don Diego could speak, a vision of loveliness floated from the house and across the flagstones of the patio. Señorita Inez Sandoval stopped beside her father, her head held high and her eyes flashing as she accepted Don Diego's courteous bow.

"I heard everything," she said. "You, Diego, are good at turning a phrase, but that does not cast aside the disaster that is coming to our house."

"Disaster?" Don Diego questioned.

"They will steal our herd," Inez told him. "And the unjust tax will still remain against us. So they will come and steal something else, perhaps the furnishings of the house and our few jewels."

Don Manuel gestured for his daughter to be silent.

"Don Diego, pardon my poor hospitality," he implored. "My

servants shall care for your horses and carriage at once, and furnish your coachman and footman with quarters and food."

"I asked my body servant, Bernardo, to follow me on his mule," Don Diego said, "for I desire to remain the night with you. Bernardo will care for me personally."

The señorita sat beside her father. Don Diego took a bench on the opposite side of the fountain. A servant appeared with wine skin and goblets.

Don Manuel saluted Don Diego, and they drank. Señorita Inez touched her pretty curved lips to the edge of her goblet, her wide eyes watching Don Diego.

Fop or not, this man was the scion of the Vegas, a family of both wealth and power. Like many another señorita, Inez Sandoval wondered whether she could not make a proper man of him, if given the chance to do so as his wife. Perhaps this visit might mean something, she thought. It was well known that Don Diego detested riding around the country. He did not make meaningless or unnecessary journeys.

"Exactly what is the situation, amigo, concerning your herd?" Don Diego asked Don Manuel.

"My vaqueros have just completed the round up, Diego. These tax-gathering scoundrels waited until the work was done before they appeared. In the morning they will drive the herd away. You heard Lopez."

"Where is the herd now?"

"In the box canyon two miles south of here. The canyon has a narrow mouth. Lopez and his rogues are camped just inside it. They drove my vaqueros away. Juan Castro, my chief vaquero, reported that my men are willing, but they cannot fight Lopez' men with any hope of victory. The scoundrels are heavily armed. I cannot ask my vaqueros to go to certain death."

"Certainly not," Don Diego agreed. "With your kind permission, amigo, we will talk of things less disturbing. To hear of troubles always fatigues me."

"You are indeed fortunate, Don Diego, that your family has no troubles of its own," Inez told him, a tinge of rebuke in her voice. "But your father is so strong in position that even the Governor dares not affront him. Others are helpless in the face of oppression."

She sprang to her feet in anger.

Don Diego rose quickly, bowing.

"I heard you speak of Señor Zorro," Inez continued defiantly. "He is riding again, righting wrongs and punishing oppressors. I wish he would ride this way to do his work! What a man he is!"

"He may be some peon rogue," Don Diego observed.

"Whatever his blood, he is a man," Inez said.

She tossed up her head and turned away.

Don Diego was escorted to a guest chamber in the great casa. Within a short time, his personal servant, the giant peon, Bernardo, arrived on his mule. Bernardo knew many secrets concerning Don Diego Vega, but never would he disclose them. Bernardo had been born dumb. He could not write.

"Everything is in readiness, Bernardo?" Diego asked in a low tone when they met in the guest chamber.

Bernardo grinned, bobbing his head in assent.

"Zorro rides tonight," Diego went on. "It is a matter of attending to some rogues and saving a herd for a friend. Do you know Juan Castro, the chief vaquero here?"

Bernardo nodded.

"Roam around and observe several things," Diego ordered. "Find where Juan Castro has his hut. Zorro may wish to speak to him after nightfall. But first help me to dress for the evening meal."

At the repast in the Sandoval dining hall, Don Diego was a languid gentleman. He glanced at Señorita Inez a few times, but she could not convince herself that his glances were ardent. She sang for him after the meal, then retired with her duenna. Diego talked to Don Manuel for a time, yawning repeatedly.

"No doubt you are fatigued from your journey, Diego, and desire to seek your couch," Don Manuel said. "I shall retire, too, for I would be up before dawn to see what happens to my herd."

Don Manuel went with Diego to the door of the guest chamber to take leave of him ceremoniously. When Don Manuel was gone, Diego closed and barred the door. Bernardo was waiting.

"You have made all plans?" Diego asked him.

Bernardo bobbed his head. The peon's dilated nostrils and deep breathing were the only signs of excitement he revealed. He waited, standing back against the wall, while Diego removed his colored sash, so it would not delay him when the time came for him to change clothes.

From his traveling case, Diego took a pistol, powder and balls. Making sure the weapon was loaded properly, he thrust it into the belt of his trousers. He placed powder flask, balls and wads in a pocket of his coat.

"You know where Juan Castro is to be found?" he asked Bernardo.

Bernardo nodded that he did.

"No doubt you have my black horse ready, and the attire of Zorro so I may change into it quickly, and Zorro's sword. Is it so?"

Bernardo nodded assent.

"We will wait until the house is quiet," Diego told him.

A few minutes later, Bernardo extinguished the burning tapers in the candelabra. Diego went to a window which opened on the patio, and looked into the moon-drenched night.

"You will go with me until I have contacted Juan Castro," Diego said. "Then you will follow on your mule, as usual. Let us slip out now."

THEY left the room, closing the door carefully. They kept to the shadows as they went across the patio to the rear of the big house. Bernardo led the way beneath huge trees to where dense brush grew beside a stone wall. In the thicket the black horse of Zorro was waiting.

Diego changed his clothing swiftly, tucked the pistol into his belt, buckled on his blade. He got into the saddle and gathered up the reins.

"Where is your mule?" he asked Bernardo. Bernardo pointed back into the brush. Beyond, a fire was burning by the group of huts where Don Manuel's vaqueros lived. Men were scattered around the flames, talking of their day's work and wondering about their herd in the distant canyon.

"Can you show me from here where Juan Castro lives?" Don Diego asked Bernardo.

The mute pointed directly at the vaquero fire, then waved his hand to the left and held up two fingers.

"The second hut on this side of the fire?"

Bernardo nodded agreement.

"Good!" Diego said. "Stay out of sight, but follow on your mule."

He urged the big black horse out of the brush, touched lightly with his spurs, and galloped toward the fire around which Don Manuel's vaqueros were sprawled, busy with food and drink. Some of the men sprang to their feet as the rider approached.

Zorro stopped within the circle of light cast by the flames and the vaqueros saw the big black horse, the man in the saddle, his attire all black, a mask over his face. They saw the blade at his side and the butt of the pistol thrust into his belt.

"I am Zorro!" the rider announced. "I have come to help you. Do not make any noise. Send Juan Castro to me immediately."

Castro, Don Manuel's chief vaquero, came hurrying to the fire.

"You are Zorro?" Castro nervously asked.

"I am. I have come to right matters for Don Manuel Sandoval, but you men must help me."

"We are yours to command, señor," Castro replied, his eyes gleaming.

"Your men do not have to fight and run the risk of death or injury," Zorro said. "Nevertheless, we will save the herd. Attend me!"

As they gathered around, Zorro spoke in low tones.

"Castro, send five or six of your men out beyond the mouth of the canyon where that dog of a Lopez holds your herd. You and the others will ride with me. We shall go to the head of the canyon and climb down into the defile on our horses. Suddenly, we will stampede the herd. The cattle will rush wildly down the canyon and over the camp of Lopez' scoundrels. When the stampede comes from the mouth of the canyon, the vaqueros we have stationed there will keep the herd running. The cattle will take to the hills and scatter. They will be so wild that for weeks no man will approach them."

"Lopez, who would despoil Don Manuel, will know it is useless to try to round up the cattle and drive them away," Castro said, his white teeth showing in a grin.

"That is right, amigo. If there is no herd to be driven away, Lopez and his jackals must return empty-handed. You, Castro, will have the hard labor of a roundup later, but the herd will be saved. Perhaps something will happen soon to prevent the rogues from despoiling Don Manuel of his other property. When it is safe, the cattle can be gathered again. Until then, they will run wild in the hills."

The vaqueros ran to their ponies.

Zorro rode away from the fire and waited. When the horsemen were ready, the band started quietly, Castro riding on Zorro's left and showing the way.

The riders who were to take stations in front of the canyon's mouth left the others, disappearing into the night. With Zorro and Castro at their head, the remaining vaqueros rode on through the shadows toward the head of the canyon.

Slowly they ascended a rough hillside, making their way around huge rocks and through dense patches of brush. Finally, they could see the box canyon below them. The moonlight revealed a slumbering herd packed densely along the dry bed of a creek.

The descent was perilous and slow, for Zorro did not want his band to be observed. But finally all were on the floor of the box canyon at its head. The herd was between them and the mouth of the canyon. A quarter of a mile inside this canyon, in its narrow part, Carlos Lopez and his men were camped about the embers of a fire.

"Have your torches ready," Zorro ordered.

Some of the vaqueros had brought along torches made of twisting dry vines together and dipping the ends in hot tallow. Once put alight, the vine wood would flame and burn for quite a time. One of the vaqueros dismounted, put his dead torch against a rock, and got flint and metal ready to strike a spark.

FAR OUT beyond the mouth of the canyon, now the other vaqueros began screeching.

Lopez' men around the fire were attracted by the howls. Their attention centered down the canyon where they feared an attack. They thought nothing of the head of the defile, where the true danger lay.

"Light the torch," Zorro ordered.

Sparks flew and caught. Castro and his vaqueros rode past the peon afoot to ignite their torches from the one he held.

"At it!" Zorro ordered.

The vaqueros scattered to right and left across the head of the canyon. As they rode, they waved the torches above their heads, shouting. They charged around the rocks and through the brush straight at the slumbering herd down the defile.

But the herd was slumbering no longer. Already nervous from the roundup and the unusual bedding ground, the cattle leaped to their feet. The animals saw the flaming torches coming toward them, heard the wild yells.

Within a space of seconds the herd broke into a stampede. Bellowing, the frightened cattle raced from those flaming torches, down the canyon, following the dry creek bed toward the canyon's mouth.

The camp Lopez and his men had made was in the path of the frenzied herd.

Guns blazed at the camp. Men screamed in terror as they tried to get their horses, saddle them and mount. But they did not have time for that. The horses, terrified by the noise, charged out of the canyon's mouth.

The frenzied herd thundered on. Behind the stampede, the vaqueros still yelled and waved their flaming torches. The dry brush caught and burst into a sea of flame, which the night wind blew down the defile.

Like an avalanche, the herd flowed over the spot where the Lopez men were camped. The mouth of the canyon was a bottleneck. There the herd swelled between the cliffs as the animals pushed one another higher and higher in the brush. Lopez' men found they could not escape the crushing hooves.

As the cattle streamed out the canyon's narrow mouth, the vaqueros waiting there rode screeching and waving torches of their own. The cattle kept moving toward the hills. None would find refuge in the brush but all would scatter over the range. Only after weeks would the stock get over their fright and commence congregating in the fertile valleys

Caros Lopez screamed as the keen blade struck

where there was water. Then Don Manuel's men would find them easily and drive them back when the danger of seizure was over.

While most of Zorro's band rode out the canyon's mouth behind the cattle, Juan Castro and a few men remained near Zorro.

"You did it, señor," Castro said. "Carlos Lopez and his rogues will not drive Don Manuel's herd away in the morning to be slaughtered. If I knew your identity, señor, I could thank you properly."

"My identity is to remain a secret, Castro," Zorro replied. "You will kindly tell Don Manuel Sandoval, when you return, that I am glad to have been of service to him. Do not follow me when I leave you, and see that none of your men do."

"It shall be as you wish, señor."

Zorro reined in abruptly. He pointed ahead. The herd had passed.

The scattered embers of Lopez' campfire glowed in the night. Two men could be seen fleeing from a narrow ledge above the camp.

"Two horses are by those rocks," Zorro pointed out. "Those rogues are trying to get to them."

He spurred his big black. Castro and his two men followed. The fugitives heard them coming. One ran into the brush on the hillside.

"Catch him!" Zorro shouted to Castro. "I'll attend to this other."

Castro and his two vaqueros began pursuit of the man in the brush. Zorro rode on toward the other, who whirled.

A gun blazed and a slug sang past Zorro's head. The man ahead could not fire again without reloading. Zorro doubted if the culprit had a second pistol in his belt.

Some of the campfire embers caught on dry grass and brush. In the light of the spreading flames, Zorro saw that the man in front of him was Carlos Lopez.

BY THE same light of the burning grass, Lopez discovered the masked horsemen approaching. The sight seemed to sting him to activity. He turned and started running, but Zorro rode like a whirlwind and turned him back.

"Stand, Lopez!" Zorro shouted in a stern voice which certainly did not resemble the usual tones of Don Diego Vega.

Lopez halted in terror. In the light of the grass fire, his face was ghastly.

"Who are you?" Lopez cried. "Who were those men with you? I am the Governor's representative."

"A poor thing of which to boast," Zorro said. "I am known as Zorro."

"You? Did Don Manuel Sandoval engage you to do this thing?"

"Don Manuel knows nothing of it," Zorro said. "I seek to punish rogues wherever I find them. I found some here."

"They are still here. Look at them!" Lopez cried, almost in hysterics, pointing to Castro's vaqueros. "There they are. Only two of us lived through the stampede. It was your doing."

"Let us say it was the cattle's doing," Zorro replied. "It is fitting that your rogues die beneath the hooves of the animals they would have stolen and slaughtered. The men with me have attended to your compatriot. They will now ride on. You will be unable to identify any of them. You can report nothing, señor, except that the cattle stampeded and ran over your camp."

"I can report that Zorro did this."

"I will make it possible, señor, for men to believe that statement," Zorro replied, whipping his blade from its scabbard.

"You have made a bad error, Señor Zorro," Lopez screeched. "You have made it possible for me to earn a rich reward. This is your end."

As he spoke, Lopez brought out a second pistol which he had hidden beneath his jacket. Zorro raked his spurs as the weapon barked and flamed. The big black horse swerved aside, and the bullet almost burned Zorro's neck.

"You failed in that, señor," Zorro said. "And now — "

"Do not slay me!" Lopez cried. He knelt quickly beside a boulder, holding up his arms imploringly, a great fear mirrored in his face.

"If I slew you there would be none to tell your story," Zorro told him. "You must give your superiors proof."

Zorro's blade darted out. The light from the fire played along the Toledo steel like dancing flame. Carlos Lopez screamed as the keen blade struck. He toppled forward, his hands going to his face.

"Get up, miserable coward," Zorro ordered. "You still have your life. And until the day of your death, señor, you will have a scar on your forehead, one that forms the letter Z."

Zorro touched his black horse with spurs, galloped through the mouth of the canyon, and turned aside to race through the moonlight night, leaving the canyon behind him, with the dead on the ground where the campfire had been.

As the vaqueros were scattering the herd in the far distance, Zorro raced back toward the Sandoval casa. At a certain spot, he stopped his tired horse, and threw a strange call through the night.

Then Zorro rode on, watching the shadows at either side of the trail. Presently, he saw one moving toward him. It was Bernardo on his mule.

They were cautious as they neared the rancho. Lights were burning in the big house. Everybody had been aroused.

In the brush, Zorro dismounted, changed his attire quickly, and left the black horse for Bernardo to attend.

Then, Don Diego Vega darted through the shadows, avoiding streaks of moonlight. He made his way to a corner of the house and finally into the patio.

He heard somebody shouting as he reached the patio, and heard Don Manuel Sandoval reply. As Don Diego opened a door and slipped into the dark guest chamber, he could hear Castro's triumphant voice tell Don Manuel that Señor Zorro had appeared and led the vaqueros.

A very few minutes later, Don Diego Vega, his hair rumpled, his eyes seemingly half glazed with sleep, yawning, came from the guest chamber to cross the patio and go to the side of the house. Don Manuel was there with Castro and some of the house servants.

As Don Diego came into view, Señorita Inez and her duenna appeared, alive with excitement.

"What is all this tumult?" Don Diego asked Don Manuel, yawning again. "People shouting, the brush afire in the distance, horses being ridden around. Have the natives started another uprising?"

"Zorro has been here, amigo," Don Manuel told him. "He worked a trick and stampeded the herd. The cattle are running wild in the hills."

"I am happy for you, but spare me the recital," Don Diego begged. "Tales of violence always upset me. Even my body servant, Bernardo, has skipped off somewhere, and is not here to bathe my forehead with perfumed water."

Zorro Runs the Gauntlet

The Fighting Hidalgo's blade and pistol flash again when he hears the cry of a girl in distress!

DON DIEGO VEGA sprawled on the silk cushions in the wide seat of his carriage. His head was tilted back, and an embroidered dust cloth was spread over his entire face. This rose and fell gently with his breathing. A thin sheet of fine linen covered his body and protected his resplendent attire from the dust of the highway.

The late afternoon sun was turning the western sky into a beautiful picture of crimson and gold. The team of spirited black horses trotted along the winding road at a steady gait. The animals were driven by Bernardo, Don Diego's native body servant, a mute who could have told many interesting things had he been able to talk. He probably would have died rather than tell them.

Don Diego had been making a visit of ceremony to an old hidalgo who lived near San Gabriel, and now was returning to his father's house in the pueblo of Reina de los Angeles. He was utterly relaxed, and half asleep.

He had the appearance and manner of a spineless fop. Most men too, who knew him, believed he was no more than that, and felt pity for old Don Alejandro Vega, his father. It seemed sad that such a fiery old hidalgo should be cursed with such a son.

Only Don Alejandro and Bernardo knew that Don Diego at times changed his attire and manner and became Señor Zorro, the masked rider who aided the oppressed, righted wrongs, and led the troopers of His Excellency, the Governor, on many a futile chase. That a large reward had been offered for his capture did not cause Señor Zorro to cease his activities one whit, but seemed rather to spur him on.

The carriage rolled around a curve in the highway, and Bernardo suddenly made a guttural sound as he checked the speed of the horses. Beside the road, a short distance ahead, was the humble adobe hut of some peon. Gathered in front of the hut were some woman and children, all of them wildly wailing.

They did not seem to notice the approach of the carriage. Being voiceless, Bernardo could not shout a warning. He was compelled to rein in the horses, lest he run down some of the ragged children. The carriage stopped in front of the hut, while the ears of Don Diego were now assailed by the wailing.

Don Diego tossed aside the linen sheet, removed the dust cloth from his face, and struggled to sit erect on the cushions.

"What tumult is this?" he demanded, stifling a yawn.

They screeched at him all the more.

Languidly, Don Diego lifted a hand in a demand for silence, and got it. He glanced around. He saw an elderly and ragged man propped up against the hut. A slender, barefooted girl was holding a gourd of water to the man's lips. Three other women and their broods had been watching, joining in the chorus of lamentations the while.

"What has happened?" Don Diego demanded. "Can none of you speak?"

The others glanced at the girl holding the gourd. She stood up and approached the carriage, and bowed.

"Woe has come to us, Don Diego," she said. "Perhaps you do not remember me? I am Inez Feliz, and this sick man is my uncle, Pedro Feliz, who once worked on the rancho of your father."

"Feliz? I seem to remember," Don Diego said, yawning again. "It was some time ago. But I do not recall you, Señorita."

"I was small then, though I kept the hut for my uncle. There are no others of our immediate family alive. My uncle left the rancho and rented a piece of land near Reina de los Angeles. He said we would raise goats and sheep, while he would work in the pueblo for wages also. In that way, we would become rich."

"And the riches did not come?" Don Diego asked.

"We were prosperous for a time, señor, for people like us. Then my Uncle was seized with an illness of the lungs. He has been growing weaker the past year. I have done all I could, Don Diego, but a girl has little chance — "

"Get to the gist of your present predicament," Don Diego implored.

"Alas, we could not pay the rental renewal. So Juan Ruiz, the magistrado, took some of our sheep, and then some more, and then our goats. And yesterday, señor, he evicted us from our hut. That was bad enough. However, friends would have taken us in. But today Juan Ruiz declared that we were vagabonds, and ordered us to quit the pueblo forever."

Don Diego sat up straighter. "He did that?"

"Sí, señor. He had us sent this far in a cart, and we were put out here. And we do not know what to do."

"Why should this Juan Ruiz, rascal though I know him to be, show such a lack of mercy in your case?" Don Diego asked. "Did he perhaps desire to rent the hut to somebody else? Even so, why order you away from the pueblo?"

"He agreed that my uncle was too ill to work, señor, but I declared I could work for us both."

"And you would not?" Don Diego asked, sternly.

"No, señor. Because Juan Ruiz, who is not a married man, said I could work only as a maid in his house. The good padre at the chapel told me that would be ill."

"It certainly would have been ill for you, my pretty one," Don Diego agreed. "Juan Ruiz, that sore on the face of officialdom, has had several pretty young girls in his house, and none left it with smiles on their faces. What can you do now, señorita?"

"We have distant cousins in San Fernando, señor, if we can manage to get there in some manner. But my Uncle Pedro is so weak."

"Whose hut is this?"

One of the women waddled forward. "It is the hut of my husband, Don Diego," she said.

Diego tossed her a gold coin.

"You will care tenderly for this man, Feliz and his niece for a little while," he ordered. He tossed another coin to the girl. "And that is for you. Stay here, eat and rest and grow calm. Perhaps a way will be found to get you to San Fernando."

They shouted blessings at him, and Inez Feliz wept and ran to the carriage, and would have kissed Don Diego's hand had he not withdrawn it quickly.

"Drive on, Bernardo!" he ordered.

Bernardo touched the blacks with the whip, and the carriage rolled on, a cloud of dust lifting in its wake. Don Diego relaxed on the cushions again. But his eyes were gleaming, while clouds of wrath were gathering in his face.

"It will be a splendid night," he observed, presently, in a voice Bernardo could hear above the pounding of the horses' hoofs. "There will be a bright moon. There will be no fog, and but little wind. The temperature should be pleasant. It will be a splendid night for a ride around the countryside."

Bernardo turned his head quickly and gave him a searching look.

"Such a night," Don Diego added, "as Señor Zorro, that confounded highwayman, might select to attend to a certain little matter."

Bernardo's face split with a wide grin, and he nodded his head vigorously.

The nod indicated assent.

Marcos Castro, the trader, reeled from the cantina on the plaza at Reina de los Angeles, with two friends standing by to catch him did he start to fall.

It had been an expensive day for Marcos Castro. His cart caravan, bound from San Diego de Alcála to Monterey, was camped at the outskirts of the pueblo for the purpose of giving the oxen a day's rest. Señor Castro had gone into town to spend the afternoon and evening and seek relaxation.

Wine, dice and cards had been his undoing, which was nothing unusual in the career of Marcos Castro. He had been almost stripped of ready cash. He would have to make a recovery in a gambling spree when he reached Santa Barbara, he had decided.

His friends helped him into his saddle, while he gathered up the reins and touched with his spurs. His horse moved slowly. Marcos Castro left the pueblo and started toward the spot where his caravan was camped.

It was a bright moonlight night, but huge trees cast shadows along the highway in spots. From one of these deep shadows appeared a masked man on a black horse. The rider was dressed entirely in black, while the moonlight gleamed from a blade he wore. The soft light also glanced off the barrel of a pistol which he presented at the head of Marcos Castro.

"Halt!" the masked man ordered.

Castro reined in, hiccupped, and roared with laughter for a moment.

"What is the cause of your merriment?" the masked rider demanded, sternly.

"It is a joke on you, señor," Castro replied. "You are a highwayman, no doubt. You believe that Marcos Castro, the trader, has much gold upon his person, and would rob him. If you seek my gold, señor, you must go to the cantina in the pueblo, for there is where I left it. The Evil One himself was in the cards and dice this day."

"I do not wish to steal gold from you," the masked man explained. "I wish to give you some."

"How is this? A highwayman wishes to give me gold? Is the world perhaps approaching its end?"

"I am known as Señor Zorro."

Castro gulped, and his eyes glistened in the light of the moon.

"You are — that is — Señor Zorro, did you say?"

"That is what I said. I wish to make a deal with you, señor. When does your caravan start toward the north?"

"About midnight," Castro replied. "We have rested all day. I will have a couple of hours sleep, then urge my men to yoke the oxen, and off we'll go. I like to travel the latter part of the night, when it is cool and the highway is not infested with riders and vehicles."

"Here are five pieces of gold," Señor Zorro said, extending a hand which held them as he pressed his black horse close beside the animal Castro was riding.

Castro took the gold and gulped again as he watched the pistol Zorro held in his other hand.

"The gold is in payment for a service," Zorro explained. "During the first two hours of your travel tonight, I'll appear to you in company with a sick man and a girl. You will make them comfortable in one of your carts and take them safely to San Fernando."

"It shall be done, señor."

"I charge you to a faithful performance of this duty," Zorro said, his voice still stern. "If you fail me, I'll seek you out, señor, wherever you may be, and visit punishment upon you. Is that understood?"

"Sí, señor. Things shall be as you say," Castro replied. "Where will I pick up the man and the girl?"

"I'll stop your caravan at some spot and deliver them to you. Say nothing of this transaction, señor, if you value your precious skin."

Before Castro could say anything more, Zorro used his spurs and was away, leaving the highway and ascending the slope at the left. Castro saw him for an instant in silhouette against the moon. Then he was over the hill and gone.

Castro put the gold away in his pouch, sagged in his saddle and cogitated. This was Señor Zorro with whom he had made a deal, and there was a huge reward offered for Señor Zorro. Because the dice and cards had not been his friends this day, Castro needed funds badly. And his was a grasping nature.

He wheeled his horse and rode at top speed back to Reina de los Angeles. He next went to the presidio, where he demanded that the corporal of the guard take him immediately to Capitán Carlos Ortega, commandante.

"I should bother the capitán at the whim of a trader who has taken too much wine?" the corporal asked.

"This affair concerns Señor Zorro," Castro whispered. "Take me to your capitán at once, or you will rue this night."

A few minutes later, Castro was telling Capitán Ortega and Sergeant Manuel Garcia, his second in command, the story of what had happened out on the road. They made him repeat the story, and Castro showed the gold he had received.

"If a capture results from this information, Castro, you will receive half the reward, as I told you," Ortega promised. "You are a good man to report this immediately."

"I shall be a dead man, capitán, if this Zorro discovers my perfidy," Castro wailed. "I demand protection."

CAPITÁN ORTEGA paced his office floor for a time, and finally stopped beside his desk.

"Garcia!" he ordered the sergeant. "You will explain this matter to three men, have them go to the caravan and ride hidden in some of the carts. They must be heavily armed. They are to protect Señor Castro, and also assault this Zorro when he appears."

"It is an order, capitán."

"In addition, you will order out the entire force of troopers. Let them leave the presidio carefully, one or two at a time, so the movement will not be observed. Have them stationed northward from where the caravan is now camped.

"We do not know at what point Zorro will stop the caravan and deliver the man and girl to Castro. As the caravan passes, each trooper will fall in behind, at a distance. When Zorro appears, all will congregate and aid in his capture."

"Understood, capitán!"

"I wish this fellow alive," Ortega said, sternly. "I know, Garcia, that you yearn to slit him with a blade, as I do myself, because he has attacked both of us in the past. But we can enjoy ourselves more to see him hang, especially if he is a caballero, as he has boasted."

Sergeant Garcia hurried away. Capitán Ortega faced Castro again.

"I know the old man and girl in this case," he told the trader. "The magistrado ordered them out of town today. If they have been in touch with this Zorro, I perhaps can get information out of them. I'll have them arrested and brought in to the presidio and thrown into the jail room."

"I am to be protected?" Castro said, nervously.

"The three troopers will go back with you to the caravan. Put them in your carts, one in the lead, one the middle and the third in a rear cart."

"And the reward — ?"

Capitán Ortega glared at him. "I promised you would have half of it for your information. It will be waiting for you when your caravan returns from Monterey."

Cautiously, Señor Zorro rode down the hill through the deeper shadows and approached the highway. For a time, he kept behind a mass of rocks and listened.

He was a short distance above the hut beside the road, where Pedro Feliz and his niece had been put out of the cart that afternoon. He hoped they had rested well, had eaten a quantity of food bought with his gold and taken good wine to give them strength.

Señor Zorro wished now to get them out of the hut, to conduct them a short distance along the highway, and wait for the arrival of Marcos Castro's caravan. He would see them on their way to San Fernando, then return to a certain spot where Bernardo would be waiting, change attire, and become Don Diego Vega again.

He heard voices as he rode slowly through a mass of shadows toward the hut. Women were wailing again, and a man's raucous voice was berating somebody. Señor Zorro dismounted, left his horse with reins trailing, and went forward afoot like a shadow drifting through other shadows.

He stopped at the rear of the adobe hut to listen. It was one of Capitán Ortega's troopers talking, he learned.

"Be glad that you are not taken to Reina de los Angeles and have your ears lopped off," the trooper was saying. "I tell you the man and girl are in league with this Zorro. That is why they have been taken back to the pueblo, to be questioned. They will reveal what they know of Señor Zorro, if my capitán has to torture them."

"But we do not know them. They but stopped here," a woman protested.

"That is fortunate for you, especially since you have given me the piece of gold I found in your possession. If this pretty Zorro rides tonight, it will be his last ride. Our capitán knows his plans. Every trooper in the presidio save one is waiting beside the highway, and three are in the carts of the caravan.

"Zorro was to have met the caravan somewhere, and turn over the man and girl to be taken to San Fernando."

"How could you know that?" the woman asked.

"The trader with whom he made the deal told our capitán."

"But, if Zorro comes here to find the man and girl — ?"

"Ha! Am I not here to welcome him? I can use the big reward his capture would bring me. And I'll have a yarn to tell."

ZORRO strode around the hut, the front door of which was open. The trooper was standing in the doorway, and his horse was just across the road. He glanced up to see the masked man before him, a pistol held ready.

"Your conversation is interesting, señor," Zorro said. "So you know my plans, eh? And you would claim the reward for my capture? Try to claim it, señor."

" 'Tis Zorro!" the trooper gasped.

"Step across the highway, señor, where I can slay you without making a mess in this hut."

"Would you shoot a man who has no opportunity to draw a blade?"

"Ah! You wish to draw blade? Do so, and I'll cross blades with you."

"I cannot fight a swordsman like you, Señor Zorro. It is death to try it," the trooper wailed. "Have mercy on me. I am but a poor soldier who has to obey orders."

"The girl and her uncle have been taken to the presidio?" Zorro asked.

"It is true, señor. By orders of Capitán Ortega. He will torture them to make them talk of you."

"They know nothing of me. I have interested myself in them merely because they are persecuted," Zorro said. "They could tell your officer nothing. And I will not have them tortured in my name."

"The capitán perhaps is at it even now," the trooper said.

"I leave you unharmed," Zorro said. "But do not frighten these good people in the hut. If you do, I may look you up later. See that you remain here for some time."

Zorro whirled away and ran into the darkness, going toward his horse. He mounted, guided the animal to the highway, and used the spurs.

If Pedro Feliz and his niece were being put to the torture, Zorro wanted to reach the pueblo and see such treatment stopped. He felt responsible, since he had made the deal with Marcos Castro and the latter had betrayed it.

The big black horse thundered along the highway through the bright moonlight. Far behind him, Zorro heard a peculiar piercing cry which rang through the night. It was a signal from the trooper he had met at the hut, though he did not know it.

Zorro dashed around a curve, and at a short distance ahead saw a rider awaiting him. The moonlight glcamed from a blade the rider swept from its scabbard.

Zorro gathered the reins and drew his own blade, then rode on. As he drew nearer, he saw the rider was a trooper.

"Halt, señor!" the trooper howled.

Zorro swept up beside him, their blades clashed an instant, then Zorro was away again. The wounded trooper was toppling out of his saddle as blood gushed from a wound in his breast.

So Zorro began running the gauntlet. At intervals, a trooper would be in the road or at the side of it. Zorro out-raced some, engaged and wounded others, heard pistols explode and slugs whistle past his head, but continued to ride unscathed.

He was nearing the caravan now, he knew, if Castro had started out when he had said he would. And three troopers were hidden in the carts of the caravan, according to what Zorro had heard.

He supposed those he had passed and were still able to sit saddle and ride were after him, but he could not be sure. He was eager to get to the pueblo and the presidio, but he wanted to punish Marcos Castro, too.

"Halt, señor!" a cry came out of the night.

Zorro saw a mounted man ahead of him, and rode toward him furi-

Castro's eyes bulged and a cry of fear bubbled from his lips.

ously. A bullet sang past Zorro's head. Then he was at the other, their mounts had clashed together, blades had rang for an instant, and Zorro rode on, leaving another wounded man behind.

At the crest of a hill, he stopped his horse. The gentle wind carried to his ears no sounds of pursuit. He looked ahead, toward the pueblo, and in the bright moonlight saw the cart caravan coming slowly toward him.

Zorro got away from the skyline and trotted his horse along the highway, keeping to the side of it where tall trees grew and there were shadows. In ambush, he waited. He looked to the pistol he had not yet used and made sure it was ready for instant service. Then he lifted his blade from its scabbard to be sure it was not stuck with the blood it had drunk.

Marcos Castro, he saw, was riding at the head of the caravan with another man, the latter not a trooper. Zorro waited until the long line of carts came within a short distance of him. He rode out from the shadows and suddenly met Castro in the bright moonlight.

"So, señor, you betrayed my trust!" Zorro cried.

Castro's eyes bulged, and a cry of fear bubbled from his lips. The man riding beside him screeched and turned his horse to spur away. Castro would have turned also, but Zorro seized his reins.

"I warned you, señor," Zorro said.

"Have mercy, good Señor Zorro! I'll return your gold."

"Because you betrayed trust, a sick old man and a girl are perhaps undergoing torture," Zorro said. "Why should I not slay you now?"

As he spoke, Zorro had been watching the line of carts. He saw the three troopers tumble from them and start forward as the rider who had been with Castro shrieked a warning. Now that he had them all in view, Zorro knew what moves he could make.

"Ride beside me," he ordered Castro. "A wrong move, señor, and you die!"

"Spare me, good Señor Zorro!"

"If you never appear in this part of Alta California again," Zorro said. "Sell your goods at Monterey, go to San Francisco de Asis, and remain there."

"I swear I'll do it!"

Zorro spurred the big black suddenly and dashed forward. A pistol exploded, and a slug missed him by scant inches. Another shot came not so close. The third man fired as Zorro bore down upon him.

Their pistols were empty now, and they had no time for reloading. Zorro spurred up to them, his blade flashing in the moonlight. They held up their hands and cried for mercy.

"Be thankful that I have no time to expend on you," Zorro said. "I'll attend to you later, if I find you guilty of persecution. I give you your lives, because you are soldiers acting under orders."

He spurred his horse again and rode on. As he neared the pueblo, he slackened speed and became more cautious. But there were no travelers on this section of the highway tonight. Zorro left the road and circled, and so came up behind the presidio building.

He dismounted and trailed the reins. Going forward afoot, he reached the presidio building and crept along the wall through the darkness. No guard was in front, and Zorro entered boldly. A girl's scream rang in his ears, and he heard a man's raucous laughter.

He followed a corridor toward that part of the building which contained the jail cells and the torture room. In front of him, he saw the trooper who had remained with Capitán Ortega. The trooper turned and saw him, and reached for his blade.

Zorro rushed forward as the trooper gave a cry of alarm. He cut the man down as Capitán Ortega emerged from the torture room, and covered the officer with his pistol.

"So, capitán, you torture a girl?" Zorro asked.

"Zorro! How come you here?"

"After riding the highway and wounding several of your men," Zorro replied. "It is my duty to come here. The girl and her uncle know nothing of Zorro. I heard of the case, and tried to help them down the highway. And because of that — "

Zorro ceased speaking and looked beyond Ortega, because another man had emerged from the torture room. He was Juan Ruiz, the magistrado.

"Come forward!" Zorro ordered, flourishing his pistol.

Ruiz' face turned greenish white in the light from the torch which burned in the corridor, and he stumbled forward like a man about to fall.

"Juan Ruiz, you are a rogue!" Zorro said. "I know how you have handled this affair. Had the maid been content to serve in your house, all would have been well with her and her uncle. Back into the torture chamber, you and the capitán!"

Zorro drove them before him, watching Ortega carefully, for the officer was not without courage. Pedro Feliz was propped against the wall, breathing heavily. Inez was shackled to the masonry, her garment had been torn from her back, and welts were across her bared shoulders.

"Fiends!" Zorro roared at the pair he had driven in from the corridor. "I tell you these people know nothing of me and my affairs. Yet you have tortured them, in an attempt to make them talk."

Holding his pistol, he picked up a whip from a bench, and faced the pair again.

"Untie the girl!" he ordered Ortega.

The capitán glared and moved forward. He loosened Inez and stepped back.

"Girl! Do as I order," Zorro said. "Fasten Juan Ruiz, the magistrado, to those shackles in the wall. Walk forward, Ruiz, and get in proper position, or I'll slay you."

Weak with fear, Ruiz pressed his body against the wall, and Inez fastened the shackles.

"Now, Ortega," Zorro ordered, "you face the wall also."

"You will kill me first," Ortega howled.

"If that is your wish, capitán, a touch of the trigger will give you your wish."

"Let us fight with blades!"

"There is no occasion for me to meet a man of your stripe in honorable combat," Zorro told him. "To carry out your duty is laudable. But to aid a rascal of a magistrado in his nefarious affairs is something else. Against the wall!"

Zorro strode toward him, held the pistol ready, and with his left hand whirled Ortega against the wall and motioned for the girl to shackle him. Her eyes gleamed as she obeyed.

"Perhaps, señores, you will appreciate your work hereafter if you know how it feels to have a lash across your backs," Zorro said.

He worked swiftly, tore the clothing from them, bared their backs, and then the whip sang through the air, and the lash cut into flesh, Juan Ruiz screeched and howled, but Ortega took the punishment with only whimpers of pain.

"Señores, I do not disrupt the workings of the law," Zorro said, "so I will return this girl and the man to their cells. It is not my intention to aid them in an escape. As I told you, they know nothing of me, and I interested myself in their case only because they are being persecuted. We'll meet again señores."

Pedro Feliz was helped to his feet. Zorro also beckoned the girl to follow, and he took them both back to the cell rooms.

"Have no fear," he whispered to Inez. "Relief will be here soon."

Zorro locked them in, then hurried through the corridor, past the unconscious trooper, and went toward the front door. As he emerged, he came face to face with Sergeant Garcia.

The meeting startled them both. Zorro had a wholesome respect for Garcia's courage and skill with a blade. Garcia had sworn to take Zorro some day. Their blades were whipped from scabbards at the same instant, met and rang, and in the light from the torch in the doorway, they fought.

Zorro had a little the better of it this time. For an instant, the light from the flaring torch blinded the sergeant. Zorro's blade darted beneath the other's guard and went home. Sergeant Garcia dropped his own weapon and reeled aside, with blood pouring from a wound in his right shoulder.

"I have no wish to slay you now," Zorro said. "Mend your hurt, Garcia, and some day we will meet again."

He ran from the building and got to his black horse, mounted, and spurred away from the pueblo. But, after a time, he circled and went to a certain spot where Bernardo was waiting for him. Swiftly, Zorro stripped off his costume, and stood revealed as Don Diego Vega. Bernardo then prepared to take the black horse away, care for him, and hide him.

"Everything has gone well, amigo," Zorro said. "But there is something to do in the morning."

DON DIEGO went then to his father's house, where Don Alejandro was waiting for him, and related his night's adventures. They made certain plans, and retired.

In midmorning the following day, Don Diego, dressed in his resplendent attire as usual, walked beside his father along the side of the plaza, bowing to friends and acquaintances, and made their way the presidio. Prior to this, Don Alejandro had sent a message by a native servant to Juan Ruiz, bidding him meet them at the presidio.

Don Alejandro and his son were admitted immediately to Capitán Ortega's presence and they found Juan Ruiz there. They exchanged the usual courtesies.

"I come on an easy, but serious matter, señores," proud, dignified Don Alejandro said. "It has reached my ears that a certain Pedro Feliz, an old workman of my rancho, and his young niece, have met with misfortune."

"Misfortune?" Ortega intoned.

"So I am informed. The man is ill, and you, Juan Ruiz, evicted him and his niece from their hut because they could not pay your rental. That is the face of things. In reality, señor, you evicted them because the comely girl would not work in your house as maid."

"Don Alejandro!" Ruiz raged.

"Do not presume to lift your voice at me, señor." Don Alejandro warned. "Your conduct, personally and officially, is a stench in the nostrils of honest men. I am surprised that Capitán Ortega will have anything to do with you. Capitán, I have been told that you have Feliz and his niece here, that they have been tortured without cause — "

"I have been trying to make them give me information concerning Señor Zorro, as is my right," Ortega broke in, rather excitedly.

"Was it necessary to torture them?" Don Alejandro asked. "I fear you overexert your authority at times, Ortega. I am inclined to petition His Excellency, the Governorship, to place a new commandant here, and perhaps to retire you in disgrace."

"I only attend to my duties, Don Alejandro," Ortega said.

"Father," Don Diego begged, "must we have all this talk? It fatigues me." He brushed a scented handkerchief across his nostrils and yawned.

"You are right, Don Diego, my son," his father said. "We shall get to the core of the matter immediately. Juan Ruiz, I am informed that you yesterday issued an order of expulsion from the pueblo against Pedro Feliz and his niece."

"That is true, Don Alejandro. They had no visible means of support."

"You will rescind the order immediately, señor," Don Alejandro declared. "I am taking Feliz and his niece out to my rancho where Feliz worked once before. I will care for them. They will be under my protection."

"In that case, they no longer are vagabonds," Juan Ruiz admitted.

"They never were vagabonds, señor!" Don Alejandro said, sternly. "The man is ill, and you took their goods a little at a time, thinking that finally you would have the girl working in your house. Capitán Ortega, you will release the prisoners at once, since the magistrado has no charge against them."

"It shall be done, señor," Ortega said.

"And for the needless torture you inflicted upon them, you will pay Pedro Feliz, from your own purse, twenty pieces of gold."

"Señor?"

"Or have my petition for your removal go to the Governor," Don Alejandro added.

"I acted only in an effort to capture this Señor Zorro," Ortega said.

"Zorro? He does nothing but help the oppressed. You would do well to ignore him and his actions, capitán. Will you make restitution for the torture, as I ask?"

"I'll make it, señor, and reimburse myself from the reward when I capture Zorro."

Don Diego yawned. "Do not try to collect interest on that, señor," he advised, "for I fear it will be some time before you catch Señor Zorro."

"I'll catch the fiend!" Ortega roared. "Last night, he wounded several of my men, and even ran Sergeant Garcia through the shoulder."

"Enough of this Zorro!" Don Alejandro roared. "Release your prisoners to me immediately, Capitán Ortega, so I can have them sent out to the rancho."

"And take this piece of gold," Don Diego added, tossing it upon the table, "and have wine bought for the men Zorro wounded, as you say. Or perhaps it would be better spent for salve for their wounds."

He yawned again, brushed his handkerchief across his nostrils, and got up and prepared to follow his father.

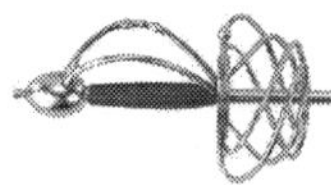

Zorro Fights a Duel

Once again Zorro's blade flashes red as an arrogant, merciless killer hurls defiance at the Fighting Hidalgo!

BY THE time Esteban Sanchez arrived at the inn on the plaza at Reina de los Angeles, the stage had been well set for his dramatic entrance.

Three hours before, a dusty rider had come off the highway to stop at the inn and announce the approach of his master, ordering the best quarters the inn could provide. The advance rider was not reticent about relating tales of his master's prowess.

"In Mexico, Señor Esteban Sanchez was the private bodyguard for a certain official of very high standing," the man reported. "To duel with my master means certain death. He slew so many in combat that it was thought best he absent himself for a year, so he came to Alta California, and has been residing in Monterey."

Esteban Sanchez was a name known to many around Reina de los Angeles. He had the reputation of being a wanton slayer. It was said he did more than protect and defend the man in whose service he had been in Mexico. He even sought quarrels, and when he could find none, made them himself.

The man's skill with a blade was well known. Certainly he was not a man to affront.

People began wondering what brought him to Reina de los Angeles, and whether he was coming solely to pick a quarrel with somebody and run him through.

News of Esteban Sanchez' approach flashed through the pueblo and out to the nearby ranchos.

There was quite a gathering around the plaza when Sanchez arrived.

He rode a splendid black horse, and an attendant on a swift riding mule followed him. This attendant, as well as the advance rider, resembled nothing so much as murderous thugs.

In front of the inn, where the advance rider now awaited him, Esteban Sanchez tossed aside his dust-covered cloak and descended from the heavy, silver-studded saddle his mount bore. He was tall and slender, and dressed in resplendent clothing. He had a thin face, piercing black eyes, and his manner was arrogant.

"Is this miserable hovel the best the place affords?" he demanded of the fat landlord, who was bowing and scraping and shivering in terror.

" 'Tis but a poor pig sty, Excellency, but the best we have," the landlord replied. "Your quarters have been prepared. You will find our food good and wholesome. I have sent out to a certain rancho for some wine much better than I usually have for sale."

"My baggage is coming on a cart which should be here by nightfall," Sanchez said. "I'll cleanse myself of the highway dirt. Let me have cold food and wine immediately, and see that this evening's repast is plentiful and well served."

The landlord bowed again and turned to lead the way into the inn. Sanchez drew himself up to his full height and glared at those who had been watching and listening. Then he started to follow the landlord.

A peon servant was standing innocently at the side of the door. He was not in Sanchez' path, but Sanchez chose to believe so. He struck savagely at the man with his heavy riding whip.

"One side, scum!" he barked. "You stench the air."

Sanchez struck again. The peon retreated with a cry of fear and pain. The newcomer finally entered the inn, where a few men were drinking wine and playing at cards and dice in the big common room.

PERFUMED hot water was now ready for Esteban Sanchez' bath. One of his men played valet, whilst the other, out in the stable, rubbed down Sanchez' horse, cooled him off, gave him water and food and led him to a stall. The stains of his journey washed away and his attire changed, Sanchez strolled again into the common room of the inn with his man in attendance.

Only a few men were in the common room, who disappeared rapidly. There remained only the landlord and a native servant who was trying to drive out the flies.

"What a hole!" Sanchez roared. "Is there no life about? Do you have no business here, landlord? Do not the men of this pueblo drink wine, play at cards and dice? I like amusement, entertainment. At night, I like lights and music, sparkling wine, the dice cup — "

"Perhaps, Señor Sanchez, everybody here is afraid of you," the landlord suggested.

"Afraid of me? If I have indeed come here to trouble some man, you may be sure he is not a hanger-on at a tavern. I do not soil my blade with such foul blood, señor."

His blade was at his side, and the landlord glanced at it. Hilt and scabbard were studded with precious stones. The landlord shuddered at thought of that blade. It had let out the life blood of many men, if reports were correct.

Sanchez drank a goblet of wine, made a wry face, and then clapped his hands to summon the man attending him.

"We will go to the presidio, so I may pay my respects to the commandante," Sanchez decided.

The presidio and troopers' barracks was only a short distance away. Esteban Sanchez walked there with his man a stride behind him. It was just after the siesta hour, and men and women were strolling around the plaza, taking the air. They beheld Sanchez' arrogant progress and saw him boot a native who got too close to him.

"If Señor Zorro hears of this man's acts — " a man whispered to another.

The mysterious Señor Zorro, it was said, dealt violently with those who mistreated or persecuted peons and natives. He had, it seemed, the strange idea that they were human beings and entitled to certain rights.

This proud, arrogant, merciless killer who had lately arrived, was the sort of man Señor Zorro liked to stretch to earth.

At the presidio, Sanchez introduced himself to Sergeant Manuel Garcia and demanded to see the commandante. He was ushered to the private quarters of Capitán Ortega, who arose and bowed as he entered.

"I have heard much of you, señor," Ortega flattered his visitor. "It delights me that I meet you at last. If I may be of service to you, command me. You are passing through?"

"I am here on important business, Capitán," Sanchez announced. "Would I travel so far to such a place as this for pleasure?"

Sanchez brought forth a document and tossed it upon the table between them. Ortega unfolded it and read, and his eyes bulged.

"So that is the way of it?" he asked.

"That is the way of it, Capitán Ortega. The Governor has decided that this Señor Zorro is too much for you and your men. He wants the rogue handled. So, I have been sent here on a special mission."

"You will slay him?" Ortega queried.

"I must contrive to have a quarrel with him and meet him," Sanchez explained. "I'll fight him, but not slay him. I'll wound him enough to render him helpless, but he is to be saved for the rope and a public hanging.

"The Governor desires to make an example of him. After I have wounded him, Capitán, you will take charge of him. The reward for his capture will go to you, half for yourself and the other half to be shared by your men."

"Ah!" Ortega said, his eyes gleaming. "I was fearing there would be no reward."

"You and your men may have it all. I am being well paid for this work," Sanchez said. "The greatest difficulty, I fear, will be to meet this Señor Zorro and fight him. I must do something to get him out into the open, possibly taunt him publicly. He may not be eager to cross blades with me, since I have a reputation as a swordsman."

"It is my opinion that he would not dare refuse an open challenge to fight," Ortega replied. "If he did that, he would lose prestige. Those he claims to befriend would deem him a coward and turn against him."

"I shall start my work at once," Sanchez said. "We must not appear too friendly, or this Zorro may scent a trap. I'll keep you advised, while you can inform me if the rascal is seen. Let my reason for being here remain a mystery. I am eager to end this task and return to Monterey. There is a señorita in Monterey who has engaged my interest. You comprehend?"

"Fully, señor," Ortega replied, his white teeth flashing in a knowing smile.

For several days thereafter, Señor Sanchez proceeded to make himself particularly obnoxious. Peons and natives learned to keep their distance from him. He was ever ready with his whip or a kick or cuff if they got within range.

He played cards and diced at the inn each evening, with passing traders and travelers off the highway, but sought a quarrel with none. But the landlord's native servants were so loath to serve him that the landlord was compelled to do it himself, making it appear that he did so as a special mark of respect.

Came an evening when the common room of the inn was crowded and Señor Esteban Sanchez was playing cards at the long table beneath the open window. Several troopers were in the place. Capitán Ortega was at the card table with Sanchez, while Sergeant Garcia watched over the presidio.

Don Diego Vega strolled into the inn, shuffling as he walked, and yawning as was his wont. He was dressed in his usual finery, and his shoulders, instead of being erect to give a hint of a caballero's hauteur, were stooped as though beneath the weight of the world.

Several men of lesser degree knuckled their foreheads in respect as Don Diego entered and went toward the counter in a corner of the common room. Here the landlord sold certain commodities.

"Who is that popinjay?" Sanchez asked Capitán Ortega.

"He is Don Diego Vega, son of Don Alejandro," Ortega whispered. "A thorn in his father's flesh! About as much spirit as a shellfish. He is a sorry jest, but must be treated with respect because of his father's standing."

"I will speak to him," Sanchez said.

Brushing aside Ortega's protests, Sanchez lurched to his feet and approached the counter, Ortega a short distance behind him. The landlord was bowing and rubbing his hands, for Don Diego visited the establishment seldom, and each visit was an event, giving the inn tone and prestige.

"A jar of that special honey, señor," Don Diego was telling the landlord. "I delight to smear it upon cold tortillas and devour it in the evenings when I am reading the works of the poets."

The landlord got a jar from a shelf. "This honey is from bees who take it from the blossoms of wild sage," he explained. "I get a small quantity of it from a man who has a hut on the edge of the desertland."

Don Diego yawned again, and tossed down a coin. He picked up the jar of honey and turned to glance around the room. At that instant, Esteban Sanchez appeared beside him.

"You are Don Diego Vega, are you not?" Sanchez asked. "Capitán Ortega so informed me. I am spending a short time in Reina de los Angeles, and was glad to have the opportunity to make your acquaintance. I am Esteban Sanchez."

Don Diego looked at him coldly. "Have I asked your name, señor?" he questioned.

"I do not like your attitude, señor," Sanchez exploded. "I am used to being treated with respect."

"Possibly by men afraid of you," Don Diego said. "I have heard of you, señor, and know something of your history. You are a hired murderer, I believe."

"Señor!" Sanchez cried. "Do not try me too far. If you do, hidalgo or no, I'll ask you to fight me."

"Fight you, señor?" Don Diego smiled a little. "Let me inform you, señor, that a man of my blood does not cross blades with such as you."

"Perhaps it is fortunate for you that you do not."

"It is quite true, Señor Sanchez, that you have slain a few poor fellows," Don Diego continued. "But there is an ancient saying that for every good blade there is a better one. In Mexico, señor, you met foes of merit. Here in Alta California, your sword arm may grow stiff with disuse. You will scarcely find foes worthy of your steel. Unless this Señor Zorro — "

"What of him?" Sanchez asked, quickly.

"He is a highwayman of a sort, according to the authorities. Capitán Ortega and his sergeant, I believe, have crossed blades with him. The Capitán can tell you of the man. He might give you an interesting moment, señor."

"Zorro? Ha! The rogue has not shown himself since I have been around Reina de los Angeles. No doubt he has his reasons. Nothing would please me more than to cross blades with the rascal. But how am I to find him?"

"That is beyond me, señor," Don Diego said, smiling. "It is said, however, that Señor Zorro attacks men who mistreat the natives and peons. If you do so, señor, perhaps he will make himself known to you."

"This Señor Zorro is more a legend than anything else," Sanchez declared, in a voice all in the common room of the inn could hear. "He has been fortunate in a few instances, so men think he is a swordsman. Here and now, I challenge him to come to me, meet me with his blade. He is an arrant coward if he does not. If any in this room know him, carry him my message."

SANCHEZ swung back to the gambling table with Capitán Ortega at his heels. Don Diego Vega calmly clutched his jar of honey and strolled forth into the night.

For several days more, Esteban Sanchez raged about the town, denouncing Señor Zorro as a coward, meanwhile kicking or cuffing a native or peon whenever he had opportunity.

Don Diego Vega heard of the man's acts continually. One afternoon, after the siesta, he had speech with Don Alejandro, his father.

"My son, this Esteban Sanchez is becoming a pest," Don Alejandro said. "This morning, I have learned, he beat a peon until the man was unconscious. And he howls continually that Señor Zorro is afraid to face him, blade in hand."

"He is a noisy fellow," Don Diego agreed.

"Regarding the Zorro matter, my son … I have heard certain whisperings. People are commencing to say that Zorro should handle this Sanchez rogue for mistreating natives and the poor peons, and that evidently Zorro is afraid to do so."

"So they think Zorro a coward, my father?"

"It amounts to that. Once people acquire an idea, it takes work to remove that idea from their minds. People know the reputation of this fellow Sanchez for skill with a blade, and possibly believe Zorro fears him."

Don Diego smiled slightly and glanced up as a servant entered the room. He was Bernardo, Don Diego's personal man. He had brought a serape for Don Diego to throw around his shoulders.

Only three men knew that Diego was Señor Zorro, that he put aside his lethargy at times and rode, using his blade in defense of the weak.

His father was one. Bernardo was another, but the native servant was a mute and could not tell the secrets he knew. He would not have told had he been able to do so. The third man was aged Fray Felipe, of Mission San Gabriel, who was Diego's confessor. So he would not speak, of course.

"My father," Diego said now, so that Bernardo could also hear, "I believe this Esteban Sanchez was sent here to kill Zorro. I have been watching and listening. He is often in conference with Capitán Ortega, and they seem to be planning something."

"That is possible, my son"

"I have heard the man is good with a blade. I do not fear for Zorro on that account. What I fear for Zorro is a trap. Perhaps, if Zorro meets this Sanchez and duels with him, he will find, if he wins, that he is surrounded by the soldiery."

"A trap is a possibility," Don Alejandro sagely admitted.

"But Zorro must do something at once, my father. I know the people are murmuring. They must not lose faith in Zorro."

"My son, let us have a decision," Don Alejandro said. "The man is a peril, so I counsel nothing. It is for you to make the decision. Because you fight for the Right, your sword arm will be given strength."

"I am Zorro, but no rogue," the masked man said.

"I have decided," Don Diego said. "Zorro will meet this boasting murderer."

Don Alejandro sighed and relaxed, and Bernardo gave a gurgle which meant he was pleased.

"I must play a game with the rogue," Diego continued. "I must make him raging mad, taunt him into a frenzy. Then I must contrive to meet him where he and I can fight it out fairly."

Diego gave Bernardo orders, and Bernardo hurried away. That night, Diego slipped from the house and went to a certain hut. There he put on his black Zorro costume over his other clothes. He donned his mask and black sombrero, making sure his pistol was in readiness and that his blade would slip easily from its scabbard. He did not intend to fight this night, but it was best to be prepared.

The pueblo grew quiet. At the tavern, men were drinking and gambling in the common room. A sleepy watchman prowled around the plaza. At the presidio, most of the troopers were asleep. The guards lounged around the entrance.

On his black horse, Zorro thundered out of the night. Down the highway from the north he rode into the town. His horse scattered barefooted natives in front of the inn. Through the open window above the card table, Zorro tossed a rock with a sheet of parchment wrapped around it. Then he was away, the thundering of his mount's hoofs dwindling in the distance.

The rock had knocked over a candelabra within a few feet of Esteban Sanchez. It was Sanchez who read the scrawl on the parchment. He gave a howl of rage and tossed it upon the table for others to read:

> Esteban Sanchez is a cowardly murderer. He beats peons and natives who are helpless against him. I would meet him in fair fight and punish him, but how am I to do so? How and where could we fight without Capitán Ortega and his troopers coming to Sanchez' aid? Let Sanchez speak his mind about this matter, and news of his talk will reach me.

"Nothing could give me greater pleasure than a chance to cross blades with the rascal," Sanchez declared, as he paced boldly around the room while the others watched him. "I'll run him through, tear off his mask and reveal his identity to the world. If any here know him, carry him this word."

Late that night, when Esteban Sanchez retired to his own rooms, he found another sheet of parchment on his couch. The scrawl on it read:

> Ride out the San Gabriel road, señor, at mid-morning tomorrow, and perhaps you will encounter me.
>
> — Zorro

Sanchez showed the parchment to his two attendants, then sent one to carry it to Capitán Ortega at the presidio. Ortega went quickly to the inn and to Sanchez' quarters, careful not to be observed.

"If the rogue contacts you, we have him," Ortega declared. "Before dawn, I'll send Sergeant Garcia and a few troopers out on the road to take up stations. They will keep in hiding and be ready to respond to an alarm."

In the middle of the morning on the following day, Esteban Sanchez mounted his horse and rode forth. One of his attendants had ridden before him on a mule, while the other followed behind at a distance.

Sanchez rode leisurely, watching ahead and to either side like a man fearful of ambush. Each clump of trees or stand of thick brush engaged his careful scrutiny.

He passed some of the ambushed troopers. But Señor Zorro did not appear. Sanchez turned back after traveling almost all the way to Mission San Gabriel, and finally came to the inn.

"This rogue of a Zorro left a warning that he would meet me this morning on the San Gabriel road," Sanchez announced to those at the inn. "But he did not disclose himself. He turned coward at the last moment, no doubt. I'll have his ears if I ever can meet him. I will pay a generous reward to any man who will tell me how he may be reached."

Late that night, as the drinking and gambling were at their height in the tavern, hoofs thundered again, and Zorro came riding into the town. Another rock sailed through the window. A man tore the parchment off it, read, and handed it to Sanchez:

> The hired murderer came out to meet me this morning with one of his thugs riding in advance and the other following. Also, troops were in ambush along the road. Is it a duel when a man must fight a small army? This Esteban Sanchez has shown himself a craven, unworthy of my steel.
>
> — Zorro

Sanchez raged like a madman as he strode around the room. The native servants kept out of his reach. One by one, those in the common room of the inn departed, fearing they might become involved in a quarrel and feel cold steel slip between their ribs.

Sanchez found, in the two days following, that men were looking at him askance. He knew they had been whispering that he had dealt unfairly by riding to a meeting with Zorro when troopers were in ambush along the way.

"How can I meet this Zorro rogue?" he shouted. "How may I bring him out of hiding? I want to meet him fairly. I do not seek to take an advantage. True, troopers were along the road the other morning, but that was because Capitán Ortega has orders to capture this Zorro if possible. If my word could reach him, I would say that I will meet him alone at any time."

For two more days, Zorro kept silent. Esteban Sanchez raged around the town, beating natives and peons when he could, strolling around the plaza at siesta hour and being ignored by the better people. He shouted that the mysterious Zorro was a coward and afraid to meet him.

THE people began murmuring discontentedly. Don Diego Vega learned of their words. Why did not Señor Zorro punish this arrogant, cruel man, they were asking. Could it be possible that Zorro feared an encounter?

"It is time. This afternoon," Don Diego told his father.

"You have made plans, my son?"

Diego nodded, then clapped his hands to summon Bernardo. Don Alejandro made sure nobody was within earshot.

"Bernardo, Zorro must attend to a rascal tonight," Don Diego said. "I must confront this Sanchez in the common room of the inn, it appears, if I ever am to meet him at all. I will appear before him at a time when there are no troopers present. You will have important things to do."

Bernardo gurgled, and his eyes gleamed.

"The fog will roll in from the sea tonight," Don Diego continued. "It will be dark and misty. You will be on your riding mule beside the patio wall at the inn. After my work is done, I'll get outdoors, and you will ride furiously, so others will believe Zorro has mounted his horse and escaped."

Bernardo bobbed his head violently to indicate he understood. It was a game they had played before.

"I will not need the black horse tonight," Diego resumed. "But, after you have ridden away and stabled your mule, return to the inn and gather up Zorro's garments from beside the patio wall."

Bernardo bobbed his head again, and withdrew. Don Diego lifted a goblet and took a sip of wine.

"Use great care tonight, my son," his father said. "This Esteban Sanchez is a scoundrel, but do not forget he is expert with a blade. He will not be like the others you have fought."

"I will use my utmost skill, my father."

"I will go to the chapel and say a prayer for you."

"I thank you, father. It is not in my mind to slay the rascal."

"If you do not, his wound will mend, and you will only have to fight him again at a later day. And once he is repaired, he will mistreat natives and peons as before."

"It would be worse than death for such a man were he so injured that he never could wield blade again," Diego said. "A slash in his sword arm at the proper place, and it would be done."

The heavy fog was rolling in from the sea before the darkness came. Few persons were abroad.

Even the peons and natives were keeping to their huts.

Don Diego read poetry until he thought the hour was right. Then he nodded to Bernardo, and the two of them slipped out of the house and went to the hut where Zorro's attire was hidden.

"Get your mule, and go to the inn," Zorro directed, in whispers, as he dressed. "Be sure you are not seen. Do not fail me tonight, Bernardo."

Bernardo bobbed his head and left the hut. Don Diego slipped on the black costume of Zorro, put on the mask, made sure pistol and blade were ready, and left the hut also.

There was a heavy mist in the air, and the few lights around the plaza were but yellow blotches in the night. Señor Zorro walked warily, listening to every sound. He slipped past the adobe huts of some natives, avoided the corner of the plaza, and finally approached the inn from the rear.

His thoughts were busy. Esteban Sanchez, he knew, whatever his character, was a swordsman of repute. This would be an affair where Señor Zorro would have to call on the last bit of his cleverness if he was to escape the ordeal unharmed.

At the corner of the long low tavern building, he stopped in the misty darkness to watch and listen. Across the plaza, some inebriated individual was singing raucously as he went home. No horses were at the hitching posts in front of the inn. It was not a night for some innocent stroller to be about and see a furtive figure slipping along the wall of the tavern toward a window.

Zorro waited until he was sure Bernardo was in position on his mule. He slipped close and whispered:

"Use great care, Bernardo. When I cry the signal, ride like a madman, circle, and put up your mule. Then slip back afoot and get my costume and blade, which I'll put here by the wall, if things go right."

Bernardo made a guttural sound to indicate that he understood, and Zorro slipped on through the night. He approached an open window through which light streamed, and stopped beside it to listen.

He could hear Esteban Sanchez plainly enough.

"More wine, landlord!" Sanchez howled. "It is a night for drinking. We must wash the fog out of our throats. And bring a cold joint and a carving knife. We can eat and drink as we dice."

ZORRO raised his head cautiously and peered into the room from the side of the window. Sanchez was sitting at the end of the gambling table, and some traders off the highway were playing with him. A few loiterers of the town were on benches in a corner, where the landlord served his cheapest wine.

No doubt they hoped to be invited to share Sanchez' bounty.

Zorro dropped down, moved to the other side of the window and peered in once again, at the other side of the big common room. A native servant was wiping goblets at the counter, while another was hanging a fresh wineskin.

The door from the kitchen was hurled open. A native entered bearing a huge platter upon which was a cold joint of roast. He carried the platter to the end of the gambling table. His eyes gleamed as he watched Esteban Sanchez, his nervousness apparent to all.

He placed the platter on the corner of the table, then put the heavy carving knife beside it, as well as a huge loaf of tough bread and a heap of tortillas. The pile of tortillas started to slip. The servant grasped them quickly, and jostled Sanchez' arm.

"Devilment!" Sanchez roared. "Clumsy lout!"

Sanchez sprang to his feet and gave the native a blow that sent him spinning against the corner of the big fireplace. He grabbed the man before he could escape, jerked him to his feet and floored him with a blow to the face.

"Crawl away, scum, and let me not see your face again!" Sanchez roared. "Go tell your friend, Zorro, that I have cuffed you! I'd cuff this Zorro also, did I only have a chance to get at the craven."

"You have the chance, señor!" a voice said at the door.

Zorro had witnessed the attack on the native, had left the window and darted along the wall of the building to the front door. He had pulled the door open, entered and closed it behind him.

But a man approaching the inn from across the plaza had seen the masked man in black as he had passed through the streak of light, and had turned to run to the presidio with the alarm, hoping to share in any subsequent reward.

There was swift silence in the room after Zorro's shout. The half-conscious native servant ceased whimpering and crawled slowly along the wall, his eyes agleam. The men on the benches in the corner and those at the gaming table acted as if suddenly turned to stone.

Esteban Sanchez braced himself against the adobe wall and bent forward slightly.

"You are the rogue they call Señor Zorro?" he demanded.

"I am Zorro. But no rogue, señor. Only a man who defends the helpless, such as the native you have just beaten. I am a caballero, señor, and you are not fit to cross blades with me. But men like you must be punished."

"And you expect to punish me, señor?" Sanchez asked, laughing.

"I should have no difficulty in doing so. You are an arrant coward, señor. You beat helpless men, and have slain a few poorer swordsmen with your blade. I have come here to meet you, taking a chance that you will not have me ambushed. I see one of your thugs in the corner."

"We'll fight fair!" Sanchez roared. "I'll slit you open, tear off your mask, see your face. Nobody is to interfere."

"I'll see to that, señor." Zorro replied. "I hold my pistol in my left hand as we fight, to use against any man who may try to attack me. Draw your blade, señor, if you have the courage."

The fat landlord was wringing his hands behind his counter. The men in the room got up quickly and flattened themselves against the walls. Esteban Sanchez gave a bellow of rage and whipped blade from scabbard, while Zorro silently drew his weapon.

The flickering tallow torches cast an uncertain light over the room. The floor of beaten earth was smooth. The blades met and rang.

The fight began!

Both Zorro and Sanchez were wary at the start, trying to feel out each other. Sanchez, however, was eager to have an end of it. His many victories gave him overconfidence. He moved in swiftly and began pressing the fight.

Zorro retreated slightly, turned, kept on the defensive until Sanchez' violent attack had spent itself. He learned the feel of the other's wrist, the strength of his swordplay. He backed away, turned aside, got to a position where the light was favorable for him.

Then, Zorro pressed the fighting in turn. His blade slithered and flashed in the light. He drove Esteban Sanchez toward a corner, and Sanchez found himself fighting desperately to ward off a fatal thrust.

GREAT beads of perspiration stood out on Sanchez' face and glistened in the light. His face became a stern mask. He knew that he had met his equal, if not his master, and for the first time knew a little fear.

"Fight, poltroon!" Zorro screeched at him from behind his mask. "Fight, hired murderer! You were sent to Reina de los Angeles to slay me, were you not?"

"Slay you I shall!" Sanchez snarled back savagely.

His attack was ferocious, but Zorro had expected it. He gave ground slightly, parried swiftly. The blades rang in a continual music. Then Zorro's steel darted in, went home, and Zorro gave a twist and jerked his red blade away. Esteban Sanchez reeled back against the wall, a cry of pain ringing from his lips.

"I could have slain you, señor," Zorro said, as he watched the others. "But it is better this way. You'll never use your sword arm again, señor. You have slain your last man with a blade. Your arm will be a useless, withered thing, its muscles ruined — "

The door was hurled open, and from the corner of his eye Zorro saw Sergeant Manuel Garcia with a couple of troopers behind him. The kitchen door was opened also, and Capitán Ortega appeared with a couple more. They had responded to the alarm by the man who had seen Zorro enter the inn.

"So, it could not be a fair fight — " Zorro began.

The soldiers crouched and started to rush from both sides. Zorro's pistol exploded, smoke belched, and a slug flew past the head of Sergeant Garcia and thudded against the wall. He hurled the empty pistol at Ortega, whirled and darted back, and sprang through the open window.

"After him!" Ortega shouted.

Outside, Zorro ran along the wall to where Bernardo was waiting on the mule. He gave a wild cry that sounded like one of defiance. Bernardo started the mule.

Tumbling out of the inn, the troopers heard the pounding hoofs. Ortega was shouting for them to get their mounts and pursue. In the rear of the building, Zorro slipped out of his black costume and put it against the wall for Bernardo to get later, put his blade beside it, then shuffled around the building to the front.

He emerged from the darkness and into the streak of light which flowed from the open door of the inn. His breathing was now back to normal. It was Don Diego Vega who appeared, his shoulders bent, his general attitude one of disgust with the world.

Don Diego stepped through the door and into the room. Sanchez was seated at the end of the table, and two men were trying to bind up his wounded arm. The soldiers had rushed out and away.

The fat landlord was rushing around, wringing his hands and moaning.

"What is the meaning of this turbulence?" Don Diego asked in a bored tone.

"Zorro has been here. He has fought with Señor Sanchez," the landlord wailed. "Right here in my inn."

Don Diego walked slowly to the table and looked at Esteban Sanchez' pale face. His lips were twisted with pain.

"For every good blade, there is a better one," Don Diego quoted.

He turned away and beckoned the landlord.

"Try to calm yourself long enough to attend to my humble wants, señor," he ordered. "I have come through the foggy night to get another jar of that special honey. Get it for me, so I may return home quickly and resume my reading. I have a new volume of poetry newly come from Spain. There is in it a delightful verse on retribution."

Zorro Opens a Cage

With reckless laugh and flashing blade the masked caballero rides into a grim trap and out again—and is none the worse!

DURING the night, a heavy fog had rolled in from the sea to drift along the canyons of Alta California. It finally enveloped the pueblo of Reina de los Angeles, and clung. When the dawn came, it was swirling, low and wet, around the adobe buildings. In grayish billows it rolled around the plaza, shrouded the chapel, and crept through doors and windows into the tavern.

At the presidio, where the troopers had breakfasted and were starting the day's duties, it seemed especially heavy. The men grumbled at its chill and dampness as they curried and brushed their horses and oiled saddles and gear.

They had enjoyed but little sleep the night before. Most of them had ridden a matter of miles into the country, had waited for a couple of hours beside a trail doing nothing, and then had ridden back to the barracks again to stable their mounts. Sergeant Manuel Garcia had commanded them. Their only pleasure was in the knowledge that Sergeant Garcia had suffered the discomforts also.

They had been told what it all meant, and sworn to secrecy. They knew better than to betray the secret. The man who did would be tied up by his thumbs and lashed. If the guilty man was not found, all of them would be treated in that same manner, so the commandante, Señor el

Garcia tried to swerve but Zorro cut him off

Capitán Carlos Ortega, might be sure the right man had been punished.

An hour after dawn, Capitán Ortega was having breakfast in his quarters. He was tall and lean, with gleaming black eyes, mustache and a spade beard. He devoured hot tortillas, fried frijoles, a ham steak, half a cold fowl, washed down the food with a goblet of wine, and belched. He wished he might have time for a more leisurely and abundant repast, but he had serious business to claim his attention this morning.

A knock came on the door, and Ortega called permission to enter. Sergeant Garcia came in, followed by a trooper named Pedro Pizzaro. They stiffened and saluted, and Ortega returned the salute with a wave of a hand which still held a chunk of fowl.

Sergeant Garcia was huge and stocky, well known to his associates and the citizenry for skill with a blade, an ungovernable temper, a cruel disposition, undoubted courage, and the fact that he hated pistols because be was an atrocious shot. He could ride like a fiend, and handled his men after the manner of a mate on a sailing vessel, with his fists and boots.

PEDRO PIZZARRO, the trooper who had entered with Garcia, was smaller than most men. Dressed in the resplendent attire of a caballero, he would have made a dapper appearance. Just now, he seemed frightened to be in the capitán's quarters.

"I hope everything is understood," Ortega told them. "Word will be spread immediately that the notorious Señor Zorro, the highwayman who has fooled us so long, was captured by our valorous troopers after a wild ride. It will be announced that we have him in a cell here at the barracks, and that will be exhibited this afternoon and tonight a cage in the plaza, for all men to see, and that at dawn tomorrow he will be taken from the cage and be hanged."

Pedro Pizzaro's eyes bulged, and he felt of his throat. Ortega laughed.

"Do not worry, good Pizzaro," Ortega said. "We will not carry our plans to that extreme. You are too good a trooper to stretch a rope. This is all a trap we have planned."

"If I dared ask the capitán to explain — " Pizzaro hinted.

Ortega waved a hand at his sergeant.

"You explain it to him, Garcia," he ordered. "Let him know what an important part he is to play. And he had better play it without error, or the lash will sing as it bites into his back!"

Garcia turned to Pizzaro.

"This accursed Señor Zorro, the highwayman who dresses in black, wears a mask and uses a black horse, who rides the highway and even invades the pueblo, and says he punishes those who mistreat natives and peons — may the fiend take him!" Garcia began.

"I have heard concerning him," Pizzaro intimated.

"Then you know we have not caught the rogue, and that the Governor has offered a reward for his hide. So far, this Zorro has evaded us. Once I managed to cross blades with him, and would have slit the scoundrel, but my foot slipped on a wet spot as we fenced, and he ran me through the shoulder."

Capitán Ortega coughed, and smiled.

"However," the sergeant continued, choking a little, "we now have a plan. You are about the size of this Señor Zorro. We have prepared garments like his, and will dress you in them, even to the mask. Then we put you in the cage in the plaza. That may fetch results."

"If my superiors will pardon me," Pizzaro said, "I'd like to suggest that possibly it will avail nothing. No doubt the real Señor Zorro will make no effort to rescue me from the cage through pity. He may sit back and laugh, expecting you to hang me in his name."

"Why must some men be born stupid and have their stupidity increase during their years?" Ortega demanded, rolling his eyes toward the ceiling as if he hoped to find the answer there. "Listen, Pizzaro! We do not expect Señor Zorro to make a wild dash and try to rescue you from the cage. But others may try it."

"How then, capitán?"

"Zorro must have many friends among the peons and natives. He could not fade from sight so quickly without help. He is given shelter somewhere. It is said natives and peons adore the rascal. So, if they think Zorro is in the cage and is to be hanged at dawn — "

"Ah!" Pizzaro exclaimed, his face brightening. "They will try to rescue the man in the cage, and you will have our troopers ready to rush out and cut them down."

"Ass!" Ortega shouted. "We will not cut them down. To make sure of that, none of our men will carry pistol or blade, only cudgels. I want the rascals alive. We will fetch them here and do some questioning. We will make some of them talk. We have ways of doing that, have we not? We'll make them tell the real identity of Zorro, then run him down and claim the reward."

"I understand now, capitán."

"The clod softens," Ortega commented. "You must play your part well, Pizzaro. Watch all who approach the cage, listen if they speak to you. But do not say a word yourself, for some of Zorro's friends may realize your voice is not his."

"I must remain in the cage all afternoon and night?"

"Unless we have developments earlier," Ortega explained. "They may try a rescue after nightfall, especially if this fog continues. I'll have troopers stationed in the tavern, seemingly roistering but ready for quick action. I'll have others hiding beside the warehouse."

NERVOUSLY Pizzaro asked another question. "And if nothing happens during the night, and the people look for a hanging at dawn?" Pizzaro questioned.

"Do as you are ordered, Pizzaro, and cease asking questions," Ortega said. "Your reward will be a piece of gold to spend at the tavern. If Zorro's friends refuse to take the bait, we'll merely return you to the barracks the next morning and tell the truth — that we were trying a trick to catch Zorro."

"Now I understand, capitán."

"The clod is softened entirely," Ortega observed.

After the siesta hour that day, the fog lifted slightly but was not dispelled. It still swirled in billows across the plaza and around the buildings.

However, despite the inclement weather, Don Diego Vega left his father's house and strolled abroad. Bernardo, his huge peon body servant, who had been dumb from birth and could not utter more than grunts, walked behind him.

One of the house servants had carried news that there was excitement in the plaza, and Don Diego had heard of it. So he directed his steps toward the plaza now, though in reality his destination was the house of elderly Don Juan Perez, an old friend of his father.

Coming to a corner of the plaza, Don Diego stopped and looked ahead. Through the swirls of fog, he could see a cage in the plaza, only a short distance in front of the tavern door. Somebody seemed to be in the cage.

Don Diego strolled on like a man half-asleep, but his keen eyes saw everything. Groups of natives and peons were scattered around the plaza, conversing as they eyed the cage. Some got out of his path as Don Diego strolled on.

Don Diego's father, old Don Alejandro Vega, was one of the most respected men in all the district. He was the pattern of a hidalgo, who shared his time between his town house in Reina de los Angeles and his great rancho a few miles out toward San Gabriel.

But this only son of his, this Don Diego, seemed to be a weakling. He was possessed of extreme lassitude, instead of having the fire of a young caballero. It was said that he read the works of poets and discussed philosophy, when he could find anybody to listen.

Nevertheless, he was treated with the respect due his station, out of deference to his father.

Don Diego strolled on toward the cage with Bernardo a step behind him, and the natives and peons watched. A trooper was loitering near the cage, and as Don Diego neared it he saw Capitán Ortega emerge from the tavern and direct his steps toward the cage also.

Don Diego reached it first, stopped a few feet from it, and inspected it and its occupant well. The cage was eight feet high and about six feet square, constructed of metal bars, with a small door guarded with a heavy lock, and usually was kept at the barracks as a means of confinement for the insane.

Don Diego took a silk perfumed handkerchief from his cuff and brushed it lightly across his nostrils, after the manner of a fop, as though the cage and what it contained carried a stench. Capitán Ortega stopped near him and bowed.

"A good day to you, Don Diego Vega," the capitán said.

"Good day," Diego muttered. "What have we here?"

"In that cage, señor, you see the famous Señor Zorro," Ortega replied. "My brave troopers finally caught him. He does not look so famous now, eh?"

"Why is he masked?" Diego asked.

"Oh, we have seen his face! But others have not. He has always been a mystery. We'll remove his mask at dawn tomorrow, when we take him out to hang him. Then everybody can see the countenance of the man who has been spreading terror and saying he did it to help oppressed natives and peons."

"So that is the famous Zorro," Diego said. "The man who rides a black horse like a fiend, carves everybody with his blade and always makes his escape."

"He didn't escape this time," Ortega pointed out.

"What a wretch!" Diego exclaimed. "Always to be upsetting peace and tranquility. I cannot understand how a man can do such things."

Ortega smiled. Don Diego seemed to flinch when he looked at the prisoner. Capitán Ortega remembered, to his disgust, that once he had suspected this spineless fop of being Zorro.

DON DIEGO, ever so languidly brushed his nostrils again with the scented handkerchief.

"Ortega, a thought occurs to me," he said, lifting his voice a little, knowing how sounds carried in the fog.

"What is that, Don Diego?"

"You have the fellow in this cage and intend keeping him there, I understand, until you hang him tomorrow morning?"

"That is the plan, señor."

"Some of the fellow's friends may try to rescue him."

"We'll be on the watch for that."

"Oh, I do not doubt that you can keep your prisoner, capitán," Diego said. "My thought was that, as an efficient officer, you might do more than hang this Zorro. You might catch some of his friends, make them confess they have aided him, and hang them also."

Ortega's eyes glittered.

"Please lower your voice, Don Diego," he begged in a whisper. "Some of his friends may hear you. This is a part of our plan. We hope they will try a rescue. If we catch them, we'll make them talk. We have methods. This Zorro may be the head of a conspiracy against the Governor. We may unearth it all."

Diego nodded and smiled slightly. He knew his voice had been heard by natives and peons in the swirling fog.

"Is it not bad weather for you to be abroad?" Ortega asked him.

"It is, capitán. But one must attend to social duties."

"Ah! Some fortunate beautiful señorita awaits your call of courtesy, perhaps?"

Diego laughed a little. "Not exactly, capitán. This is the eightieth birthday of Don Juan Perez, as perhaps you have heard. Late this afternoon, he has a private feast for some of his old friends. Later, and possibly until dawn, there will be a fiesta, at which the beautiful señoritas will appear. But it is my lot to go early and attend the private feast, representing my father, Don Alejandro."

"Your respected father is ill?" Ortega asked.

"Heaven forbid! It is a matter of business. The superintendente of our rancho came to town on important business, and it is a matter to which my father must attend. I go to represent him at the Perez table until such a time as he can get there and relieve me."

"Your reward will come later, señor, when the dancing begins in the evening."

"I shall rest for a time after the heavy feast," Diego told him. "Then I shall pay my respects to the señoritas, as a matter of courtesy. But music numbs my brain and dancing always fatigues me. These things are duties, and must be done."

Ortega almost sniffed. This young scion of a noted family, to be so spineless! With half the eligible señoritas in the district sighing after him — perhaps because of his family prestige and the fortune he would have some day.

"Well, Don Diego, take your last look at this Señor Zorro, unless you intend to be present at his hanging in the morning," Ortega said.

"Why should I look at the rogue again?" Diego asked. "It is distressing."

"Then you have seen your last of Zorro," Ortega told him.

Don Diego smiled slightly as he turned away and brushed his nostrils with his scented handkerchief again. For Don Diego Vega was the real Señor Zorro.

It was after nightfall, and the younger guests were gathering, when Don Alejandro Vega finally appeared at the Perez house. He made his excuses to his old friend, Juan Perez, thanked Diego for representing him at the private dinner, and narrowed his eyes in a manner that told Diego his father wanted speech with him alone as soon as possible.

Because of the fog, the large patio was not being much used, though there was a smaller covered one at the side of the house with a gurgling fountain, subdued lights from small tapers in candelabra, the scent of roses, and romantic couples dodging duennas.

Diego wandered into the larger patio, being sure his father saw him, kept beneath the arches out of the mist, and leaned against the masonry. Outside the patio, oblivious of the fog, servants were feasting at long tables beneath the pepper trees, eating enormous quantities of food and drinking thin wine.

Soon Diego saw Bernardo, who was always on the watch, slip through the shadows, enter the patio and approach him. He beckoned the huge mute nearer.

"Stand by," Diego ordered. "My father wants to have speech with me. You know they have Zorro in a cage in the plaza."

Bernardo nodded his head, and grinned.

"Zorro's friends may try a foolish thing and get into trouble," Diego continued. "You understand?"

Bernardo nodded that he did.

"There is a high adobe wall behind this house. It is dark and foggy tonight. A black horse would not be seen there, nor that huge mule you ride, Bernardo."

Bernardo stepped closer and made a guttural sound.

"Not yet," Diego ordered. "I must speak to my father first. Keep near me in the shadows."

Don Alejandro emerged from the house a moment later and strode to Diego's side.

"There was excitement at the house before I left, my son," he said. "The native servants were running around like mad. It seems that the troopers have captured Zorro, and Capitán Ortega has him in a cage in the plaza and will hang him at dawn."

"I stopped a moment and looked at the miserable rogue," Diego said, his face inscrutable.

Don Alejandro's eyes flickered slightly.

"If the man in the cage is not Zorro," he said, "it would be a pity to have him hang for Zorro's so-called misdeeds."

"I agree with you, my father. A man should always pay his own score."

"There is another thing about which the servants were speaking.

Zorro's friends among the peons and natives are banding together. The rascals will attempt a rescue of the man in the cage in perhaps a couple of hours. Ortega has his troopers in hiding, waiting for that. A trusted friend told me so. The friends of Zorro may be seized and tortured to make them tell all they know of Zorro."

"Ah!" Diego spoke the one syllable and his mouth remained hanging open. "That must not be," he said, an instant later.

"How can it be prevented?"

Diego turned and faced him, and lowered his voice when he replied.

"You and I know, my father, that the man in the cage is not Zorro. Either he is some poor fool who has been playing at being Zorro, else Ortega is trying a trick to capture some of Zorro's friends."

"That is my thought, my son."

"So the real Zorro must appear and turn his friends aside from the trap. And if he would be in time, he must make haste."

He turned and beckoned Bernardo. "You heard? You understand?" he asked.

Bernardo nodded.

"Make haste, then. Outside the rear wall of the house, as I told you."

Bernardo knuckled his forehead in acknowledgment of the order and hurried away through the shadows.

"It will be perilous, my son," Don Alejandro whispered.

"I'll dance and frolic for a little time, while Bernardo is busy, then do my usual trick, my father — claim a headache and fatigue and slip away somewhere to rest."

"I don't trust Capitán Ortega. He may still suspect you."

"He has brains," Diego admitted. "He is a clever rascal. Zorro fights two things — Ortega's brains and Sergeant Garcia's sword."

"Garcia?"

"I fought him with blade once, and he made me extend myself," Diego confessed.

"Not that he is so clever and well trained. But he has great strength, and fights in such an unorthodox fashion that a real fencer never knows what to expect."

"Use care," his father urged.

"Always," Diego replied, smiling at him. "Let us go in. No doubt the hearts of some of the señoritas are palpitating as they think of dancing with me."

Diego danced with several, paid them the usual empty compliments, and then began yawning.

"Music always makes my head ring, and dancing fatigues me," he said, so that a group could hear. "I'll rest for a time, and think of philosophy and the poets. I ate too much of the meal, and drank a goblet of heady wine."

One of the elderly men laughed. "At your age, Diego, your father could drink half a skin of wine and never show the effects," he said.

"My father is a grand man," Diego observed, "and I am but ordinary compared to him."

He wandered through the crowded big room, dodging the dancing couples, and got into the patio again. Keeping under the arches where it was dark, he went slowly toward the rear wall, careful not to be observed.

There was a small gate bolted on the inside. Diego shot the bolt, opened the gate carefully and went outside into the darkness, closing the gate behind him.

Through the darkness, Bernardo slipped to his side. The mute took his hand and led him a short distance, to where Zorro's big black horse waited. A bundle on the ground held Zorro's costume, his pistol and blade.

Don Diego slipped the black costume on over his resplendent clothes. He put on the mask, stuck the pistol into his belt and buckled his sword belt around him. Then he got into the saddle.

"Mount and follow," he instructed Bernardo.

The mute mounted the big mule he rode bareback, and Zorro led him a hundred yards toward the center of the pueblo.

"You will wait here," he ordered the mute. "If I come riding away from trouble, turn beside me, keep pace, and take my reins. I'll vault from the saddle, and you ride your mule on, taking my black with you. You know how to get away and where to go."

Bernardo made a guttural sound of assent. Zorro disappeared into the night.

He was no longer Don Diego Vega. He was Zorro now, a man who punished those who oppressed men unable to help themselves, who fought always for decency and honesty. He went slowly and carefully through the dark night toward the plaza.

He could not be sure whether the man in the cage was some rogue who had been pretending he was Zorro, or a lure put there by Capitán Ortega. In either case, his appearance would settle the matter. Everyone would know the man in the cage was not Zorro, though, if he had been playing highwayman, he would pay for his crimes.

Zorro got to a spot from which he could look into the plaza. Beside the cage a torch had been stuck into the ground, and the fog swirled around it, making the torch cast an uncertain light.

In front of the tavern was only one trooper's horse, and Zorro saw it was the huge, powerful white Sergeant Garcia generally rode. But as he watched, he saw Capitán Ortega ride up and give his reins to a peon as he dismounted. Ortega went into the tavern.

Only two could chase him then, Zorro thought. But he did not know the troopers would not be armed with pistols and blades, only cudgels, and he thought he might be the target for gunfire. However, the swirling fog and the uncertain light of the torch would make him a poor target.

He urged his big black nearer, watching, listening, trying to locate the groups of peons and natives he believed were gathering for the attempt at rescue. A din of loud voices and ribald song came from the inn. The man in the cage and the one trooper guarding him were the only human beings in sight now. But Zorro guessed troopers were hiding and ready to rush out.

He rode nearer, wondering where he would discover the nearest group of Zorro's friends. Suddenly he found that it was too late for that.

At a corner of the plaza, some man screeched an order. Through the swirls of fog, men began running through the streaks of dim light toward the cage. The attempt at rescue had begun.

Howling like fiends, coming from a dozen different directions, the peons and natives rushed on toward their objective. The din was so great, and magnified so by the fog, that Zorro knew he could not make himself heard above it. He could see that the men were carrying clubs, tools, anything they might use for weapons.

He sent his big black into a run and got into the plaza. He began shouting, but none gave him attention. They had worked themselves into a frenzy, heard nothing but their own howls. They were rushing toward the cage.

ZORRO urged his black to greater speed. He almost knocked over the first of the men he encountered. He was trying now to get into the circle of flickering light from the torch, where he could be seen. Many knew his black horse, his apparel, and they would see his mask.

They whirled toward him when they finally heard the beating of his horse's hoofs, thinking some troopers were upon them.

"Back, amigos!" Zorro shouted at them. "Back! It is a trick. The man in the cage is not Zorro!"

Those nearest caught sight of him, began relaying what he had shouted.

"Run!" Zorro cried at them. "Back into the darkness! The troopers will take and torture you, to make you tell of Zorro. It is a trick."

The word was spreading swiftly now. And there was a chorus of howls as troopers suddenly came charging toward them through the haze, afoot, with clubs in their hands.

Zorro urged his horse on, for one guard had got as far as the cage and had knocked down the guard there after he had fired his pistol over their heads. They had not heard the tumult behind them. They were trying to smash the lock on the cage door.

The big black almost rode down some of them.

"Back!" Zorro cried at them. "I am Zorro. It is a trick. The soldiers are coming to catch you. They will torture you."

It was enough. They saw the black horse, the masked man, and realized the truth. Screeching, they threw away their poor weapons and began running back into the fog and the darkness.

Then, Zorro heard pounding hoofs, and caught sight of Sergeant Manuel Garcia, mounted, charging at him. The troopers were chasing after the fugitive natives and peons, and Zorro did not fear them. But he found he would not have time to get away from Garcia.

It would be a duel on horseback, Zorro knew. He kicked at the black's flanks and pretended to be running away. But he knew he would not have time for that. Garcia's powerful white would overtake him when he would be at a disadvantage.

The ruse gave Zorro time to get out his blade. Behind him, a pistol exploded. But the ball went wide. Garcia was still a poor pistol shot.

Zorro swerved his horse to the right and started back. He saw by the light from the torch that Garcia had his blade out now. Zorro made no effort to use the pistol in his belt. He did not care to bring down Garcia with a shot from it.

They met and clashed near the cage. Their mounts circled, and their blades met and rang.

"This time, highwayman!" Garcia shouted.

"It will be your shoulder this time, señor!" Zorro cried in reply.

Garcia was attacking like a man in a fury. Zorro's black swung in and put the white of the sergeant off balance. Zorro, with his black horse and black attire, with even his face covered with a black mask, made the poorer target. But his blade flashed in the light from the torch, and Garcia could see that.

The sergeant's weapon whistled past Zorro's ear, in an unexpected stroke. The frenzied horses swerved again, and separated their riders. Garcia gathered his reins, put up his blade again and charged.

Zorro swerved the black slightly. He and Garcia slashed at each other as the sergeant went past, but Zorro parried the blow. He wheeled the black to pursue before Garcia could get his mount under control.

He had the sergeant at a disadvantage now. Garcia tried to swerve, but Zorro cut him off. Their mounts bumped. Their blades met and rang again. There was some quick fencing.

"The other shoulder this time, Garcia!" Zorro shouted.

His blade went in, came out red, and he wheeled his black aside as the sergeant's sword fell from his hand and Garcia reeled in his saddle.

Howls of fear and rage came from the darkness on every side of the plaza. The man in the cage was screeching for somebody to come and save him. But Zorro's work was done. Now he had only to get away.

He urged the black back toward the cage, and cut down the torch with a blow of his sword. Then he wheeled his mount again and rode it at top speed. The capitán's horse thundered along behind him. But Zorro knew where he was riding through the blackness of the night, and Ortega did not.

Zorro gave a peculiar wild yell, which was nothing less than a signal to Bernardo to be ready. He thundered on through the night, and Ortega followed.

At the appointed spot, Bernardo swerved his mule beside the black, and Zorro tossed him the reins.

"Pick up my things," Zorro said, bending toward him. "Return when it is safe."

He had gained on Ortega, who had slackened speed once to listen to hoofbeats and make sure in which direction Zorro was riding. So he slackened speed an instant himself as he came besidc the rear wall of the Perez house. He slipped out of the saddle and hit the ground, and Bernardo rushed on, riding the mule and taking Zorro's horse with him.

Crouching in the blackness beside the wall, Zorro waited. Ortega thundered past within a short distance of him. But, as Zorro quickly stripped off his costume, and put it and his blade and pistol behind a bunch of rocks against the wall, he heard Ortega pull up.

Something had made the capitán suspicious. He might return to the Perez house and make inquiries.

It was Don Diego Vega who slipped through the gate, bolted it again, and went through the shadows of the patio of the Perez house to get beneath the arches.

In the darkness, he stopped for a moment to get his breathing back to normal, and to smooth his hair with his hands. He took an extra handkerchief from a pocket and wiped the dust from his boots, and tucked the handkerchief away. Then he went on toward the door of the big main room of the house.

The party had reached its peak. The music was lively, and all the younger guests were dancing. Don Juan Perez and some of his old friends sat to one side against the wall and sipped wine and gossiped of the old days when they had been young caballeros, ready to fight, ride or make love on an instant's notice.

Don Diego was yawning as he entered the room. One of the señoritas eyed him, and Diego advanced to her and bowed.

"If you would do me the honor?" he asked.

The señorita glanced at her duenna, who nodded agreement. Diego led her upon the floor, and they began dancing.

"You feel better, Diego?" the little señorita asked.

"A great deal better," he said. "I had a touch of migraine, but I sat for a time out in the patio, and the fog and mist seem to have cleared it away. I ate too much at the feast."

"Perhaps it was the heavy wine," she hinted, smiling at him and showing her dimples.

"It could have been that, too," he admitted.

They were in the middle of the floor, hemmed in by countless other couples, when the front door opened and Capitán Ortega came in from outdoors, drawing off his gauntlets. Perez hastened to meet him.

"Welcome to my house, Señor el Capitán!" Perez greeted. "You do me honor, you, the representative of the Governor."

Ortega bowed and smiled a bit, but his keen glance had been wandering over the dancers. He saw Don Diego Vega dancing with a pretty girl, smiling at her, seemingly oblivious to the officer's presence.

"I would have come sooner, Don Juan, but was detained by official business," Ortega replied to Perez' greeting. "We soldiers are not always our own masters."

"That is true," Perez observed.

"I was just chasing a rogue. He may have scaled the wall into your garden, Don Juan."

"I'll have the servants make a search immediately with torches, capitán. Meanwhile, join in our feast. There is good food and wine, and here are the prettiest girls in all Alta California."

IT WAS at that moment that Don Diego Vega stopped at Ortega's side, having returned the señorita to her duenna.

"Ah, capitán!" Diego greeted him. "So you have come to join in the festivities of Don Juan's birthday celebration? It will perhaps take your mind over the disagreeable task you will have at dawn."

"A disagreeable task?" Perez asked, lifting his brows.

"Have you not heard, Don Juan?" Diego asked. "The capitán's troopers have caught the notorious Señor Zorro and have him in a cage, and he is to be hanged at dawn."

Ortega cleared his throat. "You will be frightening the ladies, Don Diego," he warned. "However, there is to be no execution."

"But you told me, as I was walking here late this afternoon, that you would hang the rogue at dawn," Diego protested.

"The man we caught was not Zorro, but a poor fool pretending to be he. Perhaps we shall give him a few lashes to teach him sense, and then we shall send him down the highway."

"Then this pest of a Zorro is still at large!" Diego complained. "He will be up to his nefarious tricks again. The very thought of it makes me ill. These are such turbulent times. No peace and tranquility."

Shaking his head as if at the pity of it all, Don Diego Vega turned away, seeking some señorita who would be glad to commiserate with him.

Zorro Prevents a War

The famous Fighting Hidalgo dons his cloak and rides into rapid action when there's danger of a rebellious uprising!

RIDING his big mule at a furious pace, the young Franciscan novitiate reached Reina de los Angeles in the middle of the afternoon. He rode into the pueblo off El Camino Real, the king's highway, from the south.

The mule was expending his last strength and the young Franciscan showed evidence of saddle fatigue. He had made the forty-odd miles from the mission of San Juan Capistrano in record time.

He went to the little chapel on the plaza, where he reported to the gray-haired fray in charge. As he gulped soup, devoured cold roast mutton and washed the food down with thin wine, he explained certain things and asked questions.

His tired mule was taken to a stable by a native neophyte. The novitiate left the chapel to cross the plaza, his hands in the sleeves of his robe and his head bent as if in meditation and by a circuitous route came to the house of Don Alejandro Vega.

To the native house servant who answered his knock on the door, the novitiate spoke.

"I have come from San Juan Capistrano," he said. "I have a private message from Fray Esteban for your young master, Don Diego Vega."

He was allowed to enter and wait while the servant went in search of Don Diego. He finally located him in the patio, sitting on a bench beside the gurgling fountain, a book of poetry in his lap, and seemingly half asleep.

"What is it now?" Diego demanded, yawning and rubbing his eyes with his knuckles. "Must a man be disturbed continually?"

The servant told of the visitor and the message.

"Ah, that is different!" Diego said. "Fetch the novitiate here immediately. The good Fray Esteban, now at San Juan Capistrano, is my confessor. A message from him is to be delivered to me at once at any time, night or day."

The novitiate was ushered into the patio, and approached Don Diego and inclined his head respectfully.

"It is a written message I have for you, señor," he said. "Fray Esteban charged me to deliver it to you personally."

Don Diego yawned again and accepted thc message, broke the seal, blinked and read:

My son,

It has been some time since I have had the pleasure of seeing you, and I am concerned about the state of your soul. I would be delighted if you could make me a visit at once.

The message was innocent enough. But down in a corner of it was something not quite so innocent. Three light irregular lines were there, seemingly made by accident with the end of a charred stick. And they formed a ragged letter Z.

DON DIEGO's face remained inscrutable, and he even yawned again, but his heart suddenly was pounding at his ribs. This message was a call for help.

Fray Esteban was making an appeal to Señor Zorro, the mysterious unknown who rode the highway and righted wrongs, fought for the oppressed, and was constantly pursued in futile effort by the Governor's troopers. Fray Esteban knew Diego was Zorro, had learned it in the confessional.

"How goes the world in San Juan Capistrano, my young friend?"

Diego asked the novitiate.

"These are indeed troublesome times, señor," the novitiate complained. "The natives and peons are nervous. They are getting out of hand, and there is talk of an uprising."

"There is always talk of an uprising," Diego observed.

"This seems serious, Don Diego. Fray Esteban is disturbed. He fears violence. Somebody has been inciting the natives to revolt. We have heard that soldiers are being sent to our district. A detachment from here, with Sergeant Garcia in command, will start tonight."

Diego straightened on the bench.

"Interesting," he said.

"May I now take leave of you, señor?"

Diego nodded assent, and the novitiate retired and was let out of the house.

Diego's eyes were gleaming. He read the message again, and with his thumb carefully smeared the letter Z until it was nothing but a dirty spot on the paper.

He entered the house, located his father, showed him the message and explained.

"You must go, Diego," his father decided. "Fray Esteban would not send for you unless there was a real need. He is a man of rare judgment and not easily frightened."

"I'll start at nightfall, and travel by carriage," Diego decided. "I'll take two outriders."

"Use great care. If it is learned that you are Zorro, with a price on your head, your life will be in peril, and our family and estates suffer at the hands of the present avaricious Governor."

"I'll have Bernardo, my body servant, take my black horse and the things Zorro uses. He knows trails across the hills, and will not be seen."

A bright moon came up almost as the sun went down. The Vega carriage stopped in front of the house. Servants hurried out to put cushions in it, a hamper filled with food and drink, heavy serapes to be used if the night grew chilly. Some elderly señora might have been about to make a journey instead of Diego, scion of the house of Vega, who, had he been true to type, would have made it on a prancing steed and riding like the wind.

In the house, Diego called Bernardo for a last word. Bernardo was a huge peon who had been Diego's body servant for years and knew his secret — but could not tell it had he been inclined to do so. He could hear well, and had sharp wits, but had been born a mute.

"Take my black horse, and across the saddle fasten a bundle containing Zorro's clothes, sword and pistol, powder and bullets," Diego instructed. "Ride your mule and lead the horse. Cut across the hills and get to San Juan Capistrano and hide the horse and wait for me."

Bernardo nodded that he understood.

"Soldiers may be on the highway tonight, troopers led by Sergeant Garcia, who is no fool, so use extreme care."

Diego emerged from the house with his father, and they went to the waiting carriage. The native coachman was holding in the restive horses. Two mounted armed men who were to act as outriders were ready.

"A nuisance!" Diego was complaining, for all to hear. "I must ride throughout the night. It may be the death of me."

"But a man must see his confessor at times, my son," his father replied.

Diego embraced his father and got into the carriage. The servants packed cushions around him. The driver started the horses. The carriage cut across the corner of the plaza and disappeared in a cloud of dust, one outrider ahead and the other behind, and turned southward toward San Juan Capistrano.

About midnight, Diego ordered a stop. The carriage was pulled up beside the highway near a huge pile of rocks which cut off the wind from the sea. The hamper was opened, and Diego invited the coachman and outriders to share the repast.

Before they finished eating, they heard hoofs beating the highway, and men's coarse voices raised in song.

"Riders approach, señor," an outrider said. "They are troopers. I can see their swords glistening in the light of the moon."

The troop came loping on, ten men from the barracks at Reina de los

Angeles with Sergeant Manual Garcia at their head. The sergeant shouted an order and his men stopped, hands reaching for their weapons.

"What have we here?" Garcia demanded.

He rode close to the carriage, while his men watched the coachman and outriders.

"It is Don Diego Vega!" Garcia cried. "What do you out here on the highway at midnight, señor?"

"I am on my way to San Juan Capistrano to confess my sins," Diego replied. "Old Fray Esteban, my confessor, is stationed there."

"Perhaps your sins are not heavy, Don Diego," the sergeant said, laughing. "I haven't heard of you slaying anybody recently. Why not get a confessor nearer home?"

"Fray Esteban christened me. He is my father's confessor also. He is like one of the family. I decided to make the journey in the cool of the night, but I am desperately fatigued. And why are you and your men on the highway?"

"Our destination is also San Juan Capistrano," Garcia replied. "The natives and peons down that way are at the point of revolt. We have to chastise them."

"An uprising?" Diego wailed. "I demand protection!"

"The uprising has not started yet," the sergeant explained. "I go to investigate. If a revolt is planned, no doubt the frailes of the missions are behind it, to annoy the Governor — else that rogue of a Señor Zorro."

"Zorro? The masked fiend who rides the highway?" Diego cried. "Why isn't something done about him? Why do not your troopers catch the rogue? I have even heard, Sergeant Garcia, that he thrust his blade through your shoulder — "

"He did," Garcia snapped in angry confession. "He had a lucky moment. When next we meet, I'll have his ears — and the reward the Governor has offered."

"You think he has something to do with the uprising?"

"Possibly. The natives and peons would rally to him. Perhaps the scoundrel thinks he can upset the soldiery and start an empire with himself as king. He would seize the wealth of the missions, raid the ranchos of the hidalgos, kill, use the torch."

"Your words distress me," Diego complained. "Why can we not have peace in this country? Sergeant, I ask a favor. I am about to start on again in my carriage. Will you and your detachment guard me on my way?"

"I am ordered on a certain mission, and must hasten," Garcia declared. "You will be safe enough. You should reach San Juan Capistrano by dawn. If you are waylaid and slain, I swear to avenge you."

"How will that avail me after I am slain?"

Garcia laughed, lifted his hand in signal, and led his troopers on down the dusty highway.

It was an hour after dawn when the carriage reached San Juan Capistrano and entered the mission compound. Yawning and rubbing his eyes, Diego stepped out and stretched. Natives came to care for the horses. Fray Esteban emerged from his quarters to make Diego welcome, and Sergeant Garcia was with him.

"So you got here alive, Don Diego!" Garcia called.

"But I am almost dead from fatigue," Diego replied, as he stepped toward Fray Esteban for his blessing.

GARCIA stalked away, and Fray Esteban's eyes narrowed as he motioned for Diego to enter his quarters.

"I came as soon as I received your message," Diego told him. "I noticed the scratches on the bottom of it."

"I have need of you, my son. Sergeant Garcia has been asking questions, but I withheld some things from him. We of the missions do not always see eye to eye with the soldiers. The peons and natives are only misguided children in this case. They need understanding more than punishment."

"Tell me about it," Diego said, as a novitiate brought in food and retired.

"Somebody has been stirring up the natives. I had some of my neophytes act as spies, and unearthed some of the plot. Two men have been in the neighborhood about a month. They call themselves Luis Martinez and Pedro Gonzales. They claim to be traders. They are the ones inciting the natives."

"To what purpose?" Diego asked.

"Profit, naturally. These men have been preaching the usual thing — that natives and peons work hard to enrich the missions and get little in return. The poor dupes have been told they can seize the missions, raid the ranchos of the hidalgos, become rich overnight and live like kings. The same old talk, my son."

"Where are these scoundrels?" Diego asked.

"They rented a small adobe house a short distance down the highway. I can point it out to you."

"How much does Sergeant Garcia know?"

"Only that somebody is inciting the men to revolt. He will do this own investigating, no doubt. I dare not tell the soldiers much. The politicians are not our friends, and some of the troopers would go out of their way to harm the missions. Can you do anything, my son? As your other self, which I am careful not to mention, you have the warm regard of natives and peons. You have helped them; avenged their wrongs."

"I'll do what I can," Diego agreed. "I have made certain arrangements. Has Bernardo shown himself to you?"

"Your mute servant? I have not seen him."

"He should have been here before me. He is bringing what I may need. Put me in the guest house and let me get some sleep. When Bernardo comes, send him to me. And when I awaken, let me have the latest reports from your spies."

"Ah, I knew you would help, my son!"

"I met Garcia on the highway. He thinks Zorro may be behind the trouble here. My position will be perilous."

"I hope violence may be averted," Fray Esteban said. "I know that Señor Zorro must resort to violence at times. But a little is better than a great deal. If the poor dupes are incited to revolt, there will be bloodshed. It will be an excuse for the Governor to send more troops here, and perhaps seize the mission and even say we Franciscans caused the revolt. The missions have grown wealthy through years of toil, and the politicians covet that wealth. That is the bottom of all the trouble."

"Have you learned anything at all about those rogues, Martinez and Gonzales?" Diego asked.

"Very little. I feel sure they are scoundrels. They may be working for the politicians to start trouble. But I really think this affair is a money-making enterprise of their own."

"How can they make money by starting a revolt?"

"The answer to that is beyond me," Fray Esteban replied.

Diego slept in a room of the mission guest house, and was awakened in the heat of the afternoon by Fray Esteban. Bernardo was standing in a corner of the room.

"Bernardo came a short time ago, my son," Fray Esteban explained. "It is a pity he cannot speak and explain. I brought him to you immediately."

"Has anything happened?" Diego asked.

"My neophyte spies bring word that Martinez and Gonzales are up to something. They have kept to their house the entire day. But they were overheard talking. They have planned something for tonight."

"Sergeant Garcia?" Diego questioned.

"After his usual manner, he has been bellowing questions at everybody," Fray Esteban replied. "He quizzed Martinez and Gonzales and decided they are honest traders. He has been up and at it for a couple of hours."

Fray Esteban left, and Bernardo closed the door.

"Everything is all right?" Diego asked him.

Bernard nodded assent.

"Horse and gear are safe, and will be ready when needed?"

Bernardo nodded again.

"Good man!" Diego praised. "Nothing can be done until nightfall. Rest here in this room."

BERNARDO curled up on a rug in a corner and was asleep almost instantly. Diego paced around the room, thinking.

He knew what an uprising would mean. The mission warehouse would be looted. A horde would attack the great ranchos, burn and slay, drive off herds and flocks. Soldiers would come, and the uprising would be quelled in a sea of blood. Alta California would have another stain on her name.

Diego decided on a plan of action as Señor Zorro, and waited impatiently for night. At dusk, he went to have a frugal meal with Fray Esteban.

"Have you decided on anything, my son?" the fray asked.

"Zorro rides tonight," Diego whispered. "What have your spies reported?"

"Sergeant Garcia and his troopers are acting as if they knew something. A short time ago, they saddled their horses and put them on a picket line outside the compound, with one man to guard. Garcia and the others are around their campfire, eating and drinking."

"The two traders?" Diego asked.

"They are still in the adobe house on the highway. One of my neophytes overheard bits of talk. He heard them mention the Canyon of Echoes."

"I know the place," Diego said. "It is less than five miles east of here."

"The neophyte thinks there is to be a big meeting in the canyon tonight, when plans for the uprising will be completed."

"Have your spies learned what the traders hope to accomplish, and how they will profit from the uprising?"

"Not a thing about that."

"I have decided on a course," Diego said. "It is better I do not inform you of my plans, so you will have no guilty knowledge."

The moon was coming up when Diego left Fray Esteban's quarters. He strolled leisurely around the compound and gradually approached the campfire around which Garcia and his troopers were sprawling.

"Ha! An honor to have you visit us, Don Diego!" Garcia cried, getting up to his feet.

"I have been worried, and thought perhaps you could give me information," Diego said. "How about this reported uprising? I wish to return home tomorrow. Will it be safe for me to do so?"

"I believe so, Don Diego," the sergeant replied. "But, confidentially, I'll be able to tell you better by dawn tomorrow."

"There have been developments?"

"Oh, we've learned a few things, Don Diego! You rest easy tonight.

I'll see you in the morning. I'll tell you whether it is safe to set out for home."

"These turbulent times!" Diego mourned. "You soldiers have hard lives. I must put a couple of pieces of gold to your credit at the tavern in Reina de los Angeles."

"Now that's splendid of you, Don Diego!" Garcia cried. "I and my men will toast your health with every gulp."

"I may as well go to the guest house and retire," Diego said. "It is safe to do that?"

"I think you'll live until morning without having your throat slit," Garcia said. "If the mission is attacked, I'll have my men take care of you. Would we allow you to be slain when you intend placing gold to our credit at the tavern?"

Garcia laughed, and Diego chuckled a bit, bowed and walked away toward the guest house. But the wind from the sea carried to his ears Garcia's low-voiced remark:

"What a fop! And the son of a hidalgo! And our foolish captain once suspected him of being Zorro!"

Bernardo was awake and waiting at guest house. He had eaten with the natives and peons of the mission and was ready for the night's adventure.

"We will slip out," Diego said slowly in a low tone. "I will put on the Zorro costume and mount the black horse. You will ride your mule and come with me to a certain house, and watch while I am inside. Then you wait at a certain place for me while I ride on to the Canyon of Echoes. When I return, you will take the horse on and return to Reina de los Angeles. It is understood?"

Bernardo grinned and nodded.

"You must keep from being recognized," Diego warned. "The sergeant knows you were not with me in the carriage. He would wonder how you came here and what you are doing."

THEY waited for a long time, then Diego extinguished the tapers burning in the room, and they got out a rear door, leaving it unlocked, and to the high wall of the compound. Diego swung into a tree and

"Be quiet and listen!" Zorro shouted

jumped to the top of the wall where there were deep shadows, and Bernardo followed him with the agility of a monkey. They dropped to the ground outside.

Bernardo led the way now. Keeping to the deeper shadows, they went from the mission, avoiding the regular trails. In a secluded depression in the earth about a mile away, Zorro's black horse was tethered in a grove of stunted trees.

Bernardo untied the horse and led him to a nearby spring to drink. He had shown Don Diego where the bundle containing Zorro's things had been hidden behind some rocks. Diego slipped the costume on over his other clothes, buckled on the blade, tucked the pistol into his sash, put on his mask and black hat with the tight chin strap to hold it on against the force of the rushing wind as he rode.

Bernardo mounted his half wild mule and followed. Don Diego's manner had changed. He had put on a new personality with Zorro's clothes. His eyes gleamed through the slits in the mask. His body was erect in the saddle.

They came to the highway through the drifting shadows and stopped. Zorro handed Bernardo the reins and dismounted. He adjusted his sword belt and made sure the pistol was in his sash and ready for use.

"I am going into that small house," Zorro explained. "You stay here in the dark spot and watch. Let me know if there is hint of danger."

He darted through a dark streak and got against the adobe wall of the house near a window. There was a light inside, but the window had been blacked out partially with a serape. Zorro could hear the hum of voices. He strode to the door and knocked.

As he waited, he drew his pistol from his sash and held it ready. He could hear movement inside the house. He heard a bolt shot back, and the door was opened for a few inches, and a man peered out.

Zorro acted swiftly then. He kicked the door open violently and entered, then kicked the door shut behind him. His first rapid glance revealed a single big room with a fireplace, a broken table and a couple of chairs, and two men.

The two men had recoiled at this apparition of a masked man dressed in black with a blade at his side and a pistol held ready in his hand.

"Talk in low tones," he cautioned. "I am Señor Zorro."

"You are Zorro?" one asked, his eyes bulging. "Then you are a man we are glad to see. I am Luiz Martinez, and my companion is Pedro Gonzales."

"So you call yourselves," Zorro said. "Sit down, and do not try to reach for a weapon, or you die."

The two men sat down. Both were short, fat, but Luiz Martinez seemed to be the leader. Gonzales' face had gone white, and he was shaking.

"I know what is going on," Zorro said, standing back against the wall and watching them closely. "What are you trying to do with the natives and peons, for whom I have fought so long?"

"Ah, how glad I am that you have come!" Martinez said. "We did not know how to get in touch with you, or we would have done so. Like you, Señor Zorro, we have bleeding hearts for the lowly and oppressed. We have tried to tell the men how they are being duped, how they work for nothing while others grow rich on their toil — "

"Enough!" Zorro cut in, his voice like ice. "Do you take me to be a fool? What is your scheme, señores? And where do I come into it?"

Martinez' eyes gleamed suddenly. "So that is the way of it!" he said. "Very well, Señor Zorro! We are glad to have you one with us. We know how the natives and peons adore you and will do anything you say. And we have long wondered at your reason for risking life and limb to help them. Now, we know. The time has come to cash in."

THE eyes gleamed through the holes in the mask. "I have influence with them, sí!" Zorro said.

"They will do as you say, señor. They have told as much. They have been hoping you would put in an appearance and help them in this enterprise."

"I am here," Zorro said. "Talk swiftly."

"Very well, señor. We have arranged plans for the uprising. Tonight, around midnight, we are ready to go to the Canyon of Echoes and hold a meeting. They will be there — hundreds of them. We will tell them where and how to strike."

"And the profit?" Zorro questioned.

"Ah! Now we come to it. For your aid, Señor Zorro, we give you a third of the profit. That is fair enough, is it not?"

"How will the profit be forthcoming?" Zorro asked.

"We know, señor, how little the natives and peons have of money. The necessities of life, perhaps, but none of those things which may be purchased by money alone. We have painted a glorious picture for them. Fancy cloth for their women and children, shoes for their feet, things hard to get unless they have money."

"We waste time," Zorro observed. "Soldiers are at the mission."

"I'll make haste in my speech, señor. We are traders. We have carts and oxen ready in a certain place for a caravan. We have told the natives that they are to loot the mission warehouse after attacking and bring what they can carry away to us. We will pay them in gold."

"A tenth of the real value, no doubt?" Zorro put in.

"Why not?" Martinez laughed. "One piece of gold looks huge to such folks."

"Have you thought that they might take your money and then reclaim the goods?"

"They would die by scores if they tried it, señor. And the poor fools think we are their benefactors. We have distributed a few weapons among them."

"I get a third? Very good! And you meet them in the Canyon of Echoes around midnight? I'll be there, señores. A few words from me — "

"And they will have the courage to strike," Martinez interrupted. "We'll attack the mission an hour before dawn. Gonzales and I will give special attention to the sergeant and ten soldiers from Reina de los Angeles. The sergeant questioned us, and thinks we are honest traders. We will make the troopers gifts of wine soon, and it will be potent wine to make them sleep. The throat of a sleeping man may be slit easily, and without noise."

"I leave you, then," Zorro said. "Go to the canyon and hold your meeting. I'll appear and speak to the natives and peons. And do not hope to cheat me of my third, señores, or it will be a sad day for you."

"We'll give it to you gladly," Martinez said.

"Gladly," Gonzales echoed, for the first time.

"With you to urge them on, Señor Zorro, we can sweep from one end of the land to the other," Martinez declared. "We'll have them raid ranchos, drive off herds — the profits will be enormous. Soldiers will come, and some of the poor fools will die, but what of it? We'll cover our tracks well."

Zorro backed quickly to the door.

"Until midnight, señores," he said.

He jerked the door open, darted out into the night and closed the door again.

In the saddle, and with Bernardo beside him on the mule, Zorro rode for half a mile away from the highway and stopped. From his sash he took a bit of parchment and a writing crayon, and in the bright moonlight penned a note:

> Sergeant Garcia
>
> Take your men to the Canyon of Echoes around midnight. Do not disclose yourselves at first, but watch and listen. You will learn much truth.
>
> — Zorro

Zorro wrapped the piece of parchment around a rock, tied it securely with a wisp of dry grass, and got back into his saddle.

"Return to where you had the horse hidden, and wait for me there," he instructed Bernardo. "It may be several hours. Be prepared to take the horse and Zorro's things back to Reina de los Angeles."

BERNARDO nodded and rode away quietly through the night. Zorro listened and watched a moment, then rode back to the highway and along it, the hoofs of his big black horse spurning the flinty ground.

As he approached the mission, natives scattered out of his way. He rode like a courier from San Diego de Alcala, and was taken to be such. The big gates of the mission compound were still open. Zorro stopped his horse in the gateway.

He could see the dying campfire and the soldiers sprawled around it, their weapons put aside. A wineskin was passing among them. Zorro spurred his horse and dashed forward. As he neared the fire, he tossed the rock and parchment.

"For Sergeant Garcia!" he shouted.

He wheeled his horse and rode for the gateway again, went through it and spurred away into the night.

Two hours later, Zorro entered the Canyon of Echoes, but not through its mouth. He had followed a trail over the rim and down the side to the canyon's floor, and had marked it well for the return journey.

Dancing flames showed him where campfires were burning. He could see dark shadows moving around the fires. He rode forward cautiously, keeping in the dark streaks cast by rocks that cut off the light of the moon.

At a short distance from the throng, he stopped in a patch of darkness. Luis Martinez was standing on a huge rock and talking to the natives and peons.

"Señor Zorro, who has done so much for you, is with us," he was proclaiming. "He has promised to come here tonight and urge you to victory. An hour before dawn, we'll strike at the mission. You have been told what to do. Wealth shall be yours. Why should you slave and toil and sweat — "

There was much more of it in the same vein. And Zorro, knowing this Canyon of Echoes and how it had got its name, knew also that Martinez' words were ringing down the gulch, echoing from rock to rock wall, and could be heard distinctly by anybody in hiding there. He hoped Sergeant Garcia and his troopers would not interfere too soon.

Gonzales, the second scoundrel, mounted the rock and spoke to the natives in turn, working them up to a pitch of frenzy. Zorro could see them brandishing some poor weapons the traders had given them.

He waited for a time, until the enthusiasm died down in a measure, then rode forward again, watching and listening. And suddenly his black horse emerged from the darkness and into the flickering glare of the campfires.

"Zorro is here!" he shouted.

There was a moment of silence, and then a chorus of shouts. They saw before them a man dressed in black, riding a black horse, a black mask over his face, a blade at his side.

"Back!" Zorro shouted. "Be quiet and listen to me! I have always been your friend, have I not? I have fought for you, risked freedom and life for you. I have punished your enemies."

"Zorro! Zorro!" they shouted.

"Be quiet! I ask you to trust me now, to do as I say. Will you do so?"

They chorused that they would.

"You are but poor dupes," Zorro said, his right hand straying to the pistol in his sash. "These men, Martinez and Gonzales, are not your friends. They are swindlers. They would have you risk your lives, and cheat you. Have nothing to do with them. This is Zorro telling you that."

"Why you — " Martinez shouted.

He tried to get out a pistol, but some of the peons close at hand seized him and prevented him.

"Tell us more, Zorro!" somebody called.

"This affair is known," Zorro shouted at them. "Soldiers are here now, and more will come. You are in a trap. Nothing can be gained by a show of violence. Get away quickly, and go to your homes. Trust me, your friend. Leave those two rogues for the soldiers to handle."

Martinez managed to fire his pistol, but the ball flew past Zorro harmlessly. Then both Martinez and Gonzales were being beaten down by their dupes.

Down the canyon came a thunder of hoofbeats echoing among the rocks.

"The soldiers!" somebody cried in warning.

The natives and peons melted into the shadows, scrambling up among the rocks, trying to reach the lips of the canyon and run away.

ZORRO turned his black horse and started to ride.

"You — Zorro! I want you, you rouge!" he heard Sergeant Garcia shouting at him.

"Try to catch me!" Zorro called back. "If you listened, you know the truth. Capture those two rogues and deal with them."

He used his spurs and went through the streaks of black night and moonlight, while Garcia and some of his troopers blundered along behind as the rest of the sergeant's men stopped to take charge of Martinez and Gonzales.

Zorro knew the trail, and the others did not. The troopers heard his black's hoofs strike a rock now and then. They fired their pistols to no avail. Zorro out-rode them, reached the lip of the canyon and sped away.

He was careful during his return journey, but quickly reached the spot where Bernardo was waiting. He dismounted, stripped off the Zorro clothes, made a bundle of them and his weapons, and Bernardo lashed the bundle to the black's saddle.

"Ride your mule and lead the horse," Zorro said. "Use great care.

Get you home."

In the early morning of the following day, Don Diego Vega emerged from a room of the guesthouse, yawning and rubbing his eyes. He went toward Fray Esteban's quarters for breakfast.

Fray Esteban greeted him warmly, and with his eyes twinkling.

"One of my neophyte spies reported all that happened," the fray whispered. "The soldiers have those two traders, and the natives and peons escaped. The danger is over, my son. You have spared us fire and blood and pillage, and undoubtedly have saved many lives."

"I'll start for home in an hour or so," Don Diego said. "But since I came here to confess, I should do so."

An hour after that, Don Diego went into the compound and sought out Sergeant Garcia.

"Will it be safe, think you, for me to drive home today, if I started now and make the journey by daylight?" Diego asked.

"Absolutely safe, Don Diego," Garcia told him. "There will be no uprising. We of the soldiery caught the rascals last night in a canyon and dispersed them. And we captured the two men who were fomenting the trouble, and are taking them to Reina de los Angeles for trial. We start soon. I'll be glad to have my men furnish an escort for you, Don Diego, all the way home, for we wish to ride leisurely after this great task."

So, Sergeant Garcia and his troopers escorted the carriage from San Juan Capistrano to Reina de los Angeles, thinking they were escorting Don Diego Vega, and not knowing that they escorted the Señor Zorro who had escaped them the night before.

"I thank you," Don Diego said, as the carriage stopped in front of his father's house and the troopers prepared to ride on with their prisoners. "I shall place four pieces of gold to your credit at the tavern instead of two. Good work should always be rewarded."

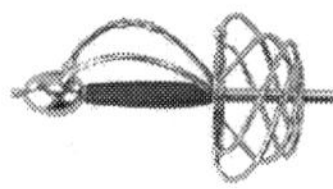

Zorro Fights a Friend

With cracking whip and flashing blade, the dauntless Hidalgo goes forth to battle against grim injustice and brutality!

AFTER the siesta hour that day, Don Diego Vega, dressed in his resplendent best, left his father's house in Reina de los Angeles and made his way slowly to the little plaza.

It was his intention to go to the chapel. Fray Felipe, his old confessor, now stationed at the mission at San Juan Capistrano, was in town on business of the Franciscan brotherhood, and Don Diego wished to pay his respects.

It was a splendid afternoon, with the warm sun beating down, birds singing in the trees and bees humming. Others were out for a stroll following the siesta, and Diego greeted friends as he sauntered along, greeted gushing señoras who had marriageable daughters and hopes of an alliance with the house of Vega, bowed to hidalgo friends of his father, and waved a hand languidly to other young caballeros he passed.

But one he did not pass. He met Rafael Reyes, the friend of his bosom, and they stopped and clasped hands and slapped each other on their backs. Diego pretending to wince at the strength of Reyes' friendly greeting.

Rafael Reyes was of good blood, a young caballero of spirit — too much spirit, many said. He was tall, slender, graceful, with broad shoulders and a fencer's arms, one of the best swordsmen in Alta California.

Diego, with the reputation of being spiritless and almost effeminate, supposed to like reading poetry rather than indulge in manly sports and pastimes, seemed to be Reyes' exact opposite. Yet some strange chain of friendship had bound them together since they were boys, and that friendship had strengthened through the years.

"Diego!" Rafael cried, seizing his shoulders in his strong hands. "I returned but two days ago from a trip to Monterey. What a time I had! Little sleep did I get there, what with the continual round of pleasure! Dice and cards and wenches! Some gorgeous new creatures but lately arrived from San Francisco de Asis. What a time I had trying to outwit duennas!"

"I rejoice, amigo, that you had great pleasure," Diego said. "No doubt its pursuit tired you. But now, since you are home, you may rest."

"Rest?" Who wants to rest?" Rafael demanded. "A man may rest when he is eighty and has great-grandchildren around his knee. How I wish my father would let me reside in Monterey all the time! But he keeps me at home. I must learn the management of the rancho, he tells me."

THERE was a strange expression on Diego's face.

"Perhaps it is best," he hinted.

"But there is little life here," Rafael complained. "It is all pleasant enough — but no adventure. However, some of us have arranged a little."

"Indeed?" Diego lifted his brows.

"This Señor Zorro, this masked highwayman who roams over the highways — the Governor is sick of him. He is sick, also, of the troopers who cannot catch him. Capitán Ortega, the commandante here, is a good man, but not good enough. This Zorro continually outwits him. And he is a fiend with the blade, it is said — and that interests me much."

"How so?" Diego asked.

"There is an offer of adventure in the situation. Capitán Ortega himself dropped the suggestion, and I took it up. I acquainted some half dozen of our friends in the matter. We are going to make an effort to capture this Zorro or lay him by his heels."

"What?" Diego seemed startled.

" 'Tis true! We drew lots, and one of us will report at the barracks each day, at noon, and stay until the next noon, when another will relieve him. Whenever an alarm comes that this Señor Zorro is abroad, one of us will be there to ride with the troopers."

"And what good will that do, if the troopers cannot catch him?"

"Perhaps we may succeed where the troopers cannot. Perhaps we can scent a trail better. Ah, Diego, there is nothing so exhilarating as a man hunt!"

"That depends on whether you are the fox or a hound," Diego observed, calmly.

"I hope to run across the rogue. I'll not pistol him. I want to cross blades with him in fair fight. 'Tis said he is good with a blade. But perchance I am better with one than some of the troopers he has bested."

"No doubt," Diego said. "Why should you wish to run him down, Rafael? Zorro has but shielded the helpless, avenged the wrongs of the weak, attacked nefarious officials — "

"Oh, I know all that! Between the two of us, Diego, I admire the fellow and his work. But the Governor has offered a reward for him, and, after all, the man takes the law into his own hands."

"Perhaps because those who should administer it fail to do so in a fair manner," Diego said.

"You seem to admire the fellow."

"Very much," Diego replied, smiling slightly.

"However, he is an outlaw. I would propose that you share this adventure with us, Diego, except that I know you abhor violence, hate to ride here and there wildly through the night, and would rather read the poets than use a blade. You are a strange caballero, amigo, yet I love you! I must hasten on. We'll meet again soon. Until then, go with God!"

Rafael Reyes hurried on across the plaza, radiating energy. Don Diego Vega walked on slowly, the faint smile still upon his lips. Rafael Reyes, his great friend, did not know that Diego was Señor Zorro.

Only three persons knew that — Diego's father, proud Don Alejandro, Fray Felipe, his confessor, and Bernardo, the peon mute who had been his body servant for years, who assisted him at times, and would have died before he would have revealed the secret, even had he been able to do so.

The encounter with Rafael Reyes worried Diego a little. He had no wish to cross blades with Reyes or any of their friends. Reyes, for instance, was almost a master swordsman. It would be an even thing to fight him, Diego knew. And Reyes, nor any of the others, would know that in the masked Zorro they were fighting one of their own kind, one of their friends.

Zorro had no wish to reveal his true identity as Don Diego Vega, for then his work must end. Nothing can be a secret when a dozen know it.

It was a secret now. His father would not reveal it even under torture, and thus put himself and his estates at the mercy of some whim of the unscrupulous governor of Alta California; Fray Felipe would not reveal it because of the seal of the confessional; and Bernardo, the mute, could not.

So, if his friends did this thing, he would have to avoid them, run away if necessary rather than fight. Knowing them as he did, Diego decided that their enthusiasm in the matter would wane in a few days. Some other idea would come to them, some situation that promised immediate excitement. Anyhow, the river need not be forded until the edge of the water was reached.

Diego greeted an elderly señora who passed, gave the eye to a pretty señorita who almost swooned because he did so, and strolled on toward the little chapel to pay his respects to old Fray Felipe.

It was three days later when Ramón Cassara, the wealthy merchant of Monterey, reached Reina de los Angeles from the south, riding a splendid horse and accompanied by two of his men on mules. Cassara had been to San Diego de Alcála on business, which had gone none too well for him, and it was plain that the man had been in a towering rage for several days.

He dismounted at the inn, and his horse and the mules of his men were cared for, and Señor Cassara was assigned the best room off the patio by the fawning innkeeper, who foresaw much profit in this visit. Cassara was rather ostentatious, and liked to fling money around to advertise his prosperity.

He announced that he would remain for a day, and possibly for two, and wanted the best of everything. A special native servant was assigned him by the innkeeper. The rarest wine in the cellar was sent to his room. A pretty native girl was sent to attend him, but Señor Cassara chased her away, saying he did not care to be bothered by a bronze wench.

The news of the rich merchant's arrival spread quickly, and certain of the town's loafers began loitering in the big main room of the inn, hoping for free wine, or for a chance to be of some service to Señor Cassara that would result in a piece of gold.

After the siesta hour, Cassara emerged into the main room of the inn, his manner that of a monarch giving his subjects the treat of looking upon his presence. He sat on a bench at the head of the longest table beneath a window, and gestured grandly to the landlord.

"Give all here a goblet of good wine, and place it to my account," he said, looking over those in the room.

The innkeeper and his servants hastened to obey. Miguel, a huge, stolid peon, carried a jeweled goblet to Cassara, bowed and placed it before him.

The innkeeper brought the wineskin and filled the goblet.

The others in the room saluted Cassara and drank, muttering their thanks and wishes for the señor's good health. Cassara sipped his wine and made a wry face, as if the stuff were beneath him and an offense to his palate.

The fat innkeeper hovered near, ready and eager to be of service, and Miguel, the big peon servant, stood close by, prepared to jump at the innkeeper's order. Señor Cassara gazed through the window at the plaza, where men and women of the town were strolling after the heat of the day.

"What a hole!" Cassara said. "The place has no spirit. Yet I must stop here to rest myself, my men, the beasts we ride. Landlord! Is there no diversion in the place?"

"What sort of diversion does the señor wish?" the landlord asked.

"Anything to keep me from falling asleep. Is there nobody in the town who likes a fling of the dice, for instance, or the flip of a card?"

"Ah! There are fiery young caballeros about, señor, and they usually drift into the inn about nightfall. They will be coming soon."

"Arrange a game for me," Cassara said. "It will serve, at least, to kill the hours."

Some of the young caballeros dropped into the inn about the hour of sunset for a glass of wine, and a game was arranged. They began playing, first with cards, then with dice, and then with cards again.

Señor Cassara was a consistent loser. He always boasted of his luck at dice and cards, and that luck seemed to have deserted him. Worst of all, it was a fair game, for he knew these sons of hidalgos were above cheating. He could afford his losses of gold, but could not endure the ignominy of defeat.

His rage became apparent in his face, and grew. He made rash bets, and lost. If he won a throw, he immediately lost thrice the amount on the next.

An hour of this, and Señor Cassara was like a wild man. He howled for more wine, berating the fat innkeeper for no fault at all. He ordered some common men at the next table to move, saying that their body stench annoyed him.

All except the young caballeros became frightened at his rage.

At this juncture, Don Diego Vega entered the inn with his body servant Bernardo behind him. He went to the counter, where the innkeeper greeted him respectfully and bowed, and rubbed his hands together in prospect of serving the scion of the house of Vega.

Diego asked for a jar of crystallized honey, saying that there was none in his father's house at the moment, and the innkeeper made haste to get it. Señor Cassara glanced across the room and saw the transaction.

"Who is that effeminate-looking popinjay?" he asked the man next him.

The caballeros glared at him.

"Careful, señor!" one whispered. "He is Don Diego Vega. His father could buy us all. A young man of rare blood, breeding and wealth, you understand."

"He does not look it," Cassara said.

"He is quiet, that is true, señor. He does not enjoy boisterous pursuits. Let us return to our game, unless you have had enough."

"Cast the dice!" Cassara growled.

Bernardo had left Diego at the counter and approached the gaming table. He always did this when he visited the inn. He liked to watch men risk their money on dice and cards, see their elation when they won and their discomfiture when they lost. It was most amusing to Bernardo.

In his eagerness to watch, he got very near the table, and Señor Cassara looked up and saw him.

"Get away, dolt!" he shouted. "How dare you approach a table where gentlemen are playing? You carry a stench."

Don Diego had left the counter, and now he stepped forward quickly and got between Bernardo and the table, and his eyes were blazing when he confronted Cassara.

"There is a stench here, señor, but my loyal servant

There was a quick exchange of thrusts

is not causing it," Don Diego said, brushing a lace handkerchief gently across his nostrils in a gesture the meaning of which was unmistakable.

"I have not the pleasure of your acquaintance, señor," Cassara said, trying to be haughty.

"As you say, it would be a pleasure — and a honor, señor," Diego told him. "You have it not, nor will you acquire it." He looked at the caballeros and smiled. "I see that some of my friends are amusing themselves investigating trash."

"Trash, señor?" Cassara roared.

Diego eyed him. "You bellow like a bull," he observed. "You look like a bull. You act like one."

"This is unbearable!" Cassara cried.

"Yet you bear it, señor." Diego turned away without another word. "Come, Bernardo," he added. "Let us get outside where the air is untainted."

Don Diego made a leisurely exit. The caballeros were smiling. Cassara's rage overflowed.

"Popinjay!" he growled.

"Careful, señor!" one of the caballeros warned. "He is one of us, and our friend. I think, señor, that we are finished playing with you."

The caballeros arose and bowed, and drifted away from the table, taking their winnings with them. Cassara's face was purple with wrath.

"Landlord! More of that swill you call wine!" he called.

The landlord motioned to Miguel, the big peon, who took up the wineskin and made haste to the table. Miguel was shaking because of the scene he had just witnessed. He slopped a little of the wine on the table, and a few drops went on Cassara's sleeve.

Cassara sprang to his feet with an angry roar. He seized a riding whip one of the caballeros had left on the end of the table. With all his strength he began beating the peon around the head and shoulders.

Cassara was expending upon the luckless peon all his accumulated rage — because of his losses at dice and cards, his conflict with Don Diego, whose evident superiority burned him, the desertion of the gaming table by the caballeros. Big Miguel could have beaten the merchant to a pulp and broken his limbs, but did not raise a hand.

Miguel only tried to protect his head with his arms, and he howled as the whip cut into his back. It was unthinkable that a man of his standing raise a hand against one like Cassara, a wealthy merchant, however unjust the attack. If he did, the soldiers would make short work of him.

Miguel's shrieks of pain attracted the attention of Don Diego as he was passing the window outside, and he stopped and peered into the room. Miguel was trying to get away. Blood was soaking through the back of his shirt. Cassara sprang forward and cut at him again, and the peon made a dash toward the kitchen door and disappeared through it.

Diego turned toward Bernardo.

"Zorro rides tonight!" he whispered. "Have everything ready."

Inside the tavern, none of the caballeros had tried to prevent Cassara giving the whipping. A peon was only a peon, though the caballeros would not have descended to beating one except for theft or insolence. But the looks they gave Cassara were far from being complimentary.

Cassara tossed the whip upon the table and returned to drink his wine.

"Give me a better servant," he told the innkeeper. "That clumsy idiot — "

"Immediately, señor!"

The caballero who owned the whip approached the table to get it.

"I gave the lout what he deserved, did I not?" Cassara asked him.

The caballero eyed him without blinking. "Señor," he said, "I would not be in your boots."

"And why not?"

"Suppose Señor Zorro is in the neighborhood and learns of this? He has a manner of dealing with men who beat peons and natives."

"Zorro? That confounded masked highwayman?" Cassara showed signs of fear in his face. "I'll call on the soldiers for help. I'll demand a guard."

"Señor Zorro has outwitted soldiers and guards before," the caballero reminded him. He smiled slightly and turned away.

Visiting the barracks before nightfall, Cassara told the story to Capitán

Carlos Ortega, and invited the capitán to dine with him at the inn. Ortega accepted. Because of his rank, he could not eat with his troopers. He was not a great favorite, and the prominent people of the town seldom invited him. And he was sick of dining alone. Moreover, Ortega had the idea that Cassara, to show his wealth, would order a sumptuous meal.

Cassara did just that. Ortega appeared, and they ate in the patio, served by three. The table was heaped with the best the landlord could supply, and the wine was the best he had.

After finishing the evening meal, they went to Cassara's room, the finest in the inn. It had a door opening into the patio, which was filled with trees and blooming flowers. There was a bright moon, which sent its light shifting through the trees in spots to augment the light cast by the reeking torches set in niches in the walls.

"Do not disturb yourself about this scoundrel, Zorro while you are in my jurisdiction, señor," Capitán Ortega told the merchant. "My sergeant, Manuel Garcia, is in charge, and has four troopers on guard with him. They have the tavern surrounded."

"That is good news," Cassara praised. "I shall mention your attention to duty when I reach Monterey."

"This Zorro is a thorn in the flesh," Ortega admitted. "He is a fiend with the blade, and he seems to dodge bullets. He has a black horse that can outrun anything we have. We never know where he will strike — that is the trouble."

"You have not learned his identity?"

"No. He apes a caballero and has said he is one, but we doubt that now. We think he came to this district from the north, possibly from San Francisco de Asis. He may be some scoundrel who was run out of that place for offenses."

They talked on, drinking the rich wine. Cassara was trying to make an impression on the capitán. In turn, Ortega was trying to make a good impression on Cassara, knowing him to be a wealthy merchant of Monterey and thinking possibly he might drop a few appropriate words in high places there and Ortega receive coveted promotion as the result.

And while they talked, a horseman approached the rear of the tavern through the deeper shadows. He dismounted and tethered his black mount to a tree in a small depression, then went forward afoot.

He avoided the streaks of bright moonlight as well as he could. A watcher would have seen that he was garbed entirely in black, and had a black mask over his face, there was a shining blade at his side.

He reached the wall of the tavern and slipped around to the rear, where there was a small gate that opened into the patio, generally used by persons delivering supplies. Through this he went, leaving it open behind him.

He was in the patio now. It was darker here than it had been outside, because of the trees and heavy vines. The intruder kept to the deeper shadows and reached the end of the row of arches before the entrances to the rooms.

Cassara's dinner table had been cleared away, and nobody was in the patio. The masked man went almost noiselessly along the walk beneath the arches, listening at any door where he saw a streak of light showing beneath. And finally he found the room he sought.

Two men were talking and laughing inside. He recognized Ortega's voice, and that of the merchant, Cassara. He glanced around again swiftly, to make sure no servant was near, then knocked on the door.

In his left hand, he held a pistol ready. In his right hand was a heavy mule whip. The blade swung at his side.

He heard steps inside the room, and the door was pulled open. A shaft of light shot out and revealed the masked man. But even as Cassara, who had opened the door, reeled back with a gasp of astonishment and fear, the intruder had darted into the room and closed the door behind him.

"Make no move, señores!" he warned, in a deep voice.

"Zorro!" Capitán Ortega cried, his face turning crimson.

"You will sit on that stool in the corner of the room, capitán," Zorro said. "You have no pistol in your sash, I see. I hold one ready. Do not compel me to use it on you, Capitán Ortega."

Ortega's eyes were gleaming dangerously as he went to sit on the stool. He would await the proper opportunity. Cassara had reeled back against the wall and stood there with his lower jaw sagging in an expression of fear, his eyes bulging, his breath coming in painful gasps.

"I have no quarrel with you, capitán," Zorro said. "I am here to punish this scoundrel who uses a whip on men unable to defend themselves. I shall give him a taste of a whip."

"Ortega, do something!" Cassara cried. "You're a soldier — the commandante here — "

"Keep your voice down, señor, else I may pistol you." Zorro warned. "Step away from the wall."

Cassara, licking at lips suddenly feverish dry, stepped toward the center of the room. Zorro glanced at Ortega again, and sensed that Ortega did not care whether the merchant was whipped, but would make a try at Zorro himself later.

"Señor, you presume on your wealth and standing to treat men like wild beasts," Zorro told Cassara. "Because you lost at dice and cards, you expended your wrath on a poor peon, who knew it would be a serious offense to lift a hand against you. In my estimation, señor, you are a human rat, and should be taught a lesson."

"Capitán — " Cassara begged, keeping his voice low.

Ortega was sitting on the edge of the stool with his feet drawn up beneath him, as if ready to spring.

"Do not be a fool, Ortega, and get your self pistoled," Zorro advised.

The whip suddenly sang through the air, and the lash cut into the fat merchant's back. He gave a suppressed howl and started toward a corner. But the lash drove him back to the center of the room again, and continued singing and cutting, the lash biting into Cassara's back, thighs, legs. Mercifully, Zorro did not use the lash on his head.

From the corner of an eye, Zorro watched Ortega continually. But Ortega made no effort to leave his stool. The pistol Zorro held never wavered, regardless of how he used the whip.

Cassara was commencing to learn how it felt to be whipped. The lash stung. It had brought blood, and the merchant's back felt like one great raw sore.

"Mercy, señor!" he begged, sobbing. "Whatever amount you wish, I'll pay you — "

The lash sang and cut deeper.

"There are some things, señor, you cannot buy with your money,"

Zorro said. "Me, for instance."

Cassara sobbed again and dropped to his knees, wrapping his head in his arms. Zorro took a few more cuts at him, and stepped back.

"Let that teach you not to beat helpless men," he said. "Do not cross my path again, señor, or you will receive much worse. Get you gone in the morning from this part of Alta California!"

Zorro backed to the door, watching Ortega carefully. He had nothing to fear from Cassara. He fastened his curled whip to his belt on the right side, back on his hip where it would be out of the way, and transferred his pistol to his right hand.

He put his left hand behind him and fumbled for the catch on the door, found it.

"Capitán Ortega, you have been a sensible man," Zorro said. Had you attacked me, I would have fired at you. Why end your career and your life by trying to rescue such a man as this Cassara?"

"The end of this is not yet, Zorro," Ortega replied. "You came here and did what you came to do. But you are not out of it, señor. There is a long distance at this moment between you and safety."

"You would try to disturb me, perhaps?" Zorro asked. "Nothing you could say would make me fear."

Zorro pulled the door open as he finished speaking, sprang out into the patio and pulled the door shut after him. And he came face to face with Sergeant Manuel Garcia.

"So!" Garcia cried. "At last I have you!"

Zorro held the pistol. There was no time for either to draw a blade. The burly sergeant stepped to one side and tried to get his pistol out of his sash. He would risk death, it appeared, in an exchange of shots.

But Zorro wished nothing like that. He sprang forward, and the barrel of his heavy pistol crashed against the side of Sergeant Garcia's head and made him reel. Zorro sprang away just as Capitán Ortega jerked the door of the room open.

"Help here! Help! Zorro is here!" Ortega shouted in a stentorian voice. "To me, troopers!"

Answering shouts came from around the tavern. Zorro darted beneath the arches, through the deeper shadows, and so came to the gate. He crouched at one side of it as a trooper came charging through in answer to the capitán's call.

There was an instant uproar in the tavern. Troopers ran into the patio, and men who had been in the big main room followed. Lights appeared.

Zorro darted noiselessly through the gate, kept to the shadows and out of the streaks of moonlight, and when at a safe distance stopped and gave a peculiar call.

That was a signal for Bernardo, who sat his swift riding mule in a spot of darkness not far away. They were playing a trick they had played often. Bernardo kicked his mule, and away he rode at high speed, the mule's hoofs resounding against the flinty ground.

"After him!" Zorro heard Sergeant Garcia cry. "Mount and we'll chase the rogue! He is making south down the highway!"

Zorro heard them running to get their horses. He knew they would never catch Bernardo. The latter would circle and return to a certain spot, and be waiting there ready to care for Zorro's horse and costume when he arrived.

THE pursuit left the tavern. Those who did not join it retired to the main room for wine. Zorro could hear Cassara lamenting of the lack of protection a man had in that country. He heard Capitán Ortega trying to soothe him.

"The rogue may return," Zorro heard Cassara say.

"He has made his getaway, but possibly this time my troopers will catch him," Ortega replied. "And three good men of mine have remained behind to guard you."

Zorro got up from his crouching position in the darkness and started toward his horse, some distance away in the depression. He went leisurely, anticipating no trouble, taking care, however, to keep in the shadows. He still held his pistol.

Slowly, he approached his horse. The big black snorted once, Zorro thought, and his caution increased. Perhaps someone was lurking in the darkness.

But he heard no sound to cause him alarm, saw nothing unusual. He walked on, and passed through a streak of moonlight to get to the horse.

"Stand there, Señor Zorro!" a stern voice called. "I am holding my pistol on you."

Zorro stopped. He could see nobody. And then a man strode out of a patch of black night and into the bright moonlight and came toward him. He was Rafael Reycs.

"So that is your trick," Reyes said. "You have a confederate who rides away. The foolish troopers chase him, and you leave the scene leisurely and in safety. But you see, Señor Zorro, I happened to stumble upon your horse, so waited for you to appear. And now, señor — "

"I am holding a pistol also," Zorro informed him.

"So I see," Reyes answered. "Should we shoot it out, do you think? I have no wish to die from a pistol ball, and I think you have not either. How about the weapons of gentlemen, señor? I have heard you are good with a blade."

"That is agreeable," Zorro replied. "We return our pistols to our sashes."

"Agreed!"

Both did so. They were standing about fifteen feet apart. As Zorro whipped out his blade, he was doing some rapid thinking.

He was compelled to make his escape. If he suffered a bad wound and was taken, or at the worst was slain, the Governor would take vengeance on his father and the Vega estates. And he did not want to hurt his friend.

Their blades met and rang before Zorro could reach a solution.

"I hope to succeed where the soldiers could not," Rafael said, as he fought.

"You toy with death, señor," Zorro replied. He was using a deep voice that was not his own.

"Less talk, señor, and more fighting!"

In the bright moonlight, they circled and fought. Their blades clashed and rang. Zorro found that in Rafael Reyes he had no mean antagonist. His friend's wrist was strong. He knew how to handle a blade. This would be no light thing like fighting with Capitán Ortega or Sergeant Garcia.

A word to Rafael, the lifting of his mask, and it would end. It would be like Rafael to insist in joining him in his adventures. But he did not want another man to know his secret. Even for his lifelong friend to know it might place him in danger. An unguarded word, a wrong move —

Zorro felt a streak of fire along his left forearm, and knew that Rafael's blade had touched him there. He redoubled his caution, felt for secure footing on the somewhat rough ground, fought his best.

"Yield!" Rafael cried.

"Never!" Zorro answered.

The ring of their blades, their cries carried on the wind, reached the ears of Ortega and his men around the tavern. They came running.

Zorro was in peril now. Ortega and his troopers would shoot him down, at least wound him enough so he could be taken. He had an instant's vision of himself incarcerated, sentenced to be hanged and that sentence approved by a vindictive Governor. He saw his father disgraced, his estates confiscated, an end of the Vega family in Alta California.

The shouts of the soldiers were coming nearer. As he fought, Zorro could hear boots pounding the hard earth. As he turned once, he caught sight of dark forms running through the streaks of moonlight toward this small grove of trees in front of which he and Rafael fought.

It was time to make an end of it. He did not wish to shoot his friend.

"Keep back! Keep away! This man is mine!" Rafael began shouting at the soldiers.

Capitán Ortega was leading three men toward the spot. Zorro retreated a few steps, and Rafael fell into the trap and forced the fighting as he advanced. Then there was a quick exchange of thrusts. The tip of Rafael's blade ripped Zorro's sleeve. The tip of Zorro's caught Rafael's right forearm and slit it, and he dropped his sword.

Zorro was away through the darkness before his blade had been thrust into its scabbard. He reached the horse, jerked the reins free and vaulted into his saddle. Ortega and his men came charging on. A hail of bullets cut leaves from the tree as Zorro gave the big black the spurs and rode through the moonlight and toward the highway.

Ortega and his men were far from their mounts, and he would be away and safe before they could make a start. Bernardo had decoyed Garcia and the other troopers toward the south. Zorro was safe again if he could reach the place of rendezvous.

He reached it in time, to find Bernardo waiting. Bernardo took the reins of the black, and Don Diego Vega stripped off the Zorro costume, the mask, and emerged himself. He gave the clothes and his blade to Bernardo to put in hiding where they kept the horse.

Then, as Bernardo rode away cautiously, Diego got through the back wall and finally entered his father's house. He heard voices in the main room, and glanced in to find his father and Fray Felipe there.

"The fellow is punished," he said. "Zorro punished him."

"You are hurt, my son!" Don Alejandro cried.

"A small slash in the left forearm. Fray Felipe can doctor me in a few minutes. We'll go to my rooms. If anyone should call for me, I am at devotions with my Father Confessor."

"Who gave you the wound?" his father asked.

Don Diego smiled softly. "The best friend I have in the world," he replied. "Only he does not know to whom he gave it."

Zorro's Hour of Peril

Once again the Fighting Hidalgo draws sword for justice!

LATE that sunny afternoon, Don Diego Vega was sitting on a bench in the patio of his father's house in Reina de los Angeles, watching the gurgling fountain play and reading poetry.

His manner was that of a quiet, rather foppishly dressed young caballero overcome with lassitude. Certainly he did not resemble other young men of his social set, who displayed an abundance of energy from sunrise until late in the night, and who thought it strange that Diego did not do likewise.

Little did they guess that Diego's attitude was a pose, that, did he so wish, he could out-ride and outfight them all. Nor did they dream that Diego was Señor Zorro, the masked man in black who, riding a wild black horse, traveled the highways righting wrongs, and thumbed his nose at the Governor's troopers when they sought to capture and hang him.

Diego read a passage, but there was a disturbing element somewhere, and he could not concentrate. Somebody was calling on his father, dignified gray-haired Don Alejandro. He could hear a calm voice, and another, having a shrill tone and a note of fear in it.

Diego arose from the bench and entered the house, making his way to the big main living room.

"Cross blades with me, will you?" cried Ybarra. "I'll slay you!"

His father was sitting at the head of the long table. Seated near him was Fray Felipe, the aged Franciscan who was Diego's confessor, who had been a friend of the family before Diego had been born.

Standing respectfully, twirling a battered sombrero with trembling, gnarled fingers, was a ragged, bare-footed peon of middle age. Diego knew the man — Pedro Castro, who worked on the Vega rancho out San Gabriel way.

"I believe the boy," old Fray Felipe was saying. "He is a good boy, and would not lie to me. Certainly not about a thing like this. I visited him in the jail room in the barracks and he told me the story."

Don Diego coughed slightly, advanced and bowed as Fray Felipe greeted and blessed him, then he sat down beside his father.

"What is all this tumult?" he asked. "I heard it from the patio."

"Pedro Castro's only son, Juan, is charged with the murder of Don Marcos Murilla," his father replied.

DIEGO's eyes widened as he looked at Castro.

"I know Juan," he declared. "He would not kill a lizard."

"He is innocent," Fray Felipe said. "But what can be done? The soldiers claim they caught him beside the body, robbing it."

"What is the story?" Diego asked.

"This is what the boy tells," Fray Felipe related. "He was coming from San Gabriel where he has been working, to visit his father here. He stretched out on the ground behind a hedge to rest, and fell asleep. Loud voices awoke him. Two men were quarreling on the other side of the hedge."

"And what did he do?" Diego asked.

"He sought for a place where he could peer through the hedge, but before he could, he heard a cry of pain, a muttered curse, then the rapid hoofbeats of a horse. He plainly saw the horseman who rode away, he told me."

"And the horseman was?" Diego questioned.

"The man who came here about a year ago and bought a rancho from heirs, this man who calls himself Don Esteban Ybarra y Sandoval — a name he has no right to claim as his own."

"I have met him," Diego said, an expression of disgust in his face, "and think him a boisterous braggart. If he has gentle blood in his veins, his actions, his words, stamp him anything but a gentleman."

"The boy," Fray Felipe continued, "got through the hedge. He saw a splendid horse standing there with reins trailing. And on the ground was Marcos Murilla, dead. A blade had been driven through his heart."

"So this so-called Don Esteban killed him?" Diego asked.

"Nobody else could have done it — unless Juan is guilty," Fray Felipe replied. "The boy ran to Murilla and knelt quickly beside him, and at that instant, Sergeant Manuel Garcia and two troopers from the presidio here came trotting along the road and stopped to investigate. Juan was tongue-tied when they accused him of slaying Murilla for the purpose of robbery, and he was the picture of a guilty man caught at the scene of his crime.

So the troopers brought him in to jail."

"A moment!" Diego said. "If this Don Esteban slew Murilla with his sword, and took the weapon away with him — "

"The killer did not use his sword," Fray Felipe broke in. "He used an ordinary sheep-skinning knife and tossed it on the ground beside the body. Every peon who works at shearing time carries such a knife, but Juan had none. So the sergeant declared the knife was his. Juan told his story — and earned a laugh. Who would believe a peon like Juan? Especially against the word of Don Esteban Ybarra y Sandoval?"

The fray looked straight at Diego, knowing, as his confessor, that Diego was Zorro. Diego glanced at Pedro Castro, the frightened father, then at his own father. Don Alejandro caught the significance of the glance.

"Castro," he said, "go to the kitchen and tell them to give you food and wine. We'll discuss your son's case and I'll see you later."

After the humble Castro had gone, the three men talked in low tones.

"This," Diego said, "seems to be an affair in which Señor Zorro should interest himself."

"I was hoping the story might come to his ears," Fray Felipe replied, smiling faintly.

"This so-called Don Esteban should be exposed, if he is sailing under false colors," Diego declared.

"He is," Fray Felipe said. "When he came here a year ago, I did not like his manner or methods. I knew he had come from Mexico, and asked for information concerning him. We Franciscans have ways of getting such. I received my information only two days ago. The man's name is Esteban Ybarra, and nothing more. The rest he invented."

"Yet he came here," Don Alejandro put in, "in a splendid carriage drawn by excellent horses. He had two carts piled high with packing cases filled with fine clothes. He wore jewels, and had more than enough gold to buy a rancho and stock it."

"Blood money," Fray Felipe interrupted. "Esteban Ybarra was for several years the bodyguard of the Viceroy in Mexico. He is said to be one of the finest swordsmen in Europe. He came to Mexico because he was no longer welcome in Spain, and the Viceroy was quick to engage him."

"So!" Diego said.

"Yes, my son. 'Tis said he would pick a quarrel with and kill anybody for a price, always under the guise of a fair duel. But it was suicide for a man to face him. I think Don Marcos Murilla knew his secret, which perhaps is why Don Marcos was killed. No doubt he ordered Ybarra to quit the district or be exposed."

"That could have been it," Diego said. "He is a cold-blooded killer, and would let no human obstacle stand in the way of his strutting around here in Alta California and playing the grandee. But he did not commit this murder in the guise of a duel, so possibly he may be brought to account."

GETTING up, Diego paced back and forth, thinking deeply. He stopped beside his father finally.

"To see this man — " he began.

"He will be here, in our house, tonight," his father interrupted.

"Here?" Diego revealed his surprise.

"Have you forgotten, my son? Several of us who own large ranchos are gathering here tonight to discuss ways of circumventing stock thieves. There has been too much stock stolen recently, and slaughtered for hides. Ybarra was invited, for he is a rancho owner and has had some losses. And Capitán Carlos Ortega, the commandante here, will also be present."

"With some of his troopers as an escort, no doubt," Diego said wryly. "Suppose Señor Zorro puts in an appearance. He would face Capitán Ortega and some of his soldiers, and Ybarra, a man who has made a bloody living with his sword, to face whom with blade in hand is supposed to be suicide."

"Perhaps Zorro had best think twice," Fray Felipe suggested gently.

"Possibly he has thought twice," Diego countered, "and is of the opinion that this Ybarra should be made to confess so Juan may go free."

Fray Felipe sighed, but his eyes twinkled.

"My father," Diego said, "if this Zorro should make an appearance, no doubt you would denounce the rogue vigorously for entering your house and annoying your guests. Such an outburst might be remembered if it ever was hinted that Zorro might be your son."

"Trust me to do so," Don Alejandro said, smiling.

"If you will excuse me now, I'll return to the patio. Send for Bernardo, my attendant. I have orders to give him."

Bernardo soon joined Don Diego in the patio. Bernardo was a huge, strong peon, who had been mute from birth. But he had a keen sense of understanding. He was one of three men on earth who knew Diego's secret, the other two being Diego's father and Fray Felipe.

Diego explained the situation in whispers, and Bernardo nodded. Then he was sent away.

Diego left the patio then and went to his own apartment on the second floor of the house, bolting the door after he had entered. He pressed a panel, and a section of the wall slipped back, disclosing a small closet. In it were Zorro's black garments, which he always put on over his other clothes, his mask which covered his entire face and even the back of his neck, his sword, dagger and always charged pistol. Diego inspected the articles and closed the panel.

When he descended to the big main room Pedro Castro had been sent away.

Fray Felipe had remained for the evening meal.

"You have considered well, my son?" Diego's father asked.

"I have, my father. There is but one thing to be done. Can Juan be let hang while the guilty man struts around?"

"This fellow is a rare swordsman, it is said."

"I have no fear of him. Perhaps what I shall say to him will unnerve him. Also, I will fight with right on my side. The main thing is to make him confess the killing of Marcos Murilla, so Juan will go free."

After the evening meal, Fray Felipe left for the little chapel on the plaza, and Diego and his father awaited the guests.

A dozen rancho owners appeared, to scatter around the room, drink wine, and eat fruit, nuts, and little cakes. Capitán Ortega came with

Sergeant Garcia and three troopers, and was made welcome.

Diego greeted the capitán without show of spirit, complained of a headache, and went out to see the big sergeant and his troopers. At the side of the house a table under the pepper trees was heaped with food. A wineskin was on one end of it.

Diego told the sergeant and troopers to help themselves.

"I know it is tedious to wait while one of these long talks is held," he explained. "Enjoy yourselves."

"Don Diego, you are a man after my own heart!" Sergeant Garcia cried. " 'Tis a shame you do not have more energy."

"You mean ride like a wild man and fight with a blade?" Diego asked, shuddering. "I prefer peace and contentment while I peruse the poets."

He drifted into the house again, just as the man who called himself Don Esteban Ybarra y Sandoval arrived.

THE man was tall, lean, with long arms. His black eyes always seemed to be gleaming malevolently. He was dressed in splendid attire, and jewels gleamed on his fingers and in the lace at his throat. They gleamed, too, on the hilt of the blade at his side and on the dagger in his belt.

Diego nodded coldly when he was presented, then stepped aside and listened while the violent death of Marcos Murilla was discussed. Esteban Ybarra had little to say, except that the peon rascal who had done the killing should be straightway hanged.

When the guards finally settled down to discuss stock thieves, Diego again complained of a headache, excused himself and went to his suite.

"Business discussions always fatigue him," his father explained by way of apology. "Those continual headaches of his sap his strength."

Diego bolted the door of his suite and hurried to a window. It was a dark night, yet he could see a shadow pass through a thin streak of light which came from one of the windows in the rear of the house, and knew that Bernardo was doing his part. The mute was astraddle his riding mule, waiting behind the patio wall.

Diego went to another window, peered down, and saw Sergeant Manuel Garcia and the troopers eating and drinking. Opening the hidden closet, Diego felt in the darkness for his Zorro costume, dressed swiftly, put on his sword belt and made sure his weapons were ready. He affixed the mask, unbolted the door, but did not open it, then darted to a window opening upon a small balcony.

Getting out upon the balcony, he went down a clinging vine and got into a tree which he descended until his feet touched the earth.

The troopers were talking and laughing, and inside the house, Diego's father and the others were discussing their troubles. Diego kept close to the wall, out of the light from the windows, and went to the front of the house.

Torches burned beside the door, but nobody was in sight. He went swiftly to the big front door, his pistol in his left hand and his naked blade in his right. With the hilt of the blade, he pounded on the door.

A servant opened the door and gave a squawk of fright. Diego, in the garb of Señor Zorro, stepped inside and kicked the door shut.

"Señores!" he greeted, in a ringing voice which was nothing like that of Don Diego Vega.

The men around the table sprang to their feet, exclamations of surprise bubbling from their lips. They beheld the black menace advancing toward them slowly, pistol and blade held ready.

" 'Tis that confounded Zorro!" some man shouted.

"Keep your voices down, señores," Zorro warned.

"What means this intrusion, you scoundrel!" Don Alejandro demanded. "How dare you enter here and disturb my guests?"

"Softly, señor," Zorro begged.

"If you have come to rob — "

"Your valuables and those of your guests are safe, señor," Zorro said. "You will sit down, señores, and put your hands flat on the table, unless you wish this pistol of mine to speak. I have serious business here — with one man."

They dropped upon benches and stools and put their hands flat upon the table as ordered. Capitán Ortega seemed hesitant.

"Be careful, Capitán!" Zorro warned. "Do not call to your troopers who are so busily eating and drinking outside. I think this little affair, Capitán Ortega, will please you. It will reveal things you will delight to know. I ask that you keep quiet and motionless while I deal with one man here. Then you may pay your personal respects to Zorro, if you still care to."

Ortega sat down, his face livid with rage. Zorro's pistol covered them all as he took another step forward. The servants were standing back against the walls, terrified.

"Nobody is to leave the room until I am done," Zorro warned.

"What is the meaning of this visit, you rogue, if it is not robbery?" Don Alejandro demanded. Diego's father was putting on a good show.

"There is one among you," Zorro said, "who is an impostor, a murderer, a man who lives grandly on blood money!"

"His name?" Don Alejandro demanded.

"He calls himself Don Esteban Ybarra y Sandoval," Zorro replied.

ESTEBAN YBARRA sprang to his feet, and found Zorro's pistol menacing him.

"How dare you, nameless rogue?" Ybarra cried. "It is safe to speak as you will when you hide behind a mask. A notorious highwayman!"

"Not half so notorious as yourself, señor." Zorro broke in, in a ringing voice. "Be seated again. If you wish to try for satisfaction after I am done, I'll accommodate you."

Ybarra sank upon the bench again and put his hands on the table. His black eyes were glittering, his nostrils distended. He was fighting hard to control his anger, knowing that every move would have to be calculated carefully.

"Say on!" he snapped at Zorro. "Let us hear what manner of yarn you have to tell. It may be amusing."

"I speak the truth," Zorro said, "and every word I shall say may be substantiated easily. You, señor, are Esteban Ybarra. And your antecedents are questionable. In Spain, you became known as a master swordsman, and made a precarious living with your blade."

"Pray continue," Ybarra said scornfully.

" 'Tis said you picked quarrels and killed men for hire. When you became too well known in Spain, you sailed to Mexico. There you became the bodyguard of the Viceroy, a man known for unsavory political deals. You slew for him, removed men standing in his way."

"Interesting!"

"Every word I speak may be substantiated, remember!" Zorro snapped. "But you were not content with the Viceroy's gold alone. You again killed for hire, señor, picked quarrels and fought, murdered men unable to stand before you and live. In this manner, you acquired gold and precious jewels. But, feeling against you presently became so strong that even the Viceroy could protect you no longer. So you ran away again, and came to Alta California."

"A pleasant place," Ybarra admitted, trying to laugh softly.

"You gave yourself a high-sounding name, flaunted your jewels and fine clothes, bought a rancho. But you cannot make a gentleman out of a nameless rascal, señor. Blood money bought your rancho, fine clothes and jewels, and fine horses and carriage. The taint of innocent blood is upon you, señor, and blood drenches your hands."

"Is this true?" Don Alejandro demanded of Ybarra.

"It is true that I served the Viceroy for a time, when he had need of a good swordsman," Ybarra admitted.

"And now," Zorro's voice rang out, "you have overstepped yourself, señor. You have murdered a friend of mine!"

"A friend of yours?" Ybarra asked scornfully. "Do you pretend to gentle blood?"

"I did not say the man you slew was of gentle blood. However, he was. And so am I, señor."

"This man you say I killed — "

"Don Marcos Murilla," Zorro said.

Ybarra laughed. "You have done some overstepping yourself, Señor Zorro," he declared. "Capitán Ortega, here, knows the truth of that. Murilla was slain by a peon with a sheep-skinning knife, and the rascal is in the jail room at the barracks. He will be hanged tomorrow."

"Juan Castro did not kill Don Marco Murilla," Zorro declared. "You slew him, señor, with the knife found beside his body. He knew your secret and threatened to expose you if you did not at once move elsewhere, and leave the air here untainted."

The expression in Ybarra's face told Zorro he had spoken truly.

"Your scene with Murilla was overheard — and observed." Zorro continued. "What have you to say now, Ybarra?"

Ybarra sprang to his feet again, but kept his hands on the table.

"Are you done with your falsehoods?" he cried.

"I have spoken the truth, señor. You pretend to be a hidalgo. Would a hidalgo allow a poor peon to be hanged for a crime he did not commit? Above all, would a hidalgo lie about something he had done, regardless of how much the truth might injure him?"

YBARRA laughed a little, sat down and looked at the others.

"I did not realize what I was doing," he explained. "I'll tell you the truth, señores. I had kept quiet because I thought it useless to create hard feelings."

"We are waiting to hear, señor." Don Alejandro said.

"Marcos Murilla desired the rancho I bought, but I purchased it before he made his desire known. We met on the San Gabriel road, and dismounted to talk. Murilla insulted me — "

"In what manner, señor?" Zorro put in.

"He said he had learned I had been the Viceroy's bodyguard, and that I was nothing but a hired murderer. So I challenged him then and there, and we fought."

"And you killed him?" Zorro asked.

"Certainly, señor. It was his life or mine. He surprised me by his skill with the blade, before I gave the thrust — "

"And the knife found beside the body?" Zorro questioned.

"No doubt it had been left there by someone. Perhaps that peon now in the jail room dropped it in his excitement. If he saw the fray, undoubtedly he thought to rob Señor Murilla's body and get gone before anybody happened along the highway."

"If you slew Marcos Murilla while he stood before you with sword in hand, how comes it," Zorro asked, "that his sword was found in its scabbard, clean of blood? Can a dead man clean his blade and return it to scabbard? Murilla was struck through the heart, and death was instant. And why did you not report the duel?"

"It was a fair fight. The troopers held a culprit, and I thought Murilla's friends would hold his death against me. I want to settle here and live in peace."

Capitán Ortega got to his feet.

"I charge you with the murder of Marcos Murilla, señor!" he said. "The boy Juan will be set free as soon as I return to the barracks."

"You dare do such a thing?" Ybarra cried. "I am not without influence!"

"I think you are, else you would not be here in Alta California," Ortega told him.

Zorro took another step forward and brought up his pistol.

"Steady, señores!" he warned. "Even if you had influence, Señor Ybarra, let me remark that a dead man cannot use influence."

"What mean you by that?"

"It is my purpose to fight with you and destroy you, señor."

"No need of that, Zorro!" Ortega cried. "I'll have my troopers take this man."

"Señores," Zorro said, "it is my purpose to fight this man who often has slain for gain. I ask that you give me a fair try at him. I ask you, Capitán Ortega, to sit at the table again, and not call on your troopers to arrest me while we fight."

"Whether you slay him or not, Zorro, I still have a claim on you." Ortega warned. "Slaying Ybarra will not make me turn kind where you are concerned. The Governor — "

"Has ordered that I be caught and hanged, and has even put up a reward of gold," Zorro said. "So be it! But I am not to be disturbed as we fight. To make sure, I shall hold my pistol in my left hand, and use it on any man who plays me false."

Esteban Ybarra sprang away from the table, his eyes aflame.

"Cross blades with me, will you?" he cried. "I'll slay you, then all here will learn the identity of this mysterious Señor Zorro."

"If you slay me," Zorro said.

"Then, as to this ridiculous charge of murder — I'll fight it and win! And I'll have this Capitán Ortega stripped of his rank and banished! On guard, señor!"

Zorro had stepped quietly to one side. The large candelabra on the table threw a flickering, wavering light as gusts of the soft breeze from the patio touched the burning tapers. Torches burned against two of the walls, also. But Zorro, of course, knew the lights, and would have a slight advantage.

He glanced swiftly at the others. Some were standing back against the wall with the affrightened servants. Others remained at the table, among them Don Alejandro. Zorro saw his father's eyes close and his hands gripping until the knuckles were white, and knew he was praying.

In the middle of the big room, their blades met and rang. Heavy rugs covered a part of the tile floor, and Zorro knew where they were, too, and where the floor might be slippery in a critical moment.

Ybarra started the fighting like a madman, as if he would make a quick end of it. Zorro gave ground cautiously before his opponent's wild charging, fighting like a machine, cold and deadly.

ZORRO knew he was facing a man who itched to kill him, a professional killer. One wrong move, and Zorro would be stretched dead on the floor, the mask torn from his face, and he would be revealed as the son of Don Alejandro Vega. His illustrious father would be disgraced, and perhaps his estates forfeited to the Governor.

Ybarra's first mad rush over, he began fighting calmly, feeling out his opponent. He had heard much of the sword play of Zorro, but thought it had been against men without much skill. He did not doubt that he could stretch Zorro lifeless.

Their blades clashed and rang, their bodies darted and writhed, as they thrust, recovered, tried all the tricks of the game.

"Hired murderer!" Zorro taunted.

Ybarra did not answer the taunt. His eyes were mere slits. He looked like a man about to make the kill.

There was a swift clash of blades, and Zorro felt a streak as of fire along his upper arm. But the cut was not deep, and he did not drop his pistol. He allowed Ybarra to force him into a slow retreat, always on the defensive.

Finally, his back was to the open door, to the patio. There as Zorro had planned, he made his stand. He continued on the defensive at first, and it took all his skill to ward off a fatal thrust. Ybarra's blade was like a live thing. The man had a wrist of steel. Zorro knew this was an hour of peril for him.

One thing was in his favor — Ybarra had done no fighting since coming to Alta California. For a year he had lived softly, and his wind was none too good.

Ybarra tried another trick or two, and Zorro retreated until he was almost in the doorway. And suddenly he assumed the aggressive. It caught Ybarra unexpectedly, for he had been anticipating a quick decision.

Light from the candelabra and torches played along Zorro's blade, as it darted in and out, clashed and rang. Ybarra tried a thrust which was warded aside.

Almost every man in the room was on his feet now. Never had they seen anything like this. Zorro was fighting fiercely, and Ybarra fell back before his vicious onslaught.

Recklessness came to Ybarra then. This unknown masked man had lasted too long, and he was proud of his reputation as a swordsman. And he had the feeling that he might be dealt with more leniently in the Marcos Murilla matter if he could kill this notorious Zorro.

He tried to force the fighting, but Zorro refused to fall back before his vicious charge. There was a rapid exchange at the patio door, then a wild cry. Ybarra's sword clattered to the tiles, and the former bodyguard of the Viceroy staggered backward, clutched at his chest, from which the blood was gushing, then tottered and fell, the life gone from him.

There was a moment of stunned silence. Zorro had a glimpse of his father fighting to hide his relief. He saw Capitán Ortega start moving.

"Señores, adios!" Zorro cried.

He sprang through the doorway into the dark patio. Ortega had jerked the front door open, and his wild yell rang into the night:

"Garcia! Troopers! Zorro is here!"

That was as Zorro would have it. Garcia and the troopers charged to the front door, putting the house between themselves and the man they sought to capture.

Zorro ran to the side of the patio, gave a peculiar shout. Beyond the wall, the mute Bernardo drove his heels into the flanks of his mule. With a clatter of hoofbeats, the mule was away, and no trooper could mount and pursue in time to catch him.

"He's riding!" Zorro heard Ortega shout. "Mount and after him!"

Lightly, noiselessly, Zorro ran from the patio, skipped along the hall, got into his own rooms, and bolted the door.

He stripped off the Zorro costume, put it and his weapons and mask away. He tore off his jacket, the left sleeve of which was stained with blood, bandaged the cut with a silk handkerchief, and put on a fresh jacket, and over it a heavy dressing gown.

On the lower floor, Capitán Ortega shouted, and men ran around shouting for servants and torches.

ZORRO was gone — but Don Diego Vega, on the floor above, mussed his hair, wiped the perspiration from his face, removed his boots and encased his feet in decorated slippers. It was Diego who unbolted and opened the door and strolled down the stairs, politely holding a scented handkerchief over his mouth as he yawned, as if just aroused from sleep.

He descended into the tumult.

"What is all this turbulence?" he complained.

"Ah, my son!" Don Alejandro cried. "You should have been here to see. Zorro appeared, and slew this rogue of an Esteban Ybarra, who confessed that he killed Marcos Murilla. The peon boy goes free! Zorro exposed Ybarra as a foul beast who lives on blood money!"

"That Zorro again!" Diego said, shuddering slightly. "Why do not the troopers catch the fellow? If they did, perhaps we could have some peace and quiet. Ah, these violent, turbulent times!"

Zorro Slays a Ghost

Don Diego Vega, far-famed Fighting Hidalgo, prepares to pit himself against a phantom horseman given to trickery!

DAWN was less than two hours away. The oxen pulling the heavy cart heaped high with bales of merchandise plodded along the dusty rough road which twisted over the hills. Their journey was to the pueblo of Reina de los Angeles from San Pedro, the place where ships put in from the sea.

Since the oxen followed the trail without command or guidance, Juan Reyes sat on the merchandise and ate heartily from a joint of cold boiled mutton. He also drank from a jug half-filled with thin sour wine. His manner of acquiring this food and drink had been slightly irregular, and he was hoping the good Franciscan fathers would not learn the truth and make him do some heavy penance.

Juan worked hard for the few pesos he received. He lived in a poor hut and had a motherless daughter to feed, and was an honest man — except when he became hungry. At such times, unguarded food and drink seemed fair loot.

Tonight, his was a tiresome journey. Another cart which had started with him from San Pedro had broken an axle, and Juan had come on alone, for there was need of haste in getting this merchandise to the warehouse.

Streaks of mist were swirling down the canyons, but the sky was clear, and a round moon was giving silvery light. A breeze rustled the dry brush beside the trail, and night birds called. Juan had an oppressive feeling of lonesomeness.

The oxen began pulling the heavy cart with its huge wooden wheels up a steep slope, straining in the yoke. They could not get off the road here, and they always stopped for a breathing spell when the top of the slope was reached. Juan tossed the mutton bone aside as the oxen stopped at the crest. He took a swig of wine, then bent forward, his crossed forearms resting upon his knees, intending to doze in contentment until the oxen decided to go on.

"Juan Reyes!" a sepulchral voice intoned suddenly.

Juan looked around quickly. Nobody was in the trail ahead or behind.

"Juan Reyes!" the call came again. The deep voice rang among the rocks, and made shivers chase up and down Juan's spine. It did not sound like a friendly voice.

Juan glanced at the right of the trail, where there was a ledge about ten feet high. And he knew sudden terror.

Atop the ridge stood a white horse. The rider wore flowing white garments, and something white obscured his head. The mist was swirling around horse and rider, and the moonlight striking through it gave them a greenish tinge.

Juan gulped and crossed himself quickly. Horse and rider had the appearance of beings from another world. Remembering the meat and wine he had stolen, Juan wondered if here was retribution.

"I am a ghost, Juan Reyes," the sepulchral voice intoned. "The ghost of a murdered man. I have a message for you."

Being incapable of speech, Juan did not dispute the assertion. And suddenly he was like a man from whom all strength had fled, so he could not jump down and run, as he felt like doing.

Juan Reyes was only a poor, barefooted peon, and superstition was so deep within him that not even the padres could root it out. The possibility that a ghost could appear and speak to him was not beyond his comprehension, nor the fact that the ghost rode a horse.

"I have something to tell you," the white spectre said. "You are to repeat it to others. If you do not I'll come each night to your hut, or wherever you are on the lonely road, and make your existence miserable."

"I — I am listening," Juan squeaked.

"I am the ghost of a man who was foully murdered by the one you and your friends know as Señor Zorro," the sepulchral voice declared. "I have come to warn you against him."

"Señor Zorro?" Juan said, in a voice that shook. "But he punishes those who oppress the poor and helpless, Señor Ghost. There must be some mistake."

"He is a murdering scoundrel," the thing on the ledge declared. "He is a ghost like myself. But he is a demon ghost instead of a good one. That is why he always dresses in black and rides a black horse. The Evil One sends him. He can materialize himself and horse and weapons."

Juan had crossed himself several times during this recital.

"He pretends to help the poor, but is only doing so to gain your confidence. When he has you well in his clutches, he will destroy you all for the Evil One. Those who grow friendly with him he will denounce to the soldiers, and all of you will be hanged."

"I cannot believe it," Juan said.

"Do you dare doubt my word?" the thing on the ledge demanded, his voice ringing angrily. "I have spoken trying to save you and your friends. Tell them all that I have said."

"Is there anything else I must do?" Juan asked.

"There is. Whatever information you have or may get concerning this Señor Zorro, give it at once to the soldiers. If they can catch him before he can dematerialize himself, they can tear off his black mask and expose him, destroy him, and you and your friends will be safe. Spread word of this as soon as you reach the pueblo."

There was another swirl of mist around the ghostly figure and the white horse suddenly wheeled, loped away and disappeared.

And one thing Juan Reyes noticed terrified him yet more — the white horse's hoofs made not the slightest sound.

Don Diego Vega, dressed in an embroidered lounging robe, sat on a bench beside the pool in the patio of his father's house in the outskirts of Reina de los Angeles.

He held a book of poetry in his lap, but seemed half asleep as he watched bees buzzing around the blooms hanging over the patio wall. He heard a step, opened his eyes, and saw Bernardo, his giant mute peon body servant standing respectfully before him.

Bernardo grinned, made a guttural sound, and pointed toward the door. So Don Diego knew his father, Don Alejandro, wished to see him, and Bernardo's gutturals informed him there was need for haste.

As Don Diego walked through the house toward the big main room, he heard voices — his father's and that of old Fray Felipe, his confessor. He quickened his step. When Fray Felipe called at this hour of the day, something unusual must have happened.

Diego entered the room and received the fray's blessing, then sprawled in a big chair and began munching fruit he took from a bowl of crystal.

"Juan Reyes, the carter, came to me this morning badly frightened and with a strange story to tell, my son," Fray Felipe told Diego. "I decided that your father and you should learn of it immediately."

The story of Juan Reyes, it appeared, had lost nothing in the telling. Urging the oxen to do their utmost, he had reached the pueblo shortly after dawn, and had sprinted to the chapel as soon as the cart stopped in front of the warehouse.

His fright and imagination had combined to concoct a wonderful tale. The fray had heard him through, and had counseled that Juan say nothing of it until later.

There had been little prospect of Juan holding his tongue. His manner would tell his friends that something had befallen him, and he would talk undoubtedly, being a big man for a moment. Not every peon received a personal visitation from a ghost who rode a white charger whose hoofs made no sound.

Fray Felipe told Juan's story, discounting the tale considerably. Diego arose and paced around the room, then returned to the table.

"Another trick in an attempt to catch Zorro," he said. "An attempt to frighten peons and natives into rushing to the soldiers and telling what they know of Zorro. But only three men know the real identity of Zorro. One is his father, from whom white irons could not tear the secret. Another is you, Fray Felipe, his confessor, and your lips are sealed by the confessional. The third is Bernardo, who is a mute and cannot speak, and, could he, would die before doing so. There is no fear that the identity of Zorro will be revealed to the soldiers. But there is another thing."

"And that, my son?" Fray Felipe asked.

"The bogus ghost must be unmasked. The peons and natives must not lose faith in Zorro, or his work will be hampered. They must be shown that this so-called ghost is but a man, an enemy of Zorro and a friend of the authorities."

"Have you any plan, my son?" Diego's white-haired father asked.

"Zorro must come face to face with this bogus ghost, unmask him. Fray Felipe, if a word could be spread — "

"What word, my son?"

"Juan Reyes has a daughter."

"Little Maria, fifteen years old," the fray replied. "A delicious child. She is admired and respected by all."

"Send for her, tell her there are no ghosts. Bid her laugh at her father and the others who are frightened. And plant an idea in her mind."

"What idea?" Don Alejandro asked.

"Have her tell them they must be sure, or Zorro would be offended and cease helping them. How can they be sure? Easy enough! If there is a ghost, he is lurking near, watching and listening while unseen. Let the peons talk among themselves, wishing they could see and hear the ghost as Juan did."

"I understand," Fray Felipe said, his eyes twinkling. "Let them arrange to meet at some place at a certain time, hoping the ghost will appear and talk to them, so they will believe Juan has not lied."

"And if the ghost appears," Diego added, "Zorro will appear also and confront him." He smiled and helped himself to more fruit.

"If this ghost is in league with Capitán Carlos Ortega, the comandante here, soldiers might be in the neighborhood of the meeting."

"That is to be expected," Diego replied.

"And Zorro might find himself in danger."

"Zorro has been in danger before," Diego told him, his face a mask.

"I'll get in touch with little Maria Reyes at once," Fray Felipe decided. "Her father adores her, and will listen to her. I'll have her suggest that the meeting be held tonight at some spot a distance from the town."

"That would be best," Diego agreed.

"As to the identity of the ghost — "

"Capitán Ortega would not play ghost nor have Sergeant Garcia or one of his troopers do it," Diego said. "He would be afraid some of Zorro's friends might be watching the soldiery. If the Governor has sent some spy here — "

He stopped as if a sudden thought had struck him, then turned swiftly and beckoned Bernardo, who had remained in a corner of the room. Bernardo hurried forward and knuckled his forehead.

"The carriage, as soon as possible," Diego said. "I will drive to the plaza and take Fray Felipe to the chapel. That will be excuse enough for the journey."

"You have some idea regarding the ghost, my son?" Fray Felipe asked.

"Perhaps. I am wondering about the man who calls himself Pedro Lucero, who came from Monterey a fortnight ago. He gave out he is a small merchant looking for a new location. He spends considerable money and wastes time. And he has been talking overmuch with peons and natives."

"You may be right," Fray Felipe said.

"If the peons and natives would go to the small canyon on the San Gabriel road at midnight, hoping the ghost would appear — "

"I'll suggest that to Maria Reyes."

"Tell her also to laugh at her father and the others for shivering at thought of a white horse galloping without making a sound. Have her tell them it is not difficult to pad the hoofs of a horse."

Diego retired to remove his robe, and returned with coat and hat. He left the house with Fray Felipe and his father, and they waited for the Vega carriage. When it came, Diego got in with the fray, and Don Alejandro returned to the house.

It was but a short drive to the plaza. When they arrived in front of the little chapel, they could see knots of men standing around in close conversation. And peons and natives came running when they saw Fray Felipe.

THE aged fray was loved and trusted. He stood among them and talked. There were no ghosts, he told them. And he made the suggestion that they gather in the canyon, to see if the ghost would appear and talk to them. So it was not necessary for Maria Reyes to be drawn into the affair at the moment.

Diego drove on to the inn and left his carriage, telling the coachman to wait. There was a laughing, jesting crowd at the inn. Men made way for Diego to enter, and he ordered a jar of sage honey from the fat landlord as an excuse for being there.

"Is it not amusing, Don Diego?" the landlord asked. "The peons think a ghost has been seen. He told them to beware of Señor Zorro."

"There is always some sort of tumult in the pueblo," Diego observed, yawning.

He saw Pedro Lucero at the gaming table. The man who said he was a merchant was tall and slender, and wore clothes a little more fashionable than a sedate merchant would wear.

Capitán Carlos Ortega strolled in, and his sergeant, Manuel Garcia, strutted at his heels.

The capitán bowed to Diego.

"Always a tumult," Diego told him. "What is this of peons and natives and ghosts?"

Ortega laughed, and explained.

"And now," he said, "they have a new idea. Fray Felipe has told them there are no ghosts. Juan Reyes declares one spoke to him, and told him to beware of Señor Zorro. They are preparing to go to the canyon on the San Gabriel road at midnight, hoping the ghost will appear."

"You will allow it, Señor el Capitán?" Diego asked.

"Why not, if it amuses them? It is none of my official business if the rascals want to hold a rendezvous with a ghost. If they held one with this confounded Señor Zorro, now, I might give the matter some attention. I

Zorro got in a position slightly above the man on the white horse and behind him.

have just received from the Governor another rebuke for not catching the rogue. But I have hopes of doing so soon."

"Hope is denied no man," Diego observed.

Pedro Lucero approached, bowing and smiling. Ortega returned his greeting coldly, and Diego merely bowed. Lucero's effort to inject himself into the conversation availed him nothing. Ortega gave him a few cold words and withdrew, but Diego saw a glance pass between them, and knew this performance was for the benefit of others.

"And what do you think of this ghost, Don Diego Vega?" Lucero asked.

"Ghosts never bother me, señor," Diego replied. "A ghost is not so much a nuisance as some humans."

Pedro Lucero's eyes glittered. "Can I find a hidden meaning in your words, señor?"

"How do I know?" Diego countered. "You may be a man of skill in such matters, for all I know, or a dolt concerning them."

"I am not sure that I like your attitude, Don Diego!"

"We cannot please everybody," Diego observed. "And allow me to assure you, señor, that whether you like my attitude does not concern me."

He turned to leave, and Pedro Lucero glowered at his back. Diego found Capitán Ortega and his sergeant waiting beside the carriage.

"Don Diego, will you ride tonight to the canyon to see the ghost?" Ortega asked, laughing.

"At midnight, señor?" Diego replied. "Scarcely. If a ghost wishes to amuse me at such an hour, he will have to appear in my bedroom. You will be obliged to ride there with your troopers, I suppose. I do not envy you your duty."

Ortega laughed again. "I have no orders from the Governor to run down ghosts," he replied. "Though he has issued orders concerning almost everything else."

"But if the peons and natives become frightened and get out of hand, señor?" Diego insinuated.

"If the rascals get unruly, you will see action enough from the soldiery," Ortega declared.

Diego got into the carriage and made himself comfortable on the silk cushions. He pretended to stifle a yawn, brushed a handkerchief across his nostrils, and bowed to the capitán.

"Home!" he ordered the coachman. "And drive slowly, rogue. When you let the horses travel swiftly, the bouncing fatigues me...."

After the evening meal, when the servants had retired and Diego and his father were alone, Don Alejandro said:

"I have been listening to the servants. All afternoon, natives and peons have been drifting out of town toward the canyon. They are afraid to look upon the ghost if he appears, yet eager to see and hear him."

"I hope he appears," Diego replied.

"Señor Zorro rides tonight?" his father asked.

"He does, my father. I already have given Bernardo his orders."

"Use caution, my son, and get back safely. Ah, that I were young again and could have such an adventure!"

"You had plenty in your time, no doubt," Diego observed, his eyes twinkling. "I have heard certain tales."

His father cleared his throat warningly, and Diego smiled.

SHORTLY after nightfall, Diego wandered through the patio and slipped away from the house when he was sure nobody was looking. Through the darkness he went until he reached a lonely hut somewhere. Bernardo was waiting.

"My black horse is ready?" Diego asked.

Bernardo answered with a guttural sound.

"Bueno! Give me my things."

Bernardo moved a small section of the hut's wall, and from an aperture took Zorro's black costume, mask, pistol and blade. Diego put on the costume over his other clothes, buckled on the blade, thrust the pistol into his sash and affixed the mask. Don Diego, the indolent scion of the house of Vega, had disappeared. In his place stood Señor Zorro, whose eyes flashed fire through the slits in the mask.

The black horse was ready in a hiding place, and they went there and Zorro mounted.

"You will follow on your mule," he instructed Bernardo. "If any see you, you are merely a superstitious peon going with the others to see the ghost."

Through the night they rode, and at a certain place Bernardo left him and turned into the highway. He rode his big mule along it, passing others on their way to the rocky canyon.

Zorro cut over the hills before the moon was up, and entered the upper end of the narrow box canyon. He moved cautiously, for if the ghost had taken the bait, he might be somewhere in the vicinity.

Capitán Ortega, Sergeant Garcia and some troopers might be hidden in the vicinity also. Zorro thought the ghost would appear and make a strong talk. And he believed some of the soldiers would be near to help the ghost if necessary, or to attack Zorro if he appeared.

Working his big black horse slowly and cautiously among the rocks, Zorro descended to the canyon's floor and moved along it almost noiselessly in the darkness.

The wind carried sounds of voices to him, and when he reached a certain spot he could see the reflection of a camp-fire on the rocky walls. The peons and natives evidently felt that a fire might protect them in a measure from a visitor from the spectral world.

Zorro approached as near as he thought safe, and got behind a huge clump of brush high on the hillside, from where he could look down upon the scene.

More than a hundred peons and natives were bunched together near the blazing fire upon which fresh fuel was being heaped continually. And more men were straggling in from the mouth of the canyon.

Zorro saw nothing of the ghost, nor of troopers. He watched the sides of the canyon where the reflection from the fire struck. The moon was just coming up, and its light gave a ghostly hue to the scene.

Keeping high on his side of the canyon, Zorro moved forward cautiously, stopping frequently to watch and listen, every sense keen. The men were crowding nearer around the fire, bunching together and talking as if nervous, waiting for midnight. Zorro rode directly opposite and above the fire and again got behind a clump of brush to watch.

Once, as he glanced across the canyon, he thought he saw a flash of white in the undergrowth. He strained his eyes, and again saw the flash of white descending the side of the canyon from ledge to ledge.

The ghost was riding into the trap! He was coming to keep the appointment.

Off to one side Zorro could see Bernardo astride his big mule, and knew he could depend on the mute for help if it became necessary. The wind was sweeping up the side of the canyon, and again Zorro could hear voices.

Above the others, he heard the shrill voice of a girl, and saw little Maria Reyes standing on a big rock at the side of her father.

"Fray Felipe says there are no ghosts!" she was calling to the men. "The thing my father saw was only a man in white garments. He is trying to get you to turn against Señor Zorro, who has helped us so much. He will get you into trouble."

"A horse whose hoofs make no sound — " somebody called.

"Fray Felipe told me that perhaps the hoofs of the horse were padded with sacks. Trust the good fray, who is so kind to us. Have no dealings with this man who claims to be a ghost. It is the middle of the night, and your ghost is not here. All day you have been talking of this meeting. If he is a real ghost, he would have been around to hear you, and he would have come here to tell you what he told my father. But he has not come."

A wild cry rang among the rocks:

"I am here!"

ZORRO's head snapped up and he looked across the narrow canyon. The white horse and rider were out on a jut of rock in plain view, bathed in the light of the moon, and with reflections of the amber firelight playing over them.

He certainly presented a ghostly figure, and there came a chorus of howls from the superstitious peons and natives. Some prostrated themselves, others turned to run but were stopped by still others pressing forward. And suddenly, as if stunned, they were motionless and quiet.

"I am here!" the sepulchral voice rang out again, to be echoed among the rocks. "I come to tell you what I told Juan Reyes on the San Pedro trail. This Señor Zorro is a demon ghost. He will gain your friendship and destroy you. Go to the soldiers and tell them all you know about this Señor Zorro. Reveal his hiding place. The soldiers will capture him and free you from all danger."

"How can they capture a demon ghost?" some brave man cried.

"They will seize him before he can dematerialize himself. They will tear off his mask and reveal him to you. He is the ghost of a foul murderer. He slew me among others. Do not let him make fools of you."

Zorro had not been idle from the moment the white spectre spoke the first words. Zorro had backed his horse away from the clump of brush and ridden away for a short distance. Then, under cover of a ledge, he had descended to the canyon floor. He crossed it without being seen, and urged the big black up the opposite side of the gulch.

"What must we do?" he heard Juan Reyes call.

"Tell the soldiers all you know!" answered the sepulchral voice.

"But we know nothing. We have seen Zorro and heard him talk, but he always disappears."

"Seize him when he appears to you next!" the man on the white horse roared. "Tear the mask from his face. Turn him over to the soldiers and claim the huge reward His Excellency, the Governor, has offered for him. And then watch the soldiers hang him for his perfidy."

Zorro finally got in a position slightly above the man on the white horse and behind him. He could cut off the masquerader's escape now. The pseudo-ghost could either stand and fight, else ride down to the floor of the canyon and make an attempt at a getaway. He could do nothing else.

"I have spoken to you!" the ghost howled. "If you obey me, you will be saved. This Zorro is a demon ghost, I have told you!"

At that moment, Zorro jumped his black horse out where those below could see. He was within forty feet of the white mount.

"Señores!" he shouted. "Here I am! Here is Zorro to give the lie to this bogus ghost. I am not a ghost, but a man of flesh and blood like yourselves. I have tried to help you, and will continue trying. This is no ghost in front of me, but a man on a white horse. He is trying to get you to betray me to the soldiers. He is a spy!"

The man on the white horse had jerked around at the sound of Zorro's voice. And now his arm went up, and a pistol exploded and flamed. The slug sang past Zorro's head.

"Does a ghost shoot a pistol, my friends?" Zorro called to the men below. "I'll seize this fellow now and turn him over to you."

He urged the big black forward. Plainly, the man on the white horse did not have a second pistol, nor time to recharge the first. He used his spurs and forced the white horse to start the descent to the canyon floor. He could not get away as he had come without coming face to face with Zorro, who had a pistol which had not been discharged.

Zorro sent the black on. The white horse was skidding down the rocky slope in a cloud of dust which looked greenish in the light of the moon.

"I am a ghost!" the man on the back of the white horse was howling.

"I am coming to get those among you who have turned against me!"

The men around the fire scattered to right and left. When the white horse reached the bottom of the slope, Zorro on the black was only a short distance behind. The white horse charged toward the fire, and Zorro was after him.

"Halt, or I fire!" Zorro called.

The rider of the white horse bent in his saddle and dashed on madly. But his wild cry rang down the canyon:

"Help, troopers! Sergeant Garcia, to me!"

So the soldiers had been placed in ambush.

Before they reached the roaring fire, Zorro was almost within touching distance of the white horse. The peons and natives who had been around the fire were running to get away, trying to scamper up the sides of the canyon.

The white horse swerved around the fire and would have continued on down the canyon. But he collided with a big mule, astride which was the mute, Bernardo.

Zorro was upon the white rider then. He threatened with his pistol, reached out and tore the white covering from the rider's head, and revealed Pedro Lucero, who had claimed to be a merchant.

"Here is your ghost, señores!" Zorro called to the frightened men in the brush and among the rocks. "A spy who came here to trap you! Pedro Lucero, who has been talking to you so much and trying to learn things."

Cries of rage came from the throats of peons and natives, now that they realized they had no supernatural being with whom to deal. They left the rocks and brush and started surging back. The white horse swerved aside, then started a mad dash forward as Pedro Lucero used his spurs.

Three men were knocked sprawling before Bernardo could contrive to have his mule bump against the white horse again. Then the white horse was seized, and men pulled a screeching Pedro Lucero from his saddle.

"Thank you, Señor Zorro!" That was little Maria Reyes screeching at him.

Zorro had done his work, and would be gone. He had exposed the bogus ghost, and men would continue to have faith in Zorro and his works. It was time now for Zorro to make his escape while the infuriated peons and natives were attending to Pedro Lucero, who was shouting in terror for the troopers to come to his aid.

Hoofs suddenly pounded the flinty ground, and the stentorian voice of Sergeant Manuel Garcia could be heard shouting orders. Troopers came thundering up the canyon from its mouth, and two bore down from one side.

Zorro realized instantly that he could not make speed enough to escape by riding toward the other end of the box canyon. The ground was too treacherous. And when he started his horse climbing out at the other end he would be an easy target for the troopers' weapons.

He shouted and gave the black the spurs, and started down the canyon, straight at the oncoming troopers. And, like a wild thing, Bernardo's big mule raced before him, Bernardo pretending to make an effort to stop him or turn him aside.

A gun exploded, and a slug whistled past Zorro's head.

"Stop, Zorro, or we shoot you down!" somebody cried.

The mule thundered on, and Zorro followed on the black. He was past the first of the troopers before they could fire, and saw that Sergeant Garcia had dropped back and left his men to go to the rescue of Pedro Lucero.

Garcia was after the big game. He called an order for Zorro to surrender, and fired his pistol. The bullet went wild. Zorro had his own pistol ready, but did not fire. That would be a last resort. He had crossed blades with the soldiery at times, but never had shot at one of them to kill.

"Sergeant Garcia!" he called. "The ghost trick did not work, eh? Better rescue your ghost before the peons slay him."

Two troopers swung their mounts toward Zorro. He fired the pistol, and they swerved aside unhurt. Then Zorro put his empty pistol in his sash, and had drawn his blade. The reflection of moon and fire showed him that Sergeant Garcia had drawn blade also.

Their mounts clashed together, and their blades met and rang. Zorro's eyes gleamed through the slits in the mask.

"We meet again, Garcia!" Zorro called. "Can you never get enough?"

Garcia was howling for some of his men to come to him. But Zorro disarmed him with a quick stroke and left him cursing, and rode on. Clever Bernardo had swung his mule aside, and now pretended that the animal was out of hand again. He swung him back directly in the path of the troopers who would have pursued Zorro.

The black raced to the mouth of the canyon and emerged from it. For a short distance, he followed the highway which ran from San Gabriel to Reina de los Angeles. Then he turned up into the hills, where Zorro knew secret trails.

He came in time to the hut a distance from his father's house, tethered the black in the usual spot in the depression, and hurried to the hut. He stripped off the Zorro costume, the mask and his weapons, and put them in the aperture in the wall.

Strolling back to his father's house, he stopped beside the patio wall to smooth his hair and brush the dust from his boots. Then he went on, and entered the house.

He had tossed his hat aside. He heard voices in the big room, and entered it, yawning. Capitán Carlos Ortega was there talking with his father.

"Diego!" Don Alejandro asked. "Where have you been? It is an hour past midnight. I have been alarmed."

"I was dreaming in the moonlight," Diego replied. "I was trying to compose a poem, and wandered far from the house. I think I have the first lines of the poem now. But what is Capitán Ortega doing here at this hour?"

"I wanted to question your servant, Bernardo," Ortega told him. "To ask him things concerning this Zorro."

"Bernardo is a mute."

"At least he can nod his head for 'yes' or 'no.' Where is he?"

"No doubt he went with others to the canyon where they hoped the ghost would appear," Diego replied. "I'll rebuke him, if you so desire. What did you wish to ask concerning this Zorro? Perhaps I can give the answers."

The capitán smiled.

"Pardon me, Don Diego, but I am sure you know nothing of this fellow Zorro and his affairs."

"What could Bernardo possibly know?" asked Diego.

"I wished to ask him routine questions, as we are asking others. I'll question him another time. But I am glad my duty brought me here tonight. Your father, Don Alejandro, has been most entertaining. I did not realize how many hours have passed. He has been telling me of the days of his youth. A gay young blade, eh, Don Alejandro? 'Tis a pity, Don Diego, that you do not have the spirit and fire your father had at your age."

"Turbulence, trouble, violence and all that — I abhor them," Diego replied, shuddering.

He held his handkerchief to his face for an instant as if to stifle a yawn, but in reality to hide a smile. His eyes sparkled as they met his father's. He realized that his father had detained Capitán Ortega here, so Zorro would have one less formidable enemy at the canyon.

"Much as I regret to leave, I must hasten," Ortega said, rising and bowing. "My sergeant and his men will be returning from the canyon, and I must have their report."

"But my poem, Señor el Capitán!" Diego protested. "I have the first lines ready. Attend me!

The moonlight shows us many things
Seen alike by fools and kings;
The breezes blow, the night bird sings —

That is as far as I got tonight. Is it not beautiful?"

"Wonderful," Ortega said.

The capitán seemed to be struggling with emotion. When he was in his saddle and a distance from the house, he burst out laughing.

But Don Diego Vega and his father were laughing louder.

About the author

Johnston McCulley

The creator of Zorro, Johnston McCulley (1883-1958) was born in Ottowa, Illinois, and raised in the neighboring town of Chillicothe. He began his writing career as a police reporter and became a prolific fiction author, filling thousands of pages of popular pulp magazines. Southern California became a frequent backdrop for his fiction. His most notable use of the locale was in his adventures of Zorro, the masked highwayman who defended a pueblo's citizens from an oppressive government.

He contributed to popular magazines of the day like *Argosy*, *Western Story Magazine*, *Blue Book*, *Detective Story Magazine*, and *Rodeo Romances*. Many of his novels were published in hardcover and paperback. Eventually he branched out into film and television screenplays.

His stable of series characters included The Crimson Clown, Thubway Tham, The Green Ghost, and The Thunderbolt. Zorro proved to be his most popular and enduring character, becoming the subject of numerous television programs, motion pictures, comic books, and cartoon programs.

In the 1950s, McCulley assigned all Zorro rights agent to Mitchell Gertz. After retiring to Los Angeles, he died in 1958.

About the illustrators

Joseph A. Farren

Joseph Farren (1884-1964) was born in Boston, the youngest of five sons. After high school, he drew comic strips and sports cartoons for various Boston newspapers. He was an avid golfer, and he competed in Massachusetts statewide tournaments. In 1926, he began drawing political cartoons for *The New York Times*. From his home art studio in Queens, he freelanced illustrations to pulp magazines such as *Clues Detective Stories*, *Detective Fiction Weekly*, *Popular Sports*, and *West*.

Farren balanced his art career and golf by a weekly routine of visiting midtown Manhattan to pick up and deliver illustrations, then heading to the golf course in nearby Flushing.

Virgil Evans (V.E.) Pyles

V.E. Pyles (1891-1965) was born in La Grange, Kentucky. He took commercial art classes while recuperating at Fort McHenry, Maryland, while recuperating from a World War I injury. He received a full scholarship to the Art Institute of Chicago.

By 1920 in New York City, he studied at the Art Students League. His first assignments were interior story illustrations for *The American Legion Monthly*, *Country Home*, and *The Saturday Evening Post*. When the Great Depression hit the slick magazine industry, he drew story illustrations for pulp magazines. After the war he illustrated men's adventure magazines, such as *Adventure*, and painted landscapes.

About the illustrators

Perego

Artist, performer, and art activist, single-named Perego has been making art and manifesting people's visions for over 28 years.

He has worked for major companies such as AT&T, Disney, Universal Studios, BET, Univision and many more. He worked in the roles of producer, art director, fine artist, performer, illustrator and activist.

Perego's fine art and murals have been included in some the most affluent homes and corporations, including Harley-Davidson, NASCAR, and themed water-parks and malls.

The Founder of an international art collective, the Art Army has over 45 outposts worldwide and broadcasts clear and wide that "Everyone is an artist" and that "We are the Art." They have produced Art Parties nationwide, with a high point being the premier party for Cirque-du Soleil in Downtown Disney.

As a performer, Perego stages high intensity live paintings and psychedelic light-shows. He has performed on several television shows including *America's Got Talent*, and he performed at Salvatore Dali's 100th birthday party at the Dali Museum in St. Petersburg, Florida.

Made in the USA
Columbia, SC
20 August 2023